# Off Script

# Off Script

## Ashley Marie

**w** by wattpad books

*W* by **wattpad** books
An imprint of Wattpad WEBTOON Book Group

Published in Canada by Wattpad Books, a division of Wattpad Corp.
36 Wellington Street E., Toronto, ON M5E 1C7

*www.wattpad.com*

First Wattpad Books edition: June 2022
ISBN 978-1-99025-915-9 (Trade Paperback original)
ISBN 978-1-99025-916-6 (eBook edition)

Library and Archives Canada Cataloguing in Publication information is available upon request.

Printed and bound in Canada
1 3 5 7 9 10 8 6 4 2

Cover design and illustration by Jessica Hartjes
Author Photo © Ashley Melonson

*Dear Granny, my loving guardian angel,*

*I know I was never supposed to read your Harlequin novels,*

*but they taught me just how meaningful a love story can be.*

*Thank you for that wisdom and for watching over me from up above.*

# 1

A burst of adrenaline pulsed through Jada's veins, the sensation familiar but unwelcome. She exhaled shakily, secretly resenting that no matter how many auditions she'd been on, her nerves kicked in every time. Five years into her career, she had perfected her routine: 1) practice relentlessly beforehand, 2) arrive early and flawlessly dressed, and 3) jam out hard core to "Lose Yourself" by Eminem for some kick-ass motivation while she waited for her turn. Yet, Slim Shady's rapid lyricism could only do so much. Once Jada left the relative comfort of the waiting area to step into the casting room, she always froze up.

Now, as she faced the stern casting director, a lump formed in her throat. Alongside the casting director, the showrunner for *Deadly Intentions* also stared at Jada, although her expression was friendlier. The whole reason why Jada had been excited to audition for this production was because the creator, Jackie Fox, had a history of putting rising stars on the map. Snagging an audition to play the lead on her newest show had been a dream come true—one that Jada was about to royally mess up. Forcing herself to snap out of her BS, Jada flashed them a confident smile.

"Hello, how are you guys? My name is Jada Berklee. I'm twenty-four. I'm really happy to be auditioning for the role of Monica today."

The team returned her greetings and ended with the typical ready when you are spiel. Arriving at the moment of truth, Jada put aside her anxiety and allowed herself to get lost in the character: her motivations, emotional conflicts, everything that played into the makeup of the street-smart detective. After they asked her to try a few more run-throughs, Jada's optimism returned. Everyone knows you don't ask for seconds unless you like what's being served on the table.

"Thank you, Jada. That was lovely," Jackie acknowledged after several takes. However, her razor-sharp eyes flicked over Jada's appearance. Based on her rule to always be flawlessly dressed, Jada assumed she was taking stock of what Jada might look like in character.

"One last question, dear. Do you usually wear your hair this short?"

Reflexively, Jada lifted her fingers, tracing the short edges of her red curls.

"Oh, well, I currently have a supporting role in Ren Kurosawa's latest film, *Love Locket*. It's a rom-com. They had a particular look they wanted for my character."

"I see. How long does it typically take for your hair to grow out?" Jackie asked innocently enough, but Jada saw the writing on the wall.

Unless she could get her curly locks bone straight and as long as Gabrielle Union's, she could kiss this role good-bye. She fought back the urge to explain the intricacies of growing out Black hair, replying with a vague "Not that long."

"Ah, I see." Jackie's courteous smile remained cemented in place, more like a bad FaceTime freeze-frame than sincere understanding. Of course Jada's answer hadn't made the cut. With an offhand "We'll let you know," they escorted her ass out the door.

Refusing to give in to the brush-off, Jada kept her head held high as she exited the building and made her way to her car. But once she slipped into the driver's seat, she rested her head on the steering wheel, a sense of defeat washing over her. To be fair, she could be overanalyzing. Yet she knew those backhanded comments and questions too well. The last time someone had made that kind of remark, the role that had been advertised for a woman of color had gone to a white woman.

"Whatever. There will be other roles, other jobs," Jada said, determined to give herself a pep talk in her rearview mirror. "Perk up, Berklee!"

Before said perking up could kick in, Jada's phone buzzed in her pocket. Her cousin, Mikayla, had sent her a text through the group chat with their other BFF, Alia. Jada had grown up next door to Mikayla back in Chicago, and had met Alia when she got her first big acting job in L.A. Back then, Jada had a supporting role on the popular fantasy show *Fallen Creatures*—with vampires and werewolves *galore!*—and Alia had been one of the staff writers. Alia became a close friend who even helped Jada and Mikayla find the apartment they currently lived in—right across the hall from Alia. The trio had become tight knit, and their group chat was a daily texting must.

**Mikayla**: Hope the audition went well! <3

**Alia**: Ohhh, same. Sending well wishes from set. Where we are currently drowning in demon blood by the way

Picturing the poised Alia covered in sticky, fake blood definitely led to a much-needed chuckle. Alia's star had continued to skyrocket after *Fallen Creatures* ended. She was now the showrunner of her own supernatural series, *Unbound*.

*It was good. Fingers crossed!* Jada typed back, deciding not to bore them with the racial microaggressions she'd experienced.

**Mikayla**: In that case . . . I thought you might want a heads-up on this . . .

Along with the ominous text, Mikayla sent a link to Jada's least favorite site. *Sip That Tea* had gone from a small, superficial blog to a digital kingpin of celeb gossip. The site's founders, social media influencers and fraternal twins Tegan and Tammy Downton, came from old-school, old-Hollywood money, which apparently meant they could spend all their free time and connections hounding and exposing everyone in the entertainment industry. Luckily, Jada wasn't high enough on the A-list to make it into their headlines often. Her ex-boyfriend, however, had his face plastered on the front page.

## DANIEL KANE SPOTTED WITH YOUNG SONGSTRESS

Sip this, Tea Fam! If you were wondering what our resident *Fallen* hottie has been up to, here's the scoop. The luscious Daniel Kane has just gotten back from filming a period drama in Germany. Aside from learning the country's mother tongue, he's also been snogging their hottest idol, Tilly Becker.

The German singer recently turned nineteen, but the six-year age gap can't stop young love! After being spotted all around Munich, Daniel brought the European beauty with him on his return flight. We're looking forward to seeing more of these two! What about you? Will they crash and burn like Daniel's past conquests or stay #relationshipgoals?

As she finished the article, a sour feeling hit Jada's stomach. Reading it brought back awful memories, but seeing Daniel's smug smirk and the redhead clinging shrink-wrap tight to his arm made it worse. The young singer was staring up at him with complete, oblivious adoration. Jada had been like that once—a lovestruck fool—until Daniel's true nature had revealed itself. Because the one thing *Sip That Tea* had gotten right was that *all* of Daniel's "past conquests" *had* ended up burned. Jada was no exception.

Alia's incoming response snapped Jada out of her sullen reverie. Her bestie had the perfect comeback to the news.

**Alia**: Way to kill the mood, Mikayla :(

**Mikayla**: I just thought she should know!

**Jada**: Thanks, but all this means is I need a serious chocolate overload when I get home

**Mikayla**: Making brownies NOW to go with our rocky road supply!

**Alia**: SAVE ME SOME. I get off at eight

With the promise of brownie sundaes, Jada shook off her crappy day and headed home. Even if she didn't have a starring role or a trustworthy boyfriend, she had her girls and a reliable sugar rush waiting for her.

—

5

The drive from her audition in Burbank to her Culver City apartment stretched by at its usual traffic-jammed pace. But when she stepped through the front door, the rich smell of double fudge brownies made up for it. Like a bloodhound, Jada picked up the scent and made her way to the kitchen. Thanks to Mikayla's artistic flair, their apartment was decked out in vibrant colors and way too much pop-culture memorabilia. Of particular note were Mikayla's beloved superhero Funko POP bobbleheads on the mantel and the Dr. Frank-N-Furter cutout Mikayla insisted on keeping in the entryway. In her own words, "Anyone who can't handle Tim Curry being iconic doesn't belong in this house." Either way, the eclectic style paired with the more sophisticated hardwood floors and marble fixtures all screamed home to Jada.

Pausing in the kitchen's doorway, Jada took in Mikayla standing at the stove, her Gordon Ramsay apron splattered with chocolate batter. Her colorful purple braids had been pulled back in a bun to keep them out of the way of her baking frenzy, and the end product looked deliciously unscathed.

"Perfect timing." Mikayla beamed at her. Even with her fashionable hair and glowing mahogany skin, Mikayla's smile was still her best feature. Her cousin's exuberance lit up the room, immediately easing some of Jada's tension.

"Damn straight," Jada said, sinking into the high-backed stool at the kitchen island. She tapped one of the ceramic bowls Mikayla had laid out. "Sundae me. Stat."

Mikayla gave her an admonishing look as she pulled the rocky road ice-cream carton from the freezer. "I knew the audition didn't go as well as you claimed."

"Unless you're psychic, I don't see how." Jada avoided her cousin's eyes as she cut a sizable brownie to dump in the bottom of her bowl. Truthfully, she shouldn't have been surprised by the astute observation. When you'd grown up joined at the hip like they had, it was hard to hide anything. Mikayla was more like a nosy little sister than her cousin. The kind who would dig around in your room looking to borrow your clothes but then ended up reading your diary.

"While I am highly spiritually attuned, it's not that. You may be an awesome actress, Jada, but you have a shitty poker face. Even your text persona radiates sweaty guilt when you tell a white lie."

"Texts don't sweat." Jada corrected her as she dug into the ice cream. "And whatever. There will be other auditions. I should be focusing on *Love Locket* anyway. How's that been going?"

While Jackie Fox may not have been a fan of Jada's hairstyle for her upcoming role, it did epitomize her character, Lana, the quirky best friend and budding scientist. Filming didn't start for her character for a few more days but Mikayla had managed to snag a costume production assistant job on the film. Well, with Jada's help. Ren had been open to hiring Mikayla since they needed someone on short notice. But at Mikayla's own conflicted expression, Jada's stomach dropped.

"What happened?" she demanded.

"Nothing! Nothing that bad. It's just . . . I don't think Ren likes me very much. I feel like he watches me like a hawk. More than Val, my actual boss. He caught me talking during a take yesterday."

"Mikayla!"

"It's not a big deal! He corrected me, and now it's over. I didn't bring it up because I knew you were focused on your own stuff."

"Still, you need to get along with everyone on set. This whole industry is about building connections."

Jada frequently wavered between being impressed by Mikayla's fearlessness and being horrified by her cousin's c'est la vie attitude. It was one thing to switch from graduating from the Pratt Institute with an art degree to trying her hand at costume design (a move in line with Mikayla's standard risk taking). It was another situation entirely to blow your first big job because of unprofessionalism, a.k.a. the scary, short-sighted side Jada could do without.

"Seriously, it turned out okay," Mikayla went on. "Tristan stood up for me, actually."

Jada shook her head at Mikayla's adoring smile. Tristan Maxwell was the star of the movie, alongside his leading lady, Angela Collins. While he was a great actor, who got his start as a teenager on the popular family comedy *Garcia Central*, Jada doubted he was as chivalrous as Mikayla's retellings of him. Like Daniel, Tristan had been the subject of several *Sip That Tea* articles regarding his infamous dating exploits. The twenty-six-year-old Colombian heartthrob picked up and dropped different women like he changed socks. Models, heiresses, even a real-life duchess, it didn't matter. They were all expendable. With his stunning blue eyes, tousled black hair, and broad shoulders, Jada could see how so many women fell into the trap of his charm and good looks. She only hoped his dating habits were the extent of the man's downsides. She'd hate to work with the guy and find out he was secretly a cannibal or a cult leader. Honestly, the dark side of Hollywood was scary as fuck sometimes.

There were only two more days until she'd start her new role and meet the allegedly heroic Tristan Maxwell up close. She couldn't wait to discover if he was as talented as everyone claimed or just lucky due to growing up as one of Hollywood's beloved childhood stars. Not that she would ever admit that to Mikayla. Giving her cousin a coy smile, Jada kept the small flurry of nervous excitement to herself.

"I guess I'll see for myself soon."

# 2

To abandon ship or sink to the bottom of the ocean. That was the real question. Unfortunately for Tristan, his current *Titanic*-like dilemma didn't come with an escape plan. Tormented by Club Oasis's cacophony of strobe lights and techno beats, Tristan longed to leave the tacky bar. Yet, his co-star's grip kept the club's exit just out of reach. Angela drunkenly clung to him with pleading, glassy eyes. He looked away from her insistent stare and down at her nails digging into his skin. How much damage would he come away with if he tried to wrestle out of her grasp? Blocking out the club's overwhelming atmosphere, Tristan struggled to reason with his companion.

"Angela, we've been over this. I'm not looking for anything serious."

"Why?" she said. "You think I'm not good enough? I've been on the 'Hottest 30 Under 30' list, won three Golden Globes, and my family's net worth could rival Bill Gates!"

She also had a torrid past of public breakdowns, several

drunk and disorderly bans from other bars, and a stray mug shot tucked under her resume. Tristan would let that slide—he wasn't perfect either—and focus on the issue at hand.

"That doesn't mean we'd be good together long term," he said.

"Then why the fuck did you hook up with me in the first place? For the movie? You're one of those fickle jackasses who uses their co-stars and then dumps them a few weeks after the press dies down."

Tristan could not argue that point. He should have never hooked up with a co-worker. Every time he did it, there were equally disastrous results. People might say he was a glutton for sadistic punishment, but he'd never intended to let things get this far with Angela. For the sake of the film they had bonded and hung out to get to know each other. A few dinners and movie nights led to a "just this once" rendezvous, which inevitably turned into more. However, what had started out as an innocent affair quickly escalated into a problematic shit show. But reasoning that they weren't right for each other would be hard with Angela already six tequilas in.

"This whole aloof act is bullshit. You're trying to hide your real feelings and act like you don't want me. Well, guess what, Tristan? You're not the only man in the world!"

With that, she sauntered away from him, snatching her latest cocktail before Tristan could steal it from her. Her drinking was not the only problem. After offering him a condescending sneer, Angela started chatting up a major creep at the other end of the bar. The beefy dude screamed textbook predator, with eyes that flickered with nefarious intentions.

"Oh shit." Tristan groaned, now reaching for his own rum and Coke.

Judging by the guy's calculating look, he'd realized who Angela was. If Angela hooked up with him, he'd definitely leak all the dirty details to the gossip rags. Having been Angela's romantic partner himself, Tristan knew just how dirty those details could get. If Tristan was as big a jerk as Angela thought, he'd leave her to that horrific fate and go home. But despite how often Angela tried to emotionally blackmail him, Tristan couldn't let that happen.

He'd never wanted to come to this obnoxious club in the first place, but Angela had insisted—even though they had just finished a long day of filming. She'd pointed out that tomorrow was their off day and said they should go out and blow off steam. She'd also mentioned needing to discuss "something important." Tristan had assumed that meant her lamenting about her dad, a massive media mogul, and their latest falling out. Their fights usually revolved around Angela's questionable behavior and her dad's obsession with their public image. However, tonight was not about her daddy issues. Instead, Tristan was on another guilt trip, watching Angela make horrible decisions. Regretfully inching closer, Tristan managed to catch a few tidbits of the awful flirting between Angela and the creepy guy.

"My God, you are gorgeous. Has anyone ever told you that you look just like Angela Collins?" the guy gushed.

"Oh honey, there's only one Angela Collins, and you're looking at her." Angela flipped her hair over her shoulder.

Upon her confirmation, of course the guy's interest increased tenfold. While Angela let out fake, tinkling laughter at his crappy jokes, Captain Skeevy started some casual groping. His hand stroked her back, then lowered down to Angela's ass. That disgusting image was more than enough for Tristan. As the new couple meandered to the door, Tristan stepped into their path.

"Angela, I think it's time I drove you home." Tristan pressed her but Angela shook her head defiantly.

"She's clearly coming with me." Skeevy snorted. He eyed Tristan the way most wannabe alphas did, trying to size him up.

"Sorry, man. That's not gonna happen," Tristan responded, keeping his tone calm. As Tristan moved to grab Angela's hand, the guy puffed up his chest in exaggerated, toxic masculinity.

"Just because you can't keep up with someone like her doesn't mean you can cockblock me. Now move."

The man made to push past him, but Tristan kept up his top-notch defense. His moves would have made any pro linebacker proud. It was also all Angela's new boy toy needed to take a swing. Tristan dodged his first attempt but that didn't stop the impending scuffle. Skeevy's next move was to tackle Tristan and wrestle him to the ground. The move went sideways, smashing Tristan and his competitor across the bar. Distantly, he could hear Angela and the other club's patrons screaming as the two men tussled, glasses and liquor crashing to the floor. Tristan's back cried out in pain as tiny glass shards embedded in his skin before he and his opponent hit the ground too. At this point, Tristan gave up all defensive niceties and went in with some jabs of his own. Trading blows, Tristan was holding his own pretty well until the guy managed to get a shot in against Tristan's cheek.

Before Tristan could retaliate the club's bouncers came to the rescue. Their strength outweighed Tristan's opponent's (and Tristan's, too, honestly). The gruff bodyguards escorted them and Angela out, kicking them onto the street. The slap of fresh air didn't help Mr. Creepo come back to reality, though, especially now that Angela was clinging to Tristan's side and fretting over his injuries.

"I should sue your ass," the guy shouted.

"Go ahead and try," Tristan challenged him. "My lawyers are so ruthless they could have gotten O. J. off the hook. Not to mention you struck first. My team and I will slap you with a shit ton of damage clauses."

Realizing his tough guy act wasn't going to get him anywhere, the man gave up, cursing them loudly as he stumbled down the street. Meanwhile, Angela leaned into Tristan's injured side, the one that had endured most of the bar collision. She devolved into a fit of giggles at the whole spectacle.

"Glad to see you're still enjoying yourself," Tristan snapped.

"Of course I am. You just showed me you do care." In a singsong voice, Angela began reciting Sandra Bullock's iconic lines from *Miss Congeniality*. The off-key refrain about her own beauty haunted Tristan all the way home after he dropped Angela back at her mansion.

He only felt true relief once he'd made it back home to his own house in Calabasas, but the feeling didn't last long. As he leaned back on his living-room couch to rest, his phone nearly buzzed off the coffee table. Thankfully, it wasn't a typo-filled text from Angela telling him to come back to her house but a text from his agent, Doug Fineman.

It read: *This You?!*, followed by a link.

**TRISTAN MAXWELL BEATDOWN**

Tristan groaned as he skimmed the post. Some trashy blog had caught wind of the night's antics, superfast. The article went on in lavish, hyperbolized detail about how Tristan got in a fistfight at a bar. It was filled with utter nonsense about him flying into a jealous rage over Angela talking with an attractive stranger.

That greasy Godzilla had been far from attractive or worth getting jealous over. Tristan sighed and texted the agent back.

**Tristan**: Evil twin doppelgänger. I swear

**Doug**: Just tell me the facts so I can spin it

**Tristan**: I was defending her from a handsy drunk after she herself was way too drunk. I intervened when things got weird. AKA no good deed goes unpunished

Tristan got stuck in a little more back and forth over whether or not he thought the other guy would press charges. He reiterated since the other man had been the one to take the first swing, Tristan doubted it. But even without a lawsuit hanging over him, the fight had been the last straw on the Angela front.

It wasn't only Angela trying to force him into a relationship that bothered him. Her drinking was getting out of hand, and she refused to acknowledge it. Tristan had seen how his own dad had succumbed to the bottle after his mom left them. He knew the signs of an alcoholic in denial. It had been bad enough watching his dad try and drink himself to death. He didn't want to witness the same thing with Angela.

Determined to banish thoughts of his childhood and bad relationships, Tristan figured his best route was to turn off his phone for the evening. He was seconds away from a cell hiatus when the damn thing buzzed again. His cheek throbbed as he winced at the GARCIA 4 LIFE group text dinging away. The tag perfectly described Tristan's relationship with his former co-stars from *Garcia Central*.

*Garcia Central* had been Tristan's first big break when he scored the role as the youngest brother in a sitcom about a loving but dysfunctional Hispanic family. Growing up beside his fellow TV brothers, Juan and Rafe, they'd bonded over so much, from gaining fame at such a young age and the behind-the-scenes madness to real-life shit like family drama and relationships. They'd stayed in touch over the years despite Juan leaving acting for a culinary career and Rafe jetting all over the world for his own projects. And true to form, they still hassled Tristan mercilessly as their troublesome little brother.

**Juan**: *¡Oye! ¿Qué es esto, bro?*

A link to the same article Doug had forwarded accompanied Juan's concerned text.

Even in a different time zone, Rafe's response came instantly.

**Rafe**: El tigre lives!

Several emojis followed: the actual tiger one, the LOL face, and then the one Tristan nicknamed The Scream for its resemblance to the famous painting. You could always figure out Rafe's stream of consciousness through his emoji game.

Tristan faked an auto reply: *Tristan is not available at the moment. He is going on a dating hiatus*

**Juan**: You really, REALLY should

**Rafe**: Wow. And that's coming from the married one in the group. But for real, dude . . . you good?

Genuine affection finally broke through Tristan's annoyance. It was probably like two in the morning wherever Rafe was, and Juan should be wiped out from his own busy life as a chef and father of three.

**Tristan**: I'm fine. *Se los juro*. If I also promise to check in with you guys tomorrow, can we all go to bed now?

With resounding messages of *Si!* and *Good night, jerk*, Tristan at last disengaged from his phone. Instead of turning in for the night, he chose to unwind first with some reruns of *Fallen Creatures*. He wouldn't admit this out loud, but it was one of his favorite shows. Pure, guilty pleasure goodness. It was exactly the kind of mindless fodder he needed.

When Jada Berklee's face came on-screen, he couldn't help smiling. Her character, Dana, achieved iconic status with her quick one-liners and smoldering persona. It had been a shame when she "left" the show in season three. The writers did a shitty job of killing her off, and the show suffered in the end for it. It sucked when networks didn't pay attention to the characters viewers saw as their favorites.

Knowing she would be joining the *Love Locket* cast on set soon, Tristan was dying to meet her and geek out completely. Somehow, he'd find a way to contain himself. As Doug had reminded him in his barrage of texts, Tristan had an image to maintain.

# 3

Bright and early Monday morning, Jada hopped out of bed, eager to head to her new job. While an acting career was often unstable, there was nothing like working on a film: the hustle and bustle, the creativity, the huge number of people coming together to make something special. Jada's first gig out of UCLA's acting program had been a role in a small indie film. She'd already been in love with the medium but working on a "real film" spurred that passion. She stacked up several small parts on similar productions before landing her biggest role yet on *Fallen Creatures*. The world of television had provided a steadier paycheck, but it had been equally hectic and complex. Returning to film filled her with a renewed purpose, especially on a larger scale production like *Love Locket*.

So, while Mikayla grouchily remarked on Jada rising "at the ass crack of dawn," Jada remained Snow White cheerful as she got ready for the day. Any Disney-friendly critters that might be lingering within their apartment walls would have gladly hummed along as she sang in the shower.

Mikayla should have been used to getting up early to arrive on time, but she'd always been a last-minute kind of girl. Even when they were actually prepared to head out, Mikayla still dragged Jada behind schedule when she couldn't find her favorite charm bracelet. She'd had it since the ninth grade and claimed it brought her luck, particularly whenever there was a clothing mishap on set. Jada merely shook her head at this and shoved her cousin out the door.

Thankfully for them, today's shoot would be taking place on one of Vignette Cinema's production lots in Burbank. Jada had been there before on other jobs, so she'd have no trouble navigating it versus if they'd been shooting on location somewhere.

Lana, Jada's character, acted as the supporting friend to the female lead, Claire, played by Angela Collins. *Love Locket* mainly revolved around Claire and Diego, played by Tristan, childhood sweethearts who were reconnecting later in life. Their path back to each other gets complicated when a time machine–type necklace makes them relive their past mistakes.

Although Jada's character played a pivotal part in helping the main characters figure out how to resolve things, Lana hadn't been needed up until now. At least, that was how the schedule had been arranged with Ren's first pick for Lana, Olivia Brooks, a client also repped by Jada's agent. When Olivia had backed out due to continued scheduling conflicts, Jada's agent had put forward Jada's name instead. Ren loved her audition, even admitting she'd done better than Olivia. That comment could have just been his resentment toward the other actress dropping out, but Jada would take it, along with the abandoned role. Now, Jada's first scenes for today would introduce her character and set her up as the confidante for Claire's love story.

On the way to Vignette Cinema's facilities, Jada peppered Mikayla for any last-minute information. Mostly, she wanted to know more about the quirks of the crew, like who else (besides Ren) might be picky to work with, which people not to chat up before they'd had their coffee, etc. Mikayla turned out to be full of more salacious gossip, like the potential love triangle forming among the lighting team and the time two PAs got in a screaming match over a missing prop. Once Mikayla recapped all the drama on set, they were rolling up to the lot's front gates. Even as Jada started to give the burly guard her name, his face lit up at the sight of Mikayla in the passenger's seat.

"Mikayla Davis, as I live and breathe," the man gushed, holding his hand over his heart. "How are you, girl?"

"Just fine, Andres. You?" Mikayla threw him her million-watt smile.

Jada shouldn't have been surprised Mikayla had old Andres wrapped around her finger; Mikayla found a way to charm practically everyone. The girl made so many friends everywhere that she might as well have her own social media network. Unfortunately, part of developing that network required endless small talk that now halted Jada's plans.

"Sorry, I didn't get a chance to bring you a Starbucks' muffin today. My ride was in a bit of a hurry," Mikayla divulged.

"No problem. Besides, it's about time I brought you something for a change."

A harried-looking driver behind them did the thing Jada didn't have the guts to, honking their horn at the delay. Andres muttered a curse about high-strung, *pendejo* producers and waved them through. From there, Mikayla helped point Jada toward Lot B.

"Okay, how do I look?" Jada said, smoothing down her wrinkle-free blouse one last time.

"Fine. You're about to be out of those clothes in a few minutes anyway," Mikayla pointed out.

"I still need to look professional," Jada muttered as they headed toward the soundstage's massive doors. "This will be Ren's first time seeing me in a while."

"That tyrant will be too busy barking orders to notice," Mikayla shot back darkly. However, the second they entered the overarching entryway, Mikayla had her charm back out in full force.

"Hey, Andrew!" She waved at their main production coordinator. "This is my cousin, Jada. She—"

"Is playing Lana Carter, and right on time," Andrew finished as he checked something off on his clipboard.

Mikayla had briefed Jada on Andrew during the car ride. A devoted cricket lover and nearly as big a perfectionist as Ren, Andrew could be counted on to stick to their schedule religiously while sporting his Team India sports cap. Despite his brusque on-the-job manner, he gave Jada a conciliatory nod.

"I'll go let Ren know," he added before hurrying off.

"And while he tracks down El Commandante, I'll steer you to our next stop."

As Mikayla walked her to one of the back rooms, Jada paused to take in the rest of the set. The soundstage had been turned into a science lab, outfitted as the setting where the characters would later do research on the locket. With microscopes, beakers, and various tools encompassing the set design, Jada could easily see all types of science-y things going down here. Aside from this area as their designated production hub, Jada's first scene with Angela's Claire character would be outside. The lot also contained exterior buildings, one of which was an outdoor café where Claire and Lana would meet.

Jada eventually pulled herself away from gawking at everything to join Mikayla in the area designated for the makeup and costume department. The space held racks of clothing, a few small changing rooms, and several vanities with bright bulb lights. A blond woman stood at one of them arranging the various cosmetics on the table. Like most makeup artists, she had her own glamorous glow, with perfectly contoured features and daring eyeliner.

"Cass, my love!" Mikayla sang as they arrived.

"Mikayla, my shining star," Cass returned in a singsong voice before spotting Jada behind her. "Oh, and you must be Jada! What a vision."

Cass studied Jada's bone structure with professional curiosity. "Oh yes. I'm gonna have fun with that face!"

"Nice to meet you, Cass." Jada laughed, not fazed by the woman's exuberance. Enthusiasm for high cheekbones and color palettes were notorious passions for makeup artists. On *Fallen Creatures*, the makeup team had often gotten caught up in heated debates on everything from skin-care regimens to blending techniques.

As Mikayla got Jada's outfit—consisting of a gray pencil skirt and gorgeous blush-colored blouse—ready, Cass studied Jada's complexion before choosing a foundation. As they fell into their regular routine, their bustle of activity didn't slow down their habitual chitchat.

"Where's Val?" Mikayla inquired about her boss, the head costume designer.

Although Val was usually around to supervise, she'd started giving Mikayla more responsibility as of late so she could "take care of other things." According to Mikayla, Val had caught her husband cheating, which had now boiled over into bitter divorce proceedings. The whole ordeal seemed to be taking a toll, causing Val to break down at the slightest mishap and then escape the set for "tea breaks." Since said tea was laced with valerian root, Val eventually ended up taking naps in her car. The costume designer also didn't get along too well with Cass, so they took turns occupying the limited space.

"Val's probably hiding from Her Highness," Cass whispered with clear distaste.

"Mmm. Ain't that the truth," Mikayla agreed.

"Who's Her Highness?" Jada asked.

"That's our code name for Angela," Cass continued in her stage whisper. "She came in *particularly* foul this morning."

"Do we know why?" Jada had heard in passing that Angela was a bit of a party girl, sometimes a diva. Still, Jada didn't want her first day to consist of walking on eggshells because of someone else's bad mood.

"Why else? Tristan." Cass rolled her eyes.

"They're 'dating.' Supposedly. I refuse to fully accept it," Mikayla explained.

"You didn't mention that in the car!"

"It's just a rumor."

"And she's in denial," Cass said.

"He can just do so much better," Mikayla said. "What are they fighting about?"

Cass's face lit up at the opportunity to share more juicy gossip. "Girl, you are not caught up on the tea. That is so not like you."

At the mention of "tea," Mikayla rushed to take out her phone, and Jada knew where this was headed. That damn gossip page.

"God, why does everyone follow that stupid website?" Jada groaned, the move upsetting Cass's work on her lips. "Sorry."

"Tristan got in a fistfight over her?" Mikayla gasped.

Cass cleared Jada's chin of the offending lipstick. Listening to them rehash the incident, Jada's spirits dipped further. Not only were the two leads in some affair that might hurt the production, Tristan was for sure not the chivalrous Adonis Mikayla made him out to be.

Eventually, Cass finished dolling Jada up, and she left the two behind. As Jada exited the makeup room, agitated whispers—that were gradually becoming much louder—caught her attention.

"Tristan, you're not being fair!" A woman's high-pitched complaint traveled around the corner. Jada stopped short at the girl's voice, not wanting to reveal herself and make whatever was going down worse.

"Life isn't fair, Angela. I've tried to be nice about this, I've tried to be reasonable. But you are refusing to accept how I feel or what I'm saying. I can't keep doing this with you."

"You're acting like everything is my fault!"

"Maybe not everything, but I wouldn't be headed back to Cass if Ren hadn't pointed out this stupid foundation isn't enough to cover up the big-ass bruise on my face."

"Ren being overly critical is not my fault," Angela protested.

"Whatever. I'm done, and I mean it this time."

If Tristan really was "done" with their conversation he might turn that corner at any moment. Jada could either a) keep going and run right into them, b) stand here like an idiot, or c) flee in the other direction. Turning on her heel, she rushed to rejoin Cass and Mikayla in the dressing room—only to stub her toe as she tried to swing the door open. Hissing at the sharp pain, she barely registered Mikayla's and Cass's looks of confusion at her failed entry. Instead, the deep male voice from earlier snapped her out of her agony.

"Oh, hey . . . you okay?"

Reluctantly, Jada turned around and came face to face with the infamous Tristan Maxwell.

Tristan's bluster from his latest altercation with Angela deflated the second he set eyes on Jada. Even though his widescreen TV at home came in high-def, the pixels on-screen didn't compare to seeing the woman in person. She was undeniably stunning, with caramel-brown skin, breathtaking hazel eyes, and curves in all the right places. Tristan dealt with beautiful actresses regularly, but something about Jada's sudden presence left him speechless. She also seemed at a loss for words as they studied each other. Not wanting their first meeting to turn into creepy awkwardness, Tristan held out his hand.

"Hi. Tristan Maxwell. You must be Jada."

"That's me." She glanced down at his hand before shaking it hesitantly. "It's nice to meet you."

"You too. I—"

"Jada!" a purposeful voice called out to them. Andrew Chaudhry arrived on the scene, his foot tapping urgently. "Ren wants to talk to you."

"Of course. I'm on my way." Jada tossed Tristan a smile and a civil nod before following Andrew.

Tristan watched her leave, then poked his head into the makeup department. Mikayla and Cass looked at him expectantly, dual smug smirks on their faces.

"Saw that, did you?" Tristan asked them.

"Mm-hmm. I must say, I'm not sure how I feel about you ogling my cousin. Unless your intentions are honorable," Mikayla warned him.

"Your cousin?"

"Yeah, I'm sure I've mentioned it. Although Jada doesn't particularly like me bragging about our family ties. She wants us to stand on our own merits."

Tristan racked his brain, trying to remember if he and Mikayla had ever talked about Jada before. He was sure they hadn't. Most of his conversations with Mikayla revolved around making fun of Ren. Tristan had a feeling Ren's admonishments of Mikayla were more charged than either of them realized, as the tension between them was too intense to solely be work based.

"What did you stop by for, hun?" Cass interrupted his thoughts.

"What else? Ren's hawk eyes." Tristan pointed to the dark circle under his own eye to bring his point home.

Cass held on to his chin, tsking unhappily. "I don't blame him. You must have been rubbing at it for it to come off like this."

"It was itchy." Tristan defended himself. While he was used to being done up for film shoots, his skin was proving extrasensitive today with the blossoming bruise. Still, Cass had little sympathy for his plight.

"Stay. Still."

After some quick foundation work and idle chatter with two of his favorite ladies, Tristan eventually got the go-ahead to return to set. He bypassed the science lab setup and headed outside. A lot of the crew had congregated on the exterior café, and Tristan spotted Ren smiling and laughing with Jada on the outdoor patio. She seemed decidedly less stiff around the director than she had been around him. The two were chatting like old friends while Angela lingered off to the side, impatiently scowling at them. As he approached, she glanced at him, her eyes red rimmed. *Oh shit*, Tristan thought. The remnants of Angela's tears meant either she was still angry and would take it out on anyone in the vicinity or she would be sulking the whole day.

"Excuse me. I'm sure you two are having an absolutely *riveting* conversation," Angela said, "but can we go over the scene we're supposed to be filming?"

*Okay, looks like she's chosen lashing out*, Tristan realized with sinking dread. Ren's easy manner evaporated as quickly as his laid-back smile.

"We are perfectly on track, Angela, but thank you for worrying," he said with mild diplomacy. "We're just waiting on— oh good, Tristan, you're back. I wanted to let you know we're going to tackle Angela and Jada's first scene, then you'll come in a bit later, also meeting Jada's character for the first time. Got it?"

"Got it, boss." Tristan threw Ren a thumbs-up. Technically, since he wasn't needed immediately, he could go chill for a bit, but he found himself wanting to stick around. He'd never seen Jada act in person, and watching this scene would help him get a feel for what their dynamic would be like when he shared the screen with her later.

As Ren went over the logistics of the scene, Angela studied Jada. The other actress remained oblivious as she nodded along with Ren's instructions. Meanwhile, Tristan was on edge, fearing Jada would become Angela's next target.

"All right. So, I know this is your first day filming together, but for this scene, we want it to feel extremely natural. Two best friends catching up on life and relationships, like they always do," Ren said, going over the logistics.

Despite the director's emphasis on friendship, Angela's scrutiny of Jada was about as subtle as a vicious piranha. Jada either remained oblivious or had decided to block it out as she paid careful attention to the blocking for how she would need to move through the scene. Still, Tristan knew better than to underestimate Angela when she was in this kind of mood. Filled with apprehension, he stayed glued to his spot off camera as the girls ran through a rehearsal and then finally took their marks, just inside of the café. After Ren yelled action, Jada and Angela exited the coffee shop to sit on the patio, drinks in hand. Perfectly in character, Jada looked attentive and excited as Angela started off with Claire's dialogue.

"Lana, the most amazing thing happened today."

"You got that big promotion at work?"

"No, he's back."

"Who?"

The girls made it to the outdoor table, and Angela sank into her seat with a dreamy sigh.

"Diego." Angela's eyes sparkled with lovestruck glee. At least until she slipped up and glanced offscreen in Tristan's direction. Her bubbly aura splintered, forcing Ren to call things to a halt.

"Angela, you're supposed to be looking at Jada, not off to the side."

"Who says I wasn't going for, like, Claire daydreaming or something?" Angela batted the criticism away.

"And that would be one direction to take, but we want this

scene to be about the chemistry between you and your best friend. Got it?"

"Sure, Ren," Angela said with false sweetness. "But I don't think that should solely fall on me."

To her credit, Jada didn't engage with her jab and stayed focused on Ren's correction. "Thanks for clarifying that, Ren. We'll try it again."

Although Jada was able to stay cool and collected, Tristan struggled to hide his annoyance with Angela. Just once, he wished she'd surprise him by showing an ounce of empathy instead of taking her resentment toward him out on their newest co-star. Knowing that would only happen once hell froze over, Tristan headed back to the soundstage as everyone reset to do the scene. Maybe his exit would take some of Angela's heat off Jada. On his way, Erica, one of the PAs, rested her hand on his arm. With bright, brown eyes and her dark hair smoothed back into a ponytail, Erica's youthful overeagerness to help with the production was well known. Her zealousness to prove herself often overlapped with chatting up Tristan.

"What's up, Erica?"

"Do you need anything? You look a little . . . tense."

"I'm just going to grab some water or something and then head to my trailer to regroup."

"Okay, we'll let you know when it's time for you to come back. But if you *do* decide you need anything else, let me know." Erica's friendly expression remained professional but Tristan noted the undertone to her offer.

For once, he didn't hop on the innuendo with a joke. Like he promised, Tristan retreated to his small oasis, going over lines and absorbed in his music playlist. He loved putting together his own idea of a soundtrack to whatever movie he was making. In the middle of him singing along to Cher's classic "If I Could Turn Back Time," Erica knocked on his trailer door to let him know they were ready for him.

When Tristan regrouped with the team at the science lab, Jada looked slightly less chipper. She still greeted Tristan pleasantly but stayed a good distance away from Angela. For her part, Angela tensed at Tristan's arrival but refused to address him outright.

"Hey, guys . . . how's it going?" Tristan asked.

"Peachy," Ren said, his brow tight with consternation. "We're picking up with Claire and Diego asking for Lana's help with the locket."

Now outfitted in a white lab coat, Jada would switch gears from being just Claire's bestie to her other responsibility as a prestigious physicist. Once the main characters realized the locket had trapped them in a time loop, they went to her for help. Ren went over the characters' motivations and what he expected before letting them launch through a few run-throughs. A while later, with beakers bubbling and the lab humming with activity, they dug into the scene.

Angela held the locket out for Jada to see, her hand shaking. "Please, you have to help us."

Jada's expression remained wary as she eyed the necklace skeptically.

"Claire, first of all, I'm not even sure what you're asking is possible. I mean, there hasn't been any proof of time travel in the real world."

Tristan stepped forward, wrapping a comforting arm around Angela's shoulders. As Tristan easily fell into the part of the distraught but protective boyfriend, Angela stayed faithful to her role this time, too, by taking solace in his embrace.

"Believe me, we're not hallucinating." Tristan jumped in with his line. "We're not delusional. There is some time warp freaky stuff happening around this thing!"

"Cut!" Ren called out. "That was good, but Mateo, I changed my mind. I'm not crazy with the lighting right now. I think it needs to be a shade more clinical."

After some adjustments and several more takes, the group dispersed for lunch. Even though Angela flounced off to lock herself in her trailer, Tristan took the reprieve as a chance to finally talk to Jada. He made an effort to walk beside her as they both headed toward the long banquet table.

"So, I'm sure you're already pretty familiar with the highs and lows of catering, but I've still got to warn you . . ." Tristan said confidentially.

"About?" Jada's eyebrows shot up at his tone.

"Avoid the mixed greens. Why? One, because salad is not a real food. And two, while it may look nice and leafy, it's a lie. Trust me." This remark earned him his first chuckle from the enchanting Ms. Berklee.

"Okay. Always good to steer clear of an E. coli emergency. Anything else?"

"Yes, actually," Tristan said as they examined the other options at the table. The viable alternatives included an array of sandwiches and a much safer bean salad. As she deliberated, Tristan decided there was no better time to ask the ultimate question.

"So . . . werewolves or vampires?" he asked innocently.

"Oh no, you're one of them, aren't you?" Jada sighed. No

doubt she'd met many *Fallen Creatures* fans pulling this schtick in the past, but Tristan couldn't help himself.

"A werewolf?" he teased. "I wish."

"No sucking blood for you then?"

"No, seems like much more fun to run naked through the woods, howling at the moon."

Tristan could have been mistaken, but Jada almost looked flustered at the mention of shifter nudity.

"Neither. I played the reincarnation of a siren. Remember?"

Tristan's mind automatically flashed back to that reveal on the show and the very skimpy outfit Jada had been dressed up in during her transformation.

"Oh yeah, I remember." He cleared his throat.

"Still, I stand by her being the best."

"Yeah. It seemed like a great ride to be on. Who was your favorite person to work with? Daniel Kane seems like a cool guy."

Jada paused in the middle of scooping up some of the bean salad as a flicker of discomfort crossed her face. "Everyone on set was great. You're right, it was a really . . . interesting time back then."

Her words might have been complimentary but there was no denying how tense Jada had grown. Before Tristan could try and backtrack, she was already moving away from him.

"Now, if you'll excuse me, I'm going to track down Mikayla. Nice talking to you, though," Jada said, walking off with her salad in hand.

*That girl is seriously awkward*, Tristan decided. But despite her weird behavior, he felt an urge to learn more about his enigmatic co-star. Maybe over the next few weeks the ice would thaw, and he'd get to know the real Jada.

# 4

The next few days on *Love Locket* were a whirlwind. Jada loved the role of Lana and spending time in the world of the film. But tension lingered beneath the surface of the production. Ren remained nice toward her, but she understood where Mikayla was coming from. The man hated any type of mediocrity and ruled with an iron fist. The real problem was that Tristan and Angela were in this bizarre dance of either trading barbs or ignoring each other—not the best combination for two romantic leads. They managed to be professionals when the cameras were actually rolling, and Jada could see how the rumor mill churned. There was a simmering attraction between them in spite of the underlying resentment from what Jada assumed was the breakup conversation she'd overheard.

Jada suspected Tristan simply had chemistry with everyone. Even when she was talking to him in passing she couldn't ignore his magnetic charm. But no matter how Tristan tried to pull her in, she refused to engage in any flirtation with him. She'd been fooled once before by one man's debonair act. The last thing she needed was a new on-set drama with Daniel 2.0.

Her time on *Love Locket* was entertaining, but Jada breathed a sigh of relief when she had her first day off. Normally, she'd spend that time enjoying the outdoors or doing yoga, but her plans for this Thursday evening were vastly different as Alia's show, *Unbound*, was premiering tonight. Already in season three, the show had a substantial following. The supernatural drama followed paranormal investigators Zane and Killian as they fell in love with each other while tracking down magical murderers. The show had received critical acclaim for its diversity and LGBTQIA+ representation.

Since she'd always been overly ambitious, these achievements alone weren't good enough for Alia. In spite of her upper-class upbringing, Alia had always worked her ass off, from clawing her way up from being a PA in Georgia's developing film industry to landing her writing position on *Fallen Creatures.* Now running her own show, Alia kept pushing the boundaries—and sometimes her own sanity—to keep the series a success. Her latest initiative involved doing a reaction video to the season premiere. She'd invited Jada, Mikayla, and various team members and actors from the *Unbound* crew to join in. Alia's apartment could have accommodated the partygoers, but the lead actor, Damien, had offered up his place instead. He played one of the main cops and exiled jinn, Zane, and adored Alia for giving him such a layered role.

As six o'clock rolled around, Alia vigorously knocked on Jada and Mikayla's front door. With her cousin caught up in perfecting her makeup, Jada let an anxious Alia inside. Well, anxious by Alia's standards. Raised as a southern debutante, from a line of Georgia's oldest and richest Black families, Alia had been trained to exude poise in any circumstance. Unlike the majority of the population, she never actually broke out in a sweat or hyperventilated when she was nervous. You had to know her pretty well to notice the telltale signs: the clench of her jaw or fidgeting fingers. Tonight, Alia was attempting to cover up her nervous ticks by letting out a long breath and clutching her purse more tightly than necessary. To any outside observer, the successful beauty still looked like a perfectly polished southern belle, with her brown skin gleaming, her red dress breathtaking, and her hair flawlessly styled. Seeing that Jada was the only one to greet her, Alia's eyes narrowed knowingly.

"Makeup?" she asked.

"Yep."

Alia let out a sigh before striding off to Mikayla's part of the suite. "Mikayla Davis, put the bronzer down and step away from the mirror!"

Jada snickered as she heard a faint protest from Mikayla, but she knew who would win this round. Making excellent time, Alia soon dragged a sulking Mikayla out of the bathroom and ushered them out the door.

"What can you tell us about this season? Does Zane find his mom? Which guest star dies first?" Mikayla pestered Alia with questions on the ride to Damien's house.

Her interrogation might have been annoying to anyone else, but it was strategic. Asking Alia about all the twists and turns for the upcoming episodes would temporarily distract her from freaking out over the premiere party, especially once Jada and Mikayla started theorizing in the hopes of teasing out spoilers.

"I bet you Killian and Zane break up *again*," Jada argued.

"Of course! They've both got so much baggage. But I want to know what happened to The Slasher."

Alia stayed tight lipped despite the temptation they threw at her. Jada and Mikayla were still in the dark about what would happen on *Unbound* when they arrived at Damien's gorgeous estate. The chic landscaping and paved driveway provided an inviting air that led them up to the front door. As they were let in by one of the other guests, they saw an interior that was in stark contrast to the outside. Damien had transformed his downstairs area into an *Unbound* fan's haven.

Memorabilia from the show—posters with the catchphrases "Release the Killer Fairies!" and fan illustrations of the show's "ships"—lined the walls. The themed food table held an eclectic range to quench anybody's appetite, from fruit punch done up like a vampire's bloody cocktail to a tiered cake in the shape of the Supernatural Crimes headquarters. Pop hits played from the speakers. The catchy music invited the attendees to jam out before the main attraction started. On a technical level, things were also on par, with rented lighting equipment and several cameras to catch the group's reactions from different angles. On top of that, a reporter from *Entertainment Hollywood* circulated around the room, interviewing various cast members.

Spotting Damien in the center of the room, Alia waved and headed over to gush over what he had put together. Of course, Alia had had some say in the setup, but the end result was worthy of in-person praise. Jada and Mikayla left her to it and tackled the food table. As Mikayla cut them a chocolate corner piece of the cops' office, the other main actor of the series, Calvin, approached them.

"Hey, now, I use that room to take down the big bads," he teased them.

"Tonight consider the big bad my stomach," Mikayla

responded as she plopped the cake on her plate.

"How are you doing, Calvin? Excited for the premiere?" Jada asked.

"Yes! I'm ready for you all to see Killian's transformation this season."

"Meaning?" Mikayla's attention got diverted from the dessert. "You can't leave us hanging with a response like that."

Calvin gave an enigmatic shrug, poured himself a vampire cocktail, and abandoned them. Clearly, he had been sworn to Alia's no-spoiler secrecy as well. As Jada shook her head at his departure, Mikayla nudged her.

"You should talk to the reporter too." Mikayla pointed out the journalist chatting with Damien and Alia.

"No . . . tonight's not about me."

"Maybe not, but we're supposed to be Alia's hype women."

"Fine. I guess I can do a shout-out on Twitter. How's that?" Jada relented. She didn't have a million followers, but her fan base did enjoy hearing from her on social media. This kind of event was perfect internet fodder. After she made sure her mouth was icing-free, Jada let Mikayla record her with her smartphone. Putting on her best influencer persona, Jada waved at the camera.

"Hi, everyone! I hope you all are doing well. I just wanted to mention that I'm celebrating the season premiere of *Unbound* with their awesome showrunner, Alia, and the amazing crew." Mikayla panned the camera to take in the crowd, pausing to do a dramatic zoom on some of the actors' faces.

"We'll be reacting to the show. You should definitely get in on the action and catch tonight's episode."

"Perfect!" Mikayla confirmed as they cut the video feed.

Their post came at just the right time as the countdown

Damien had projected on the wall flashed, alerting them the show would be starting in five minutes. People went from mingling party mode to gathering around the screen. As Jada and Mikayla settled on the couch with Alia, it was easy to get caught up in the excitement. Next to Jada, Alia's back was ramrod straight instead of relaxing into the sofa like a normal person. Sure, they would be on camera but the buttoned-up look would not help with engaging her viewers.

Jada squeezed her friend's hand in a sign of support. "It's going to be kickass. Now breathe!"

Mikayla chimed in with an exaggerated demonstration of Lamaze exercises. Alia burst into laughter, their plan of attack working beautifully. As their friend reached a minor level of chill, the countdown reached its last seconds. Everyone chanted along like it was New Year's Eve.

"Three . . . two . . . one . . ."

As the cameras in the room rolled, the iconic theme song replaced the television ads. Captivated, Jada fell into the opening scene's rhythm. As usual, Alia and the team had delivered by sucking the viewers back into last season's cliff-hanger. As Zane and Killian raced through the woods, the cast and crew threw out suggestions.

"Find a river! It'll throw The Slasher off your scent!" one of the producers, Justine, insisted.

"What they *need* to do is stop Killian bleeding or I'mma fight somebody." Calvin vouched for his own character.

As the story unfolded, the show maintained its witty, sharp edge laced with mystery and romance. By the time the episode ended, Jada's throat hurt from laughter and all the boisterous conversation. Once the preview for next week aired, the actors jumped in to address the viewers.

"We hope you enjoyed the premiere's twists and turns. Feel free to post your theories in the comments," Damien said, then turned to Alia. "Anything you'd like to add, boss lady?"

"Just that we have more in store! Thanks for watching tonight and stay tuned!" Alia gave one last wave at the cameras before the livestream ended.

The second they were off air, Jada wrapped her friend up in a hug. "It was amazing. I'm so proud of you," she gushed.

"Seconded," Mikayla added.

"Everyone did a fantastic job," Alia said. "Hopefully, this means the ratings will be on track."

As Mikayla soothed Alia's rating worries, Jada's phone buzzed in her pocket with a Twitter notification.

**@tmaxrocks:** Superjealous. We should be shipping Zillian together!

Tristan had commented on her video *and* retweeted it. More people had followed suit with other retweets and responses. Jada had also gained more followers because of it. The short message shouldn't have affected her, but a warm glow washed over her. It was strangely heartwarming that, in spite of Tristan's outward demeanor, he appeared to be a big fantasy nerd. And the fact that he even bothered to promote the show was more than a lot of Jada's past co-workers had been willing to do. Some celebrities espoused rah-rah sisterhood or stick together mantras, but rarely reached out to others when it mattered.

Jada responded: *Next time. :)*

Putting her phone away, she couldn't help smiling. Maybe there was more to Tristan than she originally thought.

# 5

When Tristan woke up Friday morning, he knew it would be busy on set. No matter how well organized, there were always a few hiccups on any film shoot—the lighting not being right or a prop temporarily going missing. He was sure today would be no exception, especially since they were diving into the trippy, time travel elements of the film. The shoot would consist of a lot of CGI and green-screen work as his character, Diego, faced the hurdles that came with purchasing the titular locket of the movie.

He'd barely gotten out of the shower, his skin still damp, when his phone rang. His first thought was the schedule had been changed, but then he saw Doug's name flashing on his screen. While Doug Fineman was a fantastic agent, willing to go to war for his clients, he was also a PR hound. There were other people in the company who could handle major stuff, but Doug preferred to be hands-on with his all-star clients. For Tristan, that meant he'd already missed one call from Doug. He had no choice but to pick up for this one.

"Doug. What's up?"

"My stress levels. That's 'what's up,' Tristan."

"What did I do now?" Tristan placed the phone on speaker so he could get dressed. At the rate things were going, it'd be best to just toss something on, matching socks be damned, and head out.

"That depends. Do you still want to be the face of Bright Futures?"

The mismatched striped socks slipped through Tristan's fingers as Doug's words hit him with chilling severity. The nonprofit organization Bright Futures assisted underprivileged children in a variety of ways, from providing donated clothes and food to fostering mentorship opportunities. Many celebrities had tons of charities they donated to or were ambassadors for, but Bright Futures wasn't just a good publicity stunt or a tax write-off for Tristan. It had started out as so much more.

When his father died from liver failure, it hit Tristan harder than he could imagine. Tristan had already relocated to pursue his career options in New York, and his relationship with his father had been distant at best. But after Tristan moved away, his dad had started to get his act together, going to AA meetings and trying to make amends. They'd been in the midst of trying to repair things between them when he got his diagnosis. Tristan's feeble hope of becoming a real family again shattered.

After his father passed away, Tristan dropped out of all his upcoming projects, falling into a hideous headspace. Thankfully, Doug and his former *Garcia* brothers kept checking in. Rafe eventually introduced him to Bright Futures through a charity gala. Meeting all of the amazing kids that the organization helped pulled on Tristan's heartstrings and inner loneliness. Working with them had guided him out of the darkness. The idea they no longer wanted him as a spokesperson, that his connection with those kids could be ripped away in an instant, nearly burned a hole through his chest.

Ignoring the lump forming in his throat, Tristan asked, "Doug, is this about that stupid bar fight?"

"You know they love you, Tristan, but this doesn't set a good example for the kids."

"Then I'll go there and give a whole damn seminar about words over fists, anti-bullying, whatever. If they drop me now, then it'll mess up our plans for the fundraiser."

He and the Bright Futures board members were in talks regarding their annual gala. Tristan had suggested doing a fair this year in Santa Monica, and they'd jumped on it after he promised to promote it. They'd been planning it for months. But it wasn't the prospect of putting on a big fundraiser that mattered to Tristan. Imagining all of the kids getting to attend a carnival in their honor had been what pushed him to make the fair a success. There was no way in hell he was going to let them down.

"I'll personally call LeeAnn later," Tristan added.

LeeAnn was the main program coordinator, and they had developed an easy rapport. LeeAnn saw beyond the movie star persona. She didn't shower him with praise for simply showing up. Instead, they talked about real ways they could help the mentees, and she consistently sent him emails about all the events. As Bright Futures' star player, she would be able to smooth things over with the board better than Tristan or Doug ever could.

With their apology tour in place, Tristan hung up and practically bolted for the door. He hated being late in general, but it would especially upset Timekeeper Kurosawa (a nickname born out of love and frustration that the director—luckily—didn't know about).

Before he could reach his trusty Mustang, which would normally get him there in a flash (by L.A. standards), his phone vibrated again. He needed to start putting it on silent right when he got up.

"What is it now, Doug?"

Tristan had answered without checking the screen this time, his main focus on unlocking the car. With the phone up to his ear, he slipped into the driver's seat and waited to hear Doug's latest request. The only reply he got was mostly static and, if he wasn't mistaken, a few deep breaths on the other end. Then the line went dead altogether.

"God, whatever," Tristan mumbled, ready to give up and throw his cell in the cup holder. But as he set it down, the phone number from the missed call jumped out at him. In bold bright red, the area code flashed at him: +57.

Bogotá. There was only one person with a Colombian phone number who would call him and then hang up. It wasn't some weird butt dial or an automated scam. It was his mother. Isabella Moreno. One of the biggest telenovela actresses of her time, and also a proud member of the Shittiest Moms Club.

Shaken to the core, Tristan couldn't start the car. All he could do was think back to the last time he'd received a call from his mom. When his dad passed away two years ago, she'd reached out to offer her condolences. His comeback included several swear words and banning her from attending the funeral. Not that she would have come. Regardless, she had no right to try and weasel her way back into Tristan's life during such a vulnerable time. If you abandoned your husband and fourteen-year-old son ages ago, you didn't get to waltz back in like nothing happened. All that being said, his stomach gnawed at him, wondering what she wanted this time.

With inner turmoil churning through him, it was a miracle that Tristan got his shit together and made it to work in one piece. Nevertheless, his day was ruined. He'd do his best to put on a happy face and go along with his job, but on the inside, his mind was a mess. Why had she called? And why had she hung up without saying a word?

Walking onto the studio lot in a daze, he ran straight into Erica juggling several cups of coffee. Tristan managed to steady her before she could topple into a hot mocha mess.

"Jeez, Tristan! If you wanted a cappuccino all you had to do was ask." She laughed, handling the situation with more grace than he would have.

"I'm sorry, Erica. You okay?" Tristan asked, checking her hands and arms to make sure she hadn't suffered any burns due to his spaced-out state. Once she reassured him that she was fine, Tristan kept walking, more carefully this time. No matter what was going on with his flaky mom or outside of work, he had to be on his game now. Resisting the urge to hide out in his trailer, Tristan mentally prepared himself for a long day and his ongoing psychological chess match with Angela.

For a while after their last altercation Angela had seemed to accept their fling was over, and had resorted to catty remarks. And yet during their last day off, she'd sent him a WYD text, clearly fishing to see if he wanted to hook up. He didn't. Instead, he'd spent that night watching Jada and her friends geek out over the *Unbound* premiere. Remembering she would be on set as well, Tristan figured she'd be the one bright spot today. However, the first person he spotted was Ren, consulting with the cinematographer, Mateo.

As he walked up to his friend and director, Ren spoke up

with a stern scowl, "She's not here yet." For a moment Tristan thought he'd read his mind about Jada, but then realized he meant Angela. *Great.* Tristan sighed inwardly. He almost would have preferred sparring with Angela versus seeing Timekeeper Kurosawa come out in full force. But it was too late. The director studied his watch again, his left foot tapping impatiently. If there was one thing Ren hated it was a lack of punctuality. Actually, as history had proven, Ren hated a lot of things. But then again, his high expectations and relentless drive were exactly why he had become such a successful director, even though he was only in his thirties.

After leaving Japan to attend USC, Ren had worked his way up from promising film student to one of Hollywood's emerging stars after his first independent film won awards at Sundance. Tristan had been at the iconic film festival to see Ren's film, *Kyōto Dreams*, at its first screening. The whole venue had been buzzing over it, calling Ren the follow-up to the original directing juggernaut, Akira Kurosawa. When they met after the showing, he and Tristan bonded over Ren hating the pressure of that comparison, and became fast friends. Over the years of their friendship, Ren insisted there was no way to get accolades and name recognition by letting your actors and crew do the bare minimum. But Angela's flagrant disregard for his ideals and proper set etiquette was definitely going to give Ren premature grays. Judging by his frustrated sigh, he wouldn't work with her again, even if his life depended on it.

"That's not surprising," Tristan teased him. Aware of his friend's antics, Ren gave him a look that had shut up or else written all over it. He jerked his head toward the dressing room.

"Hair. Makeup. Wardrobe. You know the drill," Ren said.

Like a good soldier, Tristan did as he was told. When he walked into the hair and makeup department, he found Jada was already there. Seeing her made him momentarily forget about his rough morning, his tense nerves easing as he noticed her chatting with Cass.

"Hey, Jada," he said.

And yes, he might have spoken in a slightly more suggestive tone than a friendly co-worker would. He couldn't resist flirting, even if she hadn't taken the bait so far. Wooing women had become an inclination since he'd kissed Becky Miller on the cheek in the third grade. It was the talk of the playground for weeks.

"Hi, Tristan," Jada said.

"I'll be right with you, Tristan," Cass said as she flitted around.

"Take your time. I can go slip into my costume," Tristan offered.

"That's a negatory, handsome. Val noticed a 'stain' on your shirt and sent Mikayla off on a removal mission," Cass said in her droll tone. With nothing else to do for the moment, Tristan sat down in the chair beside Jada.

"So, you're a Zillian shipper too? Best choice," he said.

Jada's face lit up. "What can I say? I like my romances risqué."

"Does that extend to a personal preference, by any chance?"

Eyes widening, Jada bit her lip self-consciously, much to Cass's frustration.

"Don't ruin my art, dear." Cass scolded her and reapplied the lipstick.

"Thank you, by the way, for sharing my tweet. My friend Alia's grateful for the support."

"Of course. It's no problem."

"You're finished, beautiful," Cass said. Jada thanked her and slipped out of the trailer, dropping Tristan's mood back to bleak again.

"You can't help yourself, can you?" Cass said knowingly. He gave her a guiltless, boyish look.

"I have no idea what you're talking about, Cass."

Cass picked up a brush and started to apply foundation to his face. "*Sure*, and that bruise is healing up nicely," she said, shaking her head. "Keep up with your womanizing and you'll end up with more than raccoon eyes. A woman scorned can rip your world to shreds."

"Several have tried and failed. I think I'll live." He winked at her.

By the time Cass finished chastising him, Mikayla had returned with his outfit. Breathless but beaming, she held up the hanger with a flourish.

"Tristan! Never fear. I have arrived," she said gallantly. Tristan inspected the shirt, and it looked spot-free.

"Mikayla Davis to the rescue as usual." He thanked her.

Despite Ren's occasional comments that Mikayla was "far too loud and doesn't take anything seriously," the girl did always manage to come through in a crisis. No matter what their prickly director said, Tristan appreciated her can-do sunniness after the morning he'd had.

"And don't you forget it," Mikayla warned him. Tristan gave her an exaggerated bow of gratitude in response.

Ducking into one of the changing rooms, Tristan took stock of the rest of his ensemble. In addition to the freshly cleaned gray shirt, he had a leather jacket and designer jeans. The clothes were comfortable, and he felt good in them, but he couldn't help but feel like something was missing. Unable to put his finger on it, he went back out to ask Mikayla what he might be missing when they compared him to the continuity photographs. But she was gone, and he didn't want to rustle through Val's things to find the photos. Rather than hang around to sort it out, Tristan decided to rejoin the crew on the soundstage. When he got there, he wished he'd lingered behind after all.

On the surface, everything looked ready to go. The green screen was up, the lighting "just so," the cameras positioned. But the crew was undeniably restless. Most likely because their fierce leader, Ren, was far from pleased. Standing by Mateo, he looked like he wanted to kill someone. He was also speaking rapidly in Japanese. Tristan assumed whatever he was saying included several swear words. Off to the side, Jada stood with her arms folded, warily watching everything unfold. Tristan sidled up next to her, trying to remain inconspicuous.

"What's going on?" he whispered to her.

"Angela *still* isn't here. They've called her a bunch of times and she's not answering. So Ren is . . ." Jada waved toward their fuming boss.

"Jesus Christ." Tristan groaned, but he also had a sinking feeling.

Angela had basically been a Hollywood golden child since birth, primarily due to her Daddy Warbucks-esque father, and that came with the widespread issues of childhood stars. She'd gone through various meltdowns and been in and out of rehab. Tristan hoped nothing awful had happened to her, but he was also sick of everyone suffering the fallout from her egotism and downward spirals. Deciding he was in no mood to get swept up in Ren's rage, Tristan went to inspect the catering table. He had just picked up a bagel when Erica came up to him, this time looking more sheepish than usual.

Off Script

"Hey, Tristan, I hate to ask, but have you heard from Angela? I'm trying to track her down, but her cell is going straight to voice mail."

"Of course it is," Tristan grumbled, then took a savage bite out of his bagel. "But no, she hasn't called me."

"Yeah, I kind of noticed you guys seemed to have a falling out but figured I'd ask anyway." Sympathy radiating from her concerned look, Erica touched his arm. "I hope you're doing okay with you guys . . . breaking up?"

Although Tristan's massive dating fumbles often ended up in the press, he didn't exactly relish sharing the details of their "falling out." Erica probably wouldn't be so bold as to actually leak whatever he told her, but it would definitely get around to the rest of the crew. However, based on the way Erica still had her hand on his arm, her fingers dancing along his skin, he had a feeling she was looking for something more than gossip.

"I think I'm past the heartbroken stage." Tristan took on a lighter tone as he laid his hand over Erica's.

"Well, if you ever *do* want to talk about it, I'm here," she said, moving closer to him.

"Now that you mentioned it, there's some time to kill. Do you want to hang out in my trailer for a while?" he offered.

They both knew damn well that talking would be the last thing on their minds once they were finally alone. But this didn't faze Erica in the least as she nodded eagerly. As discreetly as they could, they slipped out a side door, headed off to put on a private, seductive show that would be far from prying eyes.

Or so Tristan thought.

# 6

"I can't believe she's doing this to us," Jada grumbled, checking her watch for the fifth time.

"I can," Mikayla said in a singsong voice.

They were hiding out in the dressing room, trying to stay safely away from Ren. Cass had gone above and beyond in avoiding the director by going on a smoke break. The rest of the crew weren't as lucky as they scrambled to reach Angela, and the tension snowballed into a stressed fever pitch. Time was money on a film set, and even if Angela's dad was bankrolling this film, any little delay caused a ripple effect, making their already long days even more time consuming.

"She's probably hungover somewhere. Facedown in her own vomit." Mikayla swung her legs childishly as she sat in the chair. Jada kicked her foot.

"That's a horrible thing to say."

"It's true. How many times has she shown up here looking shot to hell, in last night's party dress? The woman is a train wreck. She's not like you. Talented. Responsible."

"All right. You don't have to suck up to me," Jada teased.

In reality, she loved having her cousin's unconditional support. While Mikayla could be flighty with rent and often between jobs, her love for Jada never changed. She was Jada's number one cheerleader, and Jada treasured her for that.

"I'm serious. You would be a better lead for this movie. And then you'd get to make out with Tristan Maxwell." Mikayla's eyes went dreamy.

"Not this again."

"I don't get why you won't admit how hot he is! He looks at you, too, sometimes. You should hit that. Well, if Angela wouldn't kill you afterward."

"Mikayla, you had ringside seats during the Daniel fiasco. Do you seriously think I'm that much of a masochist to ever date a co-worker again?" Jada asked.

Since Mikayla had found out about Tristan's retweet, she'd gone from casually shipping Tristan and Jada to planning out entire dates. The whole way into work Mikayla had theorized on how long Tristan had been low-key scoping out Jada's social media and when he would officially ask her out. Jada refused to give in to her cousin's matchmaking frenzy. Just because they were becoming friends didn't mean she could ignore Tristan's status as king of the Casanovas. It was much safer to stay professional than succumb to the teeny, tiny part of her that wanted to know what was underneath Tristan's cool superstar surface.

So she planned to stick to her golden rule: no dating co-workers—especially not men who melted panties but then left women in tears. No way in hell was that happening to her. She'd learned her lesson the hard way on *Fallen Creatures*, and didn't need another tutoring session. Getting caught up in another torrid love affair wasn't worth the ultimate consequence of a production going to shit or her being forced to leave another job.

Mikayla's gasp distracted Jada from her inner resolutions.

"Speaking of Tristan, look what I found! After Val got on me about the shirt, I completely forgot to give this to him!" Mikayla panicked, holding up a leather belt.

Such a plain-looking accessory might not seem important to an outsider. But in the land of film continuity, details were king. If Tristan's outfit didn't match up precisely from scene to scene, even if less observant viewers didn't notice, the cameras and cinephiles would catch the flaw.

"Oh shit. They'll have my head if I don't get this to him. A single screwup in front of Val is one thing, but if Ren finds out about this . . . you know how much he hates me," Mikayla said, clutching the belt. Upon seeing Mikayla's devastated face, Jada's fierce urge to protect her cousin overpowered her inclination to scold her.

"Don't worry. I'll take it to him. I want to go out there and check on the Angela MIA situation anyway."

Mikayla gave a sigh of relief. "That's my good old cuz. Always saving my ass."

"If I didn't, you'd be dead by now," Jada said.

In the hopes of looking less conspicuous, Jada wrapped the belt around her own waist before leaving the wardrobe department for the set. The crew was doing their best to stay busy but Angela's glaring absence couldn't be ignored. For his part, Ren seemed to have retreated to a more meditative state with Andrew plying the director with chamomile tea. Although Jada was happy to see Ren calmer, she hoped Andrew hadn't gotten the Sleepytime tea bags from Val's collection. Either way, a quick look around revealed that Tristan was nowhere in sight.

Wondering where else he could be, Jada figured the next best place to look for him was probably his trailer.

Exiting the lot, she crossed the short pathway and approached the white Winnebago. Her brisk knock caused the trailer door to swing open. Hesitant to go in without an official welcome, Jada called Tristan's name. When he didn't respond, she stepped inside to find the trailer slightly messy in the expected bachelor way. As Jada stood in the main area, she heard voices coming from the bedroom area farther inside and headed that way. If Tristan was on the phone or something, she could just drop the belt off and dash back out. A minor interruption.

What Jada wasn't planning on was catching Tristan and one of the PAs going at it. Big time. Tristan was pounding into her from behind, Erica making plenty of appreciative moans. What Jada had mistaken for a murmured conversation was an expletive-laden sexual encounter.

"Fuck yes, Tristan. Harder," Erica said.

Tristan obliged, moving faster. He was completely focused on his and Erica's pleasure . . . until he looked up and saw Jada standing there. He immediately stopped, his sexual desire deflating in shock.

"Holy shit! Jada?"

Jada froze. What answer could redeem her for being the cause of coitus interruptus?

There simply *were* no words.

Jada stood there gulping like a fish, terrified of what would come next.

"Jada, what the hell are you doing in here?" Tristan's horrified question snapped her out of her stupor. At his words, Erica looked up and noticed Jada's presence as well.

She squealed and yanked the covers up to hide.

"I—I'm sorry. Excuse me. It's just—"

As Jada fumbled for an explanation, she undid the belt around her waist. Then she realized this might look like a very forward way of her asking to join them. Blushing feverishly, Jada whipped the belt loose and flung it at the bed.

"Here!" she squeaked, then turned to run out. She'd only made it a few steps before Tristan grabbed her arm. Despite being completely nude, he was a fast runner, not letting his nakedness deter him from chasing after her.

"Wait, Jada," Tristan said.

Jada kept her eyes decidedly away from him. She'd gotten enough of a glimpse to confirm what every other woman assumed. Tristan had a very ripped, hot body underneath all those leather jackets and worn jeans.

"Erica, can you give us a minute?"

The PA nodded. Wrapped in the bedsheet, she picked her clothes up off the floor and scurried into the bathroom. The girl suddenly had modesty after screwing her co-worker while bleating like a sheep throughout the whole thing. Sleeping with Tristan had been an unprofessional, stupid move.

The fact that Tristan had let it happen—no, had probably initiated it—was equally disgusting. He was supposed to be a pro in this industry. He knew better than to have sex with PAs—during work hours, no less! Besides, he had just broken up with their lead actress. Did Tristan not care about leading people on or taking advantage of impressionable newcomers who were starstruck? If so, he'd probably bed hop his way through the whole cast and crew before *Love Locket* ended.

"Jada, are you listening?"

"No. Distracted. Still processing . . . could you please put some clothes on?"

"Oh yeah. Sorry."

But Tristan didn't appear sheepish. He was comfortable with his body and being on display. However, he did let go of her and turned his back as he looked for his pants. And okay, maybe Jada took a peek at his tush. Which was as perfect as the rest of him. When he turned back around, pants back in their rightful place, Jada was able to make eye contact.

"I didn't mean to barge in on you two. I was just trying to hand over your belt. You'll need it for the scenes today." Jada gestured to the abandoned belt on the bed, the cause of this damn catastrophe. Tristan picked up the accessory and looped it through the jean's belt holes absentmindedly, more concerned with studying her reaction.

"I apologize for what you saw. I get that it's inappropriate. I can only imagine what you must be thinking about me," Tristan said. This time he did seem embarrassed, blushing slightly.

"It doesn't matter what I think."

"It matters to me," Tristan said.

Jada didn't know what to say next. She didn't want to come off as a prude or strike him as some delicate girl who didn't know what a penis looked like and who fainted at the sight of one. She wanted to be poised, indifferent, above the entire debacle—but she felt undeniably flustered.

"Don't worry about me. None of this is my business."

"You won't tell anyone?" Tristan asked, the hope and relief clear on his face. It hit home for Jada. He wasn't worried about her sensibilities or his lack of ethics. He wanted to make sure she'd keep her mouth shut.

"Of course not," Jada said.

"Thanks. I appreciate it." Tristan squeezed her hand in gratitude. Repulsed by his selfish motives, Jada tried not to flinch at his touch.

"I'm going to head back to set. See if they're ready to shoot yet," Jada said before any extra awkwardness could form between them.

"I'm right behind you." Tristan gave her his well-known brilliant smile. One that charmed everyone—except her. Not anymore. Certainly not after this.

Jada made her escape at last, fuming on her walk back to the studio. Any positive feelings she might have had for Tristan had been stripped away. His charisma and friendly demeanor were all just to hide the fact he was an inconsiderate, conniving ass. He'd tried to emotionally manipulate her into being his confidante. It was like she'd been erroneously dragged into an old boys' club, full of casting couch scandals and cover-ups. Granted, Tristan's tryst may have been consensual, but that didn't make Jada feel any better about being roped into secrecy.

In the past, keeping secrets had done far more harm than good. Unbidden, Jada's mind drifted back to another set, another hookup, another fall out. Back to the time Jada found Daniel hooking up with another *Fallen Creatures* co-star.

The day on set had started off perfectly normal. On location in Georgia, they'd been working on season three, and Jada had been dating Daniel for almost a year. When Jada had joined the cast in season two, she and Daniel had clicked right away. As the lead vampire on the show, Daniel had shown her around, filled her in on all the gossip and office politics. Long story short, he had been disarmingly charming and she had fallen for it. However,

Daniel had been adamant about not letting their attraction "influence people's perceptions of Jada's talent."

Since it had been her first major gig, she'd taken him at his word and agreed to keep their situation low key. Even when she'd developed a closer friendship with Alia toward the end of her first year on the show, Jada had kept her lips zipped about her romantic relationship. She didn't want to put Alia in an awkward situation in the writer's room or betray Daniel's trust. So like an idiot, she settled for less, relishing the moments that supposedly made the secrecy worth it. All the clandestine dates filled with roses and gifts of jewelry. Amazing make-up sex after another round of "Why can't we tell people?" She convinced herself those gestures were enough.

But on that particular day, Jada learned Daniel had been whispering sweet nothings to someone else. She probably never would have found out the truth if she hadn't done something sneaky as well. Daniel's birthday was coming up that weekend but he had "family plans" and couldn't spend it with her. Jada had been upset but ultimately decided with all the gifts Daniel gave her, she should still get him something special.

She concocted a plan to slip her gift (a watch engraved with their initials) inside Daniel's car during the lunch break. Making her way through the parking lot, she'd been so excited to give her supposed boyfriend a surprise. When she made it to Daniel's car window, she was the one who received a massive shock. On the driver's side, Daniel had leaned his car seat all the way back while their lead actress, Maggie, straddled his lap. Despite his positioning to allow for privacy, Jada caught an eyeful of their heavy make-out session.

She'd wavered between fleeing the scene and openly

confronting Daniel. Bringing everything out in the open right now would certainly quench her thirst for revenge. However, Maggie wouldn't react well to the news that she wasn't the only one to be felt up in Daniel's brand-new Tesla. Apparently, their mutual beau cared more about the environment than fidelity. Deciding it was best to retreat for now, Jada tried to tiptoe away but she wasn't fast enough. Her movement must have registered in Maggie's peripheral vision because the actress looked up just as Jada started her getaway.

Maggie looked as startled as Jada felt but covered it quickly. Surprisingly graceful for someone who'd just been interrupted midrendezvous, Maggie climbed off of Daniel's lap and exited the car. For his part, Daniel looked ashen, unable to put his acting persona up as fast as his lover. With a lot less dignity, he scrambled out after her.

"Oh my gosh! Jada, I'm so sorry you had to see that." The actress apologized profusely as she squeezed Jada's hand.

"Don't be. I understand how an attraction can develop between co-workers," Jada said, trying not to side-eye Daniel.

"Well, it's a bit more than an attraction." Maggie gushed as she looped her arm through Daniel's. "We've been seriously seeing each other for some time now. Just keeping a low profile for the show, you know?"

*Oh, believe me, I know.* Jada held back the urge to voice this thought out loud. Instead, she smiled stiffly while her heart shattered into a million pieces.

"Really? Well, congrats. And don't worry, I won't tell anyone."

"Thanks, J. You're the best." Maggie gave Jada one more smile before turning to peck Daniel on the cheek. "And you, mister, I'll see you later. I can't wait to meet your mom."

"Yeah, can't wait. We'll catch up with you in a second, okay?" Daniel said.

Maggie nodded, then gave herself one more presentability check before walking off. When she was out of sight, Daniel reached for Jada but she slapped his hand away.

"Don't even think about it. Whatever lie that's about to come out of your mouth, just don't!"

Despite "dating" him longer, Jada had never been allowed to reveal the truth. She'd never had the luxury of being invited to a family dinner. Evidently, she'd been the dirty little secret while Maggie was the "appropriate" kind of girl to actually be seen with. Daniel attempted to save face anyway.

"Listen, I swear, this thing with Maggie . . . it just happened. When the writers decided to have our characters date this season, she started flirting with me. More and more, until . . . I'll admit I had a weak moment."

Jada laughed at his denial, the car make-out session permanently engraved in her brain. "This is more than a moment, Daniel. She's meeting your family. You're spending your birthday with her instead of me."

"She heard me making plans on the phone, and—"

"Stop! You can make whatever excuses you want for your behavior, but that doesn't change the fact that you've been stringing me along."

Thinking back, all of Jada's weak moments came to the surface: forgiving Daniel's bad behavior, the endless cancellations, the constant excuses. Well, she was done being weak. Shaking her head with finality, she laid down the law.

"It's over, Daniel."

But as she turned to walk away, Daniel grabbed her, pulling

her back into his arms. Cradling her waist tenderly, with his cheek close to hers, he made another plea.

"Don't say that. We can fix this. You still love me."

"And Maggie? Do you even realize she loves you too?" Jada challenged him. He could play dumb but the look in Maggie's eyes had been unmistakable.

"But I don't love *her*. You're the one, Jada. You're the only one for me."

Sniffling back tears, Jada almost missed the stifled sob that *didn't* come from her. Whirling out of Daniel's embrace, Jada turned around to see Maggie standing on the other side of the car. As tears streaked down the starlet's face, Jada's heart went out to her.

Having stumbled upon the same type of shocking betrayal moments ago, Jada assumed she knew how Maggie felt. That she must be furious at Daniel, heartbroken at his deception, and yes, maybe even angry at Jada. But surely, if she'd caught the full conversation, she'd realize Daniel was the one at fault.

But no. At that moment, the cold look in Maggie's eyes wasn't solely directed at her unfaithful lover. Jada also caught some of her glare as Maggie let out a bitter laugh.

"I forgot my earring. Thank God I did, huh?"

Yet Jada knew Maggie's rhetorical question wasn't about finding out the truth. It was much deeper than that. It was about revenge.

While Jada would never agree that's what God truly wanted in that instance, it didn't change anything. Soon afterward, production found out about the whole messy love triangle, and Jada eventually lost her job. Jada tried to refocus on the present, but the similarities between the two situations were too eerie. With *Fallen Creatures* and Daniel, Jada had been caught in the middle of a Shakespearean-level tragic love story. But when it came to Tristan's frivolous encounters, she didn't want to be involved at all.

When Jada finally made it back inside the soundstage, she found Mikayla nibbling on fruit at the catering table. She hoped she didn't look as frazzled as she felt.

"Did you give it to him?" Mikayla said, twisting her hands anxiously.

"Yes. But things got . . . weird."

*And X-rated*, Jada added silently.

"Weird how?"

"I'll tell you later. Is Angela here yet?"

"Yes, unfortunately. She and Ren had it out. He told her off and she locked herself in the bathroom. We coerced her into going to get her hair and makeup done." If Angela was inside her wardrobe haven bickering with Cass over blush palettes it was no wonder Mikayla had risked being seen by Ren chowing down out here.

"That's a relief. At least we'll be able to get some work done today."

They parted ways as Mikayla knew she'd have to go back to help Angela with her outfit, and Jada wanted to read her lines someplace quiet. With no personal trailer to hide or fuck around in, she sat outside the dressing room. Determined not to stew over the inequalities of social status, she prayed that she'd be able to rehearse in peaceful solitude until shooting began.

"Jada?" Erica said, walking up to her.

*No, no, no*! Jada's brain screamed in protest. She didn't want to be wrapped up in Erica and Tristan's mess. Since she had agreed not to snitch on them, she simply wanted to bury this deep down and ignore it. That way, she could move past her resentment (eventually) and pretend the incident never happened. Apparently, Erica didn't see things the way she did.

"Yes?" Jada braced herself.

"I wanted to say thanks for having my back. It's nice of you to keep our secret."

"As far as I'm concerned, there is no secret. I wasn't there," Jada hinted. *Please, please go away.*

"I know it's not exactly the right thing to do—but he's hot. Who wouldn't want to sleep with him?" Erica babbled, trying to egg Jada into camaraderie. But there was no way in hell she was going to get Jada's approval for what she'd done. Instead, Jada gave her a tight nod.

"I guess."

"To be honest, as far as I'm concerned, it was worth it," the girl continued, then leaned in conspiratorially. "He's intense. I lost myself. I also lost my underwear. I think it's in his trailer somewhere."

*OH MY GOD! This girl isn't wearing any panties?!*

It was true that Tristan did melt the poor things. Or possibly kept them as souvenirs. At this rate, Jada wouldn't put it past him. Scandalized, she couldn't believe the girl was proud of the situation. Erica's pleased expression caused Jada to say her first deprecating sentence on the scenario.

"Good for you?" she said sarcastically, with a drip of condescension. Erica didn't catch on.

"See you later, Jada. Thanks again." Erica winked at her before walking off.

Jada's temples throbbed with encroaching heat, a headache

on the rise. Just as her fingers struck up a soothing massage, her whole body tensed at hearing a familiar voice.

"That was an interesting conversation. Mind explaining to me what it was about?"

Jada turned to find Angela standing behind her. She must have just exited the dressing room because she didn't look like a train wreck. With the magic of the hair and makeup department, she'd been transformed into leading lady perfection, with shiny, blond curls and a luminescent sheen. Angela might be disguised as an angel, but she was truly *la diabla* personified when she wanted to be. Jada knew if she told the truth, Angela's hellfire would rain down on her.

"Excuse me?" Jada squeaked.

"You and Erica. I have a feeling I know who you two were talking about, but it would be nice to have confirmation before . . ." Angela shrugged. Despite the casual gesture, Jada felt her impending demise gathering around her.

Searching for an out, hope arose when she saw Andrew a few feet away. Maybe if she could signal him, he would notice Angela and usher her onto set. After waiting nearly an hour and a half for her to show up, Ren would want her there as soon as possible. Her gaze flickered from Angela's stormy face to poor attempts to make eye contact with Andrew.

"Before what?" Jada asked, keeping her voice light.

"Before I make some decisions."

"Please don't involve me in your . . . decision-making process." Jada treaded carefully while also discretely waving at the oblivious production coordinator. Andrew was too caught up in a conversation with one of the grips to notice.

"It's a yes or no question." Angela stepped forward so she

and Jada were eye to eye, effectively blocking her view of the other crew members. There was no escaping her.

"Did Tristan have sex with Erica? Did he have the audacity to do something like that right under my nose?"

"That's two questions," Jada joked weakly but Angela's quirked brow meant "Don't screw with me."

"Yes or no, Jada."

"Please, don't put me in the middle of this."

"We're friends, aren't we? Tell me the truth." Angela grabbed Jada's hands, tugging on them painfully, although Jada assumed— or hoped—it was meant to be reassuring. She held back the urge to point out that no, she and Angela were not friends. They barely spoke outside of doing scenes, and when they did, Angela addressed her with patronizing contempt.

"I—I . . ."

Way too late in the twisted game, Andrew noticed their heated exchange.

"Angela! We're ready for you," he called. The urgency in his voice alluded to the unspoken "Right the fuck now."

Angela scowled and dropped Jada's hands. Her niceties were over with.

"I don't need your answer. I can tell from the guilty look on your face. I don't know why you're covering for him, but there's no fucking point."

Angela stormed off toward the soundstage with Andrew hot on her heels, using his walkie-talkie to update Ren that their star was on the move. Jada was sure all hell was going to break loose once that crazed woman found Tristan. Rather than joining in the melee, she ran off to the dressing room to tell Mikayla the deep shit she'd somehow gotten into. If she was going to die for being the messenger, she at least wanted to make a last confession.

# 7

Tristan wasn't expecting it.

One minute he was talking to Ren and one of the producers, everything perfectly calm now that they'd been notified Angela was on her way. Then out of nowhere, a mystery object struck the back of his head, shattering. Sharp shards of glass sank into his skin as stars burst in front of his eyes. Spinning around to face his attacker, he spied a steaming Angela angrily waving the remains of a handheld microscope at him. The prop must have been left out from the other day.

"How could you?" She screamed at such a high pitch it brought everyone in the room to full attention. Despite being an actor, Tristan wasn't one for dramatic public displays of any kind. Not PDA or fights, and especially not ones involving hysterical women.

"What the hell is your problem?" he hissed, yanking the prop out of Angela's hands.

"You slept with that woman! That worthless tramp. When you had *me*. No man in his right mind would choose her over *me*!"

Angela said, before looking for another object to throw. Tristan grabbed her hands, forcing her to stop her assault.

"First of all, we are over. And second, this is neither the time nor the place to have this conversation," Tristan said, wishing their co-workers weren't listening in.

"I don't care! How could you do this? After all I've done for you!"

Tristan bit back the retort that Angela had done very little other than act like a possessive prima donna. He didn't need her to do anything because he'd never asked her for a damn thing. He couldn't hold back the frustrated sigh that was bottled up within him.

"I can't deal with you when you're being irrational."

Angela gasped—then slapped Tristan so hard, it gave him whiplash.

Several crew members pulled Angela away, dragging her out of hitting range. In the struggle, the gaffer tripped over one of the cords. As he went down, the lighting equipment came down with him. Sparks flew as the bulbs exploded and the lighting's barn door blades slashed the green screen. Tristan gawked at the wreckage as others rushed to help the gaffer up, all their hard work ruined. Angela ignored the havoc she'd caused in favor of throwing out one last threat.

"Ren, I refuse to work with him. You fire him or I'll quit! I'll walk. I swear!" Angela said, kicking and screaming the whole way. Tristan didn't know—or care—where they took her as long as it saved him—and everyone else—from her onslaught. However, he was about to face another battle when he turned around and saw Ren's face.

"What the hell did you do?" Ren growled at his leading man.

Their friendship and positive working relationship weren't going to save him from the director's wrath.

"I may have . . . hooked up with someone recently."

Ren's eyes narrowed. "How recently?"

"Like an hour ago." At his response, Ren was ready to pick up where Angela left off.

"You can't be serious. Because I know you're not stupid enough to risk your professional reputation on a one-off. People might say whatever they want about your sex life in the gossip magazines, but you shouldn't give them ammo to disgrace your actual work. Let alone the crew's work." Ren flourished his hand at the damaged set.

"This messed up relationship you two have brought onto this film is screwing everyone over. Do you think Tim deserved to be dragged into your mess?" Ren shouted in defense of the lighting team member who had fallen.

"No, I'm so sorry, Tim. I'm sorry to everyone, actually," Tristan said, knowing.

Ren was right. It killed Tristan to know he'd screwed up this bad. But he realized he wasn't the only one to blame here. He started to walk away but Ren stopped him.

"Where do you think you're going? I'm not done with you."

"You can yell at me as much as you want in a few minutes. But first I have something I need to do." Tristan shrugged Ren off and went to hunt down Jada. He found her alone, hiding in the dressing room. She started to speak, probably to make excuses, but Tristan wasn't going to let her.

"What the hell, Jada? You promised you wouldn't say anything."

"I didn't," she said, stepping back and placing some distance between them.

"Oh, but you did. I have a gaping cut in the back of my head to prove it." Tristan touched the spot to double check, and yep, he was bleeding.

"I'm sorry!" Jada sounded sincere, but it wasn't enough for Tristan. He went on, needing to share the blame with someone else.

"Why couldn't you keep your mouth shut? Why did you tell her? It must be a pact between the women here, a vindictive sisterhood, where you have to stick together and gossip behind my back."

"That's not what happened." Jada's face was set in stone. She wasn't going to let Tristan keep yelling at her without defending herself.

*Bring it on*, Tristan thought.

"Maybe not," he said. "But however it went down, you've caused a shitload of trouble. You're going to regret it."

Things probably would have gotten more heated if Ren hadn't stepped into the room.

"Now what's going on?" he asked, exasperated.

"What's going on is Jada's the one who blabbed to Angela."

"Jada, is that true?" Ren asked. From his incredulous tone, it was clear he'd thought she was too classy to spread rumors or create drama. So had Tristan.

"It didn't happen the way he's making it out to be. I—"

Ren held up his hands as Tristan and Jada started to angrily talk over each other.

"That's enough. I've had my fair share of breaking up fights. Between wrecking the green screen and equipment, Angela refusing to film scenes with Tristan, and Tim and Tristan's injuries, we're done for the day. Thanks to all of you, we're on damage control right now. You've probably cost the studio millions of dollars."

"Damage control?" Jada asked, her eyes wide after being filled in on everything that had happened.

"Yes, Mr. Collins just called. He's concerned about the issues on set as well as Angela's welfare. He insists she needs a few days off, and he'd like to discuss our working conditions with me personally. So we're even further delayed."

Tristan's stomach dropped. Angela's father, Gordon Collins, was the vice president at Sunset Pictures, the production company that was funding *Love Locket*. Angela must have called him as soon as she'd been carried off. Known for a temper that rivaled his daughter's, he would have no qualms about halting production altogether if he wasn't satisfied with Ren's explanations.

"Ren—"

"Don't." The director stopped him. "I don't want your pity or you offering to help. I will take care of smoothing things over, filing the insurance claims, all of that nonsense. What I want both of you to do is go home and think about what you've caused. And if this is how you want your careers to go."

"I don't, Ren. I'm sorry," Jada said. "The only thing I want is to do my job."

"Then you better straighten up, because you've come this close to losing it." Ren walked out, leaving the pair stunned.

Ren hadn't made the same threat to Tristan as it was too late in the game to recast a lead, and he would most likely defend Tristan in front of Mr. Collins. But guilt gnawed at Tristan as he reflected on the mess he'd made and putting Ren in this terrible position. Not to mention Jada's shock at Ren's comment. Unlike him, she could easily be recast since she had already been the previous actress's replacement. Still, he was too upset about his part in things to comfort her.

The day had hit disaster-level proportions. And Tristan had a feeling that things were going to get worse before they got better.

# 8

"I can't believe Ren's thinking about firing me!" Jada wailed into her margarita glass.

"He wouldn't dare," Mikayla insisted, flames in her eyes.

The two of them were sitting in a local bar called The Drunken Skunk. After they'd left the set, Jada had moped around at home. Eventually, Mikayla was able to drag her out of the house. The Drunken Skunk might not have had the prettiest name but the crowd wasn't as rowdy as people might think. The atmosphere held that elusive blend of edginess and comfort with well-worn leather booths, cozy lighting, and yes, sometimes sticky tables.

For now, Jada could care less about a little grime as long as they kept serving her bangin' margaritas. Besides, it was close enough to their Culver City apartment that they could stumble home. Something they couldn't do if they had gone to one of the overcrowded spots in downtown L.A. On their arrival, Mikayla had also sent an SOS to Alia, who came promptly as pity party backup.

"It's going to be okay." Alia fell into the role of comforter easily. "I highly doubt he's going to get rid of you this late into production. Didn't you say you have, like, two weeks of shooting left?"

Alia did have a point. Since Jada wasn't a major character, her scenes were supposed to wrap soon. Although, after today's destruction, she wasn't sure when they'd be back on set. Ren had promised to update everyone once he knew more. Translation: they wouldn't find out until this battle with Mr. Collins played out.

Too tired to get into the what-ifs about continuing her role, Jada nodded in response to Alia's question, then took a giant sip of her drink. Alia patted her on the back with indulgent affection.

"You're a good actress, Jada. Even if he did get rid of you, you would be able to find another job. I'm sure of it." Of course, Alia went with the logical backup plan over the doom and gloom playing through Jada's mind. Not surprising for a woman so poised under pressure—Alia had graced the "30 Under 30" list of Hollywood's up and coming stars.

"Hear, hear!" Mikayla added, raising her mug of beer.

"None of this was my fault." Jada played with her straw. "I didn't force Tristan to have sex with a young and impressionable PA, but I'm the one paying the price. He thinks he can yell at me for his indiscretions."

"Yeah, I'm shocked. I can't believe Tristan did that," Mikayla said.

"That's interesting, coming from you. Since you were hiding in one of the changing rooms, listening in on our screaming match," Jada snapped.

"Hey! I heard Ren coming, and I had to dodge. You know he hates me. But still, I thought Tristan was a good guy, and it'd all work out."

"Well, he's not." Jada nearly snarled. "He's a self-absorbed, hot-headed lothario!"

Like the good friends they were, Mikayla and Alia allowed Jada to rant for another hour and two strawberry margaritas. Topics of defamation ran from Tristan's low inhibitions to the possibility that underneath his great hair his ears were too big and the more far-fetched (but still possible, she insisted) idea that his narcissism covered up hidden sociopathic tendencies. As Jada's rambling theory on how Tristan might be the next Ted Bundy wound down, Alia let out a yawn.

"I'm sorry, guys, but I'm starting to crash. I'd love to stay and keep cursing the day Tristan Maxwell was born but I have an early start tomorrow. Forgive me?"

Jada and Mikayla pardoned their friend but weren't quite ready to leave. When Alia was out the door, Mikayla turned to Jada with a devious smile.

"What?" Jada squinted at her cousin. Mikayla had her I'm plotting something diabolical face on.

"I would have brought this up earlier, but you were too devastated. Plus, Alia was here and she would not approve. But now I think you're ready." Mikayla pulled her phone out of her pocket and waved it teasingly in front of Jada.

"What does your iPhone have to do with my shitty day?"

"It *means* that I got everything on video. Well, up until the point where Ren walked in."

Slowly, Mikayla's scheme dawned on Jada.

"No! You can't show that to anyone!"

"Why not? He deserves some backlash after the way he treated you. Say the word, and I forward this to the *Sip That Tea* tip line in ten seconds."

Jada bit her lip as she began to reconsider. It was unlike her to lash out, to take revenge. But she had a sneaking suspicion that it would feel incredibly good to avenge herself. Why was the idea appealing to her? Maybe it was because she was still pissed. Maybe it was because Tristan's distrust and anger hurt her more than she'd like to admit. Or maybe it was because of those damn margaritas.

Whatever the reason, Jada found herself saying two magically destructive words.

"Do it."


*Bang!*

*Ring!*

*Bang!*

Those were the first sounds Tristan heard as he struggled to wake up. It was a combination of battering-ram thuds and an intense doorbell assault as someone tried to break down his front door. As he groggily came to his senses, Tristan wondered who had gotten past the security gate and thought they could pull such a loud B & E on him. Tristan dragged himself out of bed and headed downstairs, ready to curse out whoever was ballsy enough to do this at seven in the morning.

Looking through the front door's peephole, he spotted Doug's shiny bald forehead quivering with angry frown lines. His attack on Tristan's innocent door proved it wasn't a friendly visit. Bracing himself, Tristan opened the door and his agent barged past him into the house and promptly started screaming.

"What is the matter with you, Tristan? Have you completely

lost it? Not that I need to ask, based on what I've seen. What everyone has seen."

"Seen what? Could you lower it about ten decibels?" Tristan asked.

After his latest altercation with Angela and the horror that had ensued, Tristan was officially done with being yelled at—and being blamed for that matter. Sure, he had slept with someone else, but he hadn't been the one blabbing people's secrets or wrecking the studio equipment. He refused to engage with Doug's bad mood. Deflecting, he went into the kitchen to grab a glass of water. Doug trailed after him, steaming.

"You know exactly what I'm talking about. The catastrophe you caused on set yesterday."

"Don't get me started about that. I've had enough guilt trips to last a lifetime." Tristan sipped his water, then paused. "Wait. Did Ren call you?"

"Oh, I talked to Ren, but that's not how I found out."

At Tristan's blank stare, Doug ran his fingers through his thinning hair with exasperation.

"You honestly don't know?"

When Tristan shrugged, Doug searched in his pockets for his phone. He muttered to himself the whole time, angrily denouncing arrogant, nitwit movie stars.

"I don't know why you people are always terrorizing me and your fans with new scandals, but here! I'm talking about *this*, you idiot!" Doug said after finally finding his phone and holding the device dangerously close to Tristan's face.

Before Tristan could say anything else, Doug pressed the Play button on a video. There he was on camera yelling at Jada. She appeared as the poor victim as she shrank away from him while he gesticulated wildly. And of course, the audio had to be crisp and clear. The viewer could hear every mean, nasty word he'd said to the girl.

"Oh God." Tristan fell back into a kitchen chair, his stomach sinking. Watching the video made him realize what a bastard he'd been. He was going to be canceled before he even had his breakfast.

"I'm screwed, aren't I?" Tristan tried to say lightly, but he winced when Doug glared at him.

"Very much, I'm afraid." Doug sat down across from him. Now that he'd delivered the bad news, some of his angry mojo had subsided. He rested his balding head in his hands, winded from his dramatic entrance.

"Why, Tristan? Why did you scream at that poor girl like that?"

"I had my reasons. She's not as innocent as she looks, and—and . . ." Tristan deflated at his unquestionable defeat. He was the jerk and loser in this situation, no matter how he tried to swing it.

"I messed up. I get it."

"Do you, though? Between the bar fight, the mess with Angela, and now this! Tristan, you keep this up and you'll be tanking fast with your fans—and with the execs. No one wants to deal with or support a disorderly divo."

"Can't I just apologize?"

Doug's responding Are you effing serious? eyebrow raise proved that no, he could not. The smear campaign would be epic. No doubt there were a dozen disparaging headlines out there this instant. And with his luck, Bright Futures would drop him for real this time.

"You didn't think this through," Doug went on. "*Rival Warriors* comes out in a few weeks. And if this damn rom-com doesn't go down in flames, you'll have that too."

*Damn*! With everything else going on, Tristan's upcoming action flick had slipped his mind. There were already TV ads and giant billboards all over the place advertising the film's release. He didn't have time to process the repercussions for that project and its poor PR team as Doug barreled on with worst-case scenarios.

"How are we going to market you as a hero if you come off as a bad guy in the press? How are we going to sell to fans that you can be a romantic lead when they see you treating women like this?"

"We could lie," Tristan blurted out. "We could lie and say I was rehearsing a scene. I think if I beg, Jada might—"

"If we made out like this was you rehearsing a scene, I've got to tell you, it looks like you went way off script," Doug said. "Besides, for all we know, Jada could have been the one who sent the video out."

He hadn't considered that possibility. Would Jada do something like that? She didn't seem the type. She was sweet and unassuming—or so Tristan had presumed before she'd ratted on him.

"Fine. What's your solution?" Tristan asked.

"We have to find a way for you to redeem yourself. Based on what Angela is bound to say and this incriminating video, you need to find a way to prove that you respect women. That you can be with one and treat her well."

"Are you saying I should pretend to be in a relationship with someone to clean up my image? To masquerade as a happily committed man? I'm sorry, but I don't see how that's going to fix the way things look between me and Jada."

Rumors abounded in this town about what couples in Hollywood were soul mates versus staging a drawn-out romance for clout. Tristan had no desire to get entangled in something so sneaky and didn't see how it would help. Furthermore, he couldn't think of anyone who'd be willing to tie their fate and career to his.

"Doug, I may be an actor but me pretending to be madly in love with one person is a stretch—even for the tabloids. And I can't see any of my exes agreeing to this."

"I wasn't talking about an ex. I'm thinking a new, blossoming romance. Possibly with the one woman whose name is synonymous with yours right now." Doug twirled his phone in his hand, a devious gleam in his eyes.

Tristan's eyebrows shot up as he put the pieces together. The resulting image was horrifying.

"You want Jada to be my lucky, new girlfriend? If we can't depend on her to tell a simple lie to cover for me, what in the world makes you think she'd go along with that?"

"We just have to sweeten the deal for her. What's the one thing that every semidecent actress in this city wants?"

"A Hemsworth brother?"

This comment—despite being 100 percent accurate—earned Tristan a shoulder smack from Doug.

"No, you fool. *More*. More fame, more fans, more everything."

That didn't sound like Jada, but it did fit quite a few actresses he'd met. His attention piqued, Tristan nodded.

"Okay, I'm listening."

With Tristan's go-ahead, Doug proceeded to explain exactly how he planned to swing it, his big, master plan, and slowly Tristan bought into it. He only hoped Jada would too.

# 9

The throbbing tap dance in Jada's brain wouldn't end. She placed her forehead in the palm of her hand, wishing doing so would alleviate the pain. While sitting at the kitchen table, Jada listened as Mikayla read her the latest headlines on the Tristan fiasco. *Sip That Tea* had snatched up Mikayla's tip, all right. Along with posting the video, they'd written a scathing exposé that sent ripples out to every other celebrity gossip outlet. Their fight had been hotly discussed on *E! News*, and trending hashtags abounded online like #DownWithMaxwell and #TeamJada.

"'Tristan Maxwell's Hot Throb Rampage.' Wow. They are ripping him a new one, aren't they?" Mikayla shook her head in disbelief.

Jada winced. In her other hand, she clutched a cup of some disgusting concoction of herbs, runny eggs, avocados, and way too much paprika, which Mikayla swore would clear up her hangover. Jada reluctantly took another sip as penance for what she'd caused.

"Here's another one. 'Fiery Celeb Goes Down in Flames.'"

"Kayla, stop. If you go on, I think I'll vomit. My stomach is queasy with regret."

Mikayla rubbed her back in reassuring circles.

"Yes, what we did was harsh, but come on! He's a big-time movie star. This won't kill him. It'll just knock him down a peg."

"I guess you're right."

"I always am." Mikayla encouraged her to take another swig. Jada decided to chug the rest. It did seem to be helping, so she might as well suck it up—literally.

Abruptly, Jada's phone started its high-pitched ringing. She frowned at the loud noise since she had no desire to speak to anyone. Unfortunately, her fumbling fingers accidentally pressed the Talk button.

"Hello?" A male voice came over the line. Swearing silently, Jada answered.

"Yes. This is Jada Berklee. Who am I speaking with?" She remained wary. This could be a reporter who'd stolen her number.

"Hey, there, Jada! I'm Doug Fineman," the man said, sounding nice instead of like he was looking for a scoop.

"Okay. What can I do for you?" Jada tried to stay polite but felt like hanging up. He wasn't speaking loudly but the man's voice was vibrating in her ear, amplifying the aching in her head.

"Well, I work for Ren. He feels terrible about what happened and he'd like to speak with you."

Jada's attention was piqued—and on guard.

"Is he still . . . did he say what he wanted?"

"Not specifically. But would you be able to meet up at Sophie's Café? Around noon."

Frankly, Ren had appeared way more preoccupied with fixing

the business side of things than worrying about her. However, if he wanted to meet with her, she couldn't say no. With no alternative, Jada promised she would be there, hung up, and gave Mikayla a look of terror.

"Who's Doug? Ren's newest, unlucky assistant?" her cousin asked once Jada relayed the message.

"Maybe. The name sounds familiar. Either way, this can't be good." Although Mikayla insisted the meeting was probably to ease the tension, Jada couldn't shake a lingering feeling of dread. Regardless, she arrived at the café promptly at noon, composing herself with nerves of steel. If Ren had decided to fire her, she didn't want to burst into tears—or end up on her knees begging for him to take her back.

Sophie's Café hadn't rung a bell when Doug had first mentioned it. It wasn't located in the hustle and bustle of downtown L.A. but on a side street that was much quieter. Stepping inside, the cool air conditioning washed over her, soothing her flushed skin. There was no one at the host station to greet her, and when she peeked into the dining area, Ren was nowhere in sight. As a waitress in a checkered green and white uniform hurried by, Jada stopped her.

"Sorry, I know you're busy. But do you know if a Ren Kurosawa is here yet?"

"Kurosawa. You mean the two guys guzzling water?" The waitress jerked her head toward the far side of the restaurant, then rushed off.

Jada squinted in the dim lighting, searching for Ren's lush, dark hair and tall frame among the patrons. As she glanced around, she sensed that someone was looking for her too. That tingling feeling you get on your neck. With goose bumps rising on her skin, Jada skimmed the lunch crowd once more and spotted someone she least expected to see. And dreaded. Tristan Maxwell was staring right at her. He'd opted to sport the celeb incognito look, wearing a Lakers snapback cap and designer shades. He'd lowered the shades to stare at her pointedly. Sitting at a table in the back corner, he was with a man who was definitely *not* Ren. Tristan nodded in her direction and said something to his companion. The older man lit up and waved her over.

Jada didn't move because it was rapidly becoming clear she had been duped. They may have given the name Kurosawa to the hostess, but their boss would not be showing up at the damn café. Now hoodwinked into facing off with Tristan, her first instinct screamed to head for the exit. But while her feet itched to make a quick getaway, another part of her knew that fleeing the scene would be like admitting that she was intimidated by him. Refusing to feel bullied any longer, Jada relented and walked over, her body tense with apprehension. The man with Tristan jumped up and pulled out a chair in a gentlemanly gesture. Tristan didn't move at all; instead, he kept watching her with those hawk eyes.

"Ms. Berklee. Thank you for coming. Please have a seat," the man, a.k.a. allegedly Doug Fineman, said.

Jada took the chair but got right to the point. "What do you want, and why did you lie to me?"

"Sorry for the subterfuge. Doug Fineman, Tristan's agent. He and I are both here to offer you our deepest apologies over what happened."

Of course this ruse had come from the mind of a 10 percent con man. It also explained why Doug's name had rung a rather foggy bell. She pushed through the remains of her hangover to try and recall what she knew about the agent. Her agent, Avery, had mentioned him in passing when Jada first got cast in

*Love Locket.* She'd called him a conniving backstabber, but then again, Avery rarely had nice things to say about her competition. For his part, Doug pulled off his repentant expression fairly well, but Jada remained on edge.

"Really? You're both sorry? Well, Mr. Fineman—"

Mr. Fineman gave a sheepish smile. "Please call me Doug."

"Well, Doug, you must be a terrible ventriloquist, because Tristan hasn't spoken a word to confirm anything you've said. I'm curious if you pull off this level of subterfuge for all your clients or if the parrot act comes as an extra charge." On a roll, Jada's prickliness rose as she turned on Tristan.

"You can speak, can't you, Mr. Maxwell? You were awfully articulate the other day when you threatened me and made me out to be a gossiping liar. Your dramatics nearly lost me my job."

"I didn't call you a liar or threaten you." Tristan's indignant frown at her claim softened when Doug cleared his throat in a back-down signal.

"*Fine.* Jada, I'm sorry I yelled and hurt your feelings."

"Hurt my feelings. What am I? A twelve-year-old?! Tristan, Ren might *fire* me. Do you know how embarrassing it was for you to scream at me on set? The whole crew knows about it."

"Thanks to that video, the whole world knows about it," Tristan muttered.

"Not. Helping," Doug hissed at him.

Jada flushed as she remembered that she wasn't entirely innocent in this scenario. She had let Mikayla send the video. Her actions might have escalated things from a terrible, isolated incident to an epic media disaster. At Tristan's reference to the damning evidence, Jada's conscience jumped to the nearest conclusion.

"You think I did it?" Jada squeaked.

She was guilty, guilty, guilty as charged—but she didn't want to own up to it. Not only would it make her a hypocrite, but more importantly, it could get Mikayla into trouble. Ultimately, her pride would have been able to withstand Tristan's rage and judgment about her part in things. But ratting on Mikayla? There was no way Jada was giving her best friend up as an accomplice.

"It's a likely theory," Tristan shot back. "And makes perfect sense."

"Don't blame me. It was probably Erica. Payback for you getting her in trouble with Angela."

Tristan frowned at her suggestion because it was also a likely theory. Jada suspected that by now Erica had been cut from the crew. Ren wouldn't have the luxury of keeping her around if he wanted Angela to come back to work. Just another example of Hollywood double standards.

"No matter who's at fault, the one thing left for us to do is move forward," Doug interjected.

"Agreed. We'll finish the movie in civil cooperation, and then go our separate ways." Done with this fiasco, Jada stood up, ready to make her dramatic exit after all. Until Doug grabbed her arm, holding her captive.

"We had a more creative idea on how to solve the current situation. It would help bolster both your reputations."

Slowly, Jada sat back down. "You want me to make him look good. How? And what would that supposedly do for me?"

"Tristan may be the one who's getting slammed in the press, but Jada, you're not coming up smelling like roses, either, dear."

"Excuse me?!" Jada said with an offended gasp.

Tristan chortled. "And you say, *I'm* the one who's not helping."

Doug was obviously flustered but went on, attempting to smooth things out. "What I mean is, right now, you're seen as this helpless victim. That might seem sympathetic at first, but in the end, you'll come off as someone who can't stand up for herself. A semidecent actress who falls short by letting herself get publicly disgraced."

"That's not—I don't . . ." Jada had never thought of it in that light. Sure, she knew she would be interpreted as the injured party—but not as some chump. A weenie who wouldn't be taken seriously. But then again, she hadn't done a deep dive into the social media comments, just the hashtags. Now that she thought about it, there were most likely hundreds of internet trolls and incels making jokes and claiming she must have done something to deserve getting berated by Tristan. And on the other side, tons of supposed feminists admonishing her for her passive attitude and saying she should have taken Tristan down.

Was Doug right? If she didn't at least release an official statement or say something, this could be bad for her image too.

"But here's the bright side!" Doug added cheerfully in response to her shock. "I think there's a way that you and Tristan can mend fences and spin this viral horror show into a media goldmine."

"How?" Jada prodded as Doug utilized a long silence to draw out the suspense.

"It comes down to a blend of careful strategy and your wonderful acting abilities."

"And whether or not you believe the logic of trope-filled rom-coms works in real life," Tristan remarked offhandedly, but Doug ignored him, his eyes alight with reassuring promise.

"Basically, I can send out a press release stating that this video is a misunderstanding. You two were rehearsing a scene from the movie or something. But after that, I think a clever move for you both would be to pretend there's a different type of tension beneath the surface."

Jada stiffened as she picked up on Tristan's hint about rom-com logic.

"Oh, hell no!" she said, shaking her head vehemently. "I'm not going to pretend like everything's okay and I'm actually dating this fool!"

"It would only be for a little while, until things have smoothed out with the film. I'll even sweeten the pot. You stick with Tristan during this time, and I know we can help you go places."

The end of Doug's ridiculous pitch left Jada stunned. The man wanted her—*her*—to date that insufferable manwhore under the guise of allegedly making them both look better. What they really wanted was to use her to alleviate the allegations surrounding Tristan. On top of that, the idea that Tristan could help her career take off if they were together was offensive.

"I'm doing fine on my own. I get jobs. I'm good at what I do. And—"

"You *are* good, Jada." Tristan interrupted her. He sounded genuine, and with his understanding eyes, he reminded her of predebacle, Twitter-friendly Tristan.

"What? You really think so?" Jada said, the momentary sincerity swaying her.

"Yes. Dead serious . . . but with my help, we'll make you ten times better." Tristan winked at her.

*Of course, not-douchey Tristan only lasts for ten seconds,* Jada reminded herself. But still curious, she asked more questions—although she instantly regretted them.

"What would I have to do?"

"We'd release a few things in the press and social media," Doug said. "You'd also go on a couple of outings so the paparazzi could see you together."

"How long would we do this?"

"Let's leave it open. When you start seeing results, we'll decide how far this should go."

Jada deliberated, wringing her hands in her lap. It would be insane to do this. There was no guarantee that Tristan would do anything concrete to help her. They could just be stringing her along. At the same time, could she afford to pass up the chance he was offering? Dating Tristan would get her that extra star power. In this town, it was all about who you knew—or who you were sleeping with. What actress didn't want to make it big? As shady as it seemed, using Tristan as a leg up might be her shot. A chance to play the lead in something meaningful and shine on center stage. It would be *her* turn to be on movie posters instead of a tiny credit line at the bottom. At the end of the day, if Tristan was willing to use her for damage control, she shouldn't feel bad for using him for something even more important.

"Okay," she blurted. The words were set free before she could second guess things or take them back.

"Wonderful! We can have a press release out this afternoon. Do we have a deal?" Doug asked.

"A deal with the devil," Jada said dryly.

"Sticks and stones, babe. Sticks and stones," Tristan said.

"That's fine with me. A few broken bones might do you some good," Jada threw back, but at Tristan's calculating expression, her fire faded. He took her by surprise, grabbing her hand and stroking it lovingly.

"Oh, honey, you don't mean that." Tristan kissed her hand jokingly but ended his taunt in a sexy growl. "Then again, I love it when you get feisty."

Jada yanked back her hand as if he'd burned her. In a way, he had, if her trembling palm was anything to judge by. Pleased that he'd rattled her, Tristan cockily leaned back in his chair.

"It's settled. I'll see you tonight at seven sharp. Be ready when I come to pick you up."

"I will be, sweetie." Jada mocked him, getting one more jab in before she walked away. "Don't forget to bring your pitchfork."

"I never leave home without it." Tristan blew her an air kiss.

Fed up, Jada let him win this round. She turned on her heel and did her best show of storming away. He may think he had the upper hand, but she'd find a way to get back at him on their date. Scheming on various avenues of revenge, Jada belatedly realized her dramatic exit from the restaurant had extended to her stomping down the sidewalk outside. She forced herself to slow down as she reflected on what she'd gotten herself into. There was a possibility that this was going to end terribly. But despite the risks, Tristan's agent was pretty slick to come up with the plan in the first place.

And that's when a horrifying epiphany struck Jada.

Her agent would have something to say about this whole debacle too. Her poor drunken decision hadn't factored in that the formidable Avery Kane would get wind of the media scandal. As a tyrannical mogul in the industry, she would not be happy to find out one of her clients was caught up in yet another scandal. Forget not being happy. She would be enraged. As if Jada's thoughts had unleashed her from the fiery depths of hell, Jada's phone rang.

Avery.

Bracing herself for the agent's impending outburst, Jada reluctantly picked up. All pleasantries were lost as Avery laid into her the second she answered.

"Jada, what the hell is going on?"

"You see . . ." Jada uneasily tried to start. "Tristan and I had an argument that got caught on camera."

"The world knows that part, Jada. What I need to hear is *why* it happened."

"It's not something I want to discuss over the phone. Plus, I'm not home right now, so . . ."

Avery let out an indignant huff. "Fine. I'll be back from London tomorrow. I want you in my office first thing in the morning. Don't you dare weasel out of coming or explaining yourself."

"I would never do that," Jada said, stung.

"Your past antics say otherwise—but whatever. Just be there."

With that, the dreadful woman hung up without letting Jada defend herself.

Always wanting the last word, Avery just had to allude to Jada being pushed out of *Fallen Creatures* every chance she got. As if Avery hadn't played a key factor in all of it. If only Jada could call the agent back and put Avery's past antics on blast.

But Jada hated thinking back on the *Fallen Creatures* debacle, back to a time when she had been so vulnerable and damn stupid. The same day Maggie found out about Daniel and Jada she'd gone to the execs. She claimed it was too awkward to work with Daniel and Jada after everything that happened. Then Daniel backtracked and took Maggie's side to save his own skin. After professing his love for Jada in the damn parking lot, he told Maggie it was all a misunderstanding. He claimed Jada had a crush on him and he'd meant he loved her as a friend.

Jada came off as an unhinged homewrecker with people either siding with Maggie and Daniel or saying they wanted to stay neutral. Alia was the only one to stand by her, and Jada felt lucky to even have that, after hiding the relationship from her friend in the first place. Alia had been hurt but, thankfully, understood. She'd been Jada's sole champion as she defended Jada to some of the producers. But eventually, Jada bowed to the pressure from the more unforgiving higher-ups and left. She hadn't wanted to, but even Avery had said it was for the best and she would find something else for Jada. In reality, Avery Kane's tactic had been about saving her son's ass and their family name.

That part was the fiery icing on top of Jada's hell cake. The reason why Daniel never introduced her to his family was because Avery would have been furious about Daniel dating one of her clients. Yet Jada had ignored the risk of Avery's anger because she'd fallen so hard for Daniel. At the end of the day, the real true love was between Mommy Dearest and her rotten son. When the choice came down to Jada or Daniel, Avery's decision had been easy. The show executives accepted Jada's resignation without batting an eye—more like with a sigh of relief—making the wrongdoing hurt even more.

And despite Avery's promises to find Jada something else, *Love Locket* was her first semiprominent role after months of shitty auditions and two-second roles on the few network shows that would have her. While Jada enjoyed working for television, she'd always loved film more. As a kid, she'd had dreams of standing before the acting greats, holding an Academy Award for Best Actress, making cinematic history. That would never happen at the rate things were going. Remembering Ren's anger over what had happened on set, Jada's stomach clenched all over again.

No wonder she'd agreed to this farce with Tristan. She couldn't lose her one shot at breaking out of TV.

Even though her mind was mostly made up, Jada's mixed emotions spurred her to make her own phone calls, one to Mikayla and the other to Alia. She insisted that the three of them meet up for a real lunch. She needed to confide in her friends if she was going to get through her showdown with Avery and this charade with Tristan. When Jada met up with them at their favorite Chinese restaurant, their reactions weren't nearly as comforting as she'd hoped.

"You're going to do *what*?" Alia yelped.

Her usually refined and smooth voice rose to a surprisingly shrill octave. Jada shushed her, looking around the restaurant for any eavesdroppers. The group of friends received a few curious glances, but the other patrons redirected their attention to their meals. Unlike the shocked Alia, Mikayla snickered joyfully.

"Oh, this is too much. I can't believe what I'm hearing. *You*, innocent Jada Berklee, agreeing to such a farce! With a man you claim to hate!" Mikayla's eyes glittered with devious glee. "This is going to be good."

While Mikayla was generally an honest person—always willing to give heartfelt advice—she did have a dangerous streak that was fascinated by intrigue. The only thing that would have made her delight more palpable would be if she rubbed her hands together while cackling maniacally.

"I do hate him," Jada reiterated. "It's just . . . well, it seemed . . . oh hell! I don't know. I guess a part of me, deep down, wondered what would happen if I agreed. If my career really would start to go somewhere more . . . profound. After *Fallen Creatures*, it just feels like my life, my career, has been . . . cast blocked."

"By Avery, you mean?" Mikayla scoffed.

"Yeah, maybe. I just feel like this could be my chance to break out of all that." She glanced at her friends pleadingly. "I'm not awful, am I? For agreeing to this?"

Alia let out a long sigh. Jada braced herself for her response. Between them all, Alia was sure to be the most critical. She might try to shame Jada into backing out.

"I suppose it isn't the first time something like this has happened in the entertainment world. Couples pair up all the time to bolster their popularity," Alia said thoughtfully as she adjusted her napkin in her lap.

"So, you don't hate me? You're not going to get all judgy or anything?" Jada cautioned.

"I don't get judgy," Alia said, affronted, as she crossed her arms over her chest. But at her friends' knowing looks, she blushed. "Okay, maybe, if it was anyone else I would, but right now, Jada, I'm worried. I don't want you to get hurt."

"What do you mean, like if Tristan betrays me and the deal?"

"No, dummy." Mikayla jumped in. "She means the guy might work his Maxwell magic on you."

"*Ha*! He's so . . . irresponsible. Frivolous and insensitive. The exact opposite of everything I look for in a man." As she rattled off her list of reasons, Jada couldn't help but flash back to when Tristan had grabbed her hand at the café table. The way he looked at her. The touch of his lips on her skin. The contact had been brief, and yet it had made her shake . . . shit. Maybe she was in trouble.

But as soon as the thought crossed her mind, Jada shook her head. There was no way she would fall for Tristan. It would be a stupid thing to do. Maintaining her resentment would be much smarter. Probably not healthy, but smarter.

"It'll be okay. Seriously." Jada smiled, resolved. "I promise that if things get too heated, I'll back out."

Alia appeared mildly mollified, while Mikayla leaned across the table—all ears for further details.

"Where's he taking you? What are you going to wear?" she asked conspiratorially.

"I have no earthly idea. To both questions." Jada frowned as she picked at her kung pao chicken.

"You need to look hot. *Muy caliente*, hot." Mikayla insisted, whipping out her remedial high school Spanish skills.

"All right then. What would you suggest?" Jada asked.

She soon regretted posing that question to Mikayla. Her cousin was full of ideas, all of which were way outside of Jada's comfort zone. After they parted ways with Alia (who had to return to work at the television studio), they went back to the apartment where Mikayla immediately started fussing over Jada's hair and clothes.

She hummed in concentration as she circled Jada, taking her in from every angle. As she faced her again, she said with surety:

"You need to show some cleavage."

"What?" Jada squawked. Her hands automatically flew up to the front of her blouse, covering her breasts protectively.

"I'm serious. I want to see you in something short and low cut. You never show off your curves," Mikayla said, shaking her head as if she pitied her.

Contrary to her cousin's allegations, Jada knew she didn't dress like a tightly buttoned-up nun. She wore revealing clothes sometimes. And for the most part, she considered herself rather stylish. She had to be, as an actress in the public eye. And maybe she did value comfort more in her off-time outside of premieres, but it wasn't like bohemian-chic Mikayla dressed in sexy, breast-baring numbers all the time either.

"I know that," Mikayla said once Jada called her out on it. "But when we do go out clubbing or whatever, I'm not afraid to show some skin. You should too. It'll drive Tristan crazy. Seeing you look sexy and available—and yet you're a hands-off hottie when it comes to him."

"I'm not trying to 'arouse' Tristan's interest in any way."

"Didn't you say you wanted to get back at him for this afternoon?" Mikayla challenged her.

"Yes," Jada admitted.

"Don't you think it's the perfect payback to leave him with blue balls for the entire evening?"

Jada bit her tongue because she couldn't lie. It definitely would be satisfying to see Tristan squirming in his pants and then leave him unsatisfied. Then again, he'd probably just pick up some other girl later after he dropped Jada off at home. Still . . .

"Trust me. We won't go overkill. I won't endanger you with a nip slip accident. We'll just give him enough to tease him." That wicked gleam was back in Mikayla's eyes. Jada got sucked into it when she imagined Tristan's reaction.

"Fine. What have you got for me?" Jada gave in.

Mikayla let out a pleased squeal, dragged Jada into her room, and started rambling through her closet, throwing potential outfit options onto the bed. Jada was shorter and smaller than Mikayla so they'd have to make some adjustments to the dresses. Luckily, Mikayla could pull it off. Along with her plethora of other jobs, she'd previously worked as a seamstress.

Some of Mikayla's choices were way too loud for Jada, like a cheetah print dress with a dangerously high slit in the skirt's front. After much haggling, they settled on a sky-blue dress that was short but not in a potentially butt cheeks—escaping manner. The front was low cut but a sequined, sheer overlay on the top of the dress left the finer points up to the imagination. With some matching neon-blue pumps and the perfect blend of smoky eye shadow, Jada was finally ready—even before Tristan's impending arrival.

It'd be a perfect setup for Tristan to meet her at the front door of her apartment. Him impatiently waiting on the other side, only for her to throw it open and stun him with her ensemble. But Jada had no desire for Tristan to come that close to her home. What if he asked to use the bathroom or something? Then he would invade her personal, sacred space, and possibly find out more about her than she would like. Agreeing to play pretend girlfriend was enough of an intimate intrusion. God forbid Tristan actually discovered Jada's giant probiotic vitamins in the bathroom or the mini-unicorn collection she'd kept from her childhood.

Determined to avoid that type of invasiveness, Jada bid good-bye to Mikayla—who demanded to hear everything about the date when she returned—and made her way downstairs to the apartment complex's elegant lobby. Although she was waiting inside, Tristan's car was unmistakable when it pulled up. She'd seen him ride to work in the electric-blue Mustang several times. With the convertible top down, his midnight-black hair was ruffled but in an undeniably sexy way.

Before he had a chance to get out of the car, Jada stepped outside.

"Hello, Tristan," she said, keeping her voice silky and confident—like she'd practiced with Mikayla.

When Tristan spotted her, his jaw dropped. Jada owed Mikayla a big thank-you because her cousin had been right all along. Tristan's dumbstruck expression proved tonight was going to be highly entertaining. Jada hid a smug smile as a thrill of forbidden excitement rushed through her.

*Payback was going to be sweet.*

# 10

Damn.

That was the only word that got through to Tristan's brain before it short-circuited. One look at Jada and all his thought processes stopped. He felt like a total idiot, sitting there drooling over her, but he couldn't resist tracking the movement of her hips as she headed his way. His heart skipped a beat as she leaned over the passenger-side door, giving Tristan an eyeful of her chest—and yet not nearly enough.

"See?" she said. "I told you I'd be ready."

"Yeah. Wow, you look nice," was all Tristan managed to get out.

Before he could think of anything else to say, she opened the passenger door and slipped into the leather seat. As she crossed her legs, Tristan realized how short her dress was. And if it was just a wee bit shorter, he might be able to see something a lot more interesting than her upper thigh. Or if she would let him, he could reach over, slide his hand up said thigh himself, and—but there was no way she would let him.

And since there was no chance of Jada giving him a peek at—or feel of—the forbidden land he was imagining, the growing bulge in his pants was of absolutely no use to him. Of course, mentally Tristan knew this wasn't a real date, but his libido clearly couldn't tell the difference. Silently commanding his body to behave, Tristan forced himself to stop staring and started the car.

"Where are we going?" Jada asked innocently. Maybe too innocently. She had to know what kind of effect she was having on him.

"We'll eat, then hit up this lounge I know," Tristan said, more gruffly than he intended. Jada, of course, didn't miss the curtness in his tone.

"Is something wrong, Tristan?" And yes, she was definitely playing games. She had her doe-eyed look out in full force.

"Nothing at all." Tristan grinned back, feigning a carefree demeanor of his own. Two could play this game. Especially since his brief overview didn't fully describe what kind of evening they were about to have.

Contrary to Tristan's implication at the café that he'd come up with the plan for tonight, a lot more input had gone into it. First, Doug had suggested they stick to a classic dinner date to start with, but the choice of where to eat basically got chosen for Tristan. The problem with having such a public scandal was that everyone you knew found out about it, *including* his *Garcia* brothers.

After Doug had barged in on him the previous morning with the initial news and they concocted their plan, Tristan had eventually faced the music and checked his own cell phone. There had been a slew of texts from Juan and Rafe of the WTF and What were you thinking variety, along with a flurry of exclamation points. His lie about him and Jada mollified his friends temporarily in terms of the holy shit, the whole world thinks you're an asshole bit. But it hadn't stopped Juan from insisting that he meet Jada once Tristan mentioned they were going on their first "public" date. Unlike Rafe, whose jet-setting lifestyle often kept him out of L.A. on other films, Juan ran a very successful Mexican fusion restaurant, La Rosa Dorada. Realizing he'd be hounded to death until Jada got the *Garcia* brothers' seal of approval, Tristan had agreed. He wasn't sure if letting Jada in on this would help her gain that family okay or just make her more anxious.

As he mulled over whether or not he should share more information with her, the car ride descended into silence. Tristan stayed focused on the road while Jada stared out the window with a glazed look. Probably counting the passing palm trees and wishing she could be murdered by their barbed branches instead of stuck with him. Then she perked up, snapping her fingers in an a-ha! gesture. Maybe she'd figured out how to make *Tristan's* death look like a freak palm tree accident.

"I forgot to mention this, but . . ." She let out a heavy sigh—immediately setting Tristan on edge.

"But what? You're not backing out, are you?"

"No, I've resigned myself to our pact, but my agent found out about the video. She's not pleased."

"Ahhh. Who's your agent again?"

"Avery Kane." Jada's look of torment said it all. Not that Tristan didn't already know the agent's reputation. Everyone did. Doug had regaled him on some of her more outlandish behavior, like when she accused another agent of stealing her dog or when she got tipsy at the Academy Awards and felt up one of the winners as her "congratulations."

"That's unfortunate," Tristan said, hiding a smirk as he imagined Avery getting slapped with a restraining order by an Oscar winner. He was about to share that particular rumor with Jada when she glared at his smug expression.

"It's not funny. She's furious and wants me to meet her at her office tomorrow to explain everything. I have no idea what to say."

"Stick to the plan. Tell her the story we put together with Doug. He sent out the press release this afternoon so she might already know what 'really' happened."

Tristan's PR team had done a good job ironing out the details in the release. It included the tidbits they'd gone over with Jada about rehearsing a scene and that they had been acting it out together due to their newfound "closeness." Also, how they'd been trying to keep their budding relationship under wraps but were now making a joint statement to clear up any misconceptions. In addition to providing a cover for his outburst, the press release had worked its magic with Bright Futures too. As promised, Tristan had given LeeAnn a call, and after some theatrical begging, the coordinator said she would talk to the board to try and smooth things over.

"I doubt she's found out yet." Jada frowned. "Avery's on London time right now. She's probably passed out before hopping on her flight back in a few hours."

"She'll get to wake up to good news and see you cleaned up this mess yourself."

"What if she doesn't buy it?"

"Of course she will. You're an actress, right? Have faith in your abilities." Jada scowled at his suggestion.

"Thanks a lot. I appreciate you making fun of me again."

Jesus! The woman was as prickly as a cactus.

"What the hell?! I'm not making fun of you. I'm serious. You're a good actress, so you can pull it off."

"Just not good enough, apparently." Jada hinted at their conversation at the café. Yep, she was ready to jump into a fight. Frankly, Tristan wanted this evening to go as smoothly as possible. If this was any other woman, the odds would have been in his favor. It was a beautiful night with perfect, light weather. The stars they could see through L.A.'s otherwise smoggy sky should have brought on a more enchanting atmosphere. But so far, between the dress and the bristling attitude, Jada wasn't planning to make things that easy.

"Are you going to hold every stupid thing I say against me? Because believe me, I say a lot of them. And if so, these next few months are going to be hell."

"Months? You think we'll be doing this for months?"

"I don't know, but don't stroke out on me. It's at least going to be a couple of weeks, so you're going to have to relax." Tristan glanced over to see Jada sitting like a petrified mummy in her seat. "Do you know how to do that?"

"I can relax," Jada said as she tried to lessen the tension in her shoulders—unconvincingly.

Her dramatics irritated him, but deep down, Tristan understood it. His skin itched, too, at the idea of being sucked into this dating scheme indefinitely. Not to mention having to defend it convincingly in front of Juan. Tristan had spent his whole life dodging being in a serious relationship. The longest he'd gone was about six months with a hotel heiress, and even that had felt stifling after she started popping up at the hotels he was staying at during various film shoots.

And now he was supposed to pretend to be madly and

monogamously in love. It'd be an acting stretch for both of them. But still, he was willing to put in the work—albeit begrudgingly. She could at least do the same. If nothing else so it would be believable to the paparazzi. As he pulled into a parking space next to the restaurant, Jada looked up at the deceptively quaint, brick building.

"La Rosa Dorada? Isn't this, like, one of the hottest fusion spots in town?" she asked.

"Yep. It's a popular spot, which my former co-star owns, so there are bound to be some paparazzi creeps sulking about. You'll need to start warming up to me way more than you have up until now. Got it?"

"Hold on. You can't just drop that on me! Which co-star?"

The second Tristan admitted his fellow *Garcia Central* actor and lifelong friend ran the place Jada's eyes widened in horror.

"Tristan, if *anyone* is going to catch on to the fact we're lying, it's him!"

"Exactly, so we need to stick to our story and the warming up bit," Tristan retorted, pushing aside the guilt of not telling Jada sooner and how shitty it felt deceiving Juan.

"Define warming up," Jada countered. "Hand holding, relative proximity, or . . . something more?"

"Fine. We'll start with hand holding and set some ground rules later. For now, can we please go inside?"

When Jada started to open the car door, Tristan stopped her. "That's my job," he said.

He swiftly jumped out of the car and rushed to open Jada's door. When he offered to help her step out of the car with a gallant hand, she took it without protest. Sure enough, as they hit the sidewalk, one of those leapfrogging slimeballs hopped out at them and began snapping pictures.

"Tristan! Jada! Are you two really together or on the outs?"

"We're stronger than ever," Tristan said, holding tight to Jada's hand and steering her inside.

"Wow, word does travel fast." Jada blinked from all the flashing lights as she stepped into the protective walls of the restaurant's lobby.

"Thanks to Doug." Tristan credited his agent as he strode over to the hostess.

"Hi, I've got a party of two, under the name—"

"Tristan Maxwell!" the hostess gushed. "Juan told us you were coming."

"Yep, that's me." Tristan threw the young girl a dazzling smile. He wrapped his arm around Jada, squeezing her more tightly than necessary to make his point.

"My girlfriend and I would like your best table, please. The one by the window."

The hostess rushed to seat them to his exact wishes. Well, more like Doug's wishes. Doug had insisted their top priority while out on the town was to be seen. So Tristan and Jada would now be dining practically in a fishbowl, with the other diners openly gawking at them. Yet Tristan tried not to *feel* like a trapped goldfish as the paps outside pressed their noses to the glass to continue staring and taking photos.

"This isn't uncomfortable at all," Jada said, meekly putting her napkin in her lap.

"Yeah, it's not the best, but you get used to most of it. I mean, it's not like this is your first time having the spotlight on you when you go out in public."

"Well, no. But it's never been quite this much." Jada lifted a warning finger at Tristan's emerging smirk. "Don't you dare say it's because of you."

"I guess I don't need to." Tristan couldn't hide his smugness. It was good that Jada saw that being with him would put her in the limelight. Delivering on her expectations would keep her playing along with the charade. And now that his mind had circled back to their relationship fraud . . .

"Juan will stop by soon to introduce himself," Tristan admitted, eyeing the kitchen's door in the hopes that Juan hadn't already been alerted to their arrival. "So we should probably know a bit more about each other than we started dating while working together."

"Hmmm, if only we could have gone over that in the car," Jada gritted out through a fake smile that must mean "You're lucky the paparazzi are watching us, you jerk."

"You were too on edge and—never mind. Let's focus on selling this thing, okay? Tell me something about yourself."

"Like what?"

"I don't know. Your favorite color or favorite movie. Something about you and Mikayla. Or whether or not you have any more dresses like this in your closet—or something a bit skimpier that you like to wear to bed. You know, any of those things."

"Color's red. Movie-wise, it would have to depend on the genre, because how can you choose an all-time, across-the-board favorite. As for the rest, it's none of your business what I wear to bed or what's in my closet. What kind of things will Juan expect me to know about you?"

"That *I* am much more open about my wardrobe, and particularly that I go to bed nude."

Jada spit out the water their waiter had dropped off, hacking in a very unladylike fashion.

"Why in the world would he know that?" Jada asked after getting her coughing fit under control.

"There was a camping incident." Tristan waved off her astounded curiosity.

"You're screwing with me, aren't you?" Jada scrutinized him.

Tristan had a whole monologue prepared about the health benefits of sleeping commando when boisterous, vibrant music filled the restaurant. As he nearly jumped out of his seat, Tristan's mouth dropped as he watched a mariachi band head toward their table. Juan himself followed the group. Unlike the smartly dressed band, Juan wore a crisp chef's uniform over his built frame—but he *did* have a violin in his hand, and was playing along with the band. Jeezus! The man may have left acting behind but his flair for the dramatic had not died.

As Jada mouthed "What's going on?" to Tristan, the mariachi band and Juan launched into singing "Besáme Mucho." Unable to clue her in without being superrude to the performers, Tristan had no choice but to hope Jada would go along with his grateful smile and nod routine. When the band's dulcet sounds reached the final notes, everyone in the restaurant applauded vigorously.

Beaming with triumph, Juan bowed. "Welcome to La Rosa Dorada, Jada."

"Um, thank you. That was amazing. Unexpected but beautiful. I appreciate it."

Blushing under the new onslaught of attention, Tristan didn't feel quite as eager to shower his friend with praise. "Really, Juan? A whole mariachi band?" he whispered once the band had dispersed.

"You know our pact." Juan invited himself to sit down at their table, then addressed Jada with a wink. "I promised Tristan I'd do a whole serenade if he ever found his soul mate."

"*Cállate, cabrón,*" Tristan snarled at Juan. He wanted to

sound firm, but he hid behind his menu to escape Jada's baffled look.

How dare Juan bring that promise up when it had been made years ago, back when Tristan's mom had gotten him hooked on watching reruns of old telenovelas, like *La fea más bella*. Tristan had been obsessed with it, including the scene where the main character gets serenaded by a mariachi band. He kept saying he wished he had his own mariachi band for scenes in *Garcia Central,* and then Juan had taken that memory ten steps too far (as usual).

"Soul mate?" Jada took another sip from her water, either parched or speechless at Juan's announcement.

"Well, he openly called you his girlfriend to me and Rafe. Not hanging out, or 'We're just talking.' So, either this is the real deal or he's pulling my leg."

"Please excuse Juan's overdramatic romanticism. Being happily married has made him insufferable." Tristan deflected, able to lock eyes with Jada now that his face no longer felt like an overheating lava lamp.

Unfortunately, none of Tristan's catty remarks could stop Juan. He settled in, making recommendations from the menu. Jada gladly took him up on his offer to try the bulgogi tacos with kimchi salsa, while Tristan stuck with his tried and true Thai basil nachos. As they waited for their food, Juan stayed put, bonding with Jada more than Tristan had. Tristan mentally took note of the new information as his bestie and his girlfriend shared a love of singing and their firm belief that dogs were better than cats. Tristan had to agree with that last one. Left to their own nefarious devices, Sphynx and calico cats would take over the world. Deceptively cute but deadly.

Off Script

Everything was light and easy with a third party to take some of the pressure off. But when Juan asked how Tristan managed to rope Jada into being his girl, whatever rapport they'd developed flew out the window. Jada's look silently screamed "He knows." Tristan shook his head slightly to reassure her, but it didn't stop beads of sweat forming on Jada's forehead.

"There's no need to rope someone in if they're really soul mates. Love at first sight, right?" Tristan's carefully crafted reply didn't ease Juan's calculating gaze.

"Okay, if you guys say so," he said after a moment, probably not wanting to make Jada too uncomfortable.

The arrival of their food saved them from any further relationship talk. The nachos, piled high with juicy chicken and cheese and covered in peanut sauce, made Tristan's mouth water. Jada's plate was equally perfect for a foodie photo op, with the juicy beef sprinkled with spicy, fragrant toppings. Jada moaned with delight when she took her first bite, and Juan gleamed with pride.

"It's good, right?"

"Amazing. I'll definitely force Tristan to bring me here more often."

"And you will always be welcome."

Happy over Jada's satisfaction with the food, Juan excused himself to go back to the kitchen. His absence and their own digging into their meals steered their conversation back to so quiet you could hear them chewing silence. Juan's nosiness had gotten a lot of basic first date talk out of the way, so Tristan didn't know what to bring up next. Usually, he was the most charismatic one in the *Garcia* trio, but his arrangement with Jada was far from being a random pickup in a bar or a hookup. At last, Tristan decided to stick with a topic more applicable to their situation.

107

"So, one of Doug's producer friends is known to hang out at the lounge we're going to. He's looking for a lead in a new film. We figured you and I could go there, schmooze it up."

"Oh wow. That's soon. What do I even say to this guy?" Jada said, her brow furrowed uncertainly.

"Keep it casual. You don't want to sound overrehearsed or like we're begging. I'll be there to steer things along, so there's no need to freak out."

Seeing Jada's frown, Tristan began to wonder if the reason Jada didn't have more prominent roles was because she lacked that shark instinct. Maybe she froze up in auditions or was afraid to put herself out there for something more challenging.

"What would be your *dream* role?" Tristan asked, eager to get to the root of what Jada's real ambitions were and why she had agreed to this.

"God, that's a big question. Something groundbreaking, that challenges me to be a better actress." A sad, distant cloud passed over Jada's face before she went on. "I've always wanted to act, since I was a kid. But I don't think I knew what that meant until I watched Thandiwe Newton in *Crash*. Everything about her was pitch perfect, her frustration and betrayal, all the little ways in which she reacted to the traumatic things that happened."

*Crash* was one of Tristan's favorite movies, too, because of the way the characters' stories wove together in the end. All the performances were fantastic but Thandiwe Newton's portrayal had stood out to him too. As he smiled at her in understanding, Jada blushed.

"I want to do that one day. I want to be capable of that kind of greatness. I mean, I know I'll probably never be like her or be the next Viola Davis, but . . ."

"You don't have to be. Everyone always wants to label the next star the 2.0 of someone else. You can just be Jada."

She brushed his compliment away, flustered at the praise. "Easy for you to say, acting is in your blood. Isn't your mom a famous telenovela actress? I've seen a few of her shows when I'm flicking channels. She seems beautiful and talented."

The +57 international code from the other day flashed in Tristan's mind. A definite no-no on a first date was lamenting how your parents got divorced. Or more accurately, how your beautiful and talented mom abandoned you, and you spent your teen years working on sitcoms just to escape watching your dad waste away at home only to have her resurface later in the form of some fucked up pocket dial. Bitterness washed over him, his next words flying out before he could control them.

"That's what she wants you to think."

"What does that mean?"

God, he could not get into his messed up past with a woman he was just getting to know. Not right now.

"It means you should know by now that what you see on-screen isn't real." Tristan wiped his greasy nacho hands on a napkin, his appetite gone. Spotting the waiter, he flagged him down.

"Is something wrong with the food, Mr. Maxwell?" the waiter asked.

"No, but we're finished now."

"What? I'm not done," Jada interjected, motioning to the remaining taco on her plate.

"That's what to-go containers are for, honey," Tristan insisted sweetly, but not even the term of endearment stopped Jada's and the waiter's mouths from dropping.

"I'd like one of those and the check, please." This time his tone denied any further contradiction. When the waiter hurried off to fulfill his command, Jada jumped on him.

"What is wrong with you? I somehow tripped into your minefield of mommy issues and suddenly I can't have dessert?"

"More like we have more important things to do," Tristan said, staring her down.

"Like what, Oedipus?" Jada shot back.

"Like if you're nervous about meeting this producer guy, it's better for us to head over there earlier to get in the networking zone before we actually talk to him." Jada remained unmoved, crossing her arms. "Come on, if we can get you an audition in this guy's next action film, you'll be well on your way to moving up. It's a big-time role."

"How big?" Jada raised a skeptical eyebrow.

"Summer blockbuster money. That's way more fulfilling than La Rosa flan. Don't tell Juan I said that, though."

"Fine. We'll go. But if this meeting *doesn't* turn out better than their *world-famous* tres leches cake, you and I are going to have a serious problem," Jada said.

As Tristan paid the bill—and Jada stormed off to the car with her leftovers—there was no doubt in Tristan's mind that they already *did* have a problem. They *had* been able to fool Juan, though, based on his latest group texts.

**Juan**: It's okay, Rafe. The girl's got good taste

**Rafe**: Are you saying that because she's actually good for baby Tristan or because she liked your kimchi salsa?

*BOTH*, Juan texted back, adding the 100 and chef's hat emojis for emphasis.

Torn over the messed-up deception, Tristan texted back a sole thumbs-up, then followed after his outraged "soul mate."

The car ride to the lounge crackled with more tension than the one to the restaurant, marking this evening as one of the biggest fake date fails in history. The blame didn't solely rest with Jada. She'd signed up for fooling strangers with a little PDA for career clout. *Not* deceiving people Tristan claimed mattered to him. Juan had been so kind and welcoming that lying to his innocent face had almost ruined the fantastic food. But seeing how Juan and Tristan interacted had softened Jada's heart. She'd been even more touched when Tristan actually cared enough to ask her what her goals were, for them to bond over their shared career path. That budding opening lulled her into enough of a false sense of security to ask about Tristan's real family. Big mistake, apparently.

Tristan's dismissiveness hadn't quelled Jada's interest. It only raised more questions. Like what his mother could have done to make him hold a grudge for this long. Maybe her life as a telenovela star had gone to her head and then rubbed off into real-life *familia* drama. Okay, that was probably not the right Spanish translation, but still! Jada's hands longed to whip out her phone and look up all she could about Isabella Moreno. She would have followed through on the impulse if she wasn't worried about Tristan glancing over and catching her. No doubt he'd end up freaking out and crashing the damn car. Truthfully, Jada shouldn't care this much about the intimate details of her fake boyfriend's life. Hell, she didn't want him digging into her past either. Nevertheless, it ate away at her how their dynamic felt like taking one timid step forward and then ten steps back.

But when Tristan pulled up in front of the lounge, he transformed from the brooding bad boy to the perfect boyfriend, hurrying to open her door. The gentlemanly gesture didn't impress Jada as much this time around. Similar to their time at dinner, photographers snapped pictures as they entered the lounge, forcing Jada and Tristan to plaster smiles on their faces. Not to mention Tristan touching the small of her back territorially—something she didn't appreciate. Like at the café, his touch unsettled her in a way that was unnerving and enticing all at once. His skin against hers was like static electricity, lighting up her nerve endings with sensual sparks.

When they passed through the lounge's doors and out of the paparazzi's sight, Jada immediately separated from him. Glancing around the room, she took in the smooth lilac walls and gleaming white furniture. It was low key but still radiated a sense of excitement with an open dance floor and a large bar, which looked enchanting with its wide array of shimmering bottles behind the counter, just waiting to help Jada escape the confines of tonight's "date."

"Where's this producer?" Jada asked, cutting to the chase. Tristan gave her a dry glance in response.

"I don't have a magic wand, Jada. I can't make him appear the second we walk in. We'll have to look around a bit. Besides, are you feeling calm enough to go meet him right now?"

"I guess I could get a drink first."

"If it will help you loosen up, then yes. Please, let's go buy some drinks. I could use one myself."

"You're driving,"

"I can handle one drink." Tristan ignored Jada's disapproving stare and headed to the bar on his own, forcing her to trail behind him.

"I'd like a scotch on the rocks," Tristan told the bartender, then gestured to Jada. "And for the lady . . . ?"

"Sex on the beach, please," Jada replied innocently, because why the hell not.

Tristan had screwed her around enough on this date, blindsiding her with surprises and emotional curveballs. It was time for her to do some teasing of her own. Sure enough, Tristan's gaze flickered down to her lips with heated interest before he repeated the order. When the drinks came at last, Tristan took a swig of his. As if the sip gave him resolve, he spoke up.

"You can't stay mad at me all night."

"And why not?"

"Because for this whole agreement to work, we have to at least tolerate each other. You know I'm not happy about this, either, but I'm willing to try and make it work."

"Ah, I see. So, *that's* why you keep yelling at me," Jada pointed out.

Maybe it was easy for Tristan to sweep everything under the rug, but the memory of their on-set fight remained fresh in her mind. If their "agreement" meant putting up with more of his temper tantrums, Jada regretted her decision.

"Okay, I'll work on that. But can we call a cease-fire for the remainder of this thing? I'd prefer it if we could handle it without you strangling me," Tristan said with a grin. Damn, how the man could go from insufferable to charming! Jada felt herself smiling, no matter how hard she fought it.

"Fine," Jada said. At her acquiescence, Tristan lifted his glass as if he was raising a white flag. Jada did the same, tapping her glass to his before taking a sip.

"But that means you have to dance with me," Tristan added, setting his drink down so he could grab her hand.

"I didn't agree to that. I thought we were supposed to be getting into the networking zone," Jada said, not budging.

"Yes, by loosening up. Live a little, Berklee," Tristan insisted as he pulled her along.

Jada let him drag her to the center of the dance floor as a new song began to play. She hoped for something that they could dance energetically to, but since it was a more laid-back lounge, "Crush" by Jennifer Paige played melodiously over the sound system. Jada remembered the '90s pop hit. As Tristan held her close in his arms, Jada listened to the lyrics.

And for some reason, for some inexplicable reason, Jada could relate to them while she danced with Tristan. The attraction between them was there, no doubt. But it couldn't be anything more than a crush. She refused to faint over him, to let her heart flutter. But being with him made her feel exhilarated, young . . . free. Just like the song said.

Jada had been staring down at her feet as they moved across the dance floor, but once she got the hang of things, she instinctually looked up at Tristan—only to find he was looking at her, too, with deep, indescribable emotion in his eyes.

Throughout the slow song they'd been mere inches away, but his strong arms drew her in closer until there was hardly any space between them. Tristan's chest brushed against her own and a tantalizing friction ignited inside of her. The closeness of their bodies paired with Tristan's mesmerizing gaze proved to be too much. Against all reason, Jada moved in, breathing him in as her lips entrancingly inched closer to his . . . close en

*Wait*! What in the world was she doing

squabbling the majority of the night, and now

in for a kiss. It made no sense for her to be sm

this was an actual date. Jada pulled away, silently reprimanding

herself for getting swept away by the music and Tristan's allure.

Her sudden jerk backward startled Tristan out of . . . whatever

that had been.

"It's getting late. Maybe we should look for that guy now," she

pointed out.

"You're right," Tristan agreed, clearing his throat. "We'll find

him."

He reached for her hand, probably so they could stick together

as they traversed the crowd. Then, as if his better judgment

kicked in, he refrained from touching her. After a few moments of

peeking at different tables, Tristan whistled in victory.

"I got him."

"Where?" Jada asked, glancing around Tristan's shoulder.

"I'll show you." Tristan did clasp her hand now so she would

follow him. Jada's reluctance sank in and she tugged back—

staying put.

"Tristan, wait. I don't know if I'm ready yet. What do I need to

know about this guy?"

Outside of the actual craft of acting, Jada's least favorite part

of her job was networking. It always felt forced and slimy, no

matter how many pointers Avery gave Jada when she first started

out. With extensive practice she'd gotten better, but this back and

forth with Tristan the whole night hadn't given her the same type

of prep time.

"He's a posh aristocrat whose main interest is making hits.

‚'s down to hire anyone he thinks can help him bring in more money."

"Okay. But what if he doesn't like me?"

"He'll like you. If you're still nervous, let me do the talking. I'll show you what to do. So, come on, grasshopper." With that last remark and an encouraging push, Tristan escorted Jada toward her fate.

Way too quickly, Jada found herself and Tristan in front of a plush, ivory booth filled with people. The glass table in the center was littered with colorful cocktail glasses, some half-full and others empty. The music was softer here, allowing the patrons' laughter to fill their little corner of the lounge. In the middle of the group's revelry, a gorgeous golden-haired man was the king. He entertained his companions with jokes, and the women fawned over him foolishly. It was obvious this was the man they were here to meet. Nevertheless, Jada fidgeted at the idea of intruding on their gathering.

"Logan Wentworth?" Tristan asked bluntly, not struck with any indecision. The man cocked his head in acknowledgment.

"Yes, that's me," he said. He had a distinctive lilt in his voice that reminded Jada of James Bond. Silky soft, commanding, and very British. Her mind also latched onto his name. She'd heard Logan Wentworth described as one of the hottest producers in the industry. While he was only in his midthirties, he'd used his family's old money ties to make his way from the UK and the BBC to join Hollywood's big hitters.

"Can I help you?"

While Logan seemed friendly, there was a firmness in his voice that implied he wasn't interested in being hassled—making Tristan and Jada's job even harder. Jada allowed Tristan to take the lead, not because he'd demanded to earlier but because she feared she might screw things up.

"I'm Tristan Maxwell. A friend of Doug's. Remember? He said we might see you here tonight, told me to stop by," Tristan said jovially.

While subtle, Logan definitely did a double take. With the mood lighting in the lounge, he probably hadn't gotten a full look at Tristan, but matching the name with the face had done the trick. Jada wasn't sure if they'd actually met in person before, but Logan certainly wouldn't turn them away now that Tristan had made his presence known and implied that they had.

"Ah yes. Maxwell. Sorry. I'm a few drinks in." Logan laughed, covering the initial awkwardness. "It's good to see you. Have a seat." His invitation forced a sort of musical chairs seating rearrangement as Tristan and Jada squeezed into the booth.

"This is my girlfriend, Jada." Tristan threw a companionable arm around her shoulders as he went on. "When I saw you, I was like, Jada, you have to meet this guy. He's great—not to mention one of the best producers in town."

"Thanks, mate. That's kind of you to say," Logan said, then his gaze fell on Jada. It seemed he approved of her—at least physically—as he took in her appearance appreciatively.

"It's nice to meet you, Jada. I hope you won't be too disappointed if I don't live up to Tristan's praise."

"Oh, I don't know. I've found Tristan usually has sound judgment." Jada hoped her inner sarcasm didn't come across out loud.

"So, what have you been up to since I saw you last?" Tristan asked. "I know your sci-fi thriller, *Prototype*, came out recently. It's a hit."

"Oh, I saw that one! It was amazing." Jada chipped in as she got into the groove of Tristan's act.

"Yeah. Not to talk business on your off-hours, but are you working on anything else like that? Something cool?"

"Well, it's always good to have something in the works. Right now, I'm exploring a big action flick. Think *Black Panther* meets Indiana Jones."

"Wow! I'm so picturing Michael B. Jordan in a fedora right now." Jada glowed when Logan laughed boisterously at her joke.

"You know, you're quiet, but also quite charming," he said to her. "Good catch on your part, Tristan."

"I like to think so," Tristan said, showering Jada with a look of love. One that she almost bought.

"Well, anyway, it sounds great." Jada tried to steer them back on topic.

Logan looked at her calculatingly.

"We're still in the early stages. Would you be interested in auditioning for a part? The female lead will have to pull off playing a badass assassin. Do you think you could handle that?" Logan asked.

"Hell, yes!" Jada put on an air of badassery, garnering another laugh from Logan.

"Sounds great, love," he said. He reached into his pocket and passed Jada his business card.

"Stay in touch. Get your agent to give me a call and we can set something up."

"Thank you!" Jada tried hard not to gush further as she took the card.

"Thanks for everything, Logan," Tristan said after they'd indulged in several more minutes of small talk. "We'll have to get together again for another drink or something."

"Sounds good." Logan lifted his glass.

With that, Tristan steered Jada out of the booth and back to the main lounge area. Jada turned to him, still shocked.

"That was way easier than I thought it would be."

"Yeah. Logan is widely known as an English Don Juan—he's worse than me. A sucker for a pretty face. I knew if I brought you over things would probably go our way."

"You're saying I only got the audition because of my looks?" Jada frowned. Tristan sighed before facing off with her.

"No. I'm saying he's a man," Tristan said. The intense heat returned to his eyes as he touched Jada's chin, studying her. "Who wouldn't fall for you?" he asked, his voice soft. It washed over her, enveloping her in warmth and something else. Something dangerous. So dangerous that she worried she would fall into it.

"What do you say? Should we have one more dance to celebrate?" Tristan asked.

Instead of answering right away, Jada averted her eyes . . . only to see her worst nightmare.

It was Daniel.

Three steps away, a short distance over Tristan's shoulder, Jada swore she saw her ex-boyfriend staring straight at her. She studied him: tall, slim, piercing hazel gaze. This was not a horrible mirage. Douchebag Daniel was here in the flesh. Locked in their staring contest, all the awful memories reemerged: Daniel's constant lies, his cheating, his nonchalance when Jada got fired. His mother's complete manipulation of the situation. Everything that led to this very moment, when Jada had to pretend to be Tristan Maxwell's girlfriend to keep the one job she had left. Sickened to her core, Jada began hyperventilating. Noticing her distraction, Tristan squeezed her hand.

"What's wrong?"

"Daniel," Jada muttered under her breath.

"King of the vamps *Fallen Creatures*' Daniel?" Tristan perked up as he spotted the person who had put Jada into a petrified trance.

"Are you not going to say hi?" Tristan asked, but his voice was a distant echo compared to the blood rushing in her ears.

She was over this.

She was over him.

But why was he here?

Whatever the reason, she wasn't going to stick around long enough to find out. She saw him open his mouth to call her name. He started to walk toward her—and that, Jada simply couldn't allow. With no regard for Tristan's questions or anything else, Jada ran away. Turning abruptly, she hurried for the lounge's outer door. Once she was outside, her breath returned to her. But not for long, because a hand on her shoulder startled her. Luckily, Tristan was the one who had come after her.

"Seriously, what's wrong with you?" he asked.

"We need to leave. Now."

"But why are you freaking out?"

"It doesn't matter. Please, take me home, Tristan," Jada pleaded. Hearing the desperation in her voice, Tristan raised his hands in defeat.

Several moments later, having dodged the remaining photographers out front, they were back in the car, cruising toward her apartment. Jada could feel Tristan throwing furtive glances her way but she ignored them. She didn't want to talk about Daniel—especially not with Tristan, of all people. And yet . . .

"Are you sure you don't want to talk about it?" Tristan asked.

"Does it look like I want to talk about it?" Jada said, tone somewhere between a snap and a sigh.

"I only wanted to make sure you're okay," he said, his voice gentle, like she was some wounded animal that could attack at any minute.

Hell, she probably was.

"Please, forget it," Jada said, more resigned this time.

She didn't want to be like how Tristan had been about his mom. Her issues with Daniel were just that: hers. She and Tristan had called a truce, so she wasn't going to ruin it by yelling at him. At least, she would try not to.

"Okay, if you say so." Tristan pulled up in front of Jada's apartment. She couldn't have been more relieved. Before she was able to escape from the car and this hellish night, Tristan rested his hand on her arm, stalling her.

"Aren't you forgetting something?" he asked.

"Like what?"

"Like saying thank you. I didn't show you a completely terrible time. It felt like things were going well up until the end," Tristan alluded ominously. Jada had no intention of taking the bait.

"Yes, well, it was quite an adventure," Jada consented.

"I'll have Doug check the press tomorrow to see what people are saying, but one date probably won't be enough. You realize that, right?" Tristan eyed her cautiously.

"I know. And we'll have to post some social media pictures, too, right?"

"Yeah, that'd be a plus." Tristan cocked an eyebrow in surprise. "Although I didn't expect you to agree so easily."

"You're keeping your promise. If things work out with this Logan guy, then I'll know you're serious about helping me." Jada reached for the car door's handle again. Tristan stopped her, clasping her hand.

"I am serious about helping you, Jada. This is all going to work out. I can feel it." Tristan spoke with more confidence than Jada could muster about the situation. His belief almost put her at ease.

"I hope so. Good night, Tristan," Jada said. Unexpectedly, Tristan kissed her hand, similar to his affectionate gesture at the café. There seemed to be sincerity behind the move this time around. The way his lips gently touched her skin felt like a silent apology for how the night had ended.

"Good night, Jada. I'll see you soon." Tristan's eyes pierced her own until Jada was forced to look away. Mumbling her final good-bye, Jada got out of the car and hustled to her apartment building's lobby door. She refused to look back, although she did hear Tristan's car start up as he drove away. When she slipped into her apartment, Jada's heart swelled with gratitude at being back in her refuge. A place where she could be alone and not have to think about Daniel or Tristan or—

"How'd it go?" Mikayla asked, suddenly jumping out of the living room doorway as Jada stood in the front hall.

"Oh my gosh! Don't scare me like that! My night has been rough enough."

"Why? What happened? Did he pull something?"

Jada ignored Mikayla's questions as she went to her room and switched her party dress for a comfortable PJ set. They were Doctor Who themed (with David Tennant, of course) and not nearly as sexy as Tristan had probably been imagining.

"Kayla, give me a second to breathe. I'll tell you about my train wreck evening, but first: ice cream."

"Oh snap. If this calls for rocky road then things *really* must have been bad." Mikayla followed Jada as they made their way to the kitchen, and eventually forced the full story out of her.

"You two almost kissed? Twice?" Mikayla gasped.

"I don't know. Maybe. I'm not sure what it was. All I know is before I could even think about going through with it, Daniel showed up."

"That shithead," Mikayla said, "has the worst timing."

"*Sip That Tea* was right. He's back in town. I thought I was fine with what happened, but the second I saw him, I freaked and ran out."

"That guy is like a cockroach." Mikayla shook her ice-cream spoon in indignation. "Extremely resistant to attempted murder and he pops his ugly head out at the worst times."

Mikayla's comparison was dead-on. Jada's tempting what-if moment with Tristan would forever be tarnished by the memory of Daniel intruding on them.

"He didn't say anything to you?" Mikayla asked.

"I didn't give him a chance. After I took off, Tristan brought me home. So that's that."

"Ugh. He should officially move to Germany with his new girlfriend."

Thinking back on the singer from the blog's picture, Jada realized she hadn't seen the pretty redhead with Daniel at the club.

"If they could rebuild the Berlin Wall to specifically keep him there, then I'd be all for it," Jada added. "I didn't think seeing him could affect me anymore. It's been months, and between our different work schedules it's rare for me to run into him like that, but . . . maybe I'll never fully get over what he did."

Jada had tried so hard to push Daniel to the back of her mind, but it wasn't truly possible. Not with his mom as her agent or with them ultimately still working in the same town and industry. It wasn't just the messy breakup that hurt. The deepest wound came from the fact they were forever bonded through their work, through *Fallen Creatures*, a show Jada had once loved and been proud of. A show she couldn't watch now without feeling betrayed.

When the writers decided to kill off Jada's character, Dana, Alia had been livid enough to stage a protest. Jada convinced her elaborate outrage wouldn't work, and instead, asked Alia to write her death scene. It was the only way to ensure her character's death would be poetic or have any meaning in the scope of the show. When the episode aired and her demise became canon, she received an outpouring of love from the viewers, saying they'd miss her. Because of their support, she'd made another mistake, agreeing to attend Comic-Con that year. When the show execs had offered her the opportunity, Jada saw it as an olive branch. A tiny part of her hoped this might mean they were thinking of reviving her character. Either way, she'd decided to attend as a way to say good-bye to the fan base.

Thankfully, Alia had come along to be on the panel, with Mikayla agreeing to be the "cheer squad" in the audience. With her girls by her side and dressed in Dana's iconic siren costume (her parting gift from the crew), she'd felt confident. As fans greeted her with so much enthusiasm as she made her way through the venue, she even felt valued, loved.

That changed the second she arrived in the conference hall for the FC panel, because her former co-stars made it clear she wasn't wanted. Maggie gave her a stiff nod while some of the other secondary actors attempted to make poor small talk. Daniel didn't speak to her at all, acting as if she didn't exist. Even though after she'd left the show he'd called her repeatedly for weeks on end, begging for her to take him back.

Jada's self-worth shriveled like a dry raisin. All she wanted to do was use Alia as a decoy so she could dash out of there. Instead, though, Jada stuck to the high road and sat down toward the very end of the long panel table. No matter what her former co-workers threw at her, she'd be okay. After all, she was supposed to be here for the fans. Unfortunately, that meant answering some very painful questions from them.

During the Q & A, a bright-faced girl with gorgeous Afro puffs stepped up to the mic.

"Hi, Jada. I'm Amaya. I wanted to know what you thought of your character's fate on FC?"

"Oh . . . well, I was sad to leave such a magical world behind but I think with where the show was trying to go it made sense."

"Really? Because I feel like killing off the one Black character on the show—a character I looked up to—kind of sucked."

"We've actually got quite a diverse cast, I feel. And we don't discriminate in terms of who bites the dust. Or gets staked." One of the producers chimed in.

Jada held back the urge to retort with the truth. By diverse cast, he meant June, who had been stuck in the Asian best friend role since season one, and Eric, the one Black guy they hired after Jada was gone. Her heart ached at the girl's crestfallen expression, still seeking out Jada's gaze, for that comradery, that connection of understanding.

"I do understand how you feel, though, Amaya. Thank you for seeing yourself in Dana. I did too . . ." Her voice puttered out pathetically, unable to fully describe how much the girl's words had meant to her. Underneath the conference table, Alia squeezed her hand—her stay-strong signal as Jada's spirits plummeted further because of having let this kid down.

Another fan, not waiting for their turn to speak, shouted, "Do you think you'll ever bring Dana back? Or that she could be resurrected?"

Jada barely had time to process the question, let alone the secret wish she'd been holding on to, before Daniel tore it to shreds.

"As Jada said, the show's been going in a different direction and she's moved on. I think you guys could tell by the finale who the main villain will be next season and what the rest of us have in store."

Smoldering scorn replaced her sorrow. Jada couldn't hold back her frustration any longer, openly glaring at Daniel from her measly end of the table. How dare he interject like that, speaking for her and the actual creator and show execs' potential vision for future seasons. But of course, no one called him out on it. Jada sat there, silently fuming during the rest of the conference's talk. When it ended, she planned to bail but got stopped by people wanting autographs and asking her more questions she couldn't answer. In all the meet and greet chaos, she lost track of both Mikayla and Alia. When she finally had the chance to seek them out so they could leave, Daniel stepped into her path.

Looking down at her with cold, perceptive eyes, he said, "Jada, I hope you enjoyed your last hurrah."

"Daniel, don't bother speaking to me. I much prefer the silent treatment you've been sulking in since I got here."

Jada started to move past him but Daniel grabbed her arm, whispering in her ear so none of the nearby fans or cast members could listen in.

"You can act as high and mighty as you want, but we both know who won here. You thought you could do better than me, but here you are. Trying to weasel your way back on the show. But you never will. I'm still the top dog, while you're off begging my mom for scraps."

Pulling out of his grip, mostly to hide the tears brimming in her eyes, Jada kept her face turned away from her ex, but her back was ramrod straight. With a steady, aloof tone, she replied, "You're right about one thing, Daniel. You're definitely a dog."

Yet, even as Jada got in the last word and walked away, Daniel's words stuck with her. Weeks later while on those crappy auditions, his words echoed in her head. They made her forget lines midmonologue and second guess every acting choice. Imposter syndrome swallowed her whole as she doubted her worth as an actor and hated herself for being weak and unable to rise above his verbal abuse and lies.

And after seeing him at the lounge tonight, Jada worried Daniel's phantom and the wound he left wouldn't stop haunting her. Lost in her negative thoughts, it took Mikayla poking her with an ice-cream spoon to get her attention again.

"Look, I know that bastard put you through the wringer, but you're stronger now. You're tough. Don't let him control you emotionally."

"You're right. I am, and I shouldn't. I'm going to go on with my life and get through this deal with Tristan," Jada said.

"Speaking of Tristan, do you feel like something may be developing between you two?"

"What can develop between us, Mikayla? It's a business arrangement. Not to mention we're not completely lily-white innocent either." Jada spoon jabbed her cousin in return over their bad judgment.

"True. I guess you're right. You'll get out of it what you can. Then move on." Mikayla agreed with her.

As the two of them sat and finished their ice cream, Jada continued to mull things over.

Yes, she had learned a lot over the past few years. In particular, the very hard lesson about not dating leading men who would ultimately lead you on. In that respect, Daniel and Tristan were the same. Daniel showing up reminded her of that fact. Both men were players and Jada would be stupid to forget that. It didn't matter how Tristan looked at her or touched her—or how her heart beat a little faster every time he did. In spite of all these things, Tristan was still a heartbreaker.

She wouldn't give him the chance to crush hers.

# 11

If Tristan's date with Jada last night hadn't been challenging enough, his mission the following day felt even more daunting. Standing outside the head office for Bright Futures, the previous warm and fuzzies he had for the nonprofit were vastly overshadowed by his anxiety over what he'd face inside. LeeAnn had come through in getting him some face time at the board members' monthly meeting. Now that it was time for him to state his case, worst case scenarios rushed through his mind.

What if it was already too late and they'd chosen to bring on someone else? Like a cookie cutter, former Disney star. They'd win Tristan's mentees over by promising the kids free trips to Disneyland, and Tristan's time with them would become a distant memory. Then again, a lot of Mouse House alums didn't have squeaky-clean records either. Some of them weren't even allowed near children anymore. Still, Tristan couldn't shake the feeling he was on a high stakes audition, trying not to be replaced by some perfect Goody-Two-shoes like Zac Efron.

Unlike a real audition, Tristan didn't have a legendary courtroom monologue to persuade the board. He would simply do his best and hope that was enough. As he stepped inside bravely, the receptionist, Xavier, greeted Tristan with his usual pep. Either he was none the wiser about Tristan's media debacle (unlikely) or working in social services had made him more forgiving. LeeAnn passed by the lobby before Tristan could feel any more uncomfortable about his current predicament.

"*Psst*! Tristan!" LeeAnn gave him an urgent wave. Bracing himself for a blast of LeeAnn's frenetic energy, he made his way over to her.

"Hey, LeeAnn, how's it going?" Tristan asked cautiously.

"Don't give me the sheepish look." LeeAnn gave him an admonishing pat on the shoulder. "You have kept me busy, sir. I spent this morning before the board meeting buttering them up for you."

"And I can't thank you enough for being in my corner," Tristan assured her.

Knowing the extent of LeeAnn's charisma, Tristan's tension eased somewhat. As she escorted him down the hallway, linking her arm through his, she insisted on hearing his answers first hand.

"Now, tell me the real story behind all this madness."

"Well, like the press release said, the whole scene on set got misconstrued. I recently broke up with Angela and sort of fell for Jada. It's just easier to rehearse scenes with her when Angela's being difficult."

"And Angela's 'difficultness' was also the reason for the bar fight?" LeeAnn asked, her tone slightly more skeptical this time.

"In my book, yes. But obviously, I don't plan on saying that in there." Tristan nodded as they stopped in front of an intimidating, closed door.

"Good idea. Stay accountable, but for the love of *God*, please don't say you'll *do better*. I'm so sick of seeing that on every Notes app or Instagram apology tour. Be sincere, say what helping the kids means to you. Got it?"

"Got it." Tristan offered a thumbs-up. With his confirmation, LeeAnn left her coaching behind and knocked briskly on the door.

Just as Tristan got his breathing under control, they were given the okay to enter. Around the polished conference table, five people stared back at him. Aside from one or two thin-lipped frowns, overall, it was too early to tell how this talk would go. Nevertheless, Tristan stayed humble and pleasant as he took the last empty seat at the table. LeeAnn didn't abandon him, stationing herself at the back of the room.

"Hello, everyone. I want to thank you for making time in your busy schedules to talk to me. First, I want to say how truly sorry I am for any trouble my personal situations have caused you or this brilliant organization."

"To be fair, they're not entirely personal. Quite public, actually," one of the stuffier board members pointed out, giving him a severe look that worked quite well with his Mr. Potato Head glasses. Luckily, Tristan remembered the man's real name and refrained from calling him after the toy namesake.

"Well, Mr. Johnson, I think we've all had things in our lives that we wish weren't public get out through the family grapevine or friends gossiping. My team has already released statements about my relationship with Jada and how I tried to *protect* my co-star at that bar."

The board president, Sharon Michaels, let out a sympathetic

sigh. "You know we love you, Tristan. The kids love you too. But just like we tell the teens in our program that violence and anger isn't the answer, we can't condone it with our sponsors either."

"I know, and I'm going to do my best to live by that philosophy from now on. I can't change how my past actions have been perceived. I can only change my behavior going forward. And if anything, talking about my experiences with the mentees will only back up what they've learned here so far."

While Tristan believed he'd conveyed accountability, the room devolved into a weighty silence. Time to pull out the big guns.

"I've also been thinking about the annual gala. After our discussion about having it as a fair, I reached out to a few people. They're willing to give us a two-week stay instead of a weekend event. My former *Garcia* co-stars are also willing to put in an appearance and make donations. We're even thinking about doing a celebrity matching campaign. We could advertise it on social media."

Tristan might not like throwing his money around, but he knew plenty of stars who would love the chance to make a big show of their generosity. With Juan totally embarrassing Tristan the other night, it had been easy to strong-arm the chef into participating, along with the rest of his former TV family. The mention of more big-time donors did the trick with the board, based off the murmured gasps and eyebrows shooting up around the table. LeeAnn proved to be the loudest.

"Oh come on, guys! Even celebrities who've been *convicted* don't put in this much redemption work!" She urged them.

"*Okay*, LeeAnn." Sharon Michaels held back her laughter. "We won't be cutting ties with you, Tristan. You're passionate and full of too many good ideas. *However—*"

"I know, I know. I'll be on my best behavior," Tristan promised.

Tristan's chest felt a million times lighter as he and LeeAnn excused themselves from the rest of the meeting. Since Tristan also had a meeting with Doug later that day, he had planned on going home and crashing for a bit, but then LeeAnn pointed out a program was underway in the activity room. There wasn't an outright "go or else," but putting in extra face time would help his case. The second Tristan poked his head into the community center's main room, several of the teens shouted in surprise. As they abandoned whatever project they were working on, the room devolved into excited chatter. His mentee, Sam, gave him the biggest welcome as he waved him over.

"Big T!" the boy exclaimed. With a bit of glittery paint on his cheek and his ecstatic demeanor, he looked much younger than fourteen.

"Hey, everybody!" Tristan waved back at the energetic group. "Sorry to interrupt, Mei-Xing," he added to the program facilitator. As the head of activities at the center, Mei-Xing always found ways to tie life lessons into art therapy and whatever else she thought the kids needed.

"That's okay. We're just talking about setting goals for the future."

Looking at the tables covered in glue and various magazine clippings, Tristan whistled. "In a very hands-on way, I see."

"Yes. We're making vision boards," Sam added, barely managing to hide his disdain as he wrinkled his nose.

"Would you like to join us, Tristan?" Mei-Xing prompted him. They both knew if Tristan joined in, the less-enthused kids might perk up a bit.

"Sure, sounds great." Tristan agreed, then nudged Sam on the shoulder.

"Scoot over, champ."

Sam did so with minor grumbling. Stealing a peek at his vision board, Tristan noticed the landscape was fairly bare. Sam's images included a Jaguar sports car, Chadwick Boseman as T'Challa, and pink glitter paint that spelled *U-m-m*. Before Tristan could ask the meaning behind Sam's few selections, Mei-Xing handed him extra supplies.

"Well, of course, we *all* know how successful you are, but your vision board can be about more than just professional or financial ambitions. It can be about your relationships, spirituality, anything. It's basically an artistic way to express what you want for yourself."

*Uh-oh.* Now Tristan got some of Sam's reluctance. With his own complicated past and current relationship disasters, Tristan tried not to think about the future in any real depth. Honestly, he was kind of afraid to. For him, self-reflection often led to disquieting thoughts. Like, why bother planning a lifetime with someone who could change their mind and leave? There was no sense in trying to map out his love life, or his entire career, either, when projects came and went all the time. But perhaps his current circumstances were an indication that he should reevaluate his devil-may-care approach to life. Reading the conflicted expression on Tristan's face, Sam snorted.

"See? How can you plan anything when shit always hits the fan?" Sam whispered to him, out of earshot of Mei-Xing.

It was no surprise Sam felt the same way Tristan did. The kid had been with Bright Futures for two years, and over that time, Tristan had gotten to know him well. Sam usually pulled off a tough guy act with everyone else but had opened up to Tristan over time. His dad had died years ago and his mom was often in and out of rehab—just like Sam had been in and out of juvie since the age of twelve. But once he'd joined the Bright Futures program as part of his probation, he'd matured so much.

Tristan had been glad to play a small part in that, from visiting when Sam was locked up to talking to him about potential colleges. Not that Tristan himself had gone to college, but stressing the importance of finding a career path was paramount to Bright Futures' mission. And given a choice between well-meaning facilitators like Mei-Xing or a movie star who could relate to his family trauma, Sam often took Tristan's perspective to heart. Over the course of their relationship, Sam had become much more dedicated to graduating high school and getting involved with a better crowd.

"That may be true, but we can give it our best shot," Tristan insisted, as he sorted through the clippings.

"Any pictures of your new bomb-ass girlfriend in there?" Sam asked while carefully gluing a cheeseburger to his creation.

"Not likely. What about you? Any romantic dreams for your future?" Tristan diverted the conversation.

"Not unless I can also find Thor in here somewhere." Sam sighed wistfully as he dug through the magazines.

Sam's previous home environment didn't leave a lot of room to share feelings or the thought that he might be gay. But after cleaning up his record and working through some things, Sam had started opening up more, relationship-wise. He could finally bring up his movie star crushes with minimal blushing.

"Mmmm, you'll find your real-life Thor someday," Tristan said decisively.

As they descended into reflective silence, Tristan wavered between several options for his board. One, he could go the Sam route and also rep some Black Panther or, two, pick a picture of a yacht, because why not? But as he thought back to his talk with the board members and his vows to change, he stopped himself. Spotting a peace sign on a picture of a girl doing yoga, Tristan cut it out and glued it smack-dab in the center of his board.

"Bam! *Growth*," Tristan muttered to himself. Although deep down he knew it would never be that easy.

After laying out his psyche on paper, Tristan met up with Doug at another local café for a quick damage control update. While the previous incident had gone viral with tons of hits, this new gossip that Tristan and Jada were a couple was trending much faster. Doug gave him a recap on how all across social media, there were comments on whether the two were *really* dating, and yes, they looked cute together. Some people mentioned Tristan's previous comments on Jada's social media as proof something had been going on prior to all this. However, Tammy and Tegan from *Sip That Tea* had bypassed tweeting or writing a simple article in favor of posting a vlog, one Doug insisted he check out.

Watching their video on his phone, Tristan took in how the twins remained fiercely dedicated to their brand. They had the overly polished makeup typical of social media influencers mixed with flashy designer clothes. Shining in a sparkly blazer and revealing leather pants, Tegan sat next to his sister, Tammy. Tammy had brought the neon eyeshadow and purple lipstick out in full force. And yet, somehow all the pizzazz worked for them.

"Okay, Tea Lovers!" Tegan started off. "Here is the latest on the Tristan Maxwell–Jada Berklee fiasco. After our superb snooping skills, we were the *first* to release the news about their on-set catfight."

"While we pride ourselves on our sources, a press release is now floating around saying the incident was no biggie, just a film thang. And apparently that these two are hot for each other offscreen," Tammy said as she raised a skeptical brow.

"Now, we could go into is this true or not true—and we certainly will. But let's go back to the timeline." As Tegan spoke, snapshots of the previous night flashed on-screen.

"Shortly after this announcement, Tristan and Jada were spotted at the super-romantic and delicious spot La Rosa Dorada. While they were out on the town—either keeping up appearances or pronouncing their love to the masses—Angela Collins, the lead in their film, had some scathing things to say."

They pulled up Angela's latest social media posts and Tammy read them off, relishing in the actress's commentary.

"'Clout chasers will do anything for attention. Can't wait until the truth comes out on the backstabbers in my life. Already writing my tell-all memoir.'"

Having seen enough, Tristan cut off the video. He didn't need to keep up with Angela's remarks as he would get an earful once they were face to face again. Aside from her and people like the Tea Twins speculating on its validity, there were plenty of other people who were accepting their explanation. A twinge of guilt washed over him at seeing his fans actually excited about him dating someone. Usually, his devout followers cracked meme-filled jokes about his dating exploits. But Doug had been right about Jada. She had a definite sweetheart vibe among her own fan base and it was— surprisingly—trickling over into his. He should have been relieved their plan was working, but the idea that strangers who adored him were rooting for their scam felt icky. He chased the bitter feeling away with a sip of his much stronger latte.

"This is damage control at its best, Doug," Tristan admitted to the agent. "You know we still have one more problem, though, don't you?"

"Don't worry. While Ren is in talks with Mr. Collins about the production's fate, I reminded him that Angela's contract stipulates point blank she isn't allowed to spread bad press that could affect the movie. Her dad might care about her hurt feelings, but he cares about money more."

"Shit, I had almost forgotten about Ren dealing with him. Does he—"

"Ren knows about the plan. I talked to him before we sent out the press release. Thanks for asking so late in the game."

Tristan blushed at the dig, although it was well deserved. With everything that had been going on, Tristan hadn't even bothered to check in with Ren. Yes, he was nervous about the director still being angry at him, but he should have reached out. He'd only met Angela's dad a few times, but his heady mixture of ego and greed made him a force to be reckoned with. Mr. Collins vs. Ren was like David and Goliath. The only thing that soothed Tristan was knowing how that particular story ended.

He pushed on, asking, "Okay, so what happens next? With the movie. Did he say anything?"

"They're placating Angela with a few mental health days while they enhance safety protocols on set, yadda, yadda. I'm sure they'll notify you soon about when you can get back to work."

Tristan breathed a sigh of relief. Things were working out far better than he deserved. Hopefully, it would be the same for Jada if she got this role in Logan Wentworth's movie.

"Well, enough about that. Tell me." At Tristan's obliviousness, Doug's typical pushy impatience reared its ugly head. "How did it go, stupid?"

"Oh, the date? It was . . . interesting."

"Interesting. That's the best you can do?" Doug squinted at him in annoyance.

"Fine. Dinner was rough. The club was better, and we made progress with your producer friend, Logan. She was happy about that, so I guess the plan is working."

"And?"

"What else do you want from me?" Tristan asked.

No matter how much Doug pestered, there wasn't very much Tristan was prepared to reveal about last night, Jada's seemingly weird history with Daniel being one of those things. The almost kiss between them was another secret he planned to keep.

"How was the atmosphere? Did you put on the Maxwell charm? Did you two . . . you know?" Doug waggled his eyebrows in a way that he shouldn't. Ever.

"Stop that. Nothing happened. She's too pissed at me. We're frenemies at best."

Jada may have been caustic at times, but that didn't negate the fact that she was beautiful and funny. Even though things were rocky between them, every genuine smile he got from her or any tiny crack in her armor enticed him. He wanted to understand what made her tick, what it was about her that kept drawing him in. He couldn't tell whether this impulse came from a need to simply make sense of the attraction or to escape it.

"Frankly, I don't care what you two do privately as long as it doesn't screw up what we're trying to do publicly. Is that clear?" Doug said.

"Crystal clear, Captain." Tristan saluted him.

"Good. When are you seeing her again?"

"I don't know yet."

"Good God. Make it soon, why don't you? The public needs to see you out together more often," Doug said. At his reprimand, Tristan thought back to how Jada mentioned facing off with her agent today.

"Maybe I should catch up with her after the meeting?" Tristan suggested after filling Doug in.

"Good idea. If she's battling Terminator Kane, she'll need all the help she can get." Doug shuddered.

*Holy crap.* Tristan paused as a slow realization crept up on him. "One last thing, Doug. Are Daniel Kane and Avery Kane related?"

"Yeah, the snot-nosed brat is her son. Why do you ask?"

"No reason." Tristan gave Doug a reassuring smile, but inside, a parade of red flags went up.

Something *very* weird was going on between Jada and the Kane family. Unfortunately, he didn't have the right to ask. Although Jada wouldn't let him pry into whatever was going on, a fierce protectiveness came over him. Forget fake-dating obligations. He sincerely *needed* to check in on Jada now that these misshapen puzzle pieces had started falling in his lap. Whether she wanted to confide in him or not after talking with Avery, Tristan would be there, waiting for her.

# 12

Jada hated waiting.

She usually considered herself a patient person, but not with this. Not with Avery. Any time Jada had a confrontation with the woman, she had to put on emotional battle armor beforehand. For the most part, Jada had gotten the hang of fending off the blows from Avery's cutting remarks. Like the catty observations about why a production had gone with someone else over Jada, or pressuring her to try out for things Jada wasn't interested in "just to pay the bills." But today she had deeper concerns other than Avery's habitual rudeness.

For starters, with Daniel in town, he might come to the office to visit his Mommy Dearest. They had run into each other here several times postbreakup, Daniel chitchatting with his mom, smugly monopolizing her time when Jada had an appointment. She could never be sure that he planned it that way but it had always felt intentionally vindictive. Another way to punish her for leaving him. She didn't want a repeat of him dropping by, especially while trying to explain her "relationship" with Tristan to Avery. And if Daniel didn't show up today, he'd still probably have told his mom about their encounter at the lounge. It would be perfect ammo for Avery to ask Jada if she could handle a relationship with a womanizer like Tristan when she'd run away at the sight of her ex.

On top of the Daniel anxiety, having to tell a lie this big made her nauseated. Some people thought of acting as artistic lying. But for Jada, being an actress didn't automatically make you a good liar. She certainly wasn't. The first time Jada had ever lied she'd been eight and had just broken her mom's favorite vase. She did a piss poor job of covering it up, and her mom shamed her into never doing it again. No wonder her conscience secretly sobbed with guilt over agreeing to date Tristan . . . *and* for releasing the video.

Oh God. The nausea was getting worse. Jada bent over, not quite putting her head between her knees because it would look superweird to the receptionist, but enough to slowly steady her breathing and rapid thoughts. Maybe Mikayla was right when she insisted over and over that so much of Jada's anxiety would go away if she left Avery for a different agent. But who would take her on? Her resume and experience were fine but not enough for an agency to want to poach her from Avery—whom most people feared. Her connections were too powerful once she chose to wield them. If she truly wanted to, Avery could blacklist Jada to the rest of the entertainment community, claiming she was unprofessional or telling her own twisted version of what happened with Daniel.

When Avery's equally frightened assistant gave her the go-ahead to enter, Jada's nerves had calmed due to the deep breathing exercises. Then they sky-rocketed all over again when she walked in and saw Avery's sour expression. The woman had an unnerving tendency of staring at people intensely over the rim of her glasses. Jada suspected she was copying Meryl Streep's iconic version of this from *The Devil Wears Prada*. It was hard to deny their intimidating resemblance.

"Avery, welcome back. How was the trip?" Jada asked.

"What the hell is going on?" Avery barked. "First, that video gets released, and now I'm hearing you and Tristan are supposedly a couple? The truth. Now," she demanded.

Jada followed through, recapping the agreed-upon story from Doug's press release. As her agent gave her a stone-faced expression, Jada struggled to get her last words out convincingly.

"So, although I don't know how that video got out, I can assure you, Tristan and I are seeing each other. This has all been blown out of proportion."

Avery unclenched at last, blowing out a loud sigh. Rubbing the bridge of her nose in frustration, she asked, "Why didn't you say so in the first place when I called?"

"It didn't seem like the right time."

"Damn it, Jada. How are we supposed to milk juicy press like this if you don't clue me in? I thought by now you would have learned something about publicity from me, but apparently, you're still oblivious."

The most ironic thing about breaking up with Daniel had been the way it had changed Avery. When Jada first started acting, Avery genuinely seemed to care about helping Jada learn the ins and outs of the business. She had heard a few whispered stories about the agent's temper, but it had never been directed at her. But postrelationship, Avery morphed into an overcritical mother-in-law, resentful that her son's "girl" couldn't keep her man happy or her house in order. It didn't matter that the two had actually broken up. Avery's perception of Jada had been tainted.

Putting on her whatever you say, Mama Kane, daughter-in-law smile, Jada said, "It's new, and I'm still not sure how it's going to go."

"Hmm. I can see why. After the way you treated Daniel, and nearly turned *Fallen Creatures* into a bad soap opera."

Ignoring the daytime drama slander—*General Hospital* was still iconic in her mind—Jada filled Avery in on meeting Logan and her upcoming audition. The agent's mood lifted from judgmental to her regular level of condescension.

"Thank God. You dating Tristan will bring us some good leads. I'll get in contact with Mr. Wentworth's team and we'll arrange something." Avery lifted a warning finger, wagging it in Jada's direction.

"However, I need you to keep me informed if anything else pops up. I want only positive outcomes from you being with the great Tristan Maxwell. Understood?"

"Understood. Anything else?" Jada asked, dying to make her escape.

Avery merely grunted a curt "No" and waved Jada away offhandedly. She took the opportunity to rush out of the office like her ass was on fire. That hadn't been nearly as bad as she'd anticipated, but Jada still held her breath as she waited for the elevator. She had to make it out of the building without any run-ins with Daniel either. Once she stepped out of the building's front doors unscathed, Jada inhaled a breath of fresh air to celebrate her freedom. It was as if she'd been released from a dragon's lair or a villainous queen's dungeon. Her joy came to a halt when Tristan waved at her from his spot on the plaza's fountain.

"What are you doing here?"

"Is that any way to greet your adoring boyfriend? I came to pick up my best gal," Tristan said.

"Gal? What are we, in the fifties?" Jada said, although secretly she felt a girlish rush that Tristan had thought of her. He'd come all the way down here to see how she was doing. She supposed she should show a little gratitude.

"Thank you for coming, but luckily, I was able to escape most of Avery's wrath," Jada said as she briefed him on her exchange with Avery.

"She sounds just as bad as Doug said," Tristan said, then gave a light shrug. "Do you have time for lunch?"

"What did you have in mind? Another ritzy restaurant? You must be craving two bites of fine cuisine like you had last night."

"Honestly, I'm getting hungry for something else," Tristan said, lifting his eyebrows suggestively. Wary, Jada backed two steps away from him.

"What do you mean?"

"Hot dogs. Let's go to Pink's and then we can swim a bit."

Her stomach grumbled instantly at the mention of the famous hot dog joint. While the place was always packed, the food made it worth it. Pink's marketed itself as a Hollywood landmark, and they weren't wrong. They had specials named after celebrities, and regular sightings of stars eating there. It was a perfect place to be spotted for their new relationship, but . . .

"I would, given our deal and all, but I don't have a swimsuit for on-the-go occasions."

"Me neither. We can go buy some."

Jada hesitated, weighing the pros and cons until Tristan turned the odds in his favor.

"Come on. You're telling me you don't want to potentially run into Queen Latifah or Betty White chilling with some chili cheese dogs?"

Highly unlikely, but a girl could dream.

"Okay, fine. If a Guadalajara Dog is involved, I'm in."

# 13

"Jada! Come on. It's been thirty minutes," Tristan whined as Jada sifted through the boutique's array of swimsuits. After his skillful persuasion, Jada had left her car safely in the agency's parking lot and come with him to a suitable shop several blocks away from the downtown business district. That was the beauty of California's sunny weather. You could easily find beachwear within a very small radius.

"Picking the perfect suit takes time, Tristan." Jada studied a sparkly white one-piece, serene and unhurried. Either retail therapy was her favorite way to relax, or Jada had been sincere when she said the meeting had gone fine. Tristan didn't want to upset her, but it was on the tip of his tongue to ask about her friction with Mama Bear and Junior Kane. To distract himself from the nagging question, he *tsked* over the bland suit she'd been about to add to her selections.

"No way. This one's boring. It doesn't highlight your, uh, 'assets.' No cleavage, no . . . nothin'." Tristan regarded the garment with disgust.

"I like it. It's simple, elegant."

"It's not nearly as bold as the dress you wore last night."

"There's nothing wrong with these," Jada said, holding her choices close to her chest. Her resistance was futile as Tristan yanked them out of her arms and started putting them back.

"Look, if people are going to believe you're *my* girl, you're going to have to reveal some skin."

Blocking out her protests, Tristan began pulling his preferences. Inwardly, he had to admit his objections had nothing to do with Jada's taste, but were about his interests. She was beautiful and should show it off . . . particularly to him. He was her "boyfriend" after all.

Teasingly, Tristan held up a midnight-black suit that was basically a thong and some strategically placed triangles.

"I'm not wearing that!" Jada said, snatching the bikini out of his arms.

"You know what they say: less is more."

Jada ignored him as she scanned the racks. She picked out a purple bikini with a tasteful skirt instead.

"Compromise," Jada insisted. They managed to pick a few things they both agreed on. After much haggling, Jada went into one of the dressing rooms to try the clothes on. At first, the wait didn't seem terribly long, but as the minutes dragged by, Tristan had a sneaking suspicion Jada wasn't trying on the suits at all.

"Did you chicken out?" he drawled through the door.

"No. This first one has a lot of strings. I don't know why I let you pick it."

"Do you need help? Those tricky little things might be crying out for an agile hand."

"Don't you dare come in here!" Jada's high-pitched warning

erupted from behind the stall door. Tristan held back a chuckle as he pressed her further.

"You have two more minutes to come out or I'm leaving you altogether." Despite her grumbles of "Fine with me" and blah, blah, blah, Jada emerged from the dressing room.

"What about this one?" Jada held up her hands with lackluster enthusiasm.

Regardless of her mood, this one was a winner. With a cherry-red and white print top and flattering bottoms, it held a balance of suggestion and fun-in-the-sun playfulness. In fact, it might have piqued Tristan's interest a little too much.

"Perfect," Tristan said around a surprising scratch in his throat.

"Good. I agree," Jada said, dropping her eyes to the floor.

Once they had that decided, they ended up in another bickering spree. Jada remained adamant about Tristan not paying for her clothes. He managed to trick her into picking out beach towels long enough to slip the saleswoman his credit card. This left Jada fuming as they stopped at Pink's. Undoubtedly, her mood would have changed if they'd actually run into some of her Hollywood faves wolfing down hot dogs, however, Tristan and Jada ended up taking pictures with several fans wanting to chat with the happy couple.

Once their cheeks hurt from smiling and their bellies were full, they headed to the Santa Monica Pier and the surrounding beach. As they made their way to the boardwalk, Jada's eyes lit up in delight. Ahead of them, warm sand led to the shimmering blue ocean. All along the beach, other couples and cheerful families reveled in the good weather. Plenty of children played in the low tide while more adventurous surfers traveled farther out.

Tristan made an exaggerated motion of sucking in some fresh sea-scented air.

"Ahhh, feel that, J? The bright sun, the gentle wind, this is exactly what we need." He threw his arm over her shoulders. Surprisingly, she didn't shrug him off and let him guide her to a perfect viewing spot.

"It is nice out today," she admitted as she laid out their striped towels.

Tristan watched—probably too avidly—as Jada lay back on her towel. Sunglasses on, she rested her head on the blanket and basked in the sun, her rich brown skin luminescent under its golden rays.

"Would you like some sunscreen, dear?" Tristan teased.

"I'm good," Jada said.

"Come on, you want to ward off skin cancer, don't you?" He retained his mild innocence as he shook the SPF bottle at her.

"Fine."

"I can take care of it for you," Tristan said, slightly suggestive.

"Don't worry. I'm a big girl. I can put it on all by myself." Jada returned his tone.

Giving in (for now), Tristan squirted a generous amount into her hand. He applied some protection of his own but didn't take his eyes off of her as she worked the creamy solution into her slim stomach. When she finished, Jada lay back out, taking in the scene, leaving Tristan restless.

"Don't you want to get in the water?"

"No."

"Can you swim?"

"Yes."

"Then you should get in. We can't go to the beach and not swim."

"You go ahead. I'm good here." Jada waved at him, remaining closed off behind her shades.

Which, of course, to Tristan, was unacceptable. There was no way he was letting Jada hang around and ignore him. He'd rather have her furious at him (as usual) than oblivious to him. He did the one thing he could to rectify the situation. Without any warning, Tristan reached over and scooped Jada up into his arms.

"What are you doing?" Jada squeaked. Despite her protests, she threw her arms around his neck to stay steady.

"I told you. We're swimming." Tristan rushed into the water despite her squeals of alarm, pulling her into its salty depths. When they were immersed in the ocean, he gave her a teasing splash. Jada did not appreciate it in the least. She returned his playful action with more force, splashing multiple waves at him.

"What's wrong with you? Don't you know Black women don't like getting their hair wet?" As soon as the words were out of her mouth, Jada reached up to touch her soaked curls, her face a mask of horror.

"You look cute either way." He gave her a wide-eyed, adoring look.

"Says the man who will not be juggling a detangler brush and flat iron later!" Jada tried to swim back to shore, but he held her back from doing so.

"Please, just for a little while."

His pleading seemed to work momentarily. Even though Jada stayed away from him, she did a halfhearted turn, swimming around in a circle until she faced him again.

"All right. What do you want to do?"

"Well . . .there's Shark Attack."

"Shark Attack?" Jada's eyebrows shot up in alarm.

"Yeah, when we weren't filming, I'd still get together with the *Garcia* fam as a kid. This was my favorite game to play with Juan and Rafe. One of us would be the shark and the others were bait. 'Swim fast or be killed' kind of thing."

"That is *horrible*. It's like you're asking for a great white to come and snap you into pieces."

"Oh yeahhh, we got in a lot of trouble. When it was his turn to be bait, Rafe would scream 'Shark! Shark!' at the top of his lungs. Everyone around us would scatter." Despite the so-called bad karma, Tristan basked in the nostalgia. He had so many warm memories of those Santa Monica afternoons, and Rafe terrorizing the tourists, it was no wonder he'd pushed to have the Bright Futures fair here.

"You sure you don't want to play?"

"No, thank you." Jada shook her head. "You might as well shout to the heavens, *Take me now, God!*"

Holding back his laughter at Jada's superstitions, Tristan started humming the theme music from the movie *Jaws* as he circled around her. She splashed more waves at him as a deterrent, but Tristan launched himself at her, channeling his childhood hammerhead persona. As he mimicked biting her neck, Jada's indignant squeals soon turned into a fit of giggles. Her amusement left her winded enough to ease into his embrace. This close to her, he could smell her familiar vanilla and cocoa butter scent mixed with the saltiness of the sea. A strange sense of peace drifted over him as Jada beamed up at him.

"Tristan, your lack of predictability is terrifying sometimes."

"Yes, I would have made Bruce so proud."

"Now, you're making *Finding Nemo* references? Who are you?"

Tristan gave her a peck on the cheek. "Your boyfriend, according to *Us Weekly*."

Her smile dimming, Jada's eyes slid away from him as she pointed over his shoulder. "There's a big one coming. Let's go."

To his surprise, Jada didn't mean heading back to shore. Instead, she dragged him farther into the water. Moments later, they were standing up, waiting for the rushing torrent to hit them from behind. It did, pushing them forward as they held hands to stay steady. The current and Jada's touch left Tristan feeling powerful, and shouting Leo's king of the world line from *Titanic*. Jada responded by sinking into the waves and screaming for Wilson so passionately it would have made Tom Hanks proud. After exhausting their at-sea movie repertoire, they held an underwater breathing contest (because whether she'd admit it to him or not, Jada was as competitive as Tristan). When Jada (inevitably) lost, she claimed fatigue, so they returned to the dry safety of the beach.

"See, wasn't this fun?" Tristan teased as he trailed after her.

"You're right. I'm having a good time." Jada fell back down, spreading out in the glowing, hot sun. Tristan rested beside her and, propping his head on his hand, leaned forward conspiratorially.

"Yeah, the only thing that would make this better is if this was a topless beach."

For once, Jada didn't glare at him as she usually did. Yes, she peeked over her shades long enough to cut her eyes at him, but her lips tilted into a begrudging grin, drawing Tristan's gaze to the sand sticking stubbornly to her cheek. He brushed the gritty flecks away without thinking. Jada didn't flinch back with an accusatory remark, but instead closed her eyes peacefully at the feel of his fingers brushing her skin. Seeing that sense of release on her face, Tristan found himself moving forward, almost close enough to graze his lips against her—

"Excuse me," a young voice called from above them. A teenage girl looked down at them with excitement as she bounced on her toes.

"You're Tristan Maxwell, right? And Jada Berklee?"

"Yes, that's us," Jada said, her voice cautious yet polite. That was the way you had to approach these fans until you found out whether they were enthusiastic or crazy.

"I know it's kind of random, and you probably don't want to, but would you take a picture with me?" Her words came out in a rush as she lifted her smartphone.

"Of course." Jada sat up straighter before Tristan even had time to fully process the girl's request. His mind foggily remained on the surreal moment between them. Meanwhile, Jada brushed the remaining sand on her body off as if she could just as skillfully shake off any lingering intimacy. All for a photo op.

The girl needed no further invitation. She plopped down on the beach, squeezing between them. Tristan silently mourned the loss of Jada's proximity but kept his fan meet and greet smile intact.

"You two are such a cute couple. I'm glad you're together," the girl rambled as she pulled up her camera app.

*We* were *together,* Tristan thought resentfully, but he put on his winning charisma.

"I am too." He winked at Jada. "And we'd love to take a picture with you."

Of course, "a picture" turned into three or four as the girl got carried away with talking to them. When she left, Tristan let out a sigh of relief and looked at Jada.

"You know how it is." She laughed.

"Doesn't make it any less intrusive."

"Isn't it good that she took the picture? I'm sure she'll post it on Instagram or something. In addition to the people who snapped shots of us at Pink's, this will all help sell our story, right?"

Tristan didn't speak for a moment, his jaw clenched as he ground his teeth in frustration. He was considering going for it, kissing Jada, and she was thinking of the spotlight and their potential strategy. But then again, he shouldn't be surprised. That was the whole purpose of them being out together. Nevertheless, the way she could swiftly leave their fun in the sun behind for business gnawed at him.

"Right. It's good. Definitely," he said in a clipped tone.

Copying her move, he lay back on his towel and pulled his sunglasses down over his eyes. He wouldn't let Jada see how truly conflicted he was. If she wanted to play the role of a carefree amnesiac, fine. He could too.

# 14

Mikayla was studying Jada as she worked on making breakfast. There was a knowing gleam in her eyes that set Jada on edge. Mikayla was going to ask about her and Tristan. Jada could feel it in her gut, but she wanted to avoid having that conversation for as long as possible. She whistled cheerfully as she prepared scrambled eggs for her and her cousin.

"I heard it might rain today. I hope that doesn't slow us down getting to work." Jada rambled to stop Mikayla from talking.

After her beach outing with Tristan, she'd come home to find an email and a voice mail from Ren's assistant. Things had been smoothed over with Mr. Collins and their previous so-called safety risks had been brought "up to code." As such, they were headed back to the studio lot to shoot the time travel scenes they hadn't been able to film. Even knowing she hadn't lost her job didn't stop Jada's nerves about going back into production. Angela would be out for blood, and she had no idea how that would affect the film.

"Anyway, hopefully today will be fun. The VFX process is so

interesting," Jada went on as she finished up the eggs.

Sliding them onto their plates, she placed them next to servings of fresh strawberries, blueberries, and kiwi.

"Ta-da!" she said as she set the decorative breakfast on the table in front of Mikayla.

"Mhmm." Her cousin hummed appreciatively, took a sip of her coffee, and then stared into Jada's soul.

"You done with the bullshit now?"

Sighing, Jada sank into her chair, grabbed her fork, and started picking at her food.

"What do you want to know?"

"I want to know why you came home singing like a frickin' tan Disney princess yesterday. You were a shade darker and way happier than normal. I know it has to do with Tristan, and I need to know why ASAP."

"There's nothing to tell. We went to the beach. I like the ocean, so I had a good time."

It had also been a huge relief to see that she and Tristan could be around each other without too much arguing. That's what had cheered her up. The possibility that they might get away with their plan if they were more considerate toward each other. Tristan could be kind and fun when he wanted to. He could do spot-on imitations about Chief Brody needing a bigger boat, and loved Jada's rendition of Dory's keep swimming anthem. If she dealt mostly with the side of him that shared her interests and sense of humor, things would go okay. And she could be forgiving of some of his crappier antics. For example, he had gotten her hair wet but she hadn't drowned him right then and there.

"You're telling me that's all that happened?" Mikayla asked, frowning in disbelief.

"Swear to God." Jada held a solemn hand over her heart dutifully.

"How boring." Mikayla sighed, shaking her head as she popped a strawberry in her mouth.

"What do you mean? We're getting along."

"Yes, but *how* along? I need things to get hella more interesting here."

"The type of interesting I think you're alluding to isn't going to happen. I'm not into Tristan that way. All I care about is him keeping his promise and us getting this film done."

"Everything will work out." Mikayla patted Jada's hand soothingly. "The shoot will end, and Tristan will keep his promise. That way, you're bound to get an even better job. Maybe you can even dump Bitchery Kane and get another agent. You'd be rid of her *and* Daniel then."

Jada chewed her eggs thoughtfully. It did sound like a good plan.

"You know what? You might be right, Kayla. We'll see what happens, but for now, let's not be late for work."

Jada picked up her empty plate and brought it over to the sink.

"Chop, chop, cuz. We've got a long day ahead of us."


Although Jada inwardly warned herself to be ready for anything, she wasn't prepared for the intense awkwardness on set. The second Mikayla and Jada stepped inside the soundstage, it was like things came to a screeching halt. While the crew should have been hustling to prepare for the day, people stopped to give her calculating and curious stares, from Andrew, who gave her a reluctant wave, to the recently healed Tim, who tensed up as if she had been the one to send him flying into the rigging. Ignoring the eerie silence at her arrival, Jada focused on Ren, the only person who was—thankfully—acting seminormal. Standing by the cinematographer, he looked up from studying the green screen to greet them.

"Morning, Jada, Mikayla." Ren nodded at them. Mikayla gave a quick hello and rushed off to the dressing rooms, but Jada hesitated.

"Morning, but . . . how come you're not like everyone else, looking at me like I'm an alien?" she whispered to him.

"Doug told me everything. Can't say I completely agree with your guys' plan, but as long as everything goes smoothly for the film, I'll keep my mouth shut."

Ren gave her a wink, something she never would have expected from the stern director, especially after their last encounter. With everything seemingly forgiven between them, it made her wonder what had happened to Erica. Jada hadn't seen her among the crew, which fueled her previous assumption that the girl had been fired. However, now probably wasn't the best time to sour Ren's mood by asking about the girl's whereabouts. Shaking off her bewilderment, Jada made her way to the makeup department, where Cass was brimming with questions.

"Jada," she hissed, and grabbed her arm to steer her to the nearest chair. "How could you hide something like this from me?"

"Technically, we were hiding it from everyone. With the public eye, and Angela, and everything." Jada went on with their lie.

"Ohhh, Angela is going to be *pissed* today," Cass said, snapping her fingers. Despite her sympathetic tone, there was a gleam of excitement in her eyes.

"Yeah, well, I'll just have to deal with her rage." Jada tried to shrug off Cass's feverish exclamations. "Can we, you know . . ."

Jada waved to the various cosmetic containers on the table.

"Of course, honey," Cass said as she began to work. "Still. I can't believe it. You and Tristan. Honestly, you're perfect for each other."

"Really?" Jada said, perplexed.

"Sure. It's the whole opposites attract thing. You're exactly what he needs to calm his ass down." Cass applied Jada's concealer. Not wanting to consider Cass's unsettling words, Jada decided to focus on the relaxation of being pampered.

"I'm going to go over my lines if you don't mind," she said, shutting down any further conversation. Cass always respected actors' memorization processes.

Thankfully, focusing on her upcoming scenes kept Jada engaged until it was time to shoot. Once she was line ready and fully outfitted with her makeup intact, she went back out, steeling herself for more strange looks, which arrived swiftly as Jada came face to face with Tristan. He was also ready for the day, dressed in his costume and standing next to Ren in front of the green screen. The director was playing referee as Angela stood on his other side, seething in quiet fury. Jada forgot about her completely as her eyes locked with Tristan's. When they did, it was as if the whole room went silent. Jada discovered it wasn't her imagination. Everyone watched eagerly as Tristan made his way over to her and wrapped a territorial arm around her waist. Kissing her on the cheek, he whispered into her ear.

"Get ready to put on the show of your life."

With that one declaration as her warning, Tristan looked out at the crew, ready to challenge them.

"Welcome back to work, everyone. Before you can all start whispering away and theorizing, I'd like to set the record straight. Jada and I are a couple, and the other day's incident was a misunderstanding. However, we would appreciate it if you would treat us as professionally as always, and respect our privacy."

"That sounds good to me," Ren interjected. "Now if we could—"

"You're right, Ren. It does sound good. Maybe even a little rehearsed," Angela said.

Ren's glare at his leading actress was so sharp Jada could almost feel the daggers shooting out of his eyes. Whatever smart remark he wanted to throw back never left his lips as Andrew rushed up to him with panicked eyes.

"Mr. Kurosawa, he's here."

"Who's here?"

Ren's answer came in the sound of a man's booming voice berating one of the PAs. The tall man heading toward them paid little heed to whatever the PA had said to him. Instead, he marched forward, talking over the lowly production assistant.

"I know they have a lot of scenes to get through today. That's why I came. Some encouragement to help things go smoothly."

As the man made it to the soundstage, Angela let out a squeal of delight.

"Daddy!" She rushed over to embrace him as if she hadn't seen him in years. Hard to imagine that was the case since she'd snitched to him only a few days ago.

"Hello, princess," he said indulgently, before moving on to the rest of the crew. With the commanding presence millionaires were known for, Mr. Collins wielded his privilege over them like it was his birthright.

"Ren, I hope you don't mind that I stopped by. Just wanted to get a feel for things on your first day back." His gaze grew sharper as he noticed Tristan's arm wrapped around Jada's waist.

"Hello, Tristan. And this is the infamous Ms. Berklee, I presume?"

"Yes, that's me, sir," Jada said. Sweat beaded on the back of her neck at his shrewd examination of her.

"Do you mind if I speak with you two for a moment?" Mr. Collins motioned for them to move a few feet away.

Given the man's authoritative—and loud—voice, Jada doubted taking a few steps to the left would stop everyone else from overhearing whatever he had to say. The one thing stopping Jada from truly freaking out was that Tristan hadn't let go of her. He kept his arm steady around her, and his own expression stayed friendly and relaxed.

"Of course, Mr. Collins," he said respectfully, then steered them off to the area the man had suggested. Fortunately, as he started into them, Mr. Collins did actually lower his voice.

"Let's get right to it, shall we? I've made it clear to Ren—and my daughter—that I want the rest of this film to go smoothly. I hope the two of you want the same thing?"

Jada and Tristan both nodded as his underlying threat rang through the question.

"Good. That being said, I won't tolerate any more bullying on this set. Or shenanigans of another nature." With this last part obviously directed at Tristan, the actor stepped up.

"Mr. Collins, I take full responsibility for my part in my past relationship with Angela. I just hope she and I can be polite to each other and make amends."

"Same," Jada added. "The amends part."

He scrutinized them a moment longer, searching their vows of repentance for any false notes. At last, he nodded. "Fine. Now that that's settled, let's make some movie magic, right?"

Tristan and Jada once again put on their aye, aye, sir act and hurried to get back to the safety of the surrounding crew. Angela remained serenely smug as the two returned properly chastised. Relieved all his stars were in one piece and their chief investor had been mollified, Ren hopped into the filming logistics.

"Okay, guys. We're taking it back from where Claire and Diego are trying to find a way to put an end to the time loop with Lana's help. But then all three of you end up getting sucked back into it. This is going to require some great imagination on your parts. We're going to need to work on your blocking and how you'll move in front of the screen."

Jada disengaged from Tristan's side and rushed to take her mark. After Ren's guidance, she moved offscreen, waiting for her cue as Tristan and Angela got into their positions. They went through several practice runs, rehearsing the blocking with ease. However, the second they began rolling, Angela fumbled her way through the scene, her facial expressions and movements much too stiff.

"Diego! I think the only way to escape is . . ." She trailed off, conveniently forgetting her lines right when Jada was supposed to enter, intentionally fucking the scene up—and everyone else over—to satisfy her whims. As Ren called cut, Angela held up her hands with feigned innocence.

"Gosh, I'm sorry, Ren. Something must be throwing me off. I don't know what it could be."

"Well, we'll be staying here as long as we need to until we can get this right. So let us know if we can do *anything* to help you along," Ren said.

His voice was calm but anger simmered beneath his cool tone. Mr. Collins's looming presence stopped him from calling her out properly. As Angela put her hands on her hips, about to protest, her father cleared his throat.

"But, Daddy!" Angela began, stung by the unspoken signals between them.

"Listen to Ren, Angela." Not princess or sweetie this time. Surprised that Mr. Collins would be the one keeping his rebellious daughter in check, Jada resisted the urge to laugh. With that small amount of criticism from her dear daddy, Angela straightened up and they managed to get through the scene. Once Mr. Collins seemed content with their progress, he excused himself, off to micromanage something (or someone) else.

After he left, Ren let them break for lunch, and Jada greatly appreciated the reprieve. She headed to the buffet table and inspected a roast beef sandwich. Her relief was short lived, though, as Angela sidled up to her.

"You sure you want to eat that? That's a lot of carbs for a girl like you."

Jada responded by taking a huge bite.

"Okay, if that's how you want it." Angela shrugged. "Just keep in mind, Tristan doesn't date anyone above a size six. And what, you're pushing a four at least, right?"

While Jada was perfectly happy with her body, Angela's fat shaming pissed her off. Like women didn't have enough body image issues without having other women picking them apart. Somehow, she resisted the urge to tell her co-star to crawl back into the hellhole she came from.

"Thanks for your advice, Angie. I'll keep it in mind."

"Good. Then again, I doubt you'll have to worry about it for too long. Your little fling is bound to be over by next week."

"Sorry to disappoint you, but Tristan and I are very happy together," Jada lied.

"That's what he wants you to think. Meanwhile, he's probably off sleeping with at least two different whores behind your back." Angela raised a pointed eyebrow as she alluded to Jada's supposed betrayal. "Tristan's always got a spare in his back pocket. And let's face it, Jada, you are neither interesting enough nor hot enough to hold his attention for much longer." Angela took a carrot stick off of a platter and bit into it with a loud crunch. She cocked her head to the side, as if her loud chewing was some kind of battle cry.

Jada gave her a warm smile in return. "Your dad seems nice. Made a whole speech to us about anti-bullying, and how we should all make amends."

Hearing how her father had not emotionally scarred Jada as she would have liked, Angela tossed the carrot in the trash.

"No thanks," she sneered, then breezed away.

Even though Jada was free of her, Angela's words reverberated in her head. Of course, Jada knew everything the woman said was bullshit. Angela was merely trying to get under her skin. But it shouldn't, because she and Tristan weren't a real couple. So why did the deli meat now feel like a heartburn-ridden wad of anxiety in her stomach?

Andrew's arrival at the buffet table was the sole reason Jada didn't throw up then and there. He gave her an acknowledging nod, then went back to examining his food options. Jada found herself hovering next to him. Still thinking about how Tristan had discarded both Angela and Erica, Jada sensed that Andrew—as the eyes and ears of the production—might have intel on something that kept bothering her.

"Hey, Andrew . . . just wondering, do you know where Erica ended up?" Jada asked.

"Turns out another film by Sunset Pictures was in desperate need of a PA. They offered Erica a lot of money to switch over to that production." Andrew kept his tone equally light, but they both knew the truth. Mr. Collins had bought Erica off with another job and a shady payout from his company.

Jada thanked him but abandoned the catering table, half-eaten sandwich still in hand. She needed air in the midst of this whole, twisted situation. Just as she made it outside the lot's main doors, someone placed their hand on her shoulder. With a cheerful smile on his face, Tristan had followed her outside.

"Hey, hon, you okay over here? You look like that hoagie challenged you to a fight."

"I'm fine." Jada sounded colder than she intended but couldn't help it. She shrugged out of his hold by throwing the sandwich in a nearby trash can. They might be on the film lot, and she should be going along with the charade, but now, suddenly everything felt wrong. As Tristan continued to speak to her, all she heard was Angela's mocking and Mr. Collins's veiled threats. She didn't see his handsome face smiling at her. All she saw was the memory of Tristan screwing Erica.

"I know Angela's dad showing up was like Freddy Krueger scary, but he went easy on us. I think things will be okay from here on out."

When Jada didn't respond to Tristan's summation, he pried further. "You sure you're okay? With everyone around, I've barely gotten to talk to you. That doesn't bode well for our image as a happy couple," he said, reaching for her hand.

Jada looked down as he intertwined their fingers. Sure, for

now, he was touching her, paying attention to only her. But when they left the set, after the demanding public was gone, who would he be seeking out then?

"Yes. God forbid we ruin the image," Jada said.

"What's wrong?" Tristan raised a quizzical eyebrow.

"Tell me, Tristan. How closely are you sticking to our deal?"

"What do you mean?"

"I mean, how many other women are you hooking up with?"

"As far as I know, you and I aren't 'hooking up.' We've barely held hands, let alone tried to hit all the bases."

Despite her growing frustration, Jada kept her voice low, in case of nearby eavesdroppers. Crossing her arms, she shook her head as Tristan remained oblivious.

"That doesn't answer my question," she said. "Do you plan on having sex with other women during our little arrangement?"

When Tristan's dumbfounded look didn't transform into an outpouring of reassurances, Jada's mouth dropped in astonishment. "Did you not even *think* about it?"

"Well, we never did get around to establishing those ground rules. And I mean, does it really matter—"

"Of course it matters, Daniel! Especially since it makes me look like an idiot for you to cheat on me."

How could this man not get how embarrassing it was for him to hook up with other women? Again! But no, he just kept looking at her with that same stupid—

"You mean Tristan?"

"What?"

"You just called me Daniel."

*Shit!* They hadn't discussed the *D* word since that night at the lounge, and a Freudian slip was not how Jada wanted to bring it back up. And yet, she'd let Angela's words suck her right into a time warp in which she apparently couldn't tell the difference between her ex-boyfriend and her faux-boyfriend. Flushing full force now, Jada cut Tristan off so he couldn't question her further.

"Whatever! You get my point. Until you decide whether or not you can keep it in your pants, don't talk to me." Before Jada could storm back inside, Tristan caught her in a hug from behind. Holding on to her hips, he spoke into her ear.

"Little hard to do that, babe, since we work together and are supposed to be in love."

Subtly, Jada gave him an elbow nudge to the gut, forcing him to let go of her.

"Well, love, absence makes the heart grow fonder."

Tristan played it smart and didn't go after her. He followed her wishes, steering clear of her outside of shooting. His obedience made Jada feel vindicated but also guilty. Deep down, she knew she had no claim on Tristan's sex life. She also knew her staunch rejection went against their agreement, but she couldn't help it. The idea that Tristan was messing around while she went along with their ruse irritated her to no end. It made her puzzle over all their previous interactions, like their great day at the beach. Had Angela had those moments, too, where Tristan played the perfect leading man? Before things had gone to shit with them, had he been just as swoon worthy and whimsical? Lulled Angela into the same deception that he could be that special someone.

Either way, after the argument, the afternoon passed without incident except for Angela's periodic attempts to stall production. But overall, the day drew to a close without too much damage befalling them. When they finished for the day, Jada dragged Mikayla off the lot in a rush.

"What's gotten into you?" Mikayla asked as Jada sped home, pushing her small, silver Infiniti to the max.

"Nothing. I'm just ready for this film to be over. Angela was testing my patience today," Jada replied, evading her cousin's questions.

Mikayla agreed, and the two launched into a debate about what exactly had caused the girl to become so selfish, especially after they'd met her dad, and, particularly, how her aristocratic upbringing must have gone awry. The infamous scene from *Gone with the Wind* in which Scarlett and Rhett's daughter suffered a traumatizing horseback riding accident, came to mind. Perhaps Angela came from a similar racist, toxic household that owned disobedient ponies? Something had to have influenced her turning out so vile. That speculation took them the rest of the way home and through their front door. Since it was Mikayla's turn to make dinner, Jada collapsed on the well-worn burgundy couch the second they entered the apartment. Resting against the soft cushions, she relished being done with both Tristan and Angela. At least for the night. She could curl up with a good book or watch *RuPaul's Drag Race* and forget all about her personal and professional problems.

Her ringing phone temporarily interfered with her plans. Glancing down at the screen, she saw Tristan was the caller.

*Hell no*, Jada thought, pressing the Reject button with more force than necessary. As the call went to voice mail, Jada closed her eyes, struggling to de-stress. Yet her shoulders clenched once more when she heard an abrasive knock on the door. Knowing Mikayla was preoccupied with making her trademark spaghetti, Jada sluggishly got up.

"I got it, Kay!" she shouted, and made her way to the door.

Most likely, it would be Alia. Being the benevolent creature she was, she'd understand Jada's mood and join her on the couch to watch good ol' Ru sass his protégés. Or maybe they'd have a spaghetti bitchfest.

But when Jada opened the door, expecting a friend, her biggest foe greeted her: a brooding Tristan, determined to be let in.

# 15

Tristan wasn't quite sure why he was subjecting himself to more of Jada's resentful attitude. Yet here he was, on her doorstep, about to face battle number seventeen—or whatever number of fights they were at now. He just knew he hadn't liked the way they'd left things. Not after they'd been making such positive strides at the beach. If they were going to go through with their plan, he refused to take any more steps backward.

So he took a step forward.

"Listen, Jada," he started as he pushed his way inside. Jada blocked his efforts, throwing up an arm to stop him.

"What do you think you're doing?"

"Coming in so we can talk things over. The way you behaved on set, shutting me out and storming away. That's not going to help our cause."

"Neither is you screwing every woman you come across," Jada shot back.

"Where are you getting this idea that I'm out seducing every girl I meet?"

"Tristan, get real, that's your MO."

Tristan rubbed the bridge of his nose, feeling a prickling headache coming on. Jada seemed determined to believe in some warped, malicious version of him that she had in her mind—the playboy who'd hooked up with both Erica and Angela. This version of Tristan also, apparently, could be confused with Daniel Kane. For him, Jada's demands for fidelity were outweighed by her owing him a real explanation.

"May I remind you that your MO was agreeing to this arrangement—of your own free will?"

Jada shut down at this part, wrapping her arms around herself. "*Fine*. I did agree to the whole fake dating thing, but that doesn't make your ambivalence toward real-life cheating okay."

"I won't," he finally admitted. "I talked it over with Doug. I think we can all agree that me being spotted hooking up with someone else would expose our relationship as a fake."

Deep down, Tristan had known that all along, but the way Jada had laid into him about it—without even hearing his side or thoughts—had caught him off guard. He'd gotten flashbacks to every other jealous woman he'd ever dated and so he'd gone on the defensive instead. Doug sure as hell had cleared that up when they'd "talked it over." He'd berated Tristan about how big a risk sleeping with someone else would be. Doug's shrill words still rang in his head: *What part of fake—yet committed—relationship didn't you understand?* Pushing Doug's admonishments to the back of his mind, he noticed Jada's relieved expression.

"Thank you," she said.

Finally relenting, she moved aside, letting him enter her home. He made sure he was fully inside, with her closing the door behind him, before he launched into his next bit.

"But that doesn't excuse what you did," he challenged her.

"What I did?" She gaped at him.

"Yes. You—" Tristan's reproach died on his lips as he looked behind Jada and spotted a cutout of Tim Curry in a corset. "What in the world . . ."

Following his gaze, Jada raised a warning finger. "Watch it, buddy. *The Rocky Horror Picture Show* is sacred in this house."

Deciding he would worry about Jada's questionable decorating later, Tristan leaped back to their previous argument. "Okay, whatever. But taking your angry insecurities out on me in *public* is what will really screw this whole thing up. You need to learn to keep your temper in check."

"This, coming from the man who exploded on me when his indiscretions came to light."

"I apologized for that. Honestly, the way you hold a grudge is—"

"*Ahem.*" Mikayla cleared her throat as she appeared in the entryway. "Hello, Tristan. I know you two lovebirds tend to have very passionate interactions, but unless you want our neighbors knowing all your personal business, I suggest you two keep it down."

"Sorry," Tristan muttered. Between Jada's attitude and Mikayla's admonishments, he felt properly chastised. But why? Why was he the one always apologizing? Especially when Jada was half the reason for his outbursts. Tristan glanced at Tim Curry's cardboard (yet perceptive) eyes as if the actor could hear his plea and back him up somehow.

"Fine. Let's talk about this in the living room." Jada motioned him to their couch but halted as Mikayla followed them.

"Alone," she clarified for her cousin.

Mikayla let out a sigh then headed back to the kitchen, mumbling about missing the show. Regardless of her grumblings, she'd surely be listening in from afar. When he and Jada were seated on the couch, at last, Tristan swore he would remain cool and collected. He would not raise his voice or get angry. He would stay rational, no matter how much this woman drove him insane.

"Look, I know neither one of us wants to be in this situation, but we are. We struck a deal, we said we'd compromise, so can we *do* that?" he said as calmly as he could. Jada wrinkled her nose, then sighed in resignation.

"You're right. I know you're right, it's just . . . the whole thing is still weird to me. Pretending we like each other—when we can't even stand each other—and acting like we're a couple when I don't even really know you."

"Get to know me," Tristan said simply.

"Get to know you how?" she asked.

"We could go old school and play Truth or Dare." At her skeptical expression, Tristan went on. "Or Never Have I Ever?"

Jada wrinkled her nose in distaste. "I think we're playing enough games as it is, don't you?"

"Fine. Then tonight, I will let you ask me three questions. You get three chances to quiz me on whatever you feel you need to know."

The second the words were out of his mouth, Tristan remembered their dinner date. Knowing Jada, she'd jump on the mom front again. "Although I get veto power!"

"That defeats the purpose!" Jada pouted.

"I get to veto one if I don't like where it's going. And I get to ask you three questions in return. You also get one veto."

"Okay, that's fair."

"And I will need tequila for this." Tristan made his last demand.

Shaking her head, Jada got off the couch and went into the kitchen. Tristan heard the rattling of cups along with a few sharp remarks to Mikayla before Jada returned. He took his shot glass with a benevolent smile and a quick thanks.

"Okay . . . what was it like acting when you were a kid? I loved watching *Garcia Central* when I was growing up," Jada said.

Having seen his mom's past roles as an actress, it felt like a natural progression to want to try his own hand at acting. His father had been a head writer for another show on the same network, which had helped Tristan score an audition. However, his mom insisted that he got the job on his own merits, not just because of his dad's connections.

While Tristan had believed her, he still wanted to stand apart from his parents' successful careers. Thankfully, they agreed when Tristan asked to be credited as Tristan Maxwell. Using his first and middle name for his acting persona over his family's last name, Moreno-Diaz, really helped him feel more independent. After his mom left, he was even more grateful for that decision. Having her name plastered next to his on his early acting credits would have been painful to look at now. However, Tristan planned to skip over all that with Jada.

"It was fun. You know, you're experiencing it all for the first time. And then when the show took off and became this big thing it was really rewarding. Although that puts a lot of pressure on you later."

While being good looking was an exalted virtue in this career path, it hadn't been easy going from cute thirteen-year-old to sudden heartthrob as Tristan hit his later teen years on the show. The second he started dating a few girls here and there, his personal life was always in the news.

"Yes, I remember my former *Seventeen* magazines having way too many pictures of you in them." Jada laughed.

"Oh, so you've been an admirer from *wayyy* back when, huh, Berklee?" Tristan asked slyly.

"Hardly!" In spite of her denial, Jada looked away, draining the rest of the tequila in her shot glass. The flush on her cheeks could either be from embarrassment or rushing through the strong drink.

"I thought you were supposed to be telling me the truth!" He poked her in the side.

"I am." Jada squirmed away, shamefaced.

"Stop lying, woman, or I'll be forced to resort to more devious means."

Realization dawning, she warned him. "Tristan, don't you dare—"

Too late. Tristan pounced and started tickling her.

Jada leaned away, her giggling leaving her breathless. Her hand accidentally hit the remote, turning on the TV at full blast. The loud noise jolted them out of the moment, and Jada scrambled to turn down the volume. She ended up switching the channel to the Spanish network, where the popular telenovela *Amor Prohibido* was playing. Tristan's heart dropped. A woman with lush dark hair and sparkling blue eyes was on-screen. Her appearance was too similar to his own for Jada to miss it.

"That's your mother, right? I heard she was on a new show, but—"

Tristan quickly released Jada and snatched the remote out of her hand to change the channel.

"What the hell, Tristan?!"

"That show's stupid. It's a dumb telenovela." Now he was the one sweating under Jada's scrutiny.

"Oh really? Is that the problem? Because this is the second time you've reacted like that to me bringing her up. What kind of Freudian problems did you guys have?"

"Freud is a hack and everyone knows it," Tristan deflected. But he could tell that, despite his earlier promise to keep his cool, the night was taking a much more volatile turn.

"Tristan, you leaped out of your skin just *looking* at her on TV." Jada pushed him.

"Because she's not that." He motioned to the TV. "She's not some beautiful, perfect star like everyone thinks. She's . . . it's more complicated than that."

"How?" Jada placed an encouraging hand on his knee. Tristan resisted the urge to push her away. If he and Jada were going to be stuck as a couple indefinitely, he might as well confess what really happened and get it over with. Maybe then she'd stop badgering him about it. Taking a deep breath, he finally laid the truth on the table.

"She left. When I was fourteen, she left. Just up and vanished on me and my dad. No explanation, no good-byes. I came home from set and she was gone. My dad never got over it . . . he was never the same."

*Neither was I*, he added silently.

"And you've never spoken to her since?" Jada asked.

"She sends me birthday and holiday cards. That's it." Tristan refused to mention the recent phone call or meet Jada's gaze. He didn't want her to see the pain in his eyes—or see the pity in hers. Regardless, she touched his chin, turning him to face her.

"I'm sorry," she said.

"It is what it is."

"It's wrong is what it is. And I'm sorry you had to go through that. No kid deserves to lose their mom." Jada held his hand, her touch soothing him.

"I've been hurt, too, you know. Not like that, but by someone I loved," she continued. "I get how someone you cared about so deeply could hurt you and leave you wrecked."

"Who?" he asked.

"My ex. The man I ran away from at the lounge."

"Daniel Kane of *Fallen Creatures* fame is your ex?" Tristan perked up at this revelation. Honestly, he'd been planning to use one of his questions to address the Daniel weirdness, but now all the ugly, crooked puzzle pieces fell into place. Her freak-out at the club, how weird Jada got about the show, and . . .

"Hmm. I guess that explains your Freudian moment this afternoon."

"Sorry, I know that was weird." Jada winced. "It's just a lot of things have been resurfacing and, anyway, I know it doesn't sound as severe as losing a family member." Jada went on. "But he almost ruined my career. I almost lost everything because of him."

Okay, with that in mind, Tristan didn't particularly *enjoy* being compared to someone like that. Hearing her explanation just brought up more questions about what Daniel had done and how she could still put up with Avery—but since she hadn't pushed him any further, he chose to return the favor. He raised his glass.

"Forget the game. Let's toast to us. To not letting someone else's betrayal define or defeat us."

"I'll drink to that." Jada grinned and clinked her glass with his.

As they leaned back on the couch, winded from the slew of

revelations, Jada pointed out that they still hadn't laid out any ground rules. Tristan groaned, sinking farther into the cushions. They'd already debated with each other tonight like attorneys on a high-profile televised crime case. He didn't have the energy to keep deliberating their "it's complicated" relationship status. Hoping to fool her, Tristan closed his eyes and promptly began snoring.

"Not buying it, Tristan!" Jada pinched his nose, effectively cutting off his oxygen.

"Jeez, woman!" Tristan sat back up impatiently. "No cheating, no yelling at each other in public. What more do you want?"

In the brief moments when he'd pretended to get some shut-eye, Jada had whipped out a notebook and pen. After scribbling down his additions, she tapped the page thoughtfully.

"Give me a moment . . ."

Tristan leaned back again, his arm draped around the back of the couch. Jada reclined as well, resting against him as she eyed their list. But as she studiously considered their newfound rules, Tristan's attention began to slip for real. His eyes shut once more as he rested his head on her shoulder.

Distantly, he heard her call his name, but he was already fading fast, falling asleep with her warmth next to him.

# 16

Enveloped in cozy warmth, Jada snuggled up to what she *believed* was her satin pillow. When she cracked her eyes open, her pillow turned out to be Tristan's chest. She jerked out of his embrace. The movement had the opposite effect of what she wanted. It woke Tristan up. Slightly disoriented, he glanced around the room blearily.

"What is it? What happened?"

"What happened is we fell asleep." Jada's eyes darted from her disheveled appearance to the empty glasses on the table.

Back in her college days, a scene like this would have suggested a hookup but the notebook next to the tequila bottle made the rest clear. After Tristan had conked out on her for real (so typical), Jada had stayed awake, pondering their new dating rules. First, she'd done an extensive map out of her boundaries, like PDA must be consensual and agreed upon prior to public appearances, also PDA did not include things like butt grabbing, and a heads-up the next time they had to trick a close friend or family member. Then she wondered if her list was going too overboard, considering she'd probably have to make concessions for it to look real to hard-core fans. She also kept replaying Tristan's emphasis on compromising, which had her crossing out several lines. Exhausted from rewriting the list several times, Jada had ended up succumbing to the late-night drowsiness too. One glance at Mikayla's Cheshire Cat wall clock made Jada spring into action.

"Oh my God. We're going to be late for work!" She urged Tristan up off the couch.

"You're good to drive back to your place, right?" she asked.

"Are you kidding me? If you think we're going to be late now, imagine if I went home to shower and get ready, *then* tried to make it to set? Did you forget we're shooting in Griffith Park? It'd be much easier if we both grabbed a quick shower here and then headed over on my bike."

Jada balked at the idea. His so-called bike was a massive Harley that Tristan had driven to work several times. At the prospect of speeding down busy streets on the back of a giant motorcycle, Jada held up her hand in protest. "You want me to ride shotgun on that deathmobile? No thanks."

"Technically, it's not called shotgun, but yes. You'll be totally safe and it's the fastest way. Now stop arguing with me so we can get out of here."

"Fine, you can take a shower in Mikayla's room, and I'll use mine."

Hustling down the hall, Jada called out for her cousin. "Kayla, are you awake?"

"In here," her cousin responded from the kitchen.

"Great," Jada turned back to Tristan. "Go to the room on the right."

She shooed Tristan down the hall, then rushed into the kitchen. Mikayla shot her a raised eyebrow.

"Well, well, well. I—"

"Please don't start, Mikayla. We overslept—and I can't believe you didn't wake us up, by the way. And now we're in a rush. I offered up your bathroom for Tristan to shower. I'm going to take a quick one myself. Can you head to the set now and let them know we might be running a little behind?"

"Fine, fine. Rush a girl out of her own home." Mikayla finished up her breakfast, headed for the door, then paused. "And I didn't wake you up because you were both superadorable and comfy on that couch."

After ushering Mikayla out, Jada rushed into her own room and stripped off her clothes in a rush. She was down to her bra and panties when she shoved open her bathroom door and walked in on a stark-naked Tristan. His eyes widened in surprise but he quickly recovered, lazily propping his elbow up against the towel rack with a cocky smirk.

"We've got to stop meeting like this."

Despite having seen it all before, Jada moved to cover her eyes—then remembered that she was nearly naked and went to cover herself instead.

"Tristan, I said the room on the left!"

"Oh. I've never been good with directions." His eyes unashamedly roved over her body, causing Jada to feel a different kind of heat rising through her.

"It's okay. I'll use the other bathroom." Jada turned to leave but Tristan's silky voice stopped her.

left and the bathroom will be through an adjoining door on the right."

"You don't have to rush off. It would be a much better idea for us to shower together. You know, to conserve water. And that way the water pressure won't get thrown off."

His tempting offer was like a siren's song, forcing Jada to turn back around—just in time to see Tristan's body had more in mind than eco-friendly bathing. If Jada stayed here any longer, she'd witness the full extent of Tristan's attraction to her. This idea didn't make her run away like it should. Instead, Jada's own lust came to the surface. Before the telltale sign of her arousal could drench her panties, Jada mastered her senses through sheer willpower.

"A *cold* shower is exactly what you need," she squeaked.

Not allowing him to make another tantalizing proposition, Jada slammed the door.

Good God! She'd almost given in to Tristan . . . in her own bathroom, while she was late for work! She might detest Tristan's torrid romantic past, but there was no denying how sexy he was. How tempting he was. The kind of hold he had over a woman's body should be illegal.

Fanning herself, Jada snatched an outfit out of her closet and then ran into Mikayla's room. Locking her cousin's bathroom door behind her, she had to face facts: she was the one who needed a cold shower. Then again, the idea of finishing what Tristan had proposed was extremely tempting. Especially as she knew he was just a few rooms over, lathering his body the same way she was washing hers. Was he thinking about her too? Maybe even touching himself the way she wanted to? Against her better judgment, Jada let the fantasy sink in, just a little bit, imagining Tristan's bare skin against hers. Her hands wandering down her curves. The thrilling sensations left her wondering how he'd caress her in the sweet downpour until the passion overtook them both.

*Get a grip, Jada!* She chided herself as she tried to refocus on the necessities. Scrub, rinse, repeat. She continued the process until she felt sane and composed instead of like a cat in heat. By the time she'd gathered herself and stepped out of Mikayla's room, Tristan was freshly showered, dressed, and nibbling on fruit in her kitchen. She didn't comment on the overly comfortable action as she was too busy trying not to picture his hands exploring her body.

*That's what you get for getting carried away.* Damn. It was like a tiny disapproving nun had somehow gotten lodged in her subconscious!

"Are you ready to go?" she mumbled, refusing to make eye contact.

"Are you? Have you ever ridden on a motorcycle before?" he asked.

"You have an extra helmet, right?" Jada asked, feeling light headed.

"Yes, and I promise you'll be safe with me." His eyes were bright and kind.

God, how she wanted to believe him. This thought echoed through her mind as they zipped in and out of traffic in their mad race to get to Griffith Park on time. While she clutched him for dear life, Jada wanted to believe that he wouldn't break her heart to bits. Or at the very least, that they could hook up and walk away relatively unscathed. But that didn't seem to be the fate for most women after dealing with Tristan. Especially if Angela's expression was anything to go by.

As the leading lady spotted Jada and Tristan walking on set

together, a grimace of pain flashed across her face but was swiftly replaced with disdain. When Jada and Tristan had first reached the blocked off part of the street, they'd taken off their helmets so security would let them through. But even the worst case of helmet hair hadn't made Tristan's hair dry any faster. That, coupled with them arriving together, added up to one conclusion in the eyes of the prying crew, not to mention the bystanders gathered behind the barricades who were snapping pictures of them.

Griffith Park was enormous and constantly busy, so they'd only been able to secure a small part of it for their outdoor scenes. While some people were taking in the other aspects of the park's vast hiking trails and pony rides, others had gathered to get a peek at their shoot. Along with the outside scenes scheduled for today, they'd also been lucky enough to score some time in the Griffith Observatory tomorrow. There, Lana would be struck with the inspiration that would help solve the case of the time traveling locket. But for now, they'd be focused on Diego and Claire meeting in the park, with Lana coming in later.

Keeping her mind on her work, Jada avoided the amused looks and smirks from the crew over their arrival and made a beeline for the dressing-room trailer. Since they were filming on location today, all the usual equipment, props, and clothes had to be lugged around this way. She felt much more at ease after she slipped inside the white caravan. For once, Mikayla and Cass had the decency not to cross question Jada.

While Cass was in the middle of transforming her face into a work of art, Jada's phone went off. Her stomach sank when she saw the caller ID: Avery Kane.

"Excuse me," she said to the makeup artist, then stepped outside to take the call.

"Hi, Avery. What's going on?"

"Logan Wentworth wants *you* to audition for the lead role in his new movie *Love and War*. It's an upcoming action flick. They've already got Donnie Ward attached as the director."

Jada resisted the urge to squeal, but before she could reply at all, Avery cut her off.

"My assistant will send the script over tonight along with the information for the audition. Please don't fuck this up."

And then she hung up. Not that Jada wanted to hold a conversation with her, but a few pleasantries would have been nice. Then again, at least Avery had said please before telling her not to fuck up. Either way, Jada's heart fluttered with joy at the prospect of this job turning into a reality. Surprisingly enough, the first person she wanted to tell was Tristan. She got the perfect chance when he also paid a visit to the on-wheels version of the makeup department.

"Guess what?" She beamed at him, the incident from this morning momentarily forgotten.

"You've realized you're madly in love with me?" He presumed.

"No." Jada swatted him. "I got a call about Logan's movie. Avery's going to send over the script for the audition."

"That's great. We should rehearse together."

"What do you mean?"

"Doug called me. Logan wants me to audition too. If things go well, we'll probably end up reading together anyway, so . . . your place? Tonight?"

Jada's brain blanked. She didn't have a real reason to tell him no, but did she want him back in her apartment? At the scene of the crime. The very naked, nearly X-rated crime.

"Um . . . sure, I guess," she faltered.

"All right. Sounds good. I'll meet you after work." He said it easily, like it was nothing for him to show up at her place again. Meanwhile, Jada's heart was doing somersaults.

Tristan, in her home again. With his lips that told her all the things she wanted to hear. With his perceptive looks showing he knew exactly what her body wanted. . . Dear baby Jesus, she was in trouble! And she told Mikayla as much on their drive home.

"He's coming over again?" Mikayla's face lit up with glee. "That's not bad. That's great!"

"What the hell is going on with you? You were on the whole boo Tristan train right with me after what he did. You were the one who wanted to release the video. And now, all of a sudden, you're all for me hooking up with him."

"I was always for you hooking up with him. That dimmed a bit after his behavior, but now . . . well, I see how happy you are around him."

"Happy? You mean more like a rabid dog."

"Okay, sure. Just know I'll be staying over at Alia's so you and Tristan can 'work.'"

"What? You can't leave me alone with him." Jada panicked. She hadn't even told Mikayla about what had happened this morning yet. Although, at this point, the revelation would be more like ammo than a valid reason for Mikayla to play chaperone.

"Look, you agreed to this arrangement. So either you manage to keep your hormones in check or you give into them." This worthless advice was Mikayla's last say on the matter.

True to her word, around seven Mikayla fled the apartment to hang out with Alia. Jada had begged, bargained, and practically chained Mikayla's feet to the floor, but it was no use. Her cousin was gone. This time, though, she hadn't advised Jada on what to wear. Jada vacillated on the decision way too long, eventually settling for a black camisole, light cardigan, and jeans. But she had bigger problems than just her wardrobe. She'd also gone over the dating rules notebook when she got home.

**RULES:**

*Stick to cover story at all costs.*

*No cheating.*

*No public fights.*

*Acceptable PDA: hand-holding, hugging, kissing on the cheek and/or lips, dependent on situation.*

*Social media posts allowed when agreed upon.*

The conditions looked acceptable to her, but finding the right opening to give them to Tristan—and most likely end up bargaining about them again—would be harder. All too soon, a fateful knock on the door interrupted her thoughts. Leaving the closed notebook on the living-room table, she went to let Tristan in. Standing at the apartment's threshold, he held up a bag of pretzels and sodas.

"Hi," she said breathlessly. Why she was breathless was anyone's guess. All he'd done was walk into the entryway with a load of carbs.

"Hey, I brought us some provisions. I figured we should stock up on some snacks for the rehearsal," he said.

His casual act killed her. He was behaving as if nothing had happened. As if they hadn't been moments away from getting to know each other intimately. *Very* intimately. Now, he was all friendly conversation. Where were the suggestive tone and smoldering look from this morning?

"Thanks," she said, setting the food on the table. "I've got the part of the script they sent over."

"I brought my copy as well." Tristan compared his copy with hers, confirming that they'd been handed the same scene. In it, her character was a rogue assassin while Tristan was a bodyguard who had been selected to protect her when her kill or be killed lifestyle caught up with her. As he skimmed the script in quiet contemplation, Jada discreetly scrutinized him. She'd placed the dating rules notebook right next to the printed screenplay, hoping to arouse his curiosity, but Tristan had completely skipped over it. Either he was avoiding the topic and their encounter this morning or he was taking this opportunity much more seriously than she'd first thought. She was surer of his dedication when Tristan abruptly launched into director mode.

"Since this scene is pretty intense between the two leads and takes place right in the middle of a big action sequence, do you mind if we really go for it?"

"Go for it?"

"As in if I sprint across your living room and potentially damage some sofa cushions, will you rip me a new one?" Tristan's wild grin came back.

"The cushions, no. My mama's china, yes. But I guess a fair bit of running around will help bring this to life," Jada said, thrilled about Tristan's enthusiastic insights.

"Great! Then let's get started." Tristan tossed aside the script.

"Wait, you're already off book?" Piercing insecurity hit her that Tristan had already finished memorizing his lines while she was still glancing down at hers.

"Oh yeah, my memory is pretty sharp. Are you ready?"

Jada nodded with a certainty she didn't feel before starting off with her first line.

"I don't need your protection! I've been taking down drug lords and dirty politicians for years. If anyone is in over their head, it's you."

Tristan cocked his head arrogantly. "Oh really? Then why are there at least three impending threats coming right at us?"

"What threats?" Jada asked.

At this point in the script, Tristan was supposed to protect her from a bomb aimed at them. Tristan modified the action by grabbing Jada and diving behind the couch. When they got back up, Tristan nodded in approval.

"That was good but maybe we can up the energy."

"More energy than couch diving?" She laughed, feeling a potential bruise blossoming on her butt.

But over the course of the next several run-throughs, Jada learned that yes, there were even higher-energy risks they could take. They dashed from the foyer to the hallway closet. A misguided test run of hiding behind the tub's shower curtain also came into play. The whole rehearsal was turning into a blast as they chased each other through the apartment, tossing lines back and forth.

Making a split-second decision, Jada navigated toward the kitchen. Tristan followed and the two of them were soon circling each other around the kitchen island. Jada said her first line and Tristan followed with his. Then in a swift motion, Tristan sailed over the kitchen island and wrapped Jada in his arms. He backed her up against the kitchen cabinets, boxing her in.

"It looks like you'll be needing me after all." He said his final line.

While they regained their breath from their escapade, they stayed locked in each other's embrace for a second too long. Long enough for the tension, the heat, to rise. That electricity was back, the air charged with the pent-up sexual frustration they'd been fighting. But the kinetic pull proved too strong as Jada closed the distance between them.

The second their mouths touched, the world caught fire. Everything that had been building since their first collision led them to this intoxicating moment. To his tongue dancing with hers and his warm, strong hands clutching her waist. It was better than any slow dance at a lounge, a day at the beach, or sexual innuendos in a shower. Because this was real. It was now. And extremely fucking urgent, Jada decided as Tristan lifted her onto the countertop and pulled her legs around his waist.

With Tristan pressed so tightly against her, Jada could feel his need. His hot desire searched out her own as he ground his hips. Thinking of them being closer, of him being inside her, caused her to let out a small, desperate sound. A moan she didn't realize she'd been holding back. But with its release, a dam broke inside her.

Her exploration of him grew bolder, more fervent, as she slipped her hands under his shirt to caress his firm abs. He responded in kind, throwing Jada's cardigan and camisole aside. With his luscious lips teasingly sucking on her neck, Jada was ready to give in to it all. Tristan could take her right here, right now. Hard, fast, deep, however he wanted. And let the consequences be damned because she wanted it. All of it.

Succumbing to her sultry fever, Jada was on the verge of giving her consent when Tristan cried out in pain.

"What's wrong?" She jerked back at the loud exclamation.

She'd been nibbling on his ear, but she didn't think that was enough to alarm him. Tristan cursed, clutching his right hand. He gestured at the stove. One of the burners had accidentally been switched on in the midst of their rendezvous.

"Oh shit!" Jada turned off the stove, then attended to Tristan. "How bad is it? I've got a first aid kit full of bandages somewhere."

Flustered, Jada searched for the case, but Tristan shrugged his injury off.

"I don't think it's serious enough for that, but it's okay. I hear this is a typical issue with kitchen make-out sessions. When the cooking gets hot, it can turn into a serious fire hazard," he teased.

Jada couldn't return his lighthearted demeanor. His burn's opportune timing proved she was right about them *not* hooking up. It was good they'd been interrupted before one of them did get romantically scorched.

"Well . . . if you're feeling better, I think you should go," she said, steadily staring at the floor. "We've rehearsed enough for now, and—"

"Jada, if you're freaking out on me—"

"I'm not freaking out. I—I need to think. I need to process what just happened." Jada continued to evade his gaze by collecting her discarded clothes. Nevertheless, she heard Tristan let out an exasperated sigh.

"What 'happened' is that we're attracted to each other. We want each other. Why does that terrify you?"

*Because this is business, not pleasure. Because even though you're not Daniel, this feels like I'm making the same mistakes all over again.* Instead of admitting this out loud, Jada turned her back to him, hiding her face so he couldn't see how much it truly did terrify her.

"Good night, Tristan," she replied, her tone final.

"Fine. You go ahead and think. Go and process. But at the end of all your overanalyzing, the only thing you'll discover is the truth you're avoiding right now," Tristan said.

With that one last verbal slap in the face, he left. She didn't turn back around until the front door closed and his heavy footfalls faded.

Once he was gone, Jada could finally breathe again, but her feelings were all over the place. It would have been nice to talk to Mikayla about all of this but she hadn't come home, probably having fallen asleep at Alia's. Heading back to the living room, Jada looked down at the notebook sullenly. Even with these stupid rules, they didn't help her *define* what was between her and Tristan. A ridiculous sheet of paper could not validate her worries about him being a Daniel 2.0 or clarify if they should stay in this weird semifriendship limbo. Unfortunately, there was a point it *did* help her come to grips with. Jada picked up her pen and added the number one rule they absolutely could not break.

*NO SEX.*

The following morning, Mikayla probed for the "dirty deets" over breakfast. In her sleep-deprived state, Jada cringed at the awful slang and insisted that she and Tristan had only rehearsed. She'd need a lot more coffee before she'd admit the weakness she had for her irresistible co-star. Because Tristan had been right. The truth was staring straight at her. They had a magnetic attraction that had been unleashed by chaos. The key word being *chaos*. No matter how much they were drawn to each other, things with

Tristan would always be messy and complicated. No amount of chemistry would be worth the inevitable heartbreak. Besides, she'd sworn she would start putting herself and her career first, and she meant it.

Her decision to stay professional grew harder to stick to when she arrived back at the park for their second day filming there. The moment she stepped into the square outside the Griffith Observatory and locked eyes with Tristan, she felt it: The overwhelming temptation. The sensual longing. The persistent, dreadful reality that she was falling for the wrong guy. Regardless, she worked up enough courage to greet him anyway.

"Hi." She loathed the way her voice came out small and unsure. Tristan nodded in return and gave her a guarded smile, warily awaiting her reaction to last night. However, Jada refused to say the actual phrase *So about last night*—and chose a more abrupt route.

"I know we're in this situation together, and I'm totally willing to keep my end of the bargain, but I think we should slow things down."

"Slow things down?" he repeated skeptically.

"Yeah, you know, maybe limit the touching and all of that stuff. I mean, we've already made it clear with the crew that we're together. People on set get it. And we've gone out a few times already."

"Twice," he corrected her.

"Yes, but I think if we took some time apart, we might be able to act this whole thing out—because it *is* acting after all—with cooler heads. I think this might help too."

Jada held out the dating rules page that she'd ripped out of the notebook. As Tristan read through it, his expression turned stormy. With his imminent dark mood, Jada prepared herself for him to fight back over what she'd written.

"Okay, Jada," Tristan said. She was so astonished by his easy surrender, she simply stood there gaping.

"You mean it?"

"Sure. If you want to go the rest of this shoot with less PDA, fine. Less hanging out together? Okay. But if the buzz we're getting dies down, our goals are going to get a lot harder. And this"—Tristan waved the paper at her—"will become as irrelevant as us once our adoring public gets bored."

"We can make it work. We've already got that big audition with Logan."

"And why do you think that is? You think it's a coincidence we were both asked to audition? They want the hottest It Couple in town starring in their summer blockbuster."

Jada knew by the sickening drop in her stomach that he was right. If she and Tristan played it cool for too long, people like Logan would lose interest. And yet . . .

"Please. I need a little more time," she said.

Ren called Tristan's name before he could respond. The crew had finished setting up, so the actors could start rehearsal for the scene.

"I'm coming!" Tristan yelled, then he gave Jada a halfhearted shrug. "Take your time then, Jada. I'll try not to watch the clock while you do."

As he walked away, Jada resisted the urge to call him back. She refused to change her mind because there was too much at stake. Her heart was now wrapped up in this fake game.

A game she feared she would lose.

# 17

Standing on the bustling Santa Monica Pier, Tristan breathed in the salty air. The glistening sun shone overhead while the captivating smell of carnival food wafted his way. Normally, spending time on the pier would be perfect for a date or relaxing on the weekend, but today's outing was all about Bright Futures.

They'd officially gotten the approval to host the festival for two weeks. Tristan had felt compelled to come along on LeeAnn's walkthrough of the space, despite this being one of his few days off from work. With the location secured, he and several other volunteers scouted the area for the event's future setup. Next to him, LeeAnn beamed at the surrounding view.

"You're right, Tristan. This place is perfect," she enthused, hugging her clipboard to her chest.

"Yep, there's plenty of space for the volunteers to man the food and game booths. The Ferris wheel is going to be a big attraction too." Tristan's attention shifted to the large contraption, the Pacific Wheel, in all its glory. The famous fixture was practically a national treasure and a staple among tourists, a.k.a. guaranteed festival traffic.

As LeeAnn took notes on where decorations and signage should go, Sam came up to them, popcorn in hand. Tristan watched with envy as the fourteen-year-old munched away.

"Some of that better be for the rest of us," Tristan warned him.

"No way. You're rolling in more popcorn money than me," the boy pointed out. "Go get your own."

Tristan didn't and used some ninja-like stealth to steal a kernel or two. Sam scowled at him halfheartedly before shoving another handful in his mouth. Apparently, it was now a competition to see who could eat the most.

"So, Samuel, how's school going?" Tristan asked in dutiful mentor fashion.

"Pretty good. Finally making some Bs after I started seeing this tutor." Tristan didn't miss the slight blush that appeared on Sam's face.

"What's his name? How Thor-like is he?" he prodded.

"That's none of your business!" Sam protested, but under Tristan's knowing gaze, he reluctantly confessed. "His name is Eric and nothing has happened yet, so, as I said, mind your business."

Resisting the urge to pry further, Tristan made a counter offer. "I'll let it go if you give me more popcorn."

Sam offered up the bag of junk food but not before getting in a dig of his own. "So, how's your little love affair going?"

"Jada's great." Tristan switched into actor mode, masking his fatigue with a placid air.

He didn't want the teen to see how much his situation with Jada was affecting him. After their talk, Jada had finished up her role in the film a few days later. To be perfectly honest, Tristan missed her like crazy. He and Angela still had another week or two left before they officially wrapped on the production phase.

While he and Jada hadn't been on a big elaborate date in some time, they had upped their social media game, posting on each other's pages. Tristan had also briefly run into Jada while going to his first audition for Logan's film. Running into him at the opportunity Tristan had helped her get must have gnawed at Jada's guilt, because she'd then invited him to stop by for "*Unbound* night." They watched the latest episode with Mikayla, and later posted pictures of themselves together, captioning it with talk of the show.

But other than those few interactions, Tristan had had to get most of his Jada updates from Mikayla at work, the latest being that Mikayla and Jada were headed to a Palm Springs resort this weekend to attend a conference their friend, Alia, was speaking at. Mikayla swore Tristan to secrecy about it, though, because she planned to call in sick with the flu. It would be a blow to her melodramatic boss, but the crew would survive without Mikayla for a day or two.

Realizing Jada had time to spend with everyone except him, Tristan had felt tempted to call or text but stopped himself. She'd said she needed time, and Tristan refused to come off as clingy or desperate. But as his phone buzzed with a news alert, Tristan discovered his attempts at being patient were making things worse. Another damn *Sip That Tea* blog was out.

## DYNAMIC DUO ON THE ROCKS?

The chai lattes are hot today, guys! An insider on the film *Love Locket* is backing up previous claims that

Tristan Maxwell and Jada Berklee's controversial, whirlwind romance was all for show. Since Miss Jada finished filming, she and Tristan have only been spotted together once. And while their social media gushing may seem like serious #couplegame, our source tells a different story. According to them, Tristan has been too busy with work to give Jada a second thought. Furthermore, the former drama with Angela Collins has died down, and there are rumors that the co-stars have gotten back together!

What's your take on this juicy new info?

Well, Tristan's take was he needed to kick somebody's ass over these bullshit lies! So, first step: find out the Tea Twins' home address and torture them to find out their so-called source. Second step: destroy this fake whistleblower's life. Before he could put his new plan into action, Sam nudged him.

"Dude, pay attention," he said, nodding at LeeAnn looking at him expectantly.

"Oh, I'm sorry. What did you say, Lee?" Tristan desperately tried to refocus but all he could think about was who had snitched. Along with the disturbing possibility that the person who leaked this information could have also sent out the video of his fight with Jada.

"I was saying, red or blue for the decorations?" LeeAnn repeated, oblivious to Tristan's dilemma. "It all depends on what kind of mood we're going for."

Already seeing red himself, Tristan opted for the safer choice. "Go with blue. Not as catchy but it's . . . more soothing."

LeeAnn nodded, prattling on about the festival planning. Meanwhile, Tristan's phone felt heavy inside his pocket. Once their organization prep was over, he needed to talk to Doug. ASAP.

—

The Palm Springs heat enveloped Jada, eager to make its sizzling presence known. Not that she wouldn't have been aware of it. The sandy dust on the streets and hills on the horizon transported her back to a Clint Eastwood, Old West flick. After Jada and the girls landed at the Palm Springs airport, their rental car ride to their hotel was well air-conditioned and short. A nice contrast to the city's "squaring off with a gunslinger on a horse," *Fistful of Dollars* style.

Entering the luxurious Blue Sierra Resort gave them some relief from the sweltering temperature. The hotel had capitalized on the land's down-home atmosphere with its decor. A rustic rug marked the entryway, and above the faux fireplace a mounted bull's head proclaimed its imposing glory. While the overall ambiance captured a heavy tumbleweed vibe, the reception desk made a point of advertising the resort's top of the line spa amenities. Offering signature mud baths and a massive sauna, the staff enticed their clients to try the expensive treatments available to them.

Mikayla squealed at their displays on mint aromatherapy, the promise of pampered relaxation working its magic. However, as much as Mikayla might enjoy indulging in the spa, she wouldn't be able to post about it or her spontaneous vacation on her social media after calling in "sick" to the *Love Locket* production. She'd packed a number of disguises that mostly consisted of giant beach hats and sunglasses. Ignoring Mikayla's gawking, Alia greeted the attendant behind the desk.

"Hi, the name is Alia Dumont. I'm here for the WIE conference."

Jada's chest filled with pride at her friend getting to be a speaker at the annual Women in Entertainment convention.

In addition to being a featured speaker on the Breaking into Television panel, Alia's room and accommodations for the weekend had been covered. Thus, the money she would have spent on attending this trip she used to set Mikayla and Jada up with their own room. Alia refused to let them reimburse her, calling it an investment in Mikayla's budding career and a mini-vacation for Jada post–*Love Locket*.

Gathering up the keys to the respective rooms, Alia checked her Hermès watch.

"According to the itinerary, we have some downtime before the mixer in a few hours. I have to make a few calls, make sure things haven't burned down in *Unbound* land, but I'll meet you guys later."

"Sounds good to me. I'll be tucked away with the room service menu," Jada said. Hotel food could be a costly rip-off, but Jada never could resist snuggling up and sampling what was available. Mikayla dismissed this plan, dumping her bags in their room and then jetting off to the spa. Somehow, the girl planned to fit in a shiatsu and facial before heading back to change for the party tonight.

Frankly, Jada relished this bit of alone time, and took advantage of the opportunity to stream Netflix and decompress. But as she waited for one of the waiters to bring her the margherita flatbread she ordered, a flicker of guilt passed through her. Here she was enjoying a weekend getaway and still semi-ignoring Tristan. Of course, she'd seen him when they both had their first auditions for *Love and War* and during the *Unbound* watch party, but since then she'd kept her distance. She hadn't mentioned the trip to him because it felt like throwing it in his face, especially since he was still in the middle of filming. He was probably too busy to care what she was doing. Were you supposed to report back to your fake boyfriend when you went out of town?

Knowing she wouldn't be able to unravel the intricate etiquette of fake dating by herself, Jada pushed these thoughts to the back burner. She found easy distractions in the delicious food and Mikayla coming back and fawning over the magic hands of her masseuse, Roland. Their downtime went by fast and soon Jada had to slip into her little black dress for the night's mixer. Mikayla glammed up in her own flowy, cocktail dress but made sure to carry her sunglasses as a precaution for potential photo ops. They made their way back down to the lobby where Alia was waiting for them. She'd taken more time to familiarize herself with the resort's layout for moving about the conference. As such, she served as their guide, navigating from the reception area to the ballroom the WIE conference had reserved for the mixer.

The room was a step up from the kitsch, western feel of the rest of the hotel. A tasteful chandelier, sans any type of animal horn, twinkled overhead. Close to the entrance, there was a table set up for check-ins, which also boasted a plethora of welcoming swag bags. When they gave their names at the check-in point, the volunteer at the station perked up at hearing Alia's name. With profuse enthusiasm, she handed them their WIE badges (decked out in a glittery clapboard logo) and their swag bags. As they made their way inside, Jada peeked in her bag and spotted what looked like an eclectic mix of facial products and CBD gummies. Only in California would those two go hand in hand at an exclusive networking event.

Jada started to remark on the strange combination to her friends, but Alia had gotten snagged in a conversation with another presenter while Mikayla made a beeline for the food. Knowing Alia would escape when she could, Jada joined Mikayla at the banquet table. From crab dip and crudités to little petits fours, there were plenty of snacking options to choose from. After scooping up as many goodies as they could carry, they searched for a free table only for Alia to wave them over to her spot with the other presenters.

"Hey, you sure it's okay for us to join you?" Jada asked her, not wanting to intrude.

"Oh yeah, we're just talking shop. Please save us from our workaholic tendencies," one of the women said. "I'm Kamila."

"Yes! Oh my gosh, I love *Preeti Goes Live!*" Mikayla gushed. *Preeti Goes Live* was a hit teen comedy about an Indian girl whose life goes viral after an online incident. The show had developed a cult following and picked up numerous accolades for Kamila Rahal, the show creator, as well as the cast.

"Thank you, but enough talk about my work. What do you do?" Kamila asked. While Mikayla discussed her journey into costume design, Alia stole a petit four off Jada's plate.

"Don't be self-conscious. This weekend is for you too," Alia nudged her.

"I know." Jada blushed. Obviously, she knew she should be superexcited to connect with all these amazing women, but it was also hard to gauge your footing when you first got dropped into a new situation. But if she didn't want to rely on Tristan to be her one way to move up the entertainment totem pole, she needed to get better at networking. Stat!

So Jada did her best to keep up with the clunky small talk until Regina Blake, one of the board members for Women in Entertainment, got up to speak. Clinking her wine glass, she gathered everyone's attention and launched into her opening remarks.

"I wanted to thank you all for coming and making such a positive step to further your careers and friendships in this tough industry. As women from many different backgrounds, we are still united in the unique struggles that we face while trying to succeed. I hope you will take this weekend as a chance to share your experiences and come out stronger and more inspired because of it."

Regina went on to talk about some of the panels that would be going on this weekend as well as thanking the panelists for donating their time. By the time she actually finished, Jada's stomach was rumbling. Excusing herself from the group, she headed back to the buffet, looking for something to make up for the petit four Alia had taken earlier. Mid-decision between strawberry cheesecake and swirled fudge, she caught another young woman staring at her intensely.

"Hi. Can I help you?" Jada tried to sound more curious than *what the hell are you staring at.*

"Sorry, it's just . . . are you Jada Berklee?" the woman asked. Her intense gaze still gave off suspicious vibes to Jada, but she answered honestly.

"Yes."

The woman let out a relieved sigh, and launched into her real reason for approaching.

"Oh, well, I'm a big fan. My name is Casey. And, like, I know this might be out of line but I really love you and Tristan. I think it's so romantic how you guys found each other despite all the trash people are saying. And I just hope it isn't true."

"That what isn't true?" Jada kept her voice even. There was no way this girl had found out her relationship with Tristan was fake.

"That you two might be breaking up. It's all over *Sip That Tea.*"

Okay, now Jada's attempts to stay calm nearly fell apart. What the hell was wrong with that stupid website? Covering her growing panic, she offered the girl a reassuring smile.

"Thanks for your concern, but Tristan and I are fine. I promise."

Denying the rumor wasn't enough to get Casey to leave, though. She continued to monopolize Jada for ten more minutes about how she wanted to be an actress, too, how Angela was definitely jealous of Jada and Tristan, could she get a picture with her?, etc., etc. When Jada managed to break away from Casey, her whole mind screamed to check *Sip That Tea.*

A quick glance online proved Casey right. Thinking back to the cast and crew of *Love Locket*, the top suspect would be Angela potentially stirring up trouble. But if it had been her, she'd have given a fake name to the reporters, so there was no use following that trail. It really was so trashy for them to take some rando's word without contacting Jada or Tristan's camps to confirm. Then again, since those attention hogs had relished posting the video Mikayla sent, obviously they'd have no qualms about repeating inaccurate allegations from someone else.

Wondering if Tristan had heard about the false story, Jada debated calling him. Technically, she was on vacation, and that included a break from obsessing over him. She still wasn't sure exactly what she felt for him, and the uncertainty continued to eat away at her. But in the end, he had been right about them losing momentum, and now the fate of their fake arrangement was at stake. Sensing she was about to receive an earful, Jada stepped away from the party and made the call anyway. Tristan picked up on the second ring.

"Jada, to what do I owe this honor?"

Yep. He knew about the article. His voice held a bristling edge at finally hearing from her.

"Nothing much. Just wanted to see if you'd been keeping up on the news about us."

"Oh, you mean our breakup?"

"Okay, you don't have to exaggerate."

"I mean, it's not that much of an exaggeration. Since I'm at home, all lonesome, while you gallivant through the desert. Can you bring back some shrooms or acid after you're done finding yourself?"

"That's not fair," Jada said, inwardly stung. Deep down, she had been looking at this getaway as a time to figure stuff out, professionally and romantically. The fact Tristan had been able to recognize that right away made her feel exposed.

"This is actually a very important networking opportunity. For my career. You know, the whole thing you said you would help me with. Besides, I doubt you're that lonely."

"You seriously believe I'm back with Angela?"

"No, but quite frankly, I don't know what you two are getting up to now that I'm not around anymore."

Damn it! That was not what she meant to say, but slipping back into their fighting was easier than she anticipated.

"*Mierda*!" Tristan muttered under his breath. "I don't deserve this, Jada. You're off doing whatever you want, and I've done nothing wrong."

This time Jada didn't reply, because he was right.

"If you're feeling guilty, that's your problem. Just let me know when you're back in town. Maybe by then you'll be brave enough to resolve this face to face," Tristan challenged.

Without another word, he hung up. Jada stared at her now lifeless cell phone, torn over what to do. A part of her wanted to call Tristan back and defend herself. Another part of her wanted to rush home and prove she was brave enough to deal with everything. The more reasonable side of her acknowledged that cooler heads needed to prevail. Playing phone tag to keep arguing would be stupid, and leaving even more so. Aside from her ambitions, she'd come to Palm Springs to support Alia. So that was what she would do. Wrapping herself back up in schmooze mode, Jada returned to the party.

# 18

Unlike Jada, Tristan didn't have the luxury of sunbathing in the desert that weekend. On Sunday, instead of God's day of rest, he wound up in bed next to Angela. The circumstances weren't due to one of his typical lapses in judgment, so at least that had to count for something. Filming for *Love Locket* was coming to an end, but of course, the film wouldn't be complete without viewers getting an eyeful of the main characters' lovemaking. They'd already shot some earlier scenes in the apartment and had since moved on to the bedroom.

The movie was rated PG-13, so the finished edit of the love scene wouldn't be extremely graphic. That didn't make hooking up with a former lover on camera any less awkward, especially when Tristan was 90 percent sure Angela was *Sip That Tea*'s mole. Upon ruminating on the situation, spreading the rumors and the video fit Angela's vindictive side perfectly. Also, she and the Tea Twins had grown up as part of Hollywood's elite families. It wasn't impossible for them to be on friendly terms. Doug had told Tristan to let the article and his hypothesis go, assuring him the whole thing would be obsolete once Jada was back and they patched things up. Yet Tristan couldn't shake his suspicions.

While Ren and Tim might be worrying about mood lighting and aesthetics, Tristan couldn't help side-eyeing his co-star for any hints of subterfuge. Angela steadfastly ignored him, fiddling with the ends of her hair, obviously not satisfied with the job the team had done. Outfitted in a lacy pink bra and skimpier underwear below the sheets, she looked like every man's dream. Tristan could see tons of people wanting to be in his place. And certainly, that paired with his bare chest, would have audiences full-on shipping them. The reality was so different from what people would see on-screen. Rather than falling into the part of the smitten Diego, Tristan calculated how to trick Angela into confessing.

"What are you staring at, Tristan?" Angela asked. She hadn't looked up from her strands of hair but Tristan's intense scrutiny must have been palpable.

"Nothing, dear," Tristan replied smoothly. "Just wondering what you're up to these days."

"Ah, so your alleged girlfriend abandons you, and now you're bursting to hear what's been going on with little old me?"

Angela's caustic tone ended up being no match for Tristan's own resentment at the mention of Jada. He'd been trying to push their phone call from the other day out of his mind but he was getting real sick of having to cover up for Jada's absence on his own. Not to mention the accusations she'd thrown around on the phone, almost as if she believed the article's claim about him and Angela being back together.

"She hasn't abandoned me. She's at a work thing right now, but trust me, our relationship is as wonderful as ever."

"Whatever, Tristan." Angela attempted to dismiss him but Tristan pierced her with a penetrating look.

"Haven't you ever heard of fake news, Angie? The real question is: Where have you been getting such wild misinformation?"

All ears, Tristan waited for Angela to reply with a spiteful but hopefully revealing remark but it never came. Ren interrupted the moment, clapping his hands to get the stars' attention.

"Okay, lovebirds, are you ready to dive into this?"

Belatedly switching back into work mode, Tristan and Angela both nodded. Ren then laid out the scenario for them. Since this was a romantic scene, there wasn't a lot of wordy dialogue. This part of the film would be more about the emotion behind the characters' actions as well as strategic camera angles.

As they began, all Tristan could think about was their previous conversation, with Angela's comments about Jada sticking in his mind. It may have been Angela reaching for him, kissing him, but his thoughts strayed to a different, more passionate moment. The heated make-out session in Jada's kitchen drifted to the forefront. How Jada had felt against him, how every touch from her set him on fire. Then her torn expression afterward, her denial of him and wanting space, then shouting at each other over a crappy cell line.

"Cut!" Ren's order sliced through his internal chaos. "Tristan—"

"I know. My head wasn't in it. Sorry."

"That's okay. I know these scenes can be tough but try and stay in the moment," Ren said.

Tristan followed his guidance, taking a few deep breaths to re-center. Banishing all thoughts of his complicated love life, he focused on playing Diego. A man who, despite the tricky ups and downs of time travel, had a much simpler love story in the end.

He was overcoming all obstacles to be with his soul mate. In this case, Tristan wished life imitated art. Finding The One should be as straightforward as it was in the movies. You stumbled upon that special person, beat the odds, and won true love.

Reflecting on this warm and fuzzy idea helped ground Tristan back into the present. As Angela moved to straddle him, he looked deep into her eyes, envisioning the sought-after Claire over the difficult actress's real persona. Their lips met, their limbs entangled in a supposedly passionate embrace, and Tristan went with it much more convincingly. After numerous takes of being intertwined with Angela—in a few moves that would have made a contortionist jealous—Ren released them for the day.

In the process of changing back into his regular clothes and gathering his belongings from his trailer, Tristan momentarily lost track of Angela. But when he headed to the parking lot, Angela was a few steps ahead of him, tapping away at her phone. Tristan sped up to match her pace, hoping he could gain new intel, but Angela stopped abruptly as his height cast a shadow over her.

"Do you mind? Seriously, what is going on with you today, Tristan?"

Damn it. Tristan was turning out to be a supershitty spy. Throwing up his hands, he abandoned all pretenses.

"What's going on is I've got a feeling you're not texting your next boy toy."

"So, you admit to being a boy toy?" Angela snickered.

"My point *is* I bet you and the Tea Twins go way back. How many lies have you been feeding them about me?"

Angela sighed. "Despite our tête–à–tête earlier, I do have other things going on, Tristan. My dad is on my ass about this movie and about . . ."

"About?" He prompted her. A flicker of embarrassment passed over her face, but then she squared her shoulders and looked at him defiantly.

"He wants me to go to AA. I told him that famous people can't just walk into church basements to bond with crack addicts over stale donuts. But he said he knows, like, an AAA."

"AAA?"

"A-list Alcoholics Anonymous. Very exclusive and private."

Bypassing the problematic crack addicts line, Tristan's heart softened. It had taken his dad years to finally give AA a try. Behind the snobbery, this was a big step for her. "That's good to hear, Angie."

"Yeah, well, I'm just saying, get over yourself. Stop stalking me and my phone activity and call your supposed bae, okay?"

With that, she waltzed off to her car. While Tristan would not be taking her advice about Jada, he did check his phone. He rarely used his cell on shoots, even on breaks, because he hated the idea that bad news would come in right before a scene. Tragic alerts at the end of the workday weren't fun either. And as he saw the missed voice mail, he knew this message was the type of ticking time bomb he'd always dreaded. Pressing Play, he held the phone to his ear, and a woman's familiar voice came over the line.

"Hi, Tristan. It's me. I know it's been a long time, and I know you told me not to call, but I'm going to be in L.A. soon. I was hoping I could see you. Just let me know if that works for you. If not . . . sorry."

That was it. This short little exchange was all that Tristan's mom left him. Entirely vague and infuriating, the whole thing made Tristan want to hurl the damn phone on the ground. When was "soon"? A day, a week? And why the sudden need to see him?

Also, the whole casualness of her tone. "It's me." That was the kind of phrase you used with a best friend you saw or talked to every other day. Not in a situation like this.

Tristan stumbled to his car in a daze, still wondering what his mother wanted. *She must be dying. That's the only explanation.* It was a morbid, sardonic thought but it filled him with a fear he hadn't felt in quite some time. He wasn't ready to bury another parent. But he also wasn't ready to face her, just to hear he had to do so. Whatever her real reasons were for wanting reconciliation, Tristan's silence was the only thing he could offer her in return.

Although Jada's first evening in Palm Springs ended on a somewhat sour note, the rest of the trip went much better. Saturday consisted of various panels and workshops that she and Mikayla devoured, from sessions on how to brand yourself to battling harassment and discrimination. Jada might have been in the industry for a while now, but it was still a great feeling to come together with such a vast number of women all hustling to achieve their dreams. Alia had been part of an opening panel and Q & A on Saturday, but Mikayla and Jada really got to cheer her on during the Breaking into Television event on Sunday. Back in the resort's large ballroom, Jada and Mikayla sat in the front row, ready to flash Alia a thumbs-up or supportive spirit fingers as needed.

At the long panel table, three other women flanked Alia. Jada barely had to consult the convention brochure she'd been given to identify them. Kamila Rahal, from the mixer, was there, as well as Dania Cruz, known for her family dramas. Unfortunately for Jada, Jackie Fox, the showrunner who hadn't cast Jada because of her hair, was also on the panel. Self-consciously, Jada double-checked for unwanted frizz or flyaways and instantly hated herself for it. All weekend long she'd been hearing pep talks about believing in yourself, and yet she couldn't shake the need to fit into outrageous beauty standards. Since *Love Locket* had ended, Jada had dyed her hair back to a midnight-black shade. A part of her wondered if that would make her stand out to Jackie. But most likely, the woman had already forgotten who Jada was.

The moderator for the panel, former soap opera star Rashida Jackson, tapped the microphone to gather everyone's attention.

"Hi, everyone! I hope you have been enjoying WIE weekend so far. This afternoon, we've gathered some truly inspiring ladies to talk about their career journeys in television, and how you can work to forge your own path."

Enthusiastic applause followed as each woman gave a self-introduction. Mikayla made sure to throw in an extraloud whoop as Alia's turn came up. Alia didn't let them down, her words as eloquent as always.

"Good afternoon, everyone. I'm the showrunner for *Unbound* and have worked on past fan favorites like *Fallen Creatures*. Despite my success, my journey as a writer and creator has been full of ups and downs. I'm looking forward to talking to you guys about them, and how resiliency and faith in yourself is key for breaking into the industry."

"That's a great point, Alia. I couldn't agree more," Jackie Fox spoke up, then launched into her own spiel. "Welcome, everyone. I'm Jackie Fox, creator of thrillers like *Murder Me Sweetly* and *Eyes on You*. I also wanted to say I'm so sorry I couldn't be here for the earlier part of the conference. I was working on my upcoming show, *Deadly Intentions*."

That explained why Jada hadn't seen her before this event. Noting the woman's bubbly excitement over her new project, Jada remembered seeing the announcement of who had been chosen for the show. Bailey Burke, frequently cast as the blond cheerleader or girl-next-door type, had secured the role Jada had tried out for. Still, Jada stomped down any lingering bitterness because there was no point in holding on to this grudge. For all she knew, the other girl truly had done a better job at her audition. Maybe Jada simply hadn't been good enough this time. But since the only real note they'd given her before sending her out the door was an implied "grow your hair out," Jada found placing the blame solely on herself hard to swallow.

Either way, Jada chose to put her negative experience with Jackie on the back burner and focus on the other panelists. Each of them had great insight into their struggles to be seen in the writers' room and what their shows meant to them in terms of finally having a voice and better representation. When they reached the Q & A portion of the event, attendees were bursting to ask the accomplished set a plethora of burning questions. In particular, Jada noticed Casey about to jump out of her seat as she waved her hand vigorously. Luckily for her, Rashida called on her before the girl could pass out from the anticipation. Grabbing the offered microphone, she leaped to her feet.

"This is more of a general question for all of you. I really want to be an actress, but also write as well. But so many people have told me you can't do both and you have to start out with just one thing. What do you say to those people who don't think you can have it all?"

Hmm, not as awful a question as Jada had predicted. At least it was on topic and not asking about the showrunners' personal lives.

"I think it's worthwhile to have certain things you want to aim for. And starting out with a particular track will keep you focused. However, there are plenty of creators who manage to do several things at once really well. I mean, look at Issa Rae or Robin Thede for example," Dania pointed out.

"Yes, but it takes time, experience, and a lot of trial and error, to get to that kind of level," Jackie interjected. "It doesn't happen overnight, so be ready to encounter some setbacks and know there's a learning curve you'll have to adjust to."

"Thank you, Jackie Downer," Jada grumbled.

Honestly, they both made good points, but since the conference was about lifting women up, Jackie could have put less Simon Cowell in her response. Alia pulled the Paula Abdul card, swooping in with some final words of encouragement.

"All of these are good points. What you're striving to do, Casey, is certainly a lot of work and there will be a learning curve, but we've all been there. I'm not an actress but I know what it's like to have big ambitions and experience the same worries. But no matter how much opposition you face, at the end of the day, you're the only one who can decide what you're capable of and how hard you'll work to achieve your goals."

On that much better note, Casey thanked them all for their advice, and the panel soon drew to a close. As the crowd dispersed, Jada and Mikayla went up to Alia.

"Fantastic job as always," Jada said, squeezing her hand.

"Thanks. I'm free for the rest of the afternoon, until the closing ceremony this evening. How about we grab lunch and maybe hit up the spa?"

"Yes, please! And actually, I suggest spa first." Mikayla raised her hand. Any of her downtime this weekend had been spent chilling in mud baths and getting more massages from the skillful and buff massage therapist Roland. Jada had stopped by for a facial and a manicure but had not been as thorough as her cousin.

"You're saying no to food?" Alia raised her eyebrows in shock.

"They have mint water and cucumber sandwiches down there. We'll live," Mikayla insisted.

Since her own stomach wasn't grumbling yet, Jada shrugged. "I'm good with that."

"Okay, fine. I'll meet you guys down there in twenty." Alia had a commitment to hang back for a while to speak to attendees who were clamoring for her attention.

As Jada turned to exit the ballroom with Mikayla, she found Jackie Fox staring at her (and pointedly ignoring the other guests who had come up to speak to her). Walking toward them, she offered Jada an inviting smile.

"Do I know you? You look familiar."

"Hi, Jackie. We have met. I auditioned to play Monica."

"Ah, yes! Jada Berklee." Jackie snapped her fingers at pinning down the recognition. "How are you?"

Jada wanted to say she was booked solid for the next year, and no longer even thought about that audition or the creator's thinly veiled remark. But the only thing she had lined up was a callback for Logan's movie after her first audition a few days ago.

"I'm great. I just finished working with Ren Kurosawa on *Love Locket* and have a few other things brewing."

"That's right," Jackie said. And Jada could have sworn the woman glanced at her hair. It was subtle enough for her to think Jada wouldn't notice but she had.

"Anyway, it was nice running into you and good luck with your new show. My cousin and I have to go to another workshop."

After a cordial good-bye, Jada looped her arm through Mikayla's and steered them out of the room.

"Jesus. Thanks for not introducing me. Isn't this whole event about networking?"

Glancing at her cousin's braids, Jada held back a snort. "Trust me. She's here for her own publicity, not to help people like us shatter glass ceilings."

"Okay . . ." Mikayla said, eyeing Jada skeptically.

Jada didn't give in to her prying look. This weekend should be about getting Mikayla excited about working in the industry, not reliving Jada's own experiences with the racism beneath the shiny surface. Whatever slight Mikayla felt got left behind as "spa time" arrived. With the trio snuggled up in fluffy terry cloth robes, Jada stood in the spa's lobby debating what to pursue first with her two friends.

"Look, I get that you and Roland have been bonding, but I don't really like to be touched by strangers. I don't care how magical their hands are." Alia scrunched her nose and shuddered with displeasure.

"In all seriousness, Mikayla, give the dude a break. His fingers are probably cramping from working out all your supposed . . . kinks." At Mikayla's scathing stare, Jada hid her chuckles behind the spa's pricing leaflet.

"What do you guys suggest then?" Mikayla asked, although she looked with longing down the hall corridor, like the majestic masseuse would come out any second.

"I heard sweating out your toxins is a great way to destress." Stinking it up in a sweaty, claustrophobic lodge didn't typically sound like Alia's cup of tea, or Jada's for that matter. However, the overworked writer was always trying to find ways to unclench.

After Jada's run-in at the panel with Jackie Fox, maybe she needed to do so as well. With two against one, Jada and Alia were able to drag Mikayla to the Blue Sierra sauna.

The sauna greeted them with its promised heat the second they stepped inside. Wood paneling and seating encircled the room, and a few women were resting against propped-up towels. Others had spread out across a few benches in their naked glory. While the sauna seemed full of patrons soaking in the heat, the trio was able to claim their own spot off to the side. Alia kept her towel wrapped modestly around her while Mikayla went the topless route. With abandon, she shrugged out of her towel and set her breasts free. At Alia's wide eyes, Mikayla glared at her.

"Hey! This was your idea."

"I know. I just wasn't ready for the bazooka show, I guess."

"They are quite impressive," Mikayla agreed, carefree as she leaned back against the wall.

"With as many times as she's disrobed down here, I think the twins would be confused if they weren't unleashed," Jada pointed out to Alia.

"At least I've been giving a peek to somebody," Mikayla countered.

"Nope. I'm not going to go there." Jada sensed where this conversation was headed.

"It's not just her," Alia interjected. "We both know you argued with Tristan as soon as you got here. I can't tell which way is up with you guys. What's going on?"

It was a good question but also something Jada couldn't answer. She'd told herself repeatedly that she'd only gone along with this farce because of the career gains Doug had promised. And yet, even when she was a hundred miles away at a conference where she should be networking her butt off, her and Tristan's undefined status weighed on her.

Stalling for a little more time, Jada noticed Mikayla opening a tin of candy she'd pulled from her discarded robe's pocket. Jada leaned over to snag a piece, chewing thoughtfully before speaking up.

"What's going on is a business arrangement. Nothing more," Jada assured them (and herself). "This weekend is not about Tristan. It's about us bonding and kicking ass."

Expecting at least one of them to agree to her sisterhood appeal, she received open-mouthed shock from Mikayla instead.

"What?" Jada said as she finished swallowing the blueberry candy.

"Jada . . . that's one of the CBD gummies from the swag bag," Mikayla said.

"Oh Jesus Christ!" A spasm of horror overtook Jada. Technically, she knew CBD gummies were mostly harmless. But aside from misguided tipsiness here and there, Jada stayed clear of things like this when she didn't know what kind of effect they would have on her. With her luck, *Sip That Tea* would somehow find out about this and twist the incident into her being a drug addict.

"Just calm down, lie back. It won't be that bad." Alia immediately fell into her mothering role.

While she resisted at first, Alia eventually persuaded Jada to lay her head on Alia's lap and take some deep breaths. Mikayla attempted to lower her anxiety further by discussing the supposed benefits CBD could have. When Jada merely glared at Mikayla's stats on the matter, the girls moved on to lighter topics. Gradually, the intoxicating steam did loosen Jada's apprehension. The haze washed over her in waves, lulling her into a state of relaxation. She stirred out of her reverie when a melodic humming broke through her daze. The tune grew more familiar as the woman began to sing.

Her soulful lament about her quest for a "lover man" sparked Jada's memory. She knew that voice. Shaking herself awake, Jada opened her eyes to take in the singer. Thin, with her hair stylishly coiffed, the lady before her was the spitting image of Billie Holiday. Blinking a few times, she waited for her vision to clear, thinking that maybe it would be Alia crooning over her instead.

Nope. The Billie Holiday look-alike then hit a note like the original Lady Day, something Alia could never do. After all, the writer was good at everything else, so it was only fair that she couldn't sing too. Also, upon second glance, "Billie" wasn't wrapped in a towel like Jada but dressed up in flawless old-school style.

"Ohhhh, got it. I'm dreaming." Jada gave in to the ridiculousness of it all and waved at her new companion. "Hi, Ms. Holiday. Nice to meet you. That's my favorite song by you."

"I would imagine so, with all the man trouble you've got at the moment, dear," Billie said.

As Jada started to reply that she did not have anything of the sort, a booming laugh startled her. To Jada's left, Hattie McDaniel seemed to be having a chuckle at her expense, and also sweating as much as Jada. For some reason, she'd also brought her Oscar, propping it up on the bench beside her. Then again, if Jada had been the first Black woman to win an Oscar, she would never let it out of her sight either.

"Take it from a woman who's had four husbands, they'll always be trouble," Hattie chimed in.

This escapade wasn't a little nap in a sauna but a full-on fever dream! Granted, she'd heard plenty of stories about people going to the desert and getting high so they could have high-quality hallucinations like this one. But after Mikayla's recited facts about the relative safety of CBD gummies, she hadn't anticipated having her own. Maybe she should just acknowledge the weirdness of it all and move on.

"Okay. While it is truly an honor to meet you both, can we skip to the part where I see a coyote and have whatever great epiphany I'm supposed to get?"

Before either of the imaginary women could respond, the door opened. Rather than Mikayla there to wake her up, Lena Horne leaned against the doorway. She wagged a finger at Jada like a schoolteacher catching a kid in a lie.

"Or we could skip the sarcasm and tackle why you run away from everything and think you can't succeed on your own?"

Instead of denying the starlet's erroneous accusations, Jada pinched herself to no avail. She barely felt it as Lena took a spot next to Billie, and they all waited for her to speak up. It was like being on trial by the Black Women Hall of Fame!

"I know I can succeed on my own . . ." Even to her own ears, Jada's voice lacked the conviction she needed to win her case. She couldn't just end it there as the league of women kept staring at her, the scary wisdom of being a deceased legend reflected in their eyes.

"It's just there are stars like you guys, and then there's me. It's a lot to live up to. And okay, maybe a part of me doesn't think I'm good enough, and that's where the whole thing with Tristan came in. And now it's morphing into something entirely different than what I set out to do."

"When you start with deceit, it will never turn out the way you hope it will," Billie said.

Ugh. It was a punch in the gut, but so damn true.

"So do I just dump this deal with Tristan and keep trying to make it by myself? What's the right answer?"

But as she looked imploringly at the Black Women Hall of Fame, Billie didn't melodically map out the pros and cons and Lena didn't soothe her savage burns with a follow-up. Instead, Hattie patted her on the shoulder.

"Be brave enough to find your own answer," she said, so wise and too damn cryptic.

Right when Jada started to ask for something more concrete, the earth moved. For a moment, Jada thought the real world had slipped back into her consciousness, and Palm Springs was having its own earthquake. In reality, her sleepy, semistoned ass had fallen off the sauna bench. From the hard floor, Jada took in Alia and Mikayla hovering above her.

"Jada, I'm so sorry. We're both kind of sweaty, and you kind of just . . . slid?" Alia lamented as she pulled Jada back up.

"It's okay." A bit sore and disoriented, Jada hadn't fully come back from her experience. "I kind of had an interesting fever dream thanks to gummy town."

"Ohhh, about what?" Mikayla asked.

Hattie's "answer" echoing through her mind, Jada shrugged. "Let's just say it was . . . enlightening."

Her hallucination might not have been the perfect ending to their weekend trip, but it would give her plenty to think about on the way home.

# 19

Gazing tenderly into Angela's eyes, Tristan fell into the illusion they were the only two people around. Standing outside the scenic clock tower on Vignette Cinema's outdoor lot, it was easy to get swept up in the film's final moments. Holding on to Angela's hands, he said Diego's lines with reverence.

"We did it, Claire. From now on, it's just you and me. Until the end of time."

Angela smiled up at him, her eyes shining with tears of joy. "Until the end of time."

Full of sentimental passion, they came together, seeking each other out for one, last kiss.

"Cut!" Ren finally called the thorough embrace to a close. Ecstatic, the director said the words Tristan had been longing to hear. "That's a wrap, everyone!"

Relief soared through Tristan. *Love Locket* was finally done. Well, done-ish. Tristan's part in the production was over at least, and it was all postwork from here.

"I want to congratulate you all on a job well done. I couldn't be more thankful to have such a great team." As Ren went on to thank the crew and cast, everyone applauded happily. Angela even had the audacity to give a magnanimous (a.k.a. pompous) bow when Ren acknowledged her.

*Good riddance*, Tristan thought to himself. However, when Ren turned to him, he hid his scowl at her with a plastered-on grin.

"And thanks to you, Ren. You have been a saint through all the . . . misadventures on this shoot," Tristan said.

"Thanks. I also wanted to let everyone know I'll be throwing you all a wrap party. This weekend, my place." Ren grinned.

The crew let out a loud cheer at his announcement. Tristan understood their surprise. Ren was such a private person, him hosting a party seemed like something out of the *Twilight Zone*. Yet, as he headed back to the dressing room, Tristan realized this invite meant he would get to see Jada.

After their Palm Springs argument, Jada had texted him when she got back into town. At that point, Tristan was feeling hella bitter over her behavior and accusations. Where did she get off implying that he was sleeping around when they had already talked about that? So, despite it being extremely petty, Tristan made up the excuse that he could only get together after this final week of filming. Until then, they'd have their PR team deny the allegations. But now with *Love Locket* officially wrapped, it was a different story. The mere idea of being near Jada—even if it would inevitably lead to more fighting—made his heart flutter. With hope or anxiety, he wasn't sure. He should have been terrified by that, but Angela snapped him out of his thoughts by yanking on his arm.

"I bet you're happy. You can finally be rid of me and run off into the sunset with Bambi eyes." Angela batted her own lashes for emphasis.

"That's the plan." Tristan didn't bother denying it. In spite of her vehement denials, he still suspected Angela was the blog's "reputable source."

"Hmm. We'll see how long it lasts." Angela started to walk away, but dying to prove her guilt, Tristan caught her arm.

"What does that mean?"

"It means we both know the longest relationship you've ever had has been with . . . yourself." Angela looked meaningfully down at Tristan's crotch. "Everything else, everyone else, is merely a brief side act in your long-running role in Me, Me, Me, and My Dick."

"You're no one to talk, Angela. Your fixation on my dick was the only thing holding our brief act together." Tristan let go and brushed past her. Still, he heard her last cutting remark.

"When you do blow it, give me a call. Not for pity sex. Just so I can laugh my ass off."

Despite his best dirt off your shoulder facade, her taunt did dig in. Granted, his relationship with Jada was fake, but even with their differences, the thought of it ending didn't sit well with him. Pushing the feeling aside, he changed back into his everyday clothes, said his good-byes to the crew, and drove off. Free from Angela Hell. On the drive, Doug's number lit up on his cell.

"What's up, Doug?" Tristan responded to the call via his Bluetooth device.

"Congrats on the wrap, my friend!"

"Thanks. I'm hoping—"

"Now what are we going to do about Jada? You said after

the shoot you guys would figure things out. Please do that soon because we've got to plan our next move."

"Doug, I've got it under control. The—"

"*People* magazine hasn't let that last blog go. They keep theorizing on why you two haven't been seen together lately. If we want to fix this, you two have to get back out there," Doug pushed. Despite wanting to throw back how Doug had clearly changed his tune about letting things blow over since the last time Tristan had brought this all up, he chose to stay on topic.

"Doug, listen to me! Everything's handled. Ren is throwing a wrap party this weekend, and I'll get together with her then."

"Weekend?!" Doug squealed. "Hell, you need to see her tonight and smooth things over. We've got a lot of catching up to do."

Tristan hesitated, worried that Jada had plans. Since they hadn't set an official reconciliation time, she might be offended that he was asking her to drop everything to see him now. Under more of Doug's pressuring, though, he gave in. After hanging up with his agent, Tristan reached out to Jada before he changed his mind.

"Tristan?" she answered hesitantly when she picked up.

"Yes, it's me. I know things have been rocky, but the shoot's done and—"

"And you and Doug are worried about our image. I read *People*, too, Tristan."

"No. I want to see you. You know, get the chance to clear the air or fight to the death. Whichever."

Hearing Jada's soft chuckle on the other line, Tristan pressed further. "Come out with me tonight."

After the longest pause of Tristan's life, Jada said, "Where?"

And in that moment, Tristan knew what had truly been bothering him for weeks. The reason he'd been so salty about Palm Springs. He'd missed Jada more than he'd been willing to admit. And now, seeing her easy acceptance of his request, he realized something else.

She'd missed him too.

Later that night, as Tristan waited impatiently outside Jada's apartment, he pleaded with God for the night to go well. This date felt make or break. He had a sense tonight would decide whether they kept this charade going or ended it all. His heart jumped when he spotted Jada coming out of the building's front entrance. She looked phenomenal as always as she walked up to the car.

"Why, hello, Ms. Berklee." He kept his tone light as he opened the door for her. Jada didn't get in, lingering shyly.

"Tristan, about everything . . ." she started.

"Maybe we should wait to have this talk until we get to our destination," Tristan suggested.

Jada acquiesced and slid into the passenger seat. Tristan hopped back in on his side and steered them toward Santa Monica.

"Trust me. Tonight will be fun," he assured her.

"Where are we going?"

"The Bright Futures Festival. It's a fair in honor of this nonprofit that assists underprivileged children. It's going to be going on for the next couple of weeks." Tristan had attended opening night earlier, doing a few interviews and promos. He'd always planned to return for another round. Going with Jada seemed like a natural choice.

"Let me guess, you're a sponsor?" Jada raised a knowing brow.

"Yes," he replied sheepishly. "But it's a superawesome cause, and the rides are great."

"There's not gonna be like, a gazillion clowns, are there?" she asked uneasily.

"Don't worry. I'll protect you from their big plastic shoes and balloon animals." He instinctively squeezed her hand. When she didn't speak right away, Tristan looked over and caught her blushing.

"I'm not scared. I mean, the movie *It* is incredibly creepy but I can handle it."

"Okay." He suppressed his laughter.

To his delight, the Bright Futures Festival was going strong. Happy families and excited children were everywhere, playing carnival games, eating cotton candy, screaming their heads off on rides. Knowing all the attention would help raise tons of money for his favorite charity was a big upside to their evening. LeeAnn had gone with Tristan's previous suggestion and blue balloons were tied to various booths, waving in the breeze. A banner bearing the Bright Futures' name and globe with a heart in the middle logo graced the entrance to the carnival. LeeAnn herself greeted them at the entrance to the festival grounds. She had taken up a station welcoming people as they came up. The press agent the organization had hired stood dutifully at her side, taking pictures.

"Tristan! It's so good to see you back. And you must be Jada." LeeAnn grinned at them. One of the festival artists had transformed her into a tiger using face paint, accentuating her smile even more.

Upon hearing their names and seeing them up close, the press agent started taking photos of them. As they endured the snapshot frenzy, Tristan realized this date was the perfect time for their own personal photo op. A social media update might help quell the rumor mill. Depending on how the night unfolded, Tristan might suggest it later. For now, they finished their small talk with LeeAnn and then scored their tickets to join the happy chaos inside.

"What do you want to do first?" Tristan said as they took in the noisy atmosphere and various aromas from different food vendors.

"First stop: funnel cake." Jada pointed at her favorite stand.

Throwing both of their diets to the wind, the two of them collected paper plates heaped with fried dough and powdered sugar. Guiding them over to one of the empty picnic tables, Tristan steadied himself for The Talk.

"Look, I know things got intense for you early on, and I understand that."

"Do you?" Jada interrupted. "It's one thing to pretend we're together. It's a completely different thing to be half-naked in my kitchen."

"Yes, but us being attracted to each other is a normal reaction, Jada. It doesn't have to be the end of the world if we hooked up."

"I don't want to be just another conquest, Tristan."

"I never said you were. I don't get why everything has to be either black or white with you." Tristan shook his head.

"Because as a Black woman, I don't get to live in gray, Tristan!" Before Tristan could shake off his shock and ask how race had literally gotten involved, Jada held up her hand.

"What I'm saying is I've been thinking about why I agreed to this. Tristan, do you know how many times I get offered roles to play a slave or be a part of some period piece about 'the struggle'?

How many times someone has tried to convince me I'll finally win some big award by playing a gang leader's crack-addicted baby mama? As if that's the only way to accomplish my dreams. I know everyone on the outside thinks things are changing in the entertainment industry, but it's still only for a select few. I have never gotten to be one of those people."

Jada's words were firm and strong, but there was no denying the devastated look in her eyes. Struck to his core, Tristan reached for her hand.

"I'm sorry. And you see me as one of those people?"

"In a way, yes. Which is why this pressure to be even more is too much."

"Okay. I'm sorry for pressuring you. But you've got to know, I do get it to an extent. Yes, I grew up in L.A. with influential parents. But honestly, my family is the only reason why I didn't end up playing a gang leader. Even with my connections, after *Garcia Central* I got offers to be a drug lord. It was either that or the sexy Latino. Big surprise which one I eventually went with, right?"

Jada laughed weakly. "Ahhh, it's all making sense now."

Tristan pinched her lightly at her teasing.

"Yes, I guess it just stuck after a while. But I promise, I do get it and, infuriating sexual tension or not, I will do my best to stand by the rules and my part of the deal."

"Thank you," Jada said. "Me too."

Her words sent a weird flutter of hope coursing through him. Despite his hesitance, he asked the question that had been weighing on him.

"So does that mean you don't want to end this?"

After a terrifyingly long pause, Jada shook her head. "No, I'm still in, because in a way, it's working. But before anything else, we should try and be friends first."

Although Tristan had sworn he wouldn't push Jada into a fling she didn't want, he couldn't resist a last chance to play devil's advocate. "You saw how that worked out in *When Harry Met Sally . . .*, right?"

"Tristan, please!"

"Deal." Tristan shook her hand. There was still so much more they could have said, but the newfound effort toward friendship forced him to easier topics. In particular, his photo-op idea.

"Since we've managed to bury the hatchet—not in each other's backs this time—I was thinking we could take a picture? Something to tide over the curious masses after all that's been going on?" Tristan asked, keeping his request light.

With their renewed alliance in place, Jada agreed. Holding up their half-eaten funnel cakes, they captured a few frames of their festival fun. Jada offered to post it first and tag Tristan. After some haggling, she settled on a caption that could push aside their naysayers:

I had a great time at the Women in Entertainment conference, but I'm so glad to be back in L.A., enjoying the Bright Futures Festival. Big props to @TristanMaxwell for introducing me to this great cause! <3

After posting his own comment, a mixture of saying he loved the current company and heart emojis, Tristan put his phone away and insisted they play a few games. Out of all the potential options, the classic Whac-A-Mole booth screamed his name. He looked at Jada meaningfully.

"You know I have to, right?"

"Fine. But you better get a superhigh score. And win me that unicorn!" Jada gushed over the ugliest stuffed animal in the booth. It was hard to make a purple unicorn hideous, but they'd succeeded.

"That one? It's totally cross-eyed!" he protested. But at her insistence, Tristan did his best. He came up a few tickets short and they chose a jester doll instead.

"Because you're such a fool," Jada replied when he asked her about her backup choice.

"I am not." He scowled.

"How would you like to be Maxwell Junior? Huh?" Jada spoke to the doll, then looked up at Tristan. "He says he likes it."

"I bet he does. So, I win you toys that you use to insult me? That's what friends do?" Tristan asked.

"That's what you get for missing the unicorn."

"Why did you want that googly-eyed monster anyway?"

"It's not a monster! Unicorns are the best. They bring hope and joy to the world."

"Jada, you know unicorns aren't real, right?" He eyed her skeptically.

"Obviously. But I used to think they were. Growing up, I had a whole collection of them. My grandma gave me my first one and told me stories about them. How each unicorn was special and full of magic. Believing in that made the rest of the world seem beautiful."

"You still have those dolls, don't you?" Tristan teased her lightly. Truthfully, the story had touched him. He could easily envision a tiny Jada enchanted by imaginary creatures. Jada blushed and whacked him on the shoulder with the jester doll.

"I did say they were collectibles, Maxwell Senior," she pointed out. "I'm surprised you didn't notice them when you snuck into my bathroom."

Offended at her implication that Tristan had snooped the morning of the shower incident, he nearly missed the sound of a woman's soft laughter floating their way.

"Well, aren't you two cute." Glancing over, Tristan noticed the woman eavesdropping on them was a fortune-teller, eyeing them from her post. He wasn't sure when she'd started listening in, but she seemed amused by their playfulness.

"Would you two lovebirds like a reading?"

"No thanks," Tristan said. That voodoo stuff wigged him out.

"I wouldn't mind one, honey," Jada countered.

Relenting, he sat down with Jada across from the woman. She deftly shuffled her decorative tarot deck, then laid out three cards before them: the Fool, the Lovers, and the Tower.

"Yes, you two are indeed a great couple," the fortune-teller began. "The early stages of your love are blossoming, with the Fool representing that you should open up your hearts to your newfound experience."

Then she tapped the Tower, frowning.

"This, however, is a bit troubling. While you two are right for each other, there's trouble on the horizon. Things you may not expect are coming your way, secrets yet to be revealed that will test everything. They will either bring you closer together or break your bond forever."

Unsure of what to say to such a foreboding message, Tristan turned to Jada. Seeing the troubled look on her face, Tristan cleared his throat. "Thanks a lot, but we're done here."

He left the woman a tip before steering Jada away from the table.

"Don't freak out. She's an old bat who's trying to stir things up."

"I guess," Jada said, but her weak response revealed the woman's predictions had rattled her. To be honest, they had freaked Tristan out too. He hated mystical shit like that. Today simply backed up his opinion.

The glimmering lights coming off the Ferris wheel caught his eye. It was exactly what they needed to take their mind off the heebie-jeebie mess they'd experienced.

"We haven't done any rides yet." He motioned to the Ferris wheel, and Jada nodded reluctantly. As they reached the front of the line, Tristan gasped in surprise. His mentee, Sam, stood at the ticket booth, another skinny teen next to him.

"Sam! Working hard or hardly working?" Tristan took in the sight of Sam casually hanging out, and low-key flirting, with his friend. Sure enough, Sam blushed and punched Tristan in the arm.

"Definitely working hard. This is Eric." Sam's underlying don't you dare fucking embarrass me went unsaid.

"Nice to meet you, Eric. This is my girlfriend, Jada." Tristan followed up with the introductions.

"Duh! The undisputed queen of *Fallen Creatures!*" Eric gushed.

As Jada and Eric engaged in fandom chitchat, Tristan strived to nod along casually instead of doing an impression of Chris Hemsworth lifting a mighty hammer. On the inside though, all he wanted to do was pull Sam aside and help the kid plot out his next move. Unfortunately, the line behind them kept growing, so they had to gather their tickets from Sam and take their seats. Once their car began to move, Tristan noticed Jada had reverted to rigid silence.

"Jada, are you still upset about those tarot cards? I mean, there's no way she can predict the future. All that doom and gloom stuff—"

"Will you *please* shut up? I don't care about some melodramatic psychic!" Jada demanded.

"Whoa. Is that necessary?"

"I'm scared of heights," Jada shouted, nearing hysterics the higher up the ride took them.

"What the hell! Why didn't you say anything before we got on?"

"I was trying not to be difficult!"

"What do you mean?"

"Well, we'd finally made up, and you've been so nice tonight. And it's our *first* night seeing each other after so long, I didn't want to ruin it by complaining." Jada kept her eyes closed the whole time she spoke.

"You can't be serious." Tristan groaned.

"Screw you! I have been nice." Jada opened her eyes long enough to snap at him.

"I know! But I was doing the same thing. Trying to be on my best behavior because I wanted tonight to go well."

Thinking back on the evening, Tristan started laughing.

"What's so funny?"

"I'm just thinking, what does it say about us that we can only get along as friends when we're both acting our asses off? Does that mean we're just great at our chosen profession or giant assholes in real life?"

Reflecting on his words, Jada burst out laughing too. Her amusement came to a halt though when the ride reached the top and stopped.

"Oh my God, are we stuck?"

"No, Ferris wheels stop intermittently. You don't know this?"

"Why *would* I if I hate heights, you ass?!" she shouted back at him, then gasped. "Oh my gosh, we really can't stop fighting with each other."

"Not if we're being honest, no. But I'd rather fight with you, the real you, and be miserable, than be miserable *and* fake."

"Yeah, me too. Even if it is a fake relationship, at least we can try and be truthful when it's just us," Jada confessed, then looked down. "And truthfully, I'm scared out of my mind right now, Tristan."

He held on to the sides of her face, forcing her to look at him instead of at the very far away ground. "Don't think about it. Focus on something else."

"Like what?"

He wanted her to focus on them, on this moment when they were truly being themselves, being vulnerable and open. And in spite of their new Harry and Sally status, he also wanted her to feel the intimacy and passion he was experiencing right now.

So he kissed her. Better yet, she kissed him back. It wasn't like their heated make-out session in her kitchen. This was softer, real, and perfect. Her warm lips against his, her hands wrapping around his neck to pull him closer, left him on a surreal high. So high that he didn't notice when the ride ended and they were safely back on the ground.

"See? Everything's okay. Are you feeling better?" he whispered to her as he unbuckled their seat belts.

"Much better," Jada said.

Her admission thrilled him, but he had no idea what it would mean for the two of them. Like these damn carnival rides, their relationship was up, down, and all over the place. But there seemed to be an unspoken agreement not to examine it tonight, to let things be. Even after he dropped Jada off at home, he couldn't get over it. Although he had no idea if they were headed into the friend zone or somewhere else, he was sure of one thing: Jada Berklee had a hold on him and wouldn't let go any time soon.

# 20

The queasiness in Jada's stomach meant she was going to throw up. That had to be the reason. It wasn't butterflies. It couldn't be butterflies. The lurch she kept getting in her gut every time she thought of Tristan absolutely, positively, could *not* be butterflies. Jada repeated this mantra to herself as she got ready for Ren's wrap party. She'd spent an embarrassing amount of time quibbling over what to wear—which also, of course, had nothing to do with Tristan. Friends don't worry about what to wear around each other. They also didn't kiss each other, but whatever! Eventually, she settled on a purple dress with a tulle skirt and a modest amount of complementary makeup. She finished sooner than Mikayla, who had gotten distracted tinkering around in the bathroom with her beauty products.

"Who are you getting all dressed up for?" Jada teased her.

"I could ask you the same thing." Her cousin paid her back in kind with an added dog whistle. "I'm sure Tristan will go all googly-eyed the second he sees you."

"Hurry up and get in the car," Jada said. "You don't want Ren to scold you for being late."

"It's a party!" Mikayla protested, then reconsidered. "Although if anyone was going to chastise a party guest, it'd be him. Let's go!"

It turned out Ren's house was something they didn't want to miss. In the luxurious land of Beverly Hills, his estate sprawled across a perfectly manicured lawn with a sparkling clean exterior. From outside, Mikayla and Jada could see the windows glowing with revelry as the party had, indeed, already started. If Jada had any doubts about Ren's wealth, they evaporated when a real, live butler greeted them at the front door.

"Good evening, ladies. May I have your names, please?" he said in the polished, sophisticated tone of someone who'd been in service for years.

"Jada Berklee and Mikayla Davis." Jada had to answer for them as Mikayla was too busy trying to see farther into the house.

Once Jeeves checked them off on his guest list, he guided them into the spacious living room. The cast and crew of *Love Locket* filled the room, talking and laughing loudly as they swigged cocktails. The raucous gathering seemed like it would be on Ren's list of the Top Worst Ways to Die, but he was the center of attention. Watching him entertaining guests with a smile on his face, Jada imagined the director was playing the social butterfly because he was delighted their disastrous film had ended. As Jada started to make her way toward him, Mikayla pulled on her arm.

"What are you doing?" she hissed.

"Saying hello. We have to at least thank Ren for inviting us," Jada pointed out. Mikayla let out an anxious groan.

"But he hates me," she insisted.

"He doesn't hate you. He just doesn't know you very well," Jada argued, but eventually gave in to Mikayla's dubious glare. "Okay. He hates you, but that's no reason to be rude. Manners, cousin." Jada proceeded to drag Mikayla over and tapped Ren on the shoulder.

"Jada, it's great to see you!" he enthused, then his gaze flickered over to Mikayla. "And you as well, Maya."

"Mikayla," her cousin corrected him, a testy edge to her voice.

"Right. Wardrobe PA. I remember," he said.

"Not very well, apparently," Mikayla grumbled, causing Jada to elbow her.

"Thanks so much for inviting us, Ren. Your house is amazing." Jada took back the conversation.

"No problem. Please enjoy yourselves. Grab a drink, dance, whatever you like," Ren said encouragingly, but soon took his leave of them to talk to someone else. Mikayla scowled after him.

"That asshole knows my name. He's trying to piss me off."

"And succeeding magnificently." Jada held back a snicker as she steered Mikayla over to the bar.

If she didn't know any better, she'd swear Mikayla had a thing for Ren. Mikayla always insisted she didn't want to go anywhere near him, but whenever she did, she pulled a petulant look-at-me act that Jada found entertaining. Despite her objections, Mikayla seemed to prefer negative acknowledgment from Ren rather than having him blow her off altogether.

"Here. Lighten up and drink up, Kayla!" Jada handed her a cocktail. Mikayla took it without protest and began chatting with another PA standing next to them. Honestly, Jada wasn't paying much attention to the conversation and she knew why. She was waiting for him. For Tristan to walk in and give her that look that set her on fire.

Right as she started to grow impatient, he strolled in. And yep, he looked at her and the flames ignited. And damn it, maybe he did give her a few butterflies, because something was flopping around inside of her as he walked toward her. Not wanting to have their meeting dissected by prying eyes, Jada moved away from Mikayla and company to go greet him.

She didn't get the chance to stammer and be nervous because the second she was within reach, he wrapped her up in a hug and kissed her forehead.

"Missed you," he said softly in her ear.

"You saw me yesterday." Jada hid her smile by burying her face against his shoulder. God, he smelled good.

"So? I can still miss you."

Jesus, forget butterflies. There was a frickin' parakeet inside her chest, squawking like crazy. A sensation that certainly shouldn't happen between two people who had decided to be "just friends." Surely, the Black Women Hall of Fame would be disappointed in her continued lack of willpower when it came to this man.

"We should talk about that. The missing, and Ferris wheel kissing . . ." Jada began.

"I know, but here?"

"We should have talked about it yesterday, but I . . ."

"Didn't want to ruin it. I know." Tristan's look of adoration quickly shifted as he spotted something over her shoulder.

"And someone else is going to ruin it right now." Tristan gestured for her to follow his gaze.

Low and behold, Angela had stepped onto the scene. Judging by her swiveling head, she was looking for them. She'd come up empty, though, as Tristan grabbed Jada's hand and steered her into another hallway. The corridor proved to be almost as rowdy as the living room, with people lining up to use the bathroom. As the noise of the crowd and the telltale sound of Angela's demonic high heels clacking followed them, Tristan changed directions and ushered Jada up to the second level of the house.

"We can't be up here. Ren will freak if he thinks we're snooping," Jada said.

"Such is the hazard of hosting a soiree. He knew that going in," Tristan pointed out. They both jumped at the high-pitched sound of Angela's voice coming closer.

"I saw him here a second ago!" Based off of Angela's shriek level, she had to be nearing the foot of the stairs.

Tristan and Jada picked up their pace on the second landing and darted behind the nearest door. Their haven turned out to be a linen closet that housed Ren's shiny white washer and dryer combo, along with numerous sheets and towels.

"You think we're safe?" Jada asked.

"Eh, safe-ish."

Jada couldn't help giggling over Tristan's triumphant smirk, but her humor dissipated as he moved in. She kept him at bay by grasping his shoulders.

"What about our talk?"

"Talking is overrated."

Jada pushed against Tristan's chest, stopping him from leaning in farther. "We both agreed. We're supposed to be platonic partners in crime, not . . . whatever this is."

"But don't you want to find out what 'whatever this is' really means? Our Bonnie and Clyde act could be much more interesting."

Jada threw him a skeptical look. "They died in a hail of gunfire."

"Semantics," Tristan purred, then pressed his lips to hers, doing exactly what she suspected he would: taking over. Over her sense of reason and any bit of decorum she had left.

Scooping her up in his strong arms, Tristan placed her on the dryer. As he stroked her breasts, her nipples tightened at his touch. The silky fabric of her dress no longer felt like a barrier. With each caress, the sane part of Jada faded away. She gave in, letting her own hands roam across Tristan's chest.

"Jada . . . I'm probably pushing my luck here, but I want to touch you." Tristan spoke in between delivering kisses to Jada's neck. Her pulse raced at his breath against her skin. She let out a nervous laugh.

"You are touching me."

"Yeah, but not here." Tristan's sneaky tone made sense when his fingers slid up the inside of her thigh. Jada tensed but her body simultaneously began to heat up, especially in one area that was about to get some much-needed attention.

"Tristan—"

Whatever Jada was going to say died on her lips when he stroked her through her panties. It felt good. Too damn good. She wanted more, even if it was a wrong time, wrong place situation. When she let out a whimper, Tristan smiled.

"Does it feel good?"

"Yes."

"It can get better," he said. Then he proved it by sliding two of his fingers inside her. Jada's warm, moist heat engulfed him, and he let out a moan of his own.

"I like being here," Tristan said. He added some force behind his words as he probed her farther, making his point. "I like exploring you. Do you enjoy it too?"

Jada gasped as he touched the holy grail of erogenous zones for the first time, rubbing the sensitive skin playfully. Not too hard, but just right. Enough to send an exciting jolt through her.

"Answer me, Jada," Tristan demanded, stopping. Jada almost whined when he ceased his movements.

"What?" she asked, foggy on what he'd originally said.

"Don't you love that I finally have my hands on you, inside you?"

Too embarrassed to answer, Jada averted her eyes and nodded. Tristan didn't let her hide for long, forcing her to look at him.

"Tell me how much," he goaded her, flicking that special spot again.

"Don't tease me. You already know." Feeling surprisingly bold, Jada spread her legs wider so he'd have more access and then pulled on his hand, grinding into it to urge him on. She'd never been this demanding during any of her past sexual encounters. Not that there had been many, but when there was one, she'd always been rather passive. But with Tristan, she felt hot, ready, uncharacteristically aggressive. Empowered.

"True. I can feel how badly you want this," Tristan said, moving his fingers through her, toying with her. His ministrations spurred on her saucy, new attitude.

"You're right. I don't want to talk anymore. Keep going or I'll scream." Jada tugged on his hair as a warning, but he smirked.

"Go ahead. I want you to," Tristan said, determined to get in the last word.

But then he shut up, kissing her fiercely and working his fingers deeper . . . harder . . . faster. Jada cried out as her orgasm rushed through her, causing her body to shudder in waves of pleasure. Tristan held her as she came down from her high to rest against the wall with her eyes closed.

"You're beautiful when you come, Jada. I knew you would be. I knew we would end up here."

His words and the sound of his zipper coming down brought Jada crashing back down to earth. No, not down to earth. Back to memories that should have lost their power long ago but that still haunted her. It wasn't Tristan standing before her anymore, it was Daniel, saying the exact same words.

"What do you mean you knew we'd end up here?" Jada said, her voice harsh, guarded.

"I mean, there's so much sexual tension between us. No matter how much we fought it, this was bound to happen."

Tristan shrugged, dismissing their current situation with ease, like it wasn't a big deal. As if Jada hadn't told him point-blank that she didn't want to be just another conquest. Here she was, freaking out about the repercussions of repeating her old mistakes, and he was fucking shrugging.

"Like I can't control myself because you're irresistible?" Jada bristled.

Tristan sighed like *she* was the problem with this scenario. To Jada, sighing was worse than shrugging right now.

"What's wrong?" he asked.

"What's wrong is that I'm not going to fuck you in a closet." At her snappy remark, Tristan's mood also shifted. He saw the writing on the wall the same way she did.

"When and where are you going to fuck me? Name the time and place. I'll be there," he said, back in asshole mode.

"You are so arrogant. Sorry to disappoint you, but we're not having sex. Ever." Jada attempted to move past him, but he boxed her in.

"Says the woman who was coming on my fingers three seconds ago." Then Tristan had the audacity to lift up said fingers, waving them in front of her face before he . . . sucked them into his mouth.

*Oh no, he didn't*, Jada thought, steamed at him for taunting her. And unsettled that his actions were inciting her arousal. She got ready to lay into him.

"Just because you're horny—"

"Don't you dare try and turn this around like I'm the only one turned on."

"Well, you're the only one with your genitals out!"

"Maybe so, but"—Tristan's eyes burned into hers as he issued his challenge—"you're still wet for me, aren't you?"

And *here* was the reason for the no sex rule. Oh, how quickly Tristan's charm vanished the second he didn't get what he wanted. He kept trying to sell himself as a good guy who just made mistakes, but only when he thought it would get him laid. Acting like a massive man-child because Jada refused to be another notch in his bedpost was a surefire way for any carnal "well" to shrivel into a dry Sahara.

Heady on a mix of fury and shame, Jada jumped down from the dryer. Her sudden movement pushed Tristan back and out of her way. His backpedaling led to a collision with Ren's laundry basket. As Tristan and the clothes tumbled to the floor, a scene that would surely have Ren aghast, Jada used the element of surprise to make her escape.

She was back downstairs in a flash, trying to find Mikayla. When it became clear her cousin was MIA, Jada sent her a quick text saying she was leaving early and would take an Uber. She was halfway down Ren's front walkway when she heard Tristan calling her name. Clearly, he hadn't stayed behind to pick up Ren's crumpled clothes. She increased her pace but he caught up to her.

"What the hell has gotten into you? You just snap out of nowhere and then run away in outrage? That's a bit overdramatic, don't you think?" he demanded, easily keeping up with her hurried steps.

"After what you just said? I don't think so," Jada hissed quietly. The majority of the other partygoers were inside, but a few smokers on the front steps could still overhear them arguing on Ren's driveway. Continuing to ignore Tristan, Jada pulled out her phone to request a ride.

"Seriously? An Uber?" Tristan said, peeking over her shoulder. "I'll drive you home. Sudden mood swings notwithstanding."

"I'll pass." Jada grew more desperate as the app on her phone wouldn't load.

"Looks like your bootleg phone is going to take forever. Plus, with the wait time until they get here, I'll pester you to death."

"Not likely!" Jada said as she headed toward the sidewalk. Up ahead, the road was extremely dark but she could make it out of Ren's subdivision and to a more populated street corner. Tristan called after her.

"Come on, don't be one of those girls," he said.

"What's that supposed to mean?"

"Don't be one of those women who gets hysterical and so angry at a man that she's willing to do something incredibly stupid—like walk home alone in the dark."

Jada didn't bother enlightening Tristan that all she wanted was better cell service and a busier cross street. Her focus stayed on evading him.

"I'll be fine. It's Beverly Hills. What's the worst that could happen?" The words had barely left Jada's mouth when a shadowy man jumped out at her from the bushes.

"*Holy shit!*" she screamed. At Jada's outcry, Tristan's arms instantly came around her, pulling her away from the potential threat. But her terror came to a screeching halt when the raggedly dressed man whipped out a camera.

"Is that Tristan Maxwell? Oh, Jada Berklee!"

"Nope! Uh-uh, not today! Get in the car, Jada." Tristan dragged her away from the paparazzo and led her over to his Mustang. She decided not to put up a fight as the photographer blinded them with shots. He only stopped when Tristan nearly ran him over with his car. After they'd sped off from the scene, Tristan glanced over at Jada.

"You still mad?"

Her response was a sniff as she looked out the window.

"So, you're not going to talk to me ever again? We have a deal, Jada."

"I don't need your help, and I can't believe I thought I did. I can't believe for one second, I thought I felt . . ."

"What?"

"It doesn't matter. This deal or the one I made with Daniel. It's all the same. You're all the same."

"What does Daniel have to do with this?" Tristan frowned.

"Because he screwed me around. He nearly destroyed my life. And you're exactly like him. You want me to believe you suddenly care about me? No, this is all about either hooking up or protecting your reputation. You want to use me and discard me when you're through. But guess what? It's not happening. Screw the deal."

At this point, they'd reached a stoplight in a livelier part of town. Jada took this as her cue. With those parting words, she jumped out of the passenger seat, leaving a shell-shocked Tristan in the car. This time Tristan didn't chase after her, but her past did, breathing down her neck. Demanding that she face it.

# 21

"I knew we would end up here," Daniel had said to Jada, shaking his head. "Let's cut our losses. I'll smooth things over with Maggie and you'll leave the show and get another gig."

Jada remembered Daniel's words so clearly. The bullshit he told her right before he spread lies about her to cover his own ass. She'd done her best to assure the execs she hadn't actually done anything wrong. She'd fought back the best way she knew how, but eventually she'd signed her resignation and walked away like a spineless coward. She'd let a spoiled man-child and his insufferable mom take away everything that mattered to her.

*Not again,* Jada thought as she relived her downfall. She had sworn she would never let another man hurt her or dictate her career. Yet, after hearing Tristan repeat those exact same words, she realized it was happening again. Tristan had an emotional hold over her, *and* their damn agreement gave him a say in her acting career. Jada thought what she'd said to Tristan during their heart to heart at the Santa Monica Pier would have made a difference, but things still hadn't clicked for him. He was still acting like a horny jerk. The incident at the wrap party just proved *again* how he was too embedded in her life, and she was giving him too much power. The same power she'd given Daniel. The power to break her.

It didn't matter that Tristan's touch lit her up inside, or that every time he looked at her she felt butterflies. From this moment on, she refused to let him possess her emotionally. Because if she let him in—even the tiniest bit—he would invade everything, consuming her thoughts, devouring her body. She would be completely his.

That frightening reality kept her up all night. It was also the reason why she'd blocked his calls this morning. She didn't dare pick up or listen to his messages. She would have caved immediately.

Jada buried her head in her pillow, suppressing a belabored sigh. She should get out of bed and do something productive, but the energy to do so wasn't there. Mikayla had hassled her about going to the gym but gave up when Jada claimed she wasn't feeling well. This excuse wouldn't deter her cousin for long, and she'd suffer through a full interrogation when Mikayla got back.

While she lay there, her phone rang again obnoxiously. She was going to send it to voice mail until she saw it was Avery calling.

"Hey, boss," Jada tried to say cheerfully.

"Don't patronize me. Explain this photo I found on TMZ."

"What photo?"

"The one of you and Tristan arguing outside of Ren Kurosawa's house."

Crap.

"Oh that was—"

"Another acting scene? Come on, Jada!"

"Okay, so we had a small tiff, but—"

"Jada, you can't afford any more tiffs. Tristan has been great for your image, snagging that audition for Logan Wentworth's film—your callback is tomorrow, by the way. Please don't fuck this up."

"I won't." Jada bristled. "Tristan and I are fine, and I'll act my butt off at tomorrow's audition." How convenient that Avery wasn't mentioning that Logan and the casting team had liked her enough—sans Tristan—to bring her in for a second run-through.

"Well—"

"Good-bye, Avery!" Jada shocked herself by actually hanging up on her.

*She* had hung up on Avery. Had she completely lost it? She'd pay for her audacity next time she met up with her ferocious agent. But that was a problem for another day. Today's dilemma included whether or not she should have a giant margarita or a big-ass glass of wine. The only people who could help her decide were her cousin and Alia.

Hence, that Sunday evening, the three of them ended up in Jada's living room, clad in their pajamas. They'd ultimately decided on experimenting with a whole lot of rum and a wee bit of strawberry daiquiri mix.

"Not that I'm not happy to have a girl's night, but what brought this on?" Alia looked on quizzically as Jada refilled their glasses.

"What else? Tristan!" Mikayla snorted.

"My life doesn't revolve around Tristan," Jada said, but it certainly felt like it did these days.

"Maybe not but he's the reason you bailed on me last night."

"I didn't bail. I couldn't find you to tell you I was leaving. Where were you by the way?"

"You first," Mikayla insisted.

"Fine. You guys were right. The Maxwell magic is working. Unfortunately."

"Called it!" Mikayla raised her glass in triumph while Alia stifled a giggle.

"It's not funny. He's the worst guy I could fall for. Our whole nonrelationship is built on a lie!"

"Lies and the truth can sometimes become the same thing." Mikayla said, slurring her words. "Besides, if you like each other, then fucking be together."

"Oh, that's a great idea, Mikayla, except for the huge messed-up thing we did! Which you seem to have conveniently forgotten."

"What are you two talking about?" Alia asked.

"The video that came out about The Incident? I did that," Mikayla confessed, guiltily fiddling with the stem of her glass.

"Kayla, how could you?!" Alia frowned.

"She let me!" Mikayla pointed an accusatory finger Jada's way. So much for family loyalty!

If Alia's sensibilities weren't scandalized before, they were now. "Jada!"

"I know, okay, but I was a little drunk."

"Then God only knows what you'll do tonight." Alia snatched Jada's glass away from her.

"See? It's such a mess, and even if I wanted something to come of it, it can't now. Not without it all blowing up in my face later."

That was the other darker part to all this. Jada had been

suppressing it, but how could she have anything real with Tristan without telling him the truth? Finding out she'd been involved with releasing that video would be the final nail in any relationship coffin. Deciding she didn't want to go over her plethora of mistakes more than she already had, Jada redirected their attention to Mikayla.

"I told you. It's your turn. Where were you last night when I couldn't find you?"

"In a hidden corner somewhere . . . making out with Ren." Mikayla had the gall to cockily sip her drink as if she hadn't dropped a bombshell on them.

"Damn it. Why is everyone else's life so much more interesting than mine?" Alia pouted.

"Because you work too much. I always tell you—"

"Don't you try to change the subject, Mikayla. Details, stat!" Jada said.

"I ran into him later on. He made me angry, so I kissed him."

"The old revenge kiss." Alia hummed in understanding.

"And he kissed you back?" Jada asked, stunned.

"At first. Then he pulled away and tried to blame the whole thing on me."

Jada could tell from Mikayla's furrowed brow that her instincts had been right. Mikayla had it bad for Ren. Whether or not it was unrequited remained to be seen. Knowing how much the tangled web of romance could torture a girl, Jada didn't press her.

"You know what? We should all be focusing on work, Alia. Screw men, screw relationship drama. I'm going to forget all about Tristan and focus on my audition tomorrow."

"You have an audition tomorrow? And you're sitting here

guzzling liquor?" This time Alia took the whole bottle of rum off the table and deposited it back in the kitchen.

"I'm fine!" Jada insisted. Although the room was starting to look . . . fuzzy. And sideways.

After a few more halfhearted complaints, Jada admitted (to herself, at least) that the room was spinning too much for comfort. She gave up the sauce and said good night to her loyal besties. As she was about to collapse into a deep slumber, she made sure to set her alarm for tomorrow. She was buzzed, not stupid. When she went to turn on the alert, she spotted another text from Tristan.

**Tristan**: Seriously, I'm sorry. What do I have to do for you to forgive me?

Against her better judgment, Jada texted back: *I could forgive you if I wasn't falling for you.*

Then she passed out before she could consider the consequences of her message.

# 22

The next morning, Jada's pounding headache brought painful clarity. Alia was right. Jada, never, *never*, should have chugged back sugary daiquiris like they were slushies from a local Gas N' Go. It wasn't as bad as the night of her video-posting folly, but it would take a lot of hydration to get her feeling right again. She had to get it together before her audition at three. When she blearily checked her phone for the time, her heart practically stopped when she saw a text notification from Tristan on the screen.

> **Tristan**: I didn't know you were a yam fan. It sucks that sweet potatoes are standing in our way . . .

"Yams?" Jada muttered. Glancing at their previous messages, she caught her faux pas.

> **Jada**: I could forgive you if I wasn't falling for yams

Holy crap! Thank *God* for misguided autocorrect. The gist of what she intended to say was there, but with the mistake, she hadn't completely given herself away. It left her with the most common excuse.

**Jada**: Sorry, had a few drinks last night with the girls. Also, yams and sweet potatoes aren't the same thing. Look it up

Three dots appeared, suggesting Tristan was trying to formulate the perfect response. They appeared, disappeared, reappeared, and then his text came through.

**Tristan**: Why do you know that???

She sent back the girl shrugging emoji. *Too many trivia nights.*

**Tristan**: So . . . can we talk?

She wanted to say no. She wanted to remind him that things were over.

**Jada**: Today's not a good day. I have my callback audition with Logan

**Tristan**: Nice! I do too. Still, we got to eat, right? If you come over, I'll whip something up. Or I could come meet you

She shook her head vigorously. She most definitely didn't want him coming over here. Too many mishaps happened when he did. At least if she met him at his place she could leave whenever she wanted.

**Jada**: At the risk of food poisoning . . . fine, I'll come over. What's your address?

Tristan gave her directions to his place in Calabasas.

Thankfully, it wasn't too far away from her place in Culver City. Nevertheless, the change in zip codes made a hell of a difference.

Jada let out a long whistle, genuinely impressed. Ren's house might have been fantastic, but Tristan's didn't fall far behind in the glamorous designer homes competition. When Tristan answered the door, Jada almost lost her breath all over again. Why was he so deliciously handsome? Even in basketball shorts and a plain T-shirt he was still one of the most enticing men she'd ever met. Outfitted in a sleek, black dress for the callback, Jada felt slightly overdressed as she hesitantly stood on the threshold.

"Thanks for coming." Her apprehension dissipated as he waved her inside.

"You did promise me food. I assume that includes coffee as well?" she asked.

"Of course," he said as he led her into the kitchen.

The large space embodied vibrant color with bright-blue paint and marble tile. A slew of the highest-quality kitchen appliances—from a state-of-the-art blender to a fancy coffee and espresso maker—also graced the smooth countertops. To his credit, Tristan poured her a full cup of rich, hot java instead of offering her a tiny espresso. Some people might love the feeling of a strong hit of caffeine in what was basically a shot glass, but Jada liked sipping her morning joe over time. Probably a side effect of always drinking the dinky brew on various sets. She added a fair amount of the hazelnut creamer he offered her.

"Breakfast isn't quite ready yet. I'm still . . . at work."

"Dear God, that sounds ominous."

"It's not! I was waiting until you got here before I got started. Chorizo Omelet de Tristan has to be eaten at the ideal temperature."

"Good to know."

As Tristan set to work, Jada sipped her coffee and studied his efforts closely. He didn't seem like a newbie in the kitchen as he whisked the eggs with practiced ease. The man even added seasoning to the mixture instead of just plopping it straight into the skillet.

"Where'd you learn how to make Chorizo Omelet de Tristan?"

His shoulders tensed but he answered anyway. "My mom. She made it all the time. She named it after me because it was my favorite."

"Well, I'm honored that you're sharing it with me," Jada said.

After a few more moments of Tristan showing off his "mad omelet flipping skills" (his words, not Jada's), they sat down to eat his self-proclaimed masterpiece, an array of fresh fruit and toast on the side. Jada had to admit that the omelet had turned out damn good, rich and filling, with the chorizo not as greasy as she'd anticipated. But even with the great breakfast in front of them, they both knew it was time to get down to the real issue. Tristan cleared his throat, starting them off.

"I wanted to say, in person, that I know I was a total douche the other night. I acted like an ass when you were upset. It's not an excuse, but I'm not . . . used to being around a woman like you."

"What do you mean?"

"Most women I . . . connect with, we don't fight like you and I do. They're a lot . . ."

"Easier?" Jada hinted.

"To an extent, yeah," Tristan admitted sheepishly. "You're not what I expected. When we first met, I had this idea of who you were, and I was wrong."

"You thought of me as the shy, quiet Jada Berklee people usually walk all over. Honestly, deep down, that's how I see myself sometimes. But you're right. With you, it's different. I'm different. Whether that's for better or worse, I'm not sure."

"I like that you're different with me," Tristan said, squeezing her hand. "It makes our relationship challenging as hell, but it's also kind of hilarious when you call me on my shit. It means I can't treat you like I have other women in the past. Your reaction the other night helped me understand that."

Jada winced. "Okay. To be fair, after all that talk about being civil and being friends, I should have tried to explain. But I was freaking out, all caught up in my feelings, and you didn't deserve it."

"Why did you freak out?" he asked.

"PTDD," she said, then expanded as he stared at her blankly. "Post-traumatic Daniel disorder."

Tristan's eyebrows shot up in surprise. "Exactly how bad was this breakup?"

Jada gave in and told Tristan the whole truth. The play by play of how Daniel and Agent Mommy Dearest had screwed her over.

"Why are you still with Avery after what she and her trashy offspring did to you?" Tristan demanded.

"I guess I thought I would eventually work my way back into her good graces. But if I leave now, she could blacklist me. Try and throw my past right back in my face or use it to badmouth me to other employers."

"Maybe Doug can—"

"Please, I can't accept anything else from you guys. I've got a handle on it."

Jada didn't let him object further as she pointed out her callback with Logan was in a few hours.

"You don't have to leave so soon. I haven't shown you the best part of the house," Tristan said slyly.

"Which is?" Jada asked, sure he was up to something. Like leading her to his bedroom. Yet, when he pulled her into what was clearly his man cave, she rolled her eyes. The "best part of the house" was the epitome of a bachelor pad, as Tristan listed its many amenities.

"State of the art sound system, fully stocked bar, and . . ." Tristan gestured dramatically at the pool table. "The best bar game known to man."

"You can't be serious. A pool table? That's what you wanted to show me?"

"This is high-quality felt, missy! I'm guessing you've never played a good round of eight-ball before."

After he needled her a bit longer, she conceded to give the game a try. She chose stripes and he took solids, and they began making their rounds around the table. It rapidly became clear that Jada had no idea what she was doing. As she made another poor shot, she glanced up and caught Tristan holding back his laughter.

"You're such an ass!" she said.

"Here, let me help you." He made his way to her side of the table, his arm brushing hers as he helped her adjust the pool cue. At his proximity, Jada tensed, and he felt it. He pulled back and looked at her steadily.

"I meant everything I said earlier, Jada. Despite what you may think, I'm not like Daniel."

Jada searched his eyes, sensing his sincerity. For the longest time, she had been lumping Tristan in with Daniel, assuming that in the end, being with him would do more harm than good. That Tristan was just as capable of ruining her emotionally and professionally.

But Daniel had never opened up to her the way Tristan had. She never met Daniel's other friends or family and the only secret he truly shared with her was their clandestine relationship. By comparison, she'd met one of Tristan's best friends, and he'd opened up about his mom. Yes, they still shared a secret, and she had another one in her back pocket that could inevitably destroy them, but . . .

She didn't want to listen to the voice inside her head shouting how everything was doomed. She wanted to be vulnerable and real with Tristan, like he had been with her. She wanted to be brave.

"I know you're not," she responded truthfully.

Without hesitation, without overanalyzing, she reached for him. He welcomed her embrace, and they were soon wrapped in each other's arms. His velvety skin on hers flourished into enchanting heat, pulling them closer together. She craved all of him. Savoring his kiss, she leaned back, ready to give herself away—only to find a striped red pool ball digging into her butt.

"Um, Tristan?"

"Yes, dear? What is it this time?" Tristan asked cautiously. He probably thought she'd throw the giant no sex rule back in his face, but she threw the rule aside instead.

"Your high-quality felt is okay and everything, but this would be nicer if . . ."

"I see. You want something more romantic. Will satin sheets do?"

"Depends on the thread count."

He gave her a "trust me" wink, then lifted her off the table and carried her down the hallway.

"You're going to hoist me off to your bedroom, all King Kong style?" She giggled.

"Yes. Well, the guest bedroom anyway. My bed is way too far away for what I want to do right now."

An electric thrill ran through her as Tristan kicked open a nearby door and they came face to face with an enormous bed, clad in the champagne-colored satin sheets he'd promised. She inspected them playfully.

"Hmm. Looks to be at least six hundred. I can work with that."

"I'm glad you're pleased," he said.

Based on the passion in Tristan's eyes, Jada would be even more pleased shortly. He didn't fail her. As he gradually unveiled her, stripping her of her clothes, he showered each exposure of her skin with reverential kisses. That alone was enough to have Jada writhing on the bed. When he teased her nipples with his skillful tongue, a new, feverish urgency took over her.

She grabbed his shorts, eager to return the favor. When he was at last bare before her, she caressed him, rubbing her wetness against his firm, sheathed member. Encircling his hips with her legs, she urged him closer but he wouldn't budge.

"I wasn't done yet," he said with an amused expression. Then he pressed his lips to her navel, licking her skin as he made his way down.

Way down.

Jada let out a startled squeak when Tristan's expert tongue flickered over her sensitive skin. Not because she didn't see it coming, but because of how damn good it felt. Caught in Tristan's lustful spell, she realized it had been too long since she'd had sex. But she was glad she'd waited. Waited until she found him.

Jada's moist heat became too much to bear. She lured him back to her, tasting her desire in his mouth. Then she guided his thick length inside her. She was so ready that he slid in with ease and hit home. She cried out at the intense, sensual sensation of Tristan moving within her.

"Damn, Jada. You feel good," Tristan said.

"You too. But you can go faster."

"You're pushy in bed. I like it."

Jada flushed. "Don't act like you don't want to. Besides, I was assuming I'd get the whole Maxwell treatment."

"Hey, whatever the lady wants . . ." Tristan laughed as he continued to move inside her. This time, his fluid movements proceeded in rapid, fierce succession as he gave her exactly what she needed.

Jada's orgasm came hard and fast, rushing through her in overpowering waves of satisfaction and contentment. Tristan's body shuddered as he came as well, swelling inside her. Afterward, they lay still. He stayed enveloped in her warmth, and she held on to him in worn out bliss.

"Just so you know, I didn't expect this to happen when you came over." Tristan traced her skin in leisurely circles. "But I'm sure as hell glad it did!"

"Me too." Jada laughed.

"Thank you, *reina*," he said, kissing her shoulder.

"Reina?"

"It means queen in Spanish."

"I'm your queen now?" She perked up.

"Mine? You'd be a queen with or without me, Jada," Tristan said, then considered it carefully. "But now that you mention it, keeping you as my own sounds perfect."

*Yep, it's official*, Jada decided as he smiled down at her. *I'm hooked on Tristan Maxwell.*

*Long live the queen.*

# 23

Ever since his first time, sex had been a game for Tristan. An intimate one, but a game nonetheless. The sensations, the curves of a woman's body, were all part of an adventure. A delightful dance, but once it had run its course, he was done. He'd move on.

Gazing into Jada's peaceful face, Tristan sensed he'd never be able to perceive it that way again. She looked so perfect lying beside him, flushed yet content. He wasn't much of a cuddler but he would have stayed there indefinitely, except for one small detail: the bedside clock glaring at him in angry red numerals.

"Jada, I'd love to snuggle up in postcoital bliss, but I'm afraid we both have somewhere to be." Tristan nodded to the clock.

"Oh shit!" Jada jumped out of bed, scrambling to collect her clothes. Watching Jada cover up wasn't as exciting as helping her undress.

"It's okay. We still have enough time to get there, especially if we—"

"Take your bike?" Jada groaned.

"Hey, hey. I am a very safe driver. Harley-Davidson and the LAPD both approve of the way I maneuver my so-called deathmobile."

Jada gave one more distrustful whimper, which Tristan chose to ignore.

"*Apúrate, mi reina.* We've got roles to score."

As Jada finished making herself presentable, Tristan did the same, donning a much more suitable outfit for the audition. Then he returned, grabbed hold of Jada's hand and didn't let go until she was safely astride his bike. At that point she became the clinger, grasping his waist tightly as he took off. Tristan faintly heard her screaming for the first few minutes, but between the bike and turbulent traffic, he missed out on most of it. She settled down the closer they got to their destination, but her grip on him remained surprisingly strong.

They made it to their audition a few minutes early, but not as much as either of them would typically like. The receptionist obviously agreed because she gave them a disapproving scowl at their near tardiness. Her opinion was ultimately unimportant when Logan spotted them in the lobby on his way down the hallway.

"Tristan! Jada!" He waved at them in excitement.

"Hi, Logan," they said in unison.

"Shouldn't you be inside for the auditions?" Tristan asked.

"I just popped out to go to the loo."

"How British of you." Jada stifled a laugh at Logan's colloquialisms. He merely winked in response.

"Since you're both here right on time, why don't you read together? Two birds with one stone and all that."

Since Tristan and Jada had already rehearsed together like crazy, this option was ideal. Furthermore, it wasn't uncommon for contenders for a role to audition jointly, usually to see if the actors had chemistry with one another. They eagerly jumped at the opportunity and Logan led them away, much to the surly receptionist's discontent.

When Logan escorted them into the casting office, a bespectacled man and a lanky woman awaited them.

"Jada, Tristan, I'd like you to meet Zora, our casting guru, and Donnie, the director of *Love and War*." Logan introduced them.

Tristan and Jada traded greetings with the execs who would decide their fate. Tristan didn't have a read on them yet, but he knew he and Jada would knock their socks off.

"You can begin when you're ready," Zora said graciously.

Tristan traded a knowing look with his partner. The piece for the callback involved their characters debating how to take down the movie's villain. But overall, the scene was merely a higher stakes performance of their previous time acting at Jada's apartment. Together, they would nail it and become the stars of this future billion-dollar film.

With ease, Tristan picked up the scene, playing off of Jada's witty sarcasm as if they'd been doing it their whole lives. Their newfound sexual discovery of one another only heightened the underlying desire between their two characters. It was undeniable: he and Jada had kick-ass chemistry.

After some suggestions from Donnie and a few more run-throughs—which they killed—Donnie thanked them for their time. Logan walked them out, giving them another sly wink.

"Great job, guys. We'll let you know later, all right?" Despite the casting team's positive response, as soon as Tristan and Jada were outside, Jada's trusty anxiety kicked in.

"Do you think it went okay?" she asked uncertainly.

"Putting a Jada Berklee–Tristan Maxwell match to the test? We aced it," Tristan said. "And, although I would love to rejoice in our victory . . . I have to go meet Doug."

"Oh." Insecurity flitted across Jada's face but she hid it swiftly.

"You can come with me, but it's going to be a boring business meeting. *Rival Warriors* comes out in a few days and he wanted to check in with me before the press junket madness starts." Tristan would have preferred hanging out with Jada over doing a PR blitz for his upcoming action film. Especially so soon after finishing *Love Locket*. But hey, that was the way of the industry and its horrific time constraints.

"Sounds like you're going to be pretty busy." Jada stared down at their feet, but Tristan touched her chin, encouraging her to look at him.

"I'm not bailing," he promised. "If you're worried that I'm going to disappear after we've connected, you're wrong. Sure, things will be busy with the film's release, but who do you think I'm taking to the premiere?"

Jada pointed at herself, feigning disbelief. The whole Who? Little old me? routine.

"Yes, you silly." Tristan pulled her in for a kiss. "You gonna be my date?"

"Eh . . . I guess if there's nothing on TV," Jada said before apprehensively hopping back on Tristan's "Doomsday Ride."

While they were both reluctant to part, they did. Tristan safely brought her back to his place, and Jada headed home in her much safer Infiniti. Tristan promised to call her later, and for once, it didn't feel like a line out of a Don Juan playbook. In high spirits, Tristan headed to his meeting with Doug, arriving at a hole-in-the-wall Indian restaurant.

He found Doug at a corner table by the window, tapping away at his smartphone.

"Hey, Doug! Beautiful day, huh?"

Doug raised a suspicious brow. "What's gotten into you?"

"Nothing. It's a nice day, that's all." Tristan gestured at the busy sidewalk outside. While the weather had been bright and sunny earlier, storm clouds were making their way across the horizon.

"If you say so. How did the audition go? Did you see Jada?"

"See her? We read lines together."

"Perfect!" Doug said. If they weren't in public, he'd probably have clapped his hands with glee.

"After Logan and the director have seen what you're like together, there's no way you won't get taken on as the leads."

"Agreed," Tristan said, tearing off a piece of naan bread. His mind flickered back to how their lively portrayals had brought intensity and life to an otherwise stale white casting room. His gut told him their success was a guarantee.

"Jada will be happy. Although this may mean you'll have to masquerade as a couple together for a lot longer than we imagined."

"That's okay," Tristan said, unfazed.

"Okay? To be shackled to a woman you aren't actually romantically involved with? What's going on, Tristan?"

"Nothing. Scout's honor," Tristan said.

No matter how close he and Doug were, he wasn't going to share what had happened between him and Jada. One, because she'd kill him. Two, because it was too special to ruin by getting nosy commentators involved. And third—

"You're falling for her, aren't you?!" Doug exclaimed, causing Tristan to choke on his water.

"Keep it down!" he said once his chest stopped burning. "And no, I'm not, but we're getting along."

Doug opened his mouth to investigate further, but Tristan held up his hand. "Didn't you mention over the phone you wanted to advise me on something for the Hot Pop radio interview tomorrow?"

"But—"

"Doug . . ." Tristan said, his dark underlying tone telling.

Doug sighed, knowing he'd lost the battle. "Fine."

They spent the next hour hashing out details about the upcoming interviews. Dinner was delicious, but it was a tedious conversation, and Tristan was glad when he could head home for a good night's sleep. Nevertheless, his last thoughts before he fell asleep were of Jada.

With his morning interview at the radio station, Tristan was thankful he'd had an early night. *Rival Warriors* was set to be released in a few days, and the announcer tackled the usual questions about the film. He'd be asked the same ones repeatedly throughout the day. Press junkets always had the same repetitive rhythm. So far, things were moving smoothly as he made his way from one appearance to another. Halfway through the day, he encountered his first engaging exchange on a panel for the E! network. As Tristan sat next to his co-star, Davie Harlson, their interviewer started them off with a game of What Would Your Character Do? Since the two played mortal enemies in the film, Tristan knew this would be entertaining.

"Okay, guys, so the gist is I'm going to ask you a bunch of questions, and you're going to tell me how your character would react to that situation. Got it?"

"Got it," Tristan and Davie said in unison, then laughed at

their joint answer. Once you did enough of these events with your co-workers, you ended up in sync.

"First question. If your character was faced with a hostage situation, would he try negotiating with the kidnappers or sneak into the danger zone to take them out?"

"Negotiating. Rick wouldn't risk lives," Davie said, speaking for his cinematic counterpart.

"Danger zone, baby! All the way," Tristan followed up.

"Great! Next question: In the film, you both kind of stumble upon the same mission and end up working together in not so perfect harmony. But if you were told straight-out you needed the help of your rival to save the world, would you team up willingly?"

Tristan reflected a bit, then responded with, "More like very begrudgingly."

"Agreed. I'd do it, but detest him the whole time," Davie added.

"But then he'd end up falling for me. His character's already in love with mine. He just hasn't realized it yet." Tristan teased Davie.

"Speaking of love and falling for someone . . ." The interviewer jumped on Tristan's response. Yeahhh, he'd walked right into that one.

"Yes?" he asked, playing innocent.

"You and Jada Berklee have been quite close these past few months. How is that going?"

Had it been that long already? It had flown by because of Jada. Usually, Tristan got bored by the two-week mark, but Jada . . . fighting with her, getting to know her, "falling" for her, it had all been such a rush, it'd passed by in a whirlwind. After some cajoling from Davie and the presenter, Tristan answered honestly.

"It's been good. Very good. We're happy." Tristan smiled, his sincerity radiating through. He didn't care about Davie's "awwws" and teasing. He meant it. He was happy with her. So much so that he planned on texting her about meeting up once the long press day ended.

# 24

Tristan's cheeks ached from all the smiles and pleasantries he'd put on during the plethora of interviews. All he wanted was to take a shower before heading over to Jada's. But before he got to the front door, he spotted something curious.

The light in his living room was on, throwing a soft yellow glow onto his front lawn. He'd heard plenty of stories about two-bit criminals breaking into celebrities' houses, but if these scumbags thought they could pull one over on him, they were in for a surprise. He'd taken his fair share of martial arts lessons for various roles and figured he could take them. On guard, Tristan unlocked his front door with a minimal amount of noise. He snatched an umbrella near the front door and headed for the living room.

"I've already called the cops, you son of a bitch!" Tristan shouted as he turned the corner, brandishing his weapon. (He totally hadn't but they didn't need to know that.)

The umbrella fell from his hands as he came face to face with Isabella Moreno.

"Mom?" Tristan croaked. His eyes flitted over her, wondering if she was, in fact, real or if he was in some weird dream. But there she was, standing by his fireplace with one of his picture frames in her hand.

"This is a nice photo of you, *pequeño*. You look happy," she said. The photo was one of Tristan smiling exuberantly as he accepted an MTV Movie Award.

A rush of rage spurred by betrayal coursed through Tristan's body. He made his way over and snatched the picture out of her hand, placing it back on the mantelpiece.

"What are you doing here? How'd you even get in?" he asked.

"The code on the door wasn't that hard to guess," she admitted.

So much for smart locks being the way to go. Tristan had specifically had one installed because it seemed like a better choice than someone picking a traditional lock. Apparently, that point was moot if you weren't creative enough. His mom had easily deduced he'd picked the premiere date of *Garcia Central*. The night it aired he'd looked up at her, tears in his eyes, and told her it was the happiest day of his life.

"I know it's strange for me to come here, but I needed to see you." His mom went on in the wake of his silence.

"You need a kidney, right? Is that why you called me?" He scoffed.

"*No me hables así*," she said tersely. "I understand that you're upset with me. You have every right to be. But I'm still your mother and you will respect me."

The sheer audacity of this woman made Tristan furious. It was one thing to leave a cryptic phone call without any explanation. But to show up at his house unannounced? She'd lost his respect a long time ago, and her dramatic entrance now wasn't helping. If she wanted parental courtesy, she'd have to work for it.

"Okay, I won't talk to you that way if you don't scold me like we're talking about a lost bike or a math test I cheated on."

A series of emotions flickered across his mother's lovely face before she locked them behind a more passive expression. Whether the look in her eyes had been one of sadness, shame, or regret, Tristan wasn't sure. After being away so long, it was as if the features he'd once known so well, and what they meant, were foreign to him now. Whatever she was feeling, she kept it in check and continued calmly.

"You're right. I didn't come here to reprimand you. I came to explain." His mother sat down on the couch, motioning for him to sit beside her. He gaped at the gesture, the act so simple and yet equally insufficient.

"It's about *twelve years* too late for explanations, Mom. The first year after you left, I waited every day for you to come back, for you to explain. But you never did."

"*Mijo—*"

"Don't mijo me. I was fourteen! *¿Y dónde estabas*, Mama? Tell me, where were you?"

"I didn't want to leave you, but your father insisted."

Tristan shook his head. He thought back to his father's misery and depression after his mom's disappearance. Toxic recollections filled his mind. Ones of coming home from long days on the *Garcia Central* set to find empty liquor bottles overflowing the trash can. His dad passed out on the couch or too out of it to ask how his day was. How Tristan's paychecks became a big source of the family income. But while his dad had his faults, he had still been a good man. He never would have forced his mother to leave. Tristan's dad mourned her absence for years and died brokenhearted. Tristan's dad never had a chance to fully reconcile things with his family. Tristan shook his head in disbelief at his mom asking for the same chance.

"You're lying. You're trying to make yourself look better."

"Why would I come all the way back here, and dredge up this pain, to lie to you?" She stood up and placed her hands on his shoulders.

"Tristan, leaving you killed me, but I'm here now. I want to finally tell you the truth."

"*Vete*," Tristan hissed. It was cruel, banishing his mother from his house. But if he didn't, he would break. He'd end up sobbing like the lost boy he'd been so long ago. He refused to go there. She didn't deserve his tears.

Isabella sighed, sensing his resignation. Nevertheless, she locked eyes with him, not letting him escape.

"If that's what you want, I'll go. But despite what you think, I love you, Tristan. Always," she said.

And with that, she left.

All over again.

The door closing behind her was like all the air being let out of the room. Tristan took in a shaky breath, finally sitting down on the couch. But as he tried not to freak out over what had just happened, his thoughts transported him back to the day his mom left. Tristan hadn't been home to witness her exit. Like the coward she was, she snuck away in the middle of the afternoon when Tristan was busy on set and his dad was at work.

At this point, *Garcia Central* had won critical acclaim for its first season and they were in the middle of producing season two. Tristan still loved every minute of it, relishing in the new scripts that came out. In their shoot that day, he'd gotten to dress up as a pineapple as part of a scheme the brothers had cooked up. As the loud resident jokester, Tristan had owned it, doing perfect pratfalls and nailing his signature catchphrase: "*¿Por qué yo?*"

Later on, he waited for his dad to pick him up so he could go home and tell both his parents all about it. Since his dad wrote for another show on the network, they carpooled together. That morning his dad had been surly as all get out, barely acknowledging his mom when they left and refusing Tristan's request to listen to the radio because he had a "headache."

But regardless, Tristan assumed his dad would still pick him up. However, the time ticked by, and his dad didn't come. It wasn't unusual for either of them to work long hours, but when his dad was running late, he usually texted. As Tristan waited in the lobby, his oldest *Garcia* brother, Rafe, and his mother, Mrs. Sanchez, hesitated when they saw him loitering there.

"Where's your dad, *hermanito*?" Rafe asked.

"Probably just busy upstairs."

Rafe's mom gave him a worried look. "Maybe we should go up to the writers' room. See what's taking him so long."

Tristan wasn't truly worried yet, but went ahead with her suggestion because Mrs. Sanchez was the show's designated mama bear. She always looked out for the kids when everyone else got caught up in other things. Making their way to the fifth floor, Tristan fully expected to see his father locked away with the other writers in their usual room. But tonight, the door stood wide open, the table mostly empty. Only Mr. Wright, the showrunner, had stayed behind.

"Oh, Tristan, if you're looking for your dad, he left hours ago."

"What?!"

"He said it was an emergency and that he'd let you know."

"Let him know what? To take a taxi?" Mrs. Sanchez scowled with disgust. "Come on, Tristan, I'll take you home."

Dread kicked in, and Tristan obeyed Rafe's mom with haste. The studio wasn't extremely far from his house, but the drive felt painfully long. What kind of emergency was so dire that his dad hadn't even bothered to tell him? Was he hurt? Or had something happened to his mom?

When Mrs. Sanchez pulled up to the house, the lit windows meant at least one of his parents was home. Tristan didn't wait for her to offer to walk him inside. Mrs. Sanchez's protectiveness was great, but whatever was going on was a private family matter. He offered her and Rafe a quick thanks and bolted into the house.

"Papa! Mama!" Tristan's voice echoed in the loud foyer but garnered no response. Following the light trickling into the hallway, he made his way to the living room. On the couch, his dad slumped forward with his head in his hands. For a moment, Tristan worried he'd passed out but then he saw the half-empty whiskey bottle on the table. Not even a glass in sight, just the open decanter.

Cautiously, Tristan tapped his dad on the shoulder. "Papa, are you okay?"

It took a few more tries but his dad gradually came to with a groan. "Tristan, that you?" He squinted up with bleary eyes.

"Yeah, of course. Are you okay? Where's Mama?"

"Gone, son. She's gone."

Horrific images flashed before Tristan's eyes. His mom's body battered from a car accident. Her fainting or being taken to the hospital. There were so many different ways to be "gone," all of them horrifying.

"What do you mean?" Tristan asked, his breathing increasingly shallow.

His father waved drunkenly upstairs, nearly tipping over in the process. "Go see for yourself."

After making sure his dad could stay propped up against the arm of the sofa, Tristan went to investigate. Did his mom pass away in her sleep? Maybe his dad was waiting for the paramedics to come while she lay pale and lifeless in bed. Nearly dizzy from a mix of hyperventilating and adrenaline, Tristan cracked open his parents' bedroom door. Only his mom wasn't tucked beneath the covers with a deathly pallor.

All of her belongings were gone. The picture of them she kept on her nightstand, the trinkets and knickknacks she kept on top of the dresser. A glance into their adjoining bathroom revealed that every single one of her expensive beauty products had also mysteriously disappeared. Already knowing what he'd find, Tristan made his last inspection of the closet. Half her clothes and shoes, along with the suitcase she stored there, were nowhere to be found.

"Gone" took on a whole new meaning. One, that in that moment, felt worse than death. At least death was final. You knew someone had passed on, which meant you could mourn. You knew what to mourn. But this . . .

Tristan sank down on his parents' bed, racking his brain to figure out what he'd done wrong. What he could have possibly done to make his mom abandon them. His mind flashed back to the hurried morning before he and his dad left. His mom had been in the kitchen, cooking up a storm. Tristan's face had lit up when he saw what was in the pan.

"You're making Chorizo Omelet de Tristan," he grinned. His

mom's signature omelet for him. She'd smiled back, her eyes tired and a bit sunken in. It was unusual for his mom to have bags under her eyes, but no matter how worn down she felt, she'd still made him breakfast. Before she could offer him a plate, though, his dad appeared in the doorway.

"He doesn't have time to eat all that crap, Izzy. We're already late." Then he'd stormed off to the car.

At his mom's sad look, Tristan ignored his dad and picked up a Tupperware container. "Serve it up, Mom. You know I won't miss out on this."

"Thank you, honey." Smiling back, she'd hurriedly transferred the omelet from the skillet to the container. Before he dashed out to the car, she wrapped him in a tight hug and kissed the top of his head.

"Good-bye, mijo."

If Tristan had known that this good-bye was the last one, he never would have left the house that day. He would have begged her to stay, to explain. But that had been years ago. Now that she'd come back to do just that, to offer some poor excuse, it was too late.

But the idea of staying home and dwelling on the past didn't sit well with him anymore. Yes, he'd been left behind, all over again. But he refused to stay that way for long. Driven by his instincts, he found himself going to the one place he knew he'd find solace.

Jada's.

When she opened the door, the stony expression on his face, combined with him being drenched from the pouring rain outside, immediately clued her into his state of mind.

"Tristan? What's wrong?" she asked. He answered in the only

way he could think of, the only way to express everything he was feeling.

"I need you," he said. At his distraught voice, she let him in and wrapped him in her arms.

"What happened?" she asked again as they made it to the couch.

"My mom . . . she came to my house. I got home from work and she was there. Appeared out of nowhere."

"Oh my God! What did she want?"

"To apologize, I guess. Or rather, to make excuses."

"What did she say exactly?"

"Does it matter? The point is she thinks she can waltz back into my life and erase everything that's happened. Like the years without her never happened."

"I get that, why you didn't want to talk to her, but . . ." Jada bit her lip uncertainly.

"But what?" Tristan asked warily.

"I know I don't know her, but I don't think she'd come back unless she was being sincere. Unless she truly loves you and wants to make amends."

"Oh yeah. She loved me just enough to leave without a trace. She made it perfectly clear that no one—not even my own mom— would ever love me enough to stick around."

The heartbreaking words flew out of Tristan before he could stop them. He instantly regretted it as pity flooded Jada's eyes. He knew if she prodded even the tiniest bit, he would end up pouring everything else out about the day his mother left. He rushed to cover his tracks.

"What I mean is, if that's all that love is to people, I don't want any part of it."

Because how could he believe in love after watching his family fall apart? Tristan got up from the couch and turned away, hiding the tears that were starting to well in his eyes. He'd come here for comfort, but maybe it would have been better to go to Juan's or call Rafe. People who already knew the depths of his damage. He didn't want Jada to see that desperate hollowness or how weak he was. She didn't let him hide for long, as she came up behind him and wrapped her arms around him in a light hug.

"Yes, some people take love for granted, Tristan. But the right kind of love does exist if you choose to believe in it," she insisted.

Tristan laughed bitterly, turning back to her. "How can you not be cynical after Daniel?"

"Because he wasn't the one. But when you find the right person, you open up to them. You fight for them, protect them, accept them for who they are. If they're truly for you, then they do the same. When love between two people is beautiful like that, you put in the work. You *choose* to stay. And Tristan, *you* are worth sticking around for."

Tristan could hardly breathe, let alone respond to Jada's heartfelt speech. She'd struck him to the core and left his heart racing. All he could do was reach out and hold her hand. When he was finally able to speak, his voice was thick with emotion. "Thank you, Jada. For listening and being here like this."

"Of course, but can I say one more thing?" she asked cautiously.

"Yes?"

"You're dripping water all over my hardwood floor." Jada pointed to their soggy feet.

"Oh shit, I'm sorry!" Tristan ran his fingers through his damp hair, frustrated with the night's whole disaster.

"It's okay. Why don't you take a shower? We can dry your clothes."

"Sounds good, on one condition."

"What?" Now it was Jada's turn to be wary.

"We finish what we started the last time I was in your bathroom."

"Tristan!" Jada slapped him on the chest. "Mikayla is here!"

"In her room. She won't hear us over the shower running."

In spite of her protests, Tristan saw the wheels turning in Jada's mind. Eventually, she gave in, and led him to her room.

As the shower began to heat up, Tristan and Jada squared off, eyeing one another. Surprisingly, Jada was the one to make the first move as she reached for his wet shirt. Lifting it up over his head, she then traced his muscular arms, feeling the goose bumps on his skin.

"Wow, you're cold."

"I'm sure you'll know how to warm me up," Tristan said innocently as he reached for the buttons on Jada's shirt. Slowly undressing her, Tristan caressed her flawless skin as he traveled across her body. From her lush breasts to her curved stomach, and eventually much lower. As he fondled her tender folds, Jada rushed to finish disrobing him.

"I think we can hop in now." Tristan took notice of the steam flowing through the room.

Jada hesitated before stepping into the tub.

"To be honest, I've never done it in the shower before. What if we fall and break our asses?" she asked nervously.

Tristan held back his experienced revelation that it was all about balance, because hell, he wasn't that stupid.

"Trust me, I've got you," Tristan said instead. Placing his

hands on her waist, he guided her into the embrace of the water.

For a while, they did dutifully scrub away. Jada made sure to shampoo Tristan's hair and anoint him in lathers of lavender soap. Its scent, mixed with Jada's intoxicating aroma and the heat, made Tristan's temperature—and other parts of his anatomy—rise. He gave up on showering and pulled Jada into a deep kiss, pushing her back against the tiled wall. They explored each other, melding their bodies together in sensual circles.

At last, Tristan headed toward home. Lifting her with her back still pressed against the wall, he rubbed his erection against her entrance until Jada stiffened.

"Tristan, I'm going to fall if we do it like this," she said, worried they were about to have more of a slip and slide accident rather than a shower sexcapade.

"I got you, babe."

At Jada's reluctant noise of uncertainty, Tristan sighed. He let go of her and eased her feet back down on the shower floor. But he didn't give up completely. Instead, he guided her to the showerhead and got her to wrap her hands around the handle.

"Can you hold on better this way?" Tristan said suggestively.

Jada nodded and Tristan lifted her once more, gripping her hips. Enveloped in exhilarating kisses, Tristan moved inside her. Her wet heat surrounding him was only rivaled by the hot water glistening on their bodies. Jada let out an intense moan, having forgotten about the slippage factor. Tristan wasn't far behind her, losing himself in the sensations of her, of them together as they both reached a fevered, moist ecstasy.

While they came down from the high, Tristan placed Jada's shaky feet back on the floor. He still kept his arms around her, not wanting to leave the warm cocoon the shower had become.

He wasn't ready to get hit with frigid air the second they stepped out of their small haven. That imminent chill would end not only his and Jada's rendezvous, but his escape from reality. His escape from the past and what might happen in the future.

So he stayed wrapped up in Jada as the wet droplets fell.

# 25

The next morning, Tristan left, headed back to his place to change and continue with his press junket. However, he left Jada with more than an afterglow of great sex. There was more to it; a deeper, inner glow. A warmth inside her chest that worried her. After seeing Tristan devastated last night, she knew whatever was between them was more than sex or physical attraction. She cared about him, hated to see him hurting. And when they made love, she felt closer to him than she ever had to any past lover. With his kiss good-bye this morning, that spark of warmth had ignited. The more she thought of him, the more it grew.

And why was that so frightening?

Because it felt like love.

Sipping her morning coffee, Jada mulled over what that meant, to be in love with Tristan. Their perspectives on love were entirely different. When she'd been talking about love existing and all that jazz last night, she realized she had been talking about her and Tristan. Meanwhile, Tristan was a commitmentphobe who scoffed at the idea of love's very existence. Most likely, he didn't feel the same way she did. To him, their arrangement was probably just business with a side of benefits.

Suddenly, her caramel latte tasted a lot like an oncoming assault of acid reflux.

"Hey, cousin!" Mikayla sauntered into the kitchen, cheerful as ever and oblivious to Jada's dilemma.

"You better have brewed a strong pot of coffee because someone kept me up pretty late last night with some noises from her boudoir."

"You heard us?" Jada asked, appalled.

"Yep, which means I expect details on how this happened! When did your relationship with Tristan . . . escalate? And why didn't you tell me?"

Jada's ringing phone saved her from answering. She shrugged helplessly and motioned to the caller ID: Avery Kane refused to be kept waiting.

"Hey, Avery," Jada said, ignoring her cousin's scowl.

"Jada, good news. You got the part."

"For Logan's movie?" she squealed.

"Well, since you haven't had any other major auditions lined up, then yes, Logan's movie."

"Oh wow! This is great. Thanks for letting me know, Avery."

"Don't thank me, thank Tristan. Logan wants you two as the leads. Something about how great your chemistry was and yadda, yadda. Everyone agrees it's a good media tactic to have you both in it. I'll send over more details later."

"Great. I—"

"And don't think I forgot you hung up on me last time." Avery cut Jada off. "So inappropriate."

Proving her own lack of propriety, Avery hung up before Jada could reply. But her snippy dismissal didn't faze Jada.

"I got the part!" she exclaimed to Mikayla.

After they jumped up and down in celebration, Jada whipped out her phone again.

"I have to tell Tristan!"

"Ahem. Speaking of . . ." Mikayla brought them back to their earlier topic.

"It's complicated."

"As in?"

"As in we're in cahoots in this whole big plot together, and we've both got baggage and secrets . . . and I might be falling in love with him," Jada blurted.

"Damn," Mikayla said.

"Exactly."

"Well, maybe you two will find a way to be together. *Really* together." Mikayla tried again.

"Kayla, can we drop it, please? I don't want to get my hopes up more than they already are," Jada confessed.

Mikayla relented sadly, and Jada texted Tristan to inform him of the news. Thrilled, he insisted they go out to dinner. While she was anxious about seeing him when her feelings were so unsettled, she agreed anyway, unable to resist him.

Around seven they met up at a local Italian hot spot. The second she saw Tristan waiting for her outside, her heart did that disturbing little flutter she was beginning to dread.

"Reina, congratulations!" he said, kissing her thoroughly, perfectly, despite the flashing bulbs of the paparazzi outside. Or was it because of them? God, she hated thinking about this! Especially when it ruined a good kiss.

Tristan didn't sense her hesitance. Oblivious, he held her hand as they walked inside. He continued to hold on to her until they made it to their seats. His newfound affection drove her crazy. She wasn't used to the PDA, and especially not the way it made her feel.

After they ordered, Tristan returned his full attention to her.

"I don't know about you, but I'm fucking excited. We did it, Jada!"

"Yes, we did. Together," Jada said, her poor, pitiful heart glowing at his smile.

"I'm so glad I was able to fulfill my promise to you. Things will only get better from here on out, I swear."

"I know they will," Jada lied to them both.

"Soon, you'll be a superstar, and you won't even need me. This whole thing will be over."

Damn. That hurt. The jackass didn't seem to notice her stung expression. Instead, he clinked glasses with her in a toast.

It would be just like that? She'd get "true fame" and then he'd bounce? Cheers! Looking back on the deal they made, Jada realized the terms on her side had changed. Like he was not supposed to leave her ever. Ugh, what would her Black Women Hall of Fame team have to say about this?

"Are you ready for the trip?" Tristan broke through her What would Lena Horne do? conundrum.

"Trip?" Jada forced herself to refocus.

"You know, the premiere for *Rival Warriors*. You're flying with me to New York, in, like, two days."

"Right, of course. I've already started packing my bags," Jada said, suspecting all over again that maybe all he cared about was the bargain. About contracts and appearances. Fake kisses and fraudulent feelings. It was so hard to equate these callous remarks with the same man who'd broken down to her about his mom, who'd shown her such tenderness in his weakest moments.

Jada looked down, placing her napkin in her lap to fight back what she was feeling. She could call him out for dismissing what they had. Then again, aside from those moments of deep pillow talk, what *did* they really have? Great sex, lies, and ambition. She knew that, and she was tired of fighting. It was better to give in this time, to let this one go.

Besides, why argue with the truth?

# 26

Sitting on the runway, Tristan gave Jada an appraising look.

"I know your track record with Ferris wheels but what about planes? You going to be okay for the next few hours?" he asked her.

"I fly often enough for different jobs, and I'm fine. The only thing that throws me off is bad turbulence," Jada replied. She avoided eye contact with him, glancing out the window.

Frowning, Tristan studied his companion. He'd been doing that a lot lately. Just looking at her. Paying attention to every expression, each movement. So quickly she'd entranced him. It was like once he finally saw her, all of her, he couldn't look away. And it wasn't just because of her beauty. It was about seeing her smile when something made her happy, the joy he got from making her laugh.

None of that was evident today.

Ever since Tristan had picked her up so they could go to the airport, Jada had been suspiciously quiet. Sullen even. It wasn't like the old days back when they'd constantly been at each other's throats. This wasn't animosity she was throwing at him. It was something more brooding. Something worse.

But as he racked his brain, he couldn't think of what he'd done to upset her. After confiding in her the night his mom waltzed back into his life, he'd felt closer to Jada than he ever had to anyone else. Today, he couldn't get a sense of her at all.

Things remained relatively uneventful for a while, aside from Jada tensing up at takeoff. She squeezed his hand but had eventually gone back to looking at the bright sky outside.

He shook his packet of peanuts at her, drawing her attention back to him.

"You think for first-class they'd spring for name brand, Planters. Want some?"

"No, thank you," Jada said politely, then turned back to the window.

"We can order whatever you want. We're big-timers after all. You want to see if I can get you some filet mignon instead?"

"What time is the premiere tomorrow?" Jada asked.

"Around seven. You in a hurry to walk the red carpet with me?"

"Of course. I wouldn't want to miss any opportunity to reach superstar status," she said nonchalantly.

Oh. It finally hit him. The other night at dinner. The stupid comments he made. To him, it hadn't meant anything, but he'd rattled her.

He bit the inside of his cheek. He couldn't find the words to explain to her that it had all been him being a thoughtless jackass. Of course he didn't want to end things with her—not after everything they'd been through together. Jada had become so much more to him than the attractive girl he'd taken his anger out on in that dressing room. Jada was more than his co-star now, more than his cohort in their scheme. She was . . .

The plane suddenly shook with unforeseen force. Like many of the other passengers, Tristan and Jada both jolted upright in their seats.

"Sorry, folks. It looks like we're about to run into a bit of turbulence. Please stay seated."

"Jeez, don't they usually give you the warning *before* the aircraft pulls the avalanche act," Tristan said to Jada, but as he glanced over, he saw her petrified face. Her eyes were squeezed shut, just like on their Ferris wheel ride.

"You're fine, Jada. I'm right here with you," Tristan said, holding her hand. He held on more tightly at her timid grip. "You can hold on to me as tight as you want."

Wonderfully, she took him up on it. She leaned against his shoulder, huddled in his embrace, as the world quaked around them. He held her like that until the storm passed. He felt her tension ease as she fell asleep on his shoulder.

Show, his ass. This had stopped being a show a long time ago. He was in deep now. He was . . .

No. Love wasn't in the cards for him. He'd decided that. But if this wasn't love, what the hell was he feeling?

By the time they landed and reached the Plaza hotel in New York, Tristan had worked himself into such an inner crisis that he was even quieter than Jada. He couldn't think of anything witty to say to cheer her up and didn't have a plan for what they should do, other than check into their room and stare at each other in the growing awkwardness. As they reached the reception desk, they were saved from that fate. Tristan's co-star, Davie, as well as their director, Bryan Ryder, were also in the lobby and noticed them immediately.

"Hey, Tristan!" Davie called with a cheerful wave. Tristan waved back as the director and actor walked toward them.

"Hey, guys, nice to see we've all arrived in one piece," he said, before placing his hand on Jada's back. "This is Jada."

For some reason it felt weird to tack on the obligatory "my girlfriend." First, because everyone here already knew about their "relationship." And secondly, because all the alarming thoughts from the plane ride hadn't stopped screaming at Tristan in bright, red letters: Commitmentphobe in COMPLETE DENIAL. No one called him out on it, though, because they were too busy gawking at Jada.

"So you're the enchanting Jada Berklee. It's nice to meet you at last. Tristan wouldn't stop gushing about you during the press junket." Davie shook her hand.

"Lies. Wild exaggerations," Tristan interjected, his internal panic still strong.

Everyone continued to ignore him, chitchatting about their flights and how nice the hotel was ("Whirlpool tubs, guys!" according to Davie). The conversation started to wind to a close as the front-desk clerk handed Tristan and Jada their key cards. The reality of Tristan and Jada coexisting in a hotel room in stony silence loomed closer until Bryan stopped them from heading up.

"Last thing, I promise. I'm not sure what you guys have planned for the evening, and I know you have some appearances tomorrow morning before the premiere, but did you hear about the Legends exhibit?"

Not much of a museum person, Tristan had not, but Jada's face lit up.

"Yes! It's the new wing in Madame Tussauds about LGBTQIA+ heroes. It finally opened?"

"Premiere is tonight, and one of my friends is being immortalized there. I can get you guys in if you want to go," Bryan offered.

Jada's head whipped toward Tristan and she gazed up at him with beseeching eyes. It was the first sign all day that her old spark might come back.

"Yeah, of course, we want to go. Thanks, Bryan."

After agreeing to meet up at Madame Tussauds that evening, Tristan and Jada made their way up to their room. Jada came back alive, chattering the whole while.

"Thank you, Tristan. I know you're not really a museum guy—"

"Hey, I like culture. Just not stuffy *old* culture." Tristan complained as he held the hotel room door open for her.

"I know. Trust me, this will be more fun." While she unpacked, Jada went on to list everything the new wing was supposed to include and what celebrities were supposed to show up. "It's going to be an extremely hot guest list. Besides, it's another good photo op for us, right?"

Tristan's genuine smile faltered. "Right," he said, trying to keep his tone light.

Jada spent the next half hour looking up other news about the exhibit as well as deciding on her outfit for that evening. Tristan used the downtime to check the times and events scheduled for tomorrow. There were a lot of appearances to put in before the premiere that night, so he wouldn't get to see much of Jada during the day. It was actually a good thing that they'd get to spend tonight out on the town. He had the unsettling feeling this might be one of the few times they'd get to truly enjoy their trip.

# 27

Working in the world of entertainment, Jada had been to plenty of her own premieres and opening events, but something about visiting Madame Tussauds for this historic exhibit gave her an extra thrill. She always found the art of creating wax masterpieces fascinating. And while other Tussauds locations had figures of Laverne Cox and other iconic people within the LGBTQIA+ community, it was completely different for a location to dedicate a whole new section.

A nagging part of her admitted it also had to do with being in New York with Tristan. Taking a trip together held a "seriously dating" vibe. When their journey first started, she kept reminding herself about Tristan's comments and that it was all pretend, but being aloof hadn't worked as well as she'd hoped. Tristan's concern about her phobia on the plane had started to melt the ice. Once he agreed to a night of museum sightseeing on her behalf, her mood thawed completely. Now, she was just excited to create this new memory with him. Even when their deal was over, at least they would have this evening as a reminder of the good times they'd had together.

Around eight o'clock, they were both dressed up and ready to go. With the Plaza only a short walk away from the museum's prime Times Square location, they decided to take in the sights. With her arm draped through Tristan's, Jada took in the majesty of the city as they traversed the bustling sidewalk. The multitude of lights from the skyscrapers and flashy awnings smiled down on them as the nighttime breeze spurred on the prospect of a new adventure. As they passed by the array of theaters and gaudy restaurants, Jada's fondness for the city reemerged. New York might not be the only city in the world, but the energy here was truly special.

"God, if it weren't for the fact that so many bigwigs still call Hollywood home, I swear I could live here," Jada confessed to Tristan. "To hell with the four-hour traffic jams and a vegan spot on every corner."

"I did live here for a while after *Garcia Central*. Had a few recurring roles here and there before my first big film. New York certainly has its charms," Tristan agreed.

Jada hummed, already knowing what charms he must be referring to. "Ah, so this is when the playboy ways picked up, huh?"

An unmistakable blush crept over his face, but Tristan marched onward. "My point is, I've always thought about getting another place here. Then we could visit whenever we wanted."

Jada stumbled, her steps coming to an abrupt halt at this revelation. She should have coolly played it off, but his casual tone had thrown her. What was wrong with this man? One minute he was reminding her they were only in a temporary arrangement, the next he was going on about buying a place for them to have their own getaway spot.

"Not that I'm making plans or anything." Tristan pivoted, his eyes wide. "What I meant was—"

"Look, we're almost there." Jada pointed ahead to the iconic building.

Madame Tussauds shone brightly, its name glowing on the outside panel. But its most distinctive features were the hands strategically placed around the building. At the front entrance, a silver hand bordered the door, while a golden one had been placed atop the roof near the titular sign. The whimsical design gave off the air that an omnipotent master dollmaker might be behind the scenes. There were plenty of people queued around the building. Some everyday customers waited for entry while members of the press interviewed the more high-profile guests who managed to bypass the line. Jada hated the idea of being seen as a "cutter," but Bryan's ability to get them around the wait time was too good to pass up. Leaving their uncomfortable conversation behind, Jada grabbed Tristan's hand and steered them toward the museum. Once the press caught sight of them, bulbs flashed in rapid succession and journalists shouted for their attention.

"Tristan! Jada! How are you enjoying your time in New York?"

"What are you looking forward to seeing tonight?"

"Tristan! Are you ready for *Rival Warriors* to come out?"

"Jada, what's your next role?"

Jada paused at this last question. Usually when the public spotted them, a lot of inquiries were directed to Tristan. This was the first time anyone had asked something so specific about her career. As Tristan went to talk to the guard at the door, Jada addressed the journalist.

"I'm actually up for a few things right now, and will be keeping people posted online once I have more news."

"Great! Do you think you and Tristan will act together again?"

*Okay, back to relationship talk, I guess*, Jada thought. Although, as everyone kept reminding her, Jada had her current project with Logan thanks to her deal with Tristan.

"Who knows? Hopefully!" Jada maintained a cheery air.

"Babe, we can go in now." Tristan came back over to fill her in.

With a few more waves and parting words, they stepped through the main doors. The lobby was packed with people waiting to be let into the new wing. Waiters circulated with cocktail-hour fare. Jada spotted several guests who would be honored tonight with a wax version of themselves. She eventually found Bryan and Davie at the bar with Kori Jones. Jada urgently pulled on Tristan's arm.

"Whoa! Watch it," Tristan warned, saving his mini quiche from hitting the floor.

"You didn't mention Bryan's in was Kori Jones!"

"I didn't know. Bryan literally knows everyone."

Jada barely registered Tristan's reply, too caught up in finding one of her favorite musicians a few feet away. As a prolific rapper, Kori Jones had made waves not just with her controversial lyrics but also as one of the few transgender artists thriving in the hip hop genre. Realizing Jada had mentally checked out on him, Tristan grabbed her hand again.

"Okay, let's go over and intro—"

That was all Jada needed to move lightning fast through the room and over to Bryan's side. The director greeted them exuberantly, raising his glass.

"Hey, so glad you guys could make it."

"Of course, wouldn't miss it."

"Kori, this is—"

"Bry, I know who they are. I'm going to see your film tomorrow, fool." Kori dazzled them with her megastar power as she held out her hand. With her avant-garde fashion and her hair done up in elaborate, colorful twists, she looked every bit like the cultural icon the Billboard charts couldn't stop talking about.

"Nice to meet you. Kori Jones."

"We know who you are too," Jada gushed. "I've still got 'Save the Nation' on repeat. Congrats on getting a statue tonight."

"Thank you. It's a little intimidating knowing I'm going to have a Mini-Me around. I'm very curious to see how it turned out."

On the verge of fangirling harder, Jada put her burning questions for Kori on hold as a bell dinged throughout the lobby. Jessie Andrews, the current leader of the museum's board, stood dressed to the nines in the entryway that led to the exhibit. Apparently, the need to make a grand opening speech was his reason for blocking their path.

"Thank you, everyone, for being here tonight. I'm going to say what we're all thinking: it's about time! As the world continues to evolve, our team at Madame Tussauds is determined to stay on the cutting edge of pop culture. With our Legends wing, we're showcasing innovative trailblazers and the groundbreaking stars you've come to love."

While the host's overall sentiment on progress was nice, Jada remained antsy, itching to go inside. At last, their host's splashy showboating ended, and Kori held out her arm to Jada.

"Shall we?" the artist asked, and Jada gladly took her offer. As they walked in together, Tristan muttered after them.

"Should I be jealous?" he asked.

"I'll give her back later. Don't worry," Kori said, unfazed. Her breezy response, and Davie and Bryan's amused chuckles, didn't satisfy him. Instead, Tristan quickened his step to stay on Jada's other side.

The Legends wing had been broken down into several themes. Toward the front, Madame Tussauds had gone with a historic approach. They'd created an elaborate backdrop of the Stonewall Inn. The faux brick building had a lit-up sign with the bar's name alongside rainbow flags. The figurines placed here were a slew of different activists, some holding up picket signs or raised firsts. Marsha P. Johnson stood out in the middle of the scene, wearing a replica of one of her beautiful flower crowns.

Farther into the hall, the landmark imagery of historical moments gave way to pop culture montages. Iconic moments from *The L Word*, *Queer Eye*, *Will & Grace*, and *Pose* paraded across screens. Several of the shows' most famous scenes were highlighted on the projector while figures of the directors and performers were also on display. Then things shifted more toward the typical Madame Tussauds expertise with celebrities, and they finally came across Kori's own statue.

"Well?" Kori asked, standing next to her model. For the statue, they'd chosen to go with her outfit from the previous year's Grammy Awards. The tailored suit sparkled with vivid pinstripes, with a corset instead of a typical vest, and matching fedora.

"Mini-Me perfection, for sure," Jada promised.

"Let's just hope she doesn't come alive and try and take over your life," Tristan added forebodingly.

Kori took several pictures with her wax counterpart, and Jada snuck in a shot with them too. Several of Kori's other fans also wanted to get in on the action, strategically pushing Jada out of the way. Sensing that she probably had taken up a lot of the rapper's time, Jada made her way back over to Tristan, who welcomed her into his arms.

"Having fun?"

"Yes, are you?"

"It's definitely better than the MOMA or a million marble penises."

"So rude." Jada chastised him by poking him in the stomach. "But also, thank you for bringing me."

"Mmm, I'm glad you remembered that. I thought I was about to lose you to the superstar over there."

Jada winced. "Sorry, it's hard not to freak out around her."

"I think I need more than a thank you, though." At Tristan's continued sulking, Jada kissed him on the cheek. Still not satisfied, Tristan pulled her to him for something more thorough. Jada closed her eyes as he came in for the landing but felt nothing. Peeking up at him, she saw that Tristan's face had taken on a stormy shade.

"What is it?" she asked.

"*Them*." Tristan nodded at two people standing next to the Queer Eye franchise.

Jada's heart stopped as she saw who he was staring at.

The Tea Twins were here. She shouldn't have been surprised since the *Sip That Tea* founders had a huge following. Obviously, they would jump at the chance to cover a star-studded event like this. And with Tristan giving them the death glare, they were only moments away from noticing Tristan and Jada too.

"Don't. They're not our problem." Jada cautioned him.

"Not our problem? Jada, they've been trashing us for weeks

with bad intel. You may be able to shrug it off, but I want answers."

Tristan twisted out of her embrace and headed toward the two influencers. Jada followed him, praying Tristan didn't cause another damaging outburst. When she caught up to them, Tristan had started in on Tammy and Tegan.

"I want a name," he demanded. "Tell me who you've been talking to."

"Honey, no matter how macho you want to act, we can't reveal our sources," Tammy countered, then turned to Jada. "J, please tell your roid rage boyfriend the truth."

Forget her heart stopping. For a moment, Jada felt her soul leave her body. Tammy had just sworn they wouldn't rat out their informants but had put Jada on blast. Mikayla had promised she'd sent the video of Tristan and Jada fighting anonymously, but clearly Tammy had pieced it together. Was she willing to throw Jada under the bus about the first leak to protect their other insider?

"The t-truth?" Jada stuttered, shaking in shock.

"That hassling people like this is what caused his problems in the first place," Tegan said, placing a protective arm around his sister.

"You're the ones prying into people's private lives and spewing lies," Tristan insisted. "Just because somebody like Angela feeds you a rumor—"

"Maxwell, you are so far off. Angela is not the real problem. Although she did warn us you were getting pretty wild with your accusations."

"Baby brother, he's not *that* far off. We'll give you a hint since you're superadamant. The snake in your garden? Their initials are A. C."

Tristan didn't get the chance to interrogate them further

because another journalist called out to the two bloggers. Probably desperate to share some other juicy gossip. Tristan watched them go with a furrowed brow.

"A. C. is definitely Angela Collins, right, Jada? They're just trying to confuse me. I mean, who else has those initials?" While Tristan puzzled over what they'd learned, Jada struggled to get her inner hysteria under control. The twins might not have known about Jada's role in releasing the video, but this encounter proved one thing: Jada's plausible deniability would not last indefinitely. Tristan seemed determined to find out what was really going on with *Sip That Tea* and their snitches.

If he found out that one of the aforementioned snitches had been Jada. . . . Now sick to her stomach, she tapped Tristan on the shoulder.

"Do you think we can go outside? Maybe get some fresh air?" she asked.

Tristan agreed and went to tell Bryan they were heading out. Meanwhile, Jada tried to keep her roiling revulsion at bay.

So much for tonight being about creating a special memory. The only thing she had to reflect on now was borrowed time.

With the Tea Twins officially souring the mood, Tristan fully supported Jada's decision to leave. That shitty clue they had given him left him stewing over whether he could pin down the culprit with that meager information. It was only when the chilly air hit them outside and he noticed Jada shivering that Tristan regained a bit of his senses.

"I'm sorry. I guess we didn't account for how cold it would get later."

As Tristan wrapped his arms around her to warm Jada up, she leaned into him wordlessly. Obviously, she'd been affected by Tammy and Tegan's toxicity too. Tristan geared up to ask if she wanted to simply head back to the hotel, but after the night starting off so well, he hated to leave things as they were. Glancing down the street, he saw another gaudy sign twinkling at them. With the name *Celia's* flashing at them, Tristan found a way to save the evening.

"Jada, I hope those are your get-down pumps." Tristan motioned to Jada's sparkly gold high heels.

"What in the world are you talking about?"

He pointed to the brick building. "Because we're going dancing."

"I see. Are you trying to drag me to a discotheque, Mr. Warhol?" Jada eyed the building suspiciously.

"Better. It's this great little salsa place. I forgot it was in this part of town."

"You can dance salsa too?"

"A little." He shrugged. "I had to learn for one of my movies. I picked up one or two things."

"Sorry, but I'm not really in a dancing mood," Jada said, confirming Tristan's suspicions regarding the effect of the terrible Tea Twins. Regardless, he refused to accept defeat.

"Come on. They've also got kick-ass margaritas. I know how you feel about margaritas, Miss Yams."

Jada flushed, but then relented. "Fine. You'll dance. I'll drink. How's that?"

That concession was fine with Tristan. Especially when he and Jada entered Celia's, and Jada's sullen air lifted. Named after the magnificent Cuban singer Celia Cruz, the place was adorned with pictures of her and her famous performances. Portraits of other important Latin artists also lined the walls, everyone from Selena and Calle 13 to Mexico's sweetheart, Angélica María. Beneath the extensive collage, the walls were decked out in splashes of bright red and yellow, and the dance floor was full of exultant bodies swaying to the live music.

After Jada fulfilled her part of the deal by drop kicking a giant margarita and a handful of salty tortilla chips, Tristan insisted that she get out on the floor with him. Luckily, the music had switched to a slower number as he guided her around the floor. Everything was light and easy until the band moved into their next song and the tempo changed. As a quick cha-cha struck up, Tristan moved faster. Jada managed to keep up as he twirled her into a graceful and impressive dip.

"You told me you could only dance a little," Jada said, already out of breath.

"Depends on your definition of a little." Tristan shrugged lightly, not wanting to reveal the truth: his mom had started teaching him different Latin dance styles right about the same time he learned to walk.

"Why, Tristan Maxwell, you're full of surprises." Jada laughed.

Looking down at her joyful smile, a different truth slipped out of him.

"And you have been the best surprise of my life, Jada Berklee."

Touched, Jada lowered her eyes, trying—and failing—to hide her emotions. She looked back up and swooped in for a passionate kiss.

"I think I'm ready for a different kind of dance," Jada said after pulling away.

"What do you mean?"

"Like the bedroom tango," she said mischievously.

"We just got here!" Tristan laughed.

"Are you complaining?"

"I'd never go against my queen's wishes." Tristan held his hand to his chest in a sign of loyalty.

Giving in to her desires, they made their way back to the hotel. The task took far too long, and once they arrived, the accommodations felt lackluster. Sure, the bed was comfy and the room was clean, but something was missing.

"Well, babe, I'm sorry there are no rose petals or champagne. Didn't have time to plan this out," Tristan said.

"Hey, at least, there's not a pool ball digging into my butt."

"Or that waterpark hazard that freaked you out but that you ended up *loving*," Tristan teased.

"Shut your filthy mouth, Mr. Maxwell!" Jada said in mock anger, but he pulled her toward him.

"You love my filthy mouth and all the things it can do to you." He nipped at her bottom lip and she opened up for him.

When they pulled away, the heat of the moment had come back for both of them.

"It's still okay like this though, isn't it?" Jada asked shyly. "Even without the perfect ambiance with chocolate or sexy rain, being together, just us, is nice . . . right?"

"Just us is perfect," he reassured her. Staring into her sparkling eyes, his emotions running through him, the truth hit him. It finally hit him and he knew for sure now.

He did love Jada.

He could feel the words on the tip of his tongue. He should say them now before the moment passed. Hell, before he changed his mind or lied to himself.

"Tristan, are you okay?" Jada prompted when he continued to stand there like an idiot.

"Jada, I . . ." Tristan started, ready for his true feelings to pour out.

*Say it, damn it.*

But as Jada's expectant, caring eyes stared up at him, the beautiful confession he wanted to make remained trapped on his tongue.

What the hell should he say now?

# 28

As Jada and Tristan stood in the hotel room, a sense of foreboding crept over Jada. Tristan wasn't saying anything, and it was seriously freaking her out.

"What is it, Tristan?" She searched his face anxiously.

Was them being together actually not perfect like he claimed? Was he going to turn around and reaffirm everything he'd said at that dinner? He'd make it clear that all of this was temporary. Having that confirmation from him could be for the best. It would hurt like hell, but at least she could retreat before things got any deeper.

"I was going to say that these last few weeks with you have been special. Better than I could have imagined. Thank you for giving me a shot," Tristan said at last.

Jada was about to respond but Tristan cut her off with a kiss. They'd had quite a few since they'd started the romantic side of their relationship, but none like this. This was some next level shit. Passion ran through every stroke of his tongue, in the way he caressed her face and pressed her against him like they would never be close enough. They weren't even naked yet but it felt like he was making love to her with every inch of his body through this one kiss.

As they undressed each other, there was a sense of both urgency and longing, as if Tristan couldn't get enough of her. As if he never would. Jada relished that feeling, praying for it to be true. Maybe Tristan didn't have finesse with words, but the way he expressed himself through actions spoke louder.

He made love to her that night in a way he never had before. He'd always been tender and mind blowing, but tonight, he was even more thorough. Savoring every curve of her body, committing it to memory. Filling her more deeply in an attempt to remain there always.

It was spiritual.

It confirmed that she truly was his.

Before she fell asleep wrapped in Tristan's arms, she faintly heard him whisper, "*Te quiero*," in her ear.

She wasn't sure what that meant, but she did know she would never love another man like this again. Tristan Maxwell had her heart.

Forever.


Jada remained eternally grateful that despite his dashing good looks, Tristan was relatively low maintenance. He gave her dominion over the hotel bathroom as she prepared her ensemble for the night's premiere. Technically, the grand suite's abode left room for the both of them to get ready, but she was positive if they undressed around each other, they'd miss the film's big night altogether.

Seriously, the way Tristan had made love to her yesterday. . . The sex between them was always good, but last night had been different. Deep down, she was sure he'd felt the shift between them, too, but she didn't dare ask.

After Jada gathered her thoughts, got ready, and stepped out of the bathroom, she expected a trademark once-over of appreciation from Tristan. She found herself doing one for him, as he looked exceptionally debonair tonight: the perfect leading man.

"You look amazing," Tristan said, sincerity radiating in his warm gaze. He held out his arm to her. "Would you do me the honor of escorting you tonight?"

"I suppose so," Jada said, stifling an amused giggle.

They made it to the red carpet in record time, and their arrival brought out the works in terms of flashing lights and excited screams from the crowd.

While doing a few interviews and signing things for the adoring public, Jada felt as if she and Tristan were the stars of the night. Reporters flooded Tristan with questions about *Rival Warriors* but also asked them both about *Love Locket*. A perky reporter from *Deadline Hollywood* even moved past the what really happened on set questions.

"So, Jada, after your whirlwind romance, do you feel you and Tristan will still be walking the red carpet together when *Love Locket* premieres?" the woman asked.

Knowing the release of the film wouldn't be any time soon, it was a good question. One Jada didn't have the answer to. Would she and Tristan still be keeping up this charade a year from now? It was highly doubtful, but Tristan offered the reporter a broad smile.

"There's no one else I'd rather share that night with." Tristan answered for them. Unfortunately, Tristan's skillful save got overshadowed by a new eruption of screaming at another couple's arrival farther down the red carpet.

That couple being none other than Angela . . . and Daniel.

Angela popping up at the mere mention of *Love Locket* proved that manifestation was no joke. But bringing Daniel along with her? That was an awful, karmic twist. How did they even know each other? And why—why the *hell*—was she here at all?

The answer became clear when she threw Tristan and Jada a small nod, her eyebrow raised in a cocky challenge. The conniving bitch knew exactly what she was doing: piercing Jada's heart in one fatal blow. Daniel's gaze followed Angela's, and Jada found herself locking eyes with him. Was he here to gloat, too, after the way she'd dissed him at the club? To remind Jada that despite how far she'd come he would always be around as a symbol of her downfall. Just as her emotions began to overflow, she felt a firm, strong arm wrap around her shoulders. Tristan held her close and whispered in her ear.

"Don't you dare give them the satisfaction of seeing you sweat. This is your night, Jada. Do you hear me?" he said.

"Technically, I believe it's your night," she said in meek gratitude.

"From now on, what's mine is yours." With that as his final decree, he led her into the auditorium, leaving their malicious adversaries far behind. Truthfully, as the night went on, Jada almost forgot about them. The two chuckleheads weren't seated next to them inside the theater, and the film itself was so engaging Jada lost herself in all the action. Tristan had done a fantastic job as usual. Witty, handsome, totally badass: the perfect action star.

As the lights finally came up and the raucous applause started, she couldn't help but kiss him. For his brilliance as an actor, but also just for him. For him being there with her. For simply being her Tristan. He welcomed her affection and raised their intertwined fingers in a victory salute to the pleased audience. The crowd grew even more ecstatic when Bryan announced there would be an afterparty at the Plaza.

As people began to disperse, Tristan temporarily disengaged from her.

"Let me talk to Bryan for a minute and then we can head to the party. Okay?"

Jada agreed and patiently waited as he walked off to discuss premiere affairs with his co-stars and the director. That small reprieve from his warmth was long enough for a clammy hand to come down on her shoulder. Turning, she came face to face with Daniel.

"Jada, I—"

"I have nothing to say to you," she said, cold and firm.

"But I need to talk to you. After we ran into each other at the lounge, I just wanted to get close enough to tell you—"

"To what? Lie to me all over again? News flash, Daniel: I *liked* not having seen you in forever. And now that I finally have, you're hanging out with the queen of sleaze."

"Look, I know I messed up, but what if I want you back?" His false attitude of contrition matched with such a ludicrous proposition caused Jada to let out a loud, sarcastic laugh. Leave it to Daniel to come sniffing around Jada after seeing her cozied up with Tristan in the tabloids.

"You can't be serious. Does your Munich teenybopper know you're taking other women to events while also trying to hook up with your ex? I mean, this is an ambitious amount of womanizing even for you."

"Tilly and I broke up. Mainly because I still haven't gotten over you."

"Well, I am over it." Her denial should have been enough to end the conversation but Daniel continued pleading with her.

"Come on, Jada. You honestly think Tristan will be any better in the long run? The man's a dog. He's only using you to make himself look good."

"And he's going to drop you the second he gets bored," Angela chimed in as she sidled up to them and looped her arm through Daniel's. "Seriously, you should take Daniel back. Tristan will only make you cry. We're just trying to help you see reason."

"That's funny coming from you, Angela. The entitled princess of Hollywood wants to talk to me about seeing reason? The same woman who berated and belittled me on set day in and day out— even before Tristan became an issue between us?"

"Jesus, Jada. That happened ages ago."

"Try weeks." Jada shook her head in disbelief. It was pointless standing here arguing with this woman. Angela lived in a world with no accountability and nothing Jada said today would change that.

"So, I was rude, and you were a boyfriend thief. That doesn't change the fact that I came here to tell you something else. Something way more important."

"Thanks, but I'm not interested." Jada started to walk past them, but Angela's next words chilled her to the bone.

"Not even if I know who *Sip That Tea*'s mole is?"

Jada froze, her throat closing up as she became speechless with fear. She didn't dare ask the question on her lips, "Which mole?" Had Angela only found out the identity of A. C. or was this her way of ratting Jada out too? Looking into the blond beauty's knowledgeable gaze, Jada couldn't be sure. Either way, if this was a vendetta or Angela's attempt at a redemption tour, the truth would break whatever real connection Jada shared with Tristan. The mere thought of him acted like a beacon as Tristan's sharp voice pulled her back to reality.

"What the hell are you two saying to her?" Tristan came up, protectively standing between Jada and the interlopers.

"Nothing. Just having a little chat. But I think I've left Jada with enough things to consider. Ta-ta for now. Congrats on the mediocre action flick, Trist," Angela said as she steered Daniel away.

"You okay? Do you want to go back to the hotel?" Tristan asked her, worry creasing his brows. All Jada could do was nod silently, still too shaken to speak. Once they'd reached the hotel room, her mute demeanor had put Tristan's anxiety at an all-time high.

"Jada, please. Talk to me. What did they say to you?"

"Nothing that wasn't true," she said numbly.

"What do you mean?" he asked, sitting beside her on the bed. She couldn't bear to have him that near to her. Not when she was realizing how she was never going to escape the truth about what she'd done or the fact that she and Tristan were not a real couple. They weren't in love. They were . . . nothing.

"Jada, talk to me. Do . . . do you still have feelings for Daniel?" Tristan asked.

"No, it's not that."

"Then don't go near him anymore. If he bothers you again, come get me. I won't let him hurt you again," Tristan said. He tried to pull her closer but she resisted, shaking her hand out of his grasp.

He was getting almost as worked up as she was, although for different reasons. His was jealousy, while hers was . . . well, a plethora of things. Aside from Daniel's and Angela's harsh words scarring her, Jada couldn't shrug off her dark thoughts. Tristan would never forgive her for hiding her connection to *Sip That Tea*. And honestly, Jada would never forgive *herself* if she kept stalling and let Tristan eventually find out about her deception from Angela or the Tea Twins.

As Tristan stared at her with such earnestness, Billie Holiday's words from Jada's fever dream echoed in her head. *When you start with deceit, it will never turn out the way you hope it will.* Imaginary Billie had been right, and now was the time. Time to blow all of this open and face the truth.

"Who are you to talk about hurting me? This is all a big game to you," she said. While it killed Jada to do it, she reluctantly fell into a new role: the backstabber. It was the only way to save face, to prepare her heart for Tristan's future hatred.

"What the hell are you talking about?" Tristan frowned.

"I'm talking about several things. Like how you don't actually care about me. How I'm not your real girlfriend. How this is going to end soon. I don't understand why you're pretending like I matter to you. We both know that's not true."

Tristan didn't get the chance to refute her argument as she went full steam ahead, driving their relationship further off the tracks. Ready for things to go down in flames.

"Maybe it's the whole being an actor thing. But guess what? You don't have to play the role of the doting boyfriend when we're alone. Unless it's about the sex, which you can get from someone else anyway."

She could see it. Rage and hurt boiled up inside Tristan,

marring his strong features. She could practically hear his thoughts. Is that what she thought about him? Yes, for now, it had to be.

"All right." Tristan nodded before going on slowly. "So according to you, I'm a callous bastard who doesn't give a shit about anything, and I'm only using you for professional and sexual gratification. Do I have that right?"

"Something like that, yes."

"Then I have one question for you, Jada. Why the fuck are you still here? You're acting superior, but you're only in this for your career. The sex must be good for you, too, or else it wouldn't have gone on this long. Get off your high horse, because you're using me too."

"You're right, Tristan. I have been using you. For longer than you know."

"Meaning?"

"Meaning the Tea Twins were elated when I gave them the inside scoop—or should I say, behind the scenes video—about us."

Boom. It was done. Everything they ever could have had was dead.

She knew this immediately from Tristan's look of betrayal.

"It was you? This whole time, through everything, it was you?"

"Just the first leak, but yes. I'm the traitor you've been looking for," Jada said as coldly as she could manage, hoping the tears brimming in her eyes weren't too obvious.

Tristan closed his own, probably trying to hide whatever he was feeling. For an excruciatingly long moment he was silent, his jaw working angrily as he held back whatever he wanted to say. Probably to call her a bitch, tell her that he hated her, that she was a terrible human being. What he said, in the end, was far worse.

"I never want to see you again." His icy stare bored into her soul, finding it lacking. Disgusting even. After that heart-shattering admission, Tristan headed for the door, then turned back. "Oh, and don't you dare accept the role from Logan. You only got that gig because of me, and I'll be damned if I'll let you keep it."

Jada started to argue, but her words fell on deaf ears as Tristan slammed the door on his way out. Sitting back down on the bed, she looked around. She was alone, heartbroken, and jobless once again. Only this time, she couldn't blame Daniel. She couldn't even blame Tristan. This one was on her. She'd gotten herself into this lovelorn mess, and there would be no knight in shining armor to fix everything she'd wrecked.

From now on, she'd have to save herself.

# 29

Back in California, Jada's first order of business was to unload on Mikayla and Alia. As she suspected, her friends' mouths dropped in horrified shock at her tale. The Daniel and Angela debacle, her guilty confession, Tristan's vow to kick her off the film. The whole scenario garnered the appropriate expletives, gasps, and sympathetic groans.

"But—but you *can't* turn down this role, Jada. It's a game changer," Alia insisted.

"Alia, you damn workaholic! Fuck that! Her heart is broken." Mikayla cuddled up to Jada in a comforting hug. However, the only embrace she wanted was the one she'd never get again.

"You both make good points." Jada bridged the gap. "But two things are clear. Getting over Tristan will be hard but it's a must. Giving up on my career again isn't."

"There's my girl!" Alia hooted.

"I'm not letting a man dictate what I do with my career ever again." Jada nodded.

"That's all well and good, and I fully support you, but . . . what if Tristan issues an ultimatum and Logan chooses him over you?" Mikayla asked hesitantly.

"That's a risk I'll have to take. I'll just hope that someone bets on me for a change, because I'm sure as hell going to bet on myself."

Jada's words weren't faux courage either. On the long plane ride home, she'd had a lot of time to mull over her pain and make this decision. While true love was hard to find, scoring awesome acting jobs was even harder. Despite how enraged Tristan would be, she had no intention of abandoning the film. She might have been in the wrong for releasing the video, but she wasn't going to run away in shame. This time she'd face the consequences head-on and prove that she deserved her place in that movie.

Ironically enough, her time with Tristan had been what clarified her resolve. Fighting with him, standing up to him, and loving him had made her stronger. She'd rediscovered her backbone and she wouldn't let anyone break it.

So with her head held high, Jada arrived at Avery Kane's office the next day to fill out the contract. Technically, she could have e-signed the document, but Avery insisted she wanted to talk to Jada about the role in person. In response to Avery's grating request, Jada blew by the receptionist and gave a brisk knock on the agent's door. Avery glared at her in distaste.

"You couldn't wait five minutes until I called you in?"

Knowing Avery only made people wait as a power move, Jada smiled at her brightly. "What can I say? I'm just so eager to meet with you today."

Avery raised a skeptical brow but motioned Jada in anyway. As she dug around for the paperwork, she prattled on about Jada's manners and work ethic.

"Now, Mr. Wentworth seems pretty excited to take you on for this, but let me tell you, this isn't your run of the mill straight to the bargain bin film. This is no made for TV two-bit gig. This is the big time, do you understand?" Avery said as she whipped out the paperwork.

Jada nodded, remaining silent as she mulled over the legalese. Her lawyer had already given the contract a once-over but Jada took a moment to review things anyway. As she perused, Avery continued to admonish her.

"And since this *is* the big time, you can't mess up. You can't pull a hysterical breakdown on this set like you did in New York and on *Love Locket*."

Jada's pen froze midair. "Excuse me?" she said with a tight smile. Avery gave one back, a disappointed gleam in her eye.

"I know that you saw Daniel at Tristan's premiere. Seriously, Jada. You think you could say a simple hello instead of screaming and storming out in tears."

"In tears?" Jada repeated.

"Bawling like a baby in the theater. It's entirely unprofessional and uncalled for. Especially since Daniel went there to make amends."

Jada set the pen down, steeling herself.

"You know what's unprofessional, Avery? You. Every fucking thing about you."

"What did you say?" Avery gasped at Jada's boldness. Without a doubt, none of Avery's clients had ever spoken to her this way. But for Jada, it was long overdue—and felt damn good.

"You heard me. You treat me like shit, all because you think I wronged you."

"Where are you going with this little tantrum, Jada?" The

agent had reined in her shock and was now reclining in her chair with seeming indifference. But there was an edge to her voice as her eyes darted away from Jada's accusatory glare.

"You know exactly what I mean. I made you look bad by secretly dating your son and supposedly almost destroying *Fallen Creatures*. But guess what? My mistakes don't justify your son's indiscretions. They don't absolve him, and you don't get to punish me in his place."

As the truth poured out of Jada, she felt the burdens she'd been carrying for so long finally lifting. She'd dealt with Daniel and confessed to Tristan. At last, she'd worked up the courage to confront Avery, to reveal the real reasons behind the woman's resentment. Avery kept up the charade on her end, examining Jada coldly.

"Trust me, Jada. I don't spend my spare time thinking of ways to sabotage you. You do that all on your own."

"Maybe so," Jada admitted. "But that doesn't change the fact you are a *sucky* agent. That you have never pulled your own damn weight in this relationship."

Avery's face turned a very interesting shade of maroon. Jada had struck the nerve to set off the agent's powder keg. The older woman shot up out of her chair, attempting to tower over Jada.

"That's it! You can't talk to me like that! You're—"

"Fired? Never going to work in this town again?" Jada jumped up from her chair as well, staring her fearsome adversary down.

"No, Avery. *You're* fired. You don't own me, Bitchery Kane. And I'll be damned if I let you run my life—or my career—anymore."

"Well, we'll just see what Logan Wentworth has to say about that," Avery shot back.

"Don't worry. I'll let you know," Jada said, waving her cell phone at her.

Then she turned on her heel and marched out of that office like a fucking boss and loving every minute of it. As she made her way out of the building, she managed to nab Logan's assistant and explain her situation. The CliffsNotes version, of course. The lady was perfectly pleasant, saying how Logan had mentioned his desire to work with Jada. She assured Jada he'd still be open to signing her, and to let them know if she found different representation.

At "different representation," only one name came to mind. After a few excruciatingly long rings, Doug picked up her call.

"Jada! It's great to hear from you."

"Really?" she said, surprised.

"Why the shock, lollipop?"

"One, please don't ever call me that again. And two, didn't Tristan tell you?"

At Doug's obliviousness, Jada took a deep breath and launched into the torrid story all over again. Doug also made the pertinent exclamations at the right moments.

"So, you see why I'm in a bit of a pickle," she said as she reached the end of her recap. "I don't want to stir up anything between you and Tristan, but I also can't go back to Avery. But honestly, if we're talking cold, hard business, you know taking me on is a good deal."

"That it is." Doug hummed in agreement.

"I want this job, Doug, and I also want you as my new agent."

"Why, Jada! That's the surest I've ever heard you sound about anything."

"Thanks!" Jada laughed. "It's the new me. But I'm not sure

how to make this new deal between us and Tristan work."

"Well, at the end of the day, as you said, this is business. Give me a day and let me talk to him. But whatever you do, don't tear up that contract!"

"Got it. Thanks, Doug."

As Jada hung up, she was filled with equal amounts of relief and apprehension. She was proud of herself for coming this far, acting so quickly, and taking a stand. But just *hearing* Tristan's name and wondering what he thought about her hurt. All she could hope was that her new agent was as savvy as he promised.

# 30

When the pounding assault on Tristan's front door began, he knew exactly who was on the other side of the expensive wood. Scowling, Tristan set his scotch down on the coffee table and went to let in his enraged agent. This time, Tristan had some rage of his own to match.

"What?" he snapped the second he came face to face with Doug.

"Don't you 'what' me!" Doug snapped right back. "You know exactly why I'm here."

At Tristan's blank stare, Doug clarified with exasperation. "Jada!"

Her name immediately had Tristan headed back to the couch for his liquor.

"I don't want to talk about it," Tristan said, taking a long sip. The familiar burn sliding down his throat was just the hit he needed. It masked the real reason for the pain in his chest.

"Tell me what happened," Doug demanded.

"She's the one, the rat. She posted the video that started this whole shit show."

"Damn." Doug sat down to pour himself a glass uninvited. "She didn't tell me that part over the phone."

"Because she's a liar. And why were you talking to her anyway?"

"She's my new client," Doug said so nonchalantly that Tristan gawked in astonishment.

"Are you frickin' serious? After everything she did, you're going to take her on?"

"Yep. The bad blood between you two has nothing to do with the percentage that'll be in my pocket after you two do this movie."

"I can't believe this. You really are a snake, Doug. You two deserve each other."

"Get off it, Tristan. There wouldn't have been a video for Jada to post in the *first place* if you hadn't taken your anger out on her."

Tristan scoffed, looking at the television. ESPN's lukewarm commentary wasn't enough to drown his agent out.

"That's right. Roll your eyes and blow me off," Doug went on angrily. "You want to blame everyone else for this mess and what's going on, but this started with you. With you and your immaturity. So, if you want, blame everyone else. Blame the whole world. But you'll never learn how to truly forgive and love someone until you take responsibility for your actions."

"Who said anything about love?" Tristan swiveled back to Doug as he found himself latching onto the word that had been terrifying him.

"Are you really trying to pretend like you're not crazy about that girl?" Doug asked incredulously.

That was exactly what Tristan intended to do. Sure, he might have thought he was falling for Jada, but that got shot to hell the second she confessed. Doug might have come here with his bulldozing, hash-it-out energy, but Tristan didn't have to put up with it. He hadn't even worked up the nerve to tell Juan and Rafe the truth about everything—people he actually would have trusted for love advice. He certainly wasn't going to take some from Doug, who'd just stabbed him in the back.

"You know what? If you want to take Jada on, that's your problem. I, on the other hand, have some things to reconsider."

Leaving Doug with that foreboding statement, Tristan headed for the front hallway, knowing the agent would follow him.

"Is that supposed to be a threat, Tristan?" Doug asked, some of his resolve wavering.

Doug might see Jada as a new cash cow, but he and Tristan had been through a lot more together. Doug had been there for Tristan when his dad died and had seen him through the hardest parts of his career. Tristan didn't have the heart to actually drop him right this second, but he needed an impetus to get Doug out of his house.

"What it means is I'm going for a walk. So . . ." Tristan let the sentence dangle as he opened his door.

Shaking his head, Doug stepped back outside and gave Tristan a sad, parting look. "You really won't be happy until you burn it all to the ground, will you?"

"Good night, Doug," Tristan said, his throat tight as Doug's words hit him square in the gut.

After Doug got in his car and drove off, Tristan felt so unsettled he decided to take a walk after all. The ritzy neighborhood was safe enough to stroll through at night with most of his other rich and famous neighbors cozied up behind their estates' security gates. As Tristan walked in the cold evening air, he did see Cory Fuego's place buzzing with activity. The rock star was the most hated resident on the block after turning his house into a lime-green monstrosity. Whenever he was home from touring, people came in and out at all hours, and there had been multiple noise complaints filed against him.

Tonight, dear Fuego was back in town and in the middle of another rager. Approaching the house brought the heady scent of weed wafting Tristan's way. Outside, there were a few partygoers loitering in the driveway and tossing beer bottles into the air for God only knows what reason. Wincing at the noise as the bottles shattered against the pavement, Tristan planned to duck his head and hurry on by. But when he saw a woman hunched over on the sidewalk, that strategy evaporated.

In the darkness, he could have been mistaken, but the young woman with her head in her hands bore a resemblance to Angela. Honestly, after the shit she'd pulled in New York, Tristan had no desire to talk to her, especially if her slumping stature was due to another drinking binge. However, the fact that it *might* be, coupled with Angela's previous comment about going to AA, swayed him in the end. When he stepped forward to tap her on the shoulder and say her name, Angela stared up at him with haunted eyes. Yep, she was definitely on a bad trip. And knowing how Cory rolled, Angela was probably on something heavier than her usual chosen poisons.

"Tristan? What are you doing here?" At least she'd recognized him. That was a start.

"Angela, this is my neighborhood. You've been here before."

Angela squinted at their dark surroundings. "I don't remember.

All I remember is coming here and . . . I fucked up, Tristan."

As tears streamed down her face, Tristan pulled Angela to her feet. "Come on, let's go back to my house. We'll get you some water and—"

"No, I have to tell you something." Angela pulled away from him.

"And it's something you can't tell me inside?"

Angela crossed her arms, shivering. "Fine. It is kind of cold out here."

Since they weren't that far up the street, it was a short walk back to Tristan's place. Depositing Angela on the couch, Tristan went to grab her water like he promised, only to find her eyeing the scotch he'd left on the coffee table earlier. He handed her the water and hastily got rid of the scotch. When he returned, Angela's shaking had calmed and, surprisingly, she opened up without more prying on Tristan's part.

"I don't know why you're being so nice to me after what I did."

*No kidding*, Tristan thought. But now wasn't the time to lash out at her, and even if it had been, he didn't have the energy. Still, he couldn't resist asking the question that had been bothering him.

"Why did you come to the premiere, Angela? It took the whole bitter-ex angle way too far."

Ashamed, Angela shifted her gaze, choosing to stare down at her water glass. "I was already in New York, visiting friends. My dad and Daniel's mom have been trying to get us to do a movie together. So when my dad found out Daniel was also in the city, he demanded we hang out. I kind of . . ."

"Decided you two should crash the party and terrorize Jada," Tristan finished.

"Okay, yes! That was part of it." Angela's confession came out in a rush. "But it wasn't the only reason I came. Before any of that, Tegan called me the night of the Legends opening. He told me about how you confronted them at Madame Tussauds. We met up later to rag on you some more, and he told me who the real leak is. I was going to tell you at the premiere, but then Jada pissed me off, and I stuck with the vindictive route."

Too bad Tristan had found out the hard way who the real leak was. But then again, Jada had said she'd only released the first video. Which meant the true A. C. of the later incidents was still out there. Against his better instincts, Tristan pressed on.

"So, who is it?"

"Andrew Chaudhry."

"Andrew?" Tristan balked.

Kind, hardworking Andrew had been the one badmouthing them? He'd been so steadfast on the job and courteous to Tristan. It was hard to imagine him as a *Gossip Girl*esque vigilante.

"He's friends with Erica, apparently. Even though my dad *generously* offered her another job, neither of them was happy about how it all went down."

"I guess that makes sense."

Placing himself in Andrew's shoes, Tristan could see how this type of revenge would appeal to the guy. It was still a shitty thing to do, but so was pushing out Erica. And since so much else had happened and no permanent damage had been done (compared to Jada's bombshell), Tristan no longer felt the need to go track the perpetrator down.

"Is that everything?" Tristan asked Angela.

When she nodded, Tristan sank down on the couch next to her. The past few days, not to mention the past hour or so, had been draining as hell. For a moment, he just sat there in silence, processing. For her part, Angela was not in a hurry to leave yet either. She continued to sip her water, then changed the TV from ESPN to *Entertainment Tonight*.

"Thank you for telling me." Tristan spoke up. "But about tonight . . . being at Fuego's . . . I thought you said—"

"I know, but sobriety is harder than it looks, okay?"

"Even with AAA?" Tristan asked. He hoped his comment would lighten things up, but she shook her head solemnly.

"I still haven't gone yet, but I will."

Now that the attention had shifted to her, Angela developed second thoughts about hanging around. "Thanks for letting me crash, but I should probably go."

Although Tristan offered to let her stay until her ride arrived, Angela chose to wait outside, claiming she needed the fresh air. Tristan sensed she just wanted to be alone to mull over the decisions that awaited her. His suspicion was confirmed as she gave him a final, regretful smile.

"I know we caused each other a lot of harm, Tristan, but—"

"We're even, Angela. Don't worry about it." Tristan assured her. As far as he was concerned, their chapter in each other's lives was over. She'd given him a sense of closure to the rest of the *Sip That Tea* debacle, and, hopefully, he had given her some encouragement to get the support she needed. Tristan still kept an eye out, though, to make sure Angela's ride pulled up, before making his way back to his couch.

Considering calling it a night, Tristan reached for the remote. Right when he was about to turn off the television, he saw his mother's shining smile gracing the screen, with a caption saying the illustrious star was still in town. As he watched his mom on camera, Doug's words flooded back to him. *You'll never learn how to truly forgive and love someone until you take responsibility for your actions.*

"Well, Doug, if I have to take responsibility for my actions, then so does everyone else," Tristan murmured.

This whole roller coaster ride with Jada had indeed taught him that actions had consequences. It was time to face his, but the only way to start doing so was by facing his mother. Still staring at his mother's face on-screen, Tristan pulled out his phone to call the number that had been haunting him for weeks.

It was hard confronting your deepest wounds. But as Tristan sat down with his mom the following afternoon, he knew it was for the best. When he'd called last night, his mom had eagerly agreed to meet, providing Tristan a terrifying opportunity to confront his past trauma. With the two of them in his living room again, Tristan prayed take two of this conversation would play out differently. Finding a way to *start* the conversation was the most difficult part. For a while, the echoing tick of the wall clock was the only sound. Its maddening persistence forced Tristan to break the ice.

"Um, do you . . . do you want something to drink? Or eat? I think I have . . . water," he asked dumbly.

What he wanted was his Jack Daniel's. However, if he kept using alcohol to cope with difficult situations, he knew where that slippery slope could lead.

"No, I'm fine. Thank you," she said. As she looked at him, Tristan memorized her features in a way he hadn't been able to in their previous encounter. Taking her in fully this time, he saw she looked the same; a little older, but her smile was the same.

The love in her eyes was the same, as if his doting mother had never left.

How ironic.

"So . . . I thought about what you said, and you're right. I should hear you out. What did you want to tell me the other day?" Tristan asked.

"I want you to know my leaving was never because I didn't love you or didn't want to stay. Things just got complicated."

"Complicated how?"

"I fell in love. With someone other than your father, obviously. What you don't know, Tristan, is your father was a very possessive man. He was never physically abusive; you would have seen that. His methods were more subtle chastisements, controlling what I wore, who I talked to. Eventually, I felt suffocated and ended up meeting someone else. When your father found out, well, of course, he wasn't happy. And that's when he finally did hit me. When it crossed that line, we both knew I couldn't stay. Not without things ending badly."

Tristan took it in. It was hard to imagine his father hurting his mother. His dad had always been a little on the militant side but raising his hand to her? And yet, Tristan remembered the morning his mom left. The bags under her eyes hadn't been from lack of sleep at all. His father's sullen anger that morning hadn't been about a headache. And maybe his father's downward spiral after his mom's disappearance had been more about guilt than loneliness. Thinking of this, he couldn't deny her words like he had the previous time she'd come to his house. This time it didn't feel right. Her words felt true.

"Well, who is this man?" The man who'd ruined his family. "Are you still with him?"

"Alejandro and I moved abroad so I could continue my career. But he passed away a few years later in a car accident."

Tristan found himself reaching out to hold his mother's hand. All of this must have been difficult to relive.

"So everything you went through was for nothing."

"Oh no, Tristan. Despite how hard it was to leave you, I don't regret falling in love with Alejandro. Not once."

"Even though doing so destroyed our family?"

"When you find true love, you don't let it go, mijo. I just hoped one day you would be able to forgive me. To this day, the only part I wish I could change is taking you with me."

Tears welled in Tristan's eyes at hearing the words he'd always longed for. But it wasn't just the confirmation that his mom never stopped loving him. He knew exactly where he'd heard similar rhetoric about not letting go of true love. The night he went to Jada's apartment because of this very same woman and her betrayal. But was it a betrayal for his mom to get herself out of a bad marriage? Tristan never would have wanted for things to get worse, or for his father to continue to hurt her. Her leaving wasn't as black and white as his fourteen-year-old self believed.

"I understand if you can't, though. If it's been too long." His mother's voice shook him out of his thoughts. As she began to pull away, Tristan hugged her.

"*Te perdono*, Mama."

"Really?" she asked. The tears brimming in her eyes nearly brought Tristan to tears as well.

"Really. I mean, trusting you again will take some time, but I *can* forgive you. I can't hold you living your truth against you. Not when I'm finally able to put myself in your shoes. Especially not when I've fallen in love myself."

"Oh, mijo, that's wonderful! With who?"

"With a woman who is infuriatingly complicated and just as stubborn as me. The thing is, so much has happened between us, so much hurt, that I don't know if I can fix things."

Looking back on everything that had taken place between him and Jada, Tristan was torn between the depth of his feelings for her and the fear that laying his heart on the line ultimately wouldn't be worth it. And yet he kept thinking back to the sincerity in Jada's eyes when she said he was worth sticking around for. Deep down, he knew she was too. As if she could read the emotions on his face, Tristan's mom squeezed his hand reassuringly.

"You will. If you truly love her, fight for her, Tristan. Hold on to her and cherish what you have."

While it was the first motherly advice he'd gotten in years, Tristan rediscovered that mothers still held fundamental wisdom.

"I will, Mama. And I can't wait for you to meet her soon," Tristan promised.

Full of newfound resolve, Tristan left his mother welcome to stay at his house, and then made his way to Jada's. The sun had just dipped below the horizon but the darkening sky didn't faze him. The route had become so familiar he drove there with quick ease, but a very unwilling Mikayla refused to let him in.

"What do you want?" She scowled at him.

"You know what I want. I need to speak to Jada."

"Why? To keep bullying her out of a job? She doesn't need to hear anything else from you."

"Not even how I've realized I'm a giant ass. How I'm ready to do anything for us to start over?"

"That *is* a start, but Jada's not here."

"Do you know where she went?"

"You just missed her, she left ten minutes ago. All she said was she needed to go confront her fears so she could move past everything and reach greater heights. It was all very existential."

Tristan puzzled over this revelation until it all clicked.

New heights . . .

"Okay, got it," he said excitedly. "Thanks, Mikayla."

"Oh, and Tristan," she called after him before he could rush off. "It was my idea to release the video, and I'm sorry about that now, by the way. Jada was drunk and hurt when we did it. She's basically an innocent snowflake who had a moment of weakness."

Reflecting on his mom's mistakes and everything else he'd learned, Tristan smiled. "We all do."

Mikayla's guarded stance softened in surprise at his response. She didn't get to question him further as Tristan left her behind to go find his true love.

# 31

Taking in the scenic fairgrounds, Jada thought back to when she and Tristan came here. Revisiting the places where they'd been and the things they'd done together was heartbreaking, but Jada had come here anyway. Technically, the Bright Futures Festival had ended, but the pier still felt like their "spot." Sitting at one of the few open tables, Jada glanced down at her finished letter. The whole concept of writing a Dear John letter for Tristan had come from Alia. After days of Jada moping around, Alia had pointed out that if Jada *did* plan on doing a second film with Tristan, she needed to get everything out in the open.

Actually *giving* Tristan the letter wasn't the point of this coping exercise. Her motivation was to gather her thoughts about their breakup, then come up with a better apology for when they met in person. Her eyes flowed over her message, giving it one more critical read-through.

*Dear Tristan,*

*There are no words to fully express how sorry I am for everything. I wish I could explain why I'm such a mess. Why I lash out then run away. Why I completely fuck up everything I touch, including us. The best—but still pathetic—excuse I can give is I've never been strong. I've never been able to live up to the ideal of the strong, Black woman who is proud, daring, and never cares what people think of her.*

*I care way too much. And right now, I care that you probably see me as someone who planned it all from the start, right? That I did something totally malicious and then capitalized on it when the opportunity with you and Doug fell in my lap.*

*I don't want you to think it was all a lie. Yes, I had those dreams about being like Thandiwe Newton and Viola Davis, of standing on stage and being honored for my work. But I'm no longer obsessed with getting into the Black Women Hall of Fame.*

*Because now I know I already belong there. I'm good enough just as I am.*

*Me questioning my self-worth the whole time we were together is still no excuse for me tearing you down too.*

Jada shoved the page back in her jeans pocket, unable to finish reading what else she'd written. If she did, she'd end up sobbing in front of everyone at the pier.

Turning her attention to her next step, she took in the massive Pacific Wheel. The lights glimmered at her as the small seats rotated. It was the place where she and Tristan had felt like a real couple for the first time, where they'd shared their first real kiss. Here, Jada had faced one of her greatest fears and overcame it because of him. Because of Tristan's strength, she'd felt safe. She'd been able to take on anything. Now she would use the courage he'd given her one last time.

To say good-bye.

With one last ride, she swore to herself she would let go of the past, of all her hang-ups and fears. One last ride and she would emerge as a new, stronger Jada. She'd be able to fight for her right to participate in Logan's movie and face whatever else might come in life or with Tristan.

Jada stepped up to the conductor. "One ticket, please."

"Make that two." A voice she knew all too well spoke up from behind her.

"Tristan! What are you doing here?" she asked, wheeling around.

"Talking to you," he said simply.

"I don't think so." Jada hurriedly grabbed the piece of paper from the confused ticket seller and climbed into the nearest seat. Letter or not, she was not prepared for a real-life confrontation. But before she could put the bar down, Tristan slid in beside her. She didn't get the chance to protest or leave as the conductor pressed the lever, sending them up as the ride started.

"I take it you've talked to Doug," Jada said to Tristan, although she refused to look at him. Instead, she stared out at the vast scenery, the ground slowly falling away from them. However, she didn't mind as much as before. She worried that had to do more with the man beside her than her so-called new bravado.

"Yes, I did."

"Well, I'm taking that role, Tristan. I'm sorry about releasing the video and everything that's happened. You have no idea how much I wish . . ." Jada held back the swell of emotions rising in her, unable to formulate that elusive, perfect apology. "I wish things had been different. But I'm not giving up this part."

"I want you to have it, Jada."

She jerked back in surprise, "What?"

"You've earned that role, Jada. You deserve it."

"So, you're backing out then?"

"No. We're going to do this together."

Jada searched Tristan's face for any sign that he'd take his words back and state his real purpose for coming. But when he kept staring at her with open sincerity, her heart began to beat faster, fluttering with what was sure to be ill-fated hope.

"I don't see how that's possible," she admitted at last.

"It's possible if we forgive each other. If we finally put the past in the past and see there's so much more to each other than we thought."

"What are you saying, Tristan?"

"I'm saying there's potential here. I think there's hope for us."

Tristan took her hand, interlacing their fingers. Despite how good and natural it felt, she had to pull away.

"There never was an us, Tristan."

"I thought you might say that," Tristan said, heaving a sigh. With resignation, he reached into his jacket pocket and pulled out the hideous unicorn from the game booth. In shock, she took it from him. The small toy truly was ugly, but right now, she clutched it, touched.

"I may not believe in unicorns, but I believe in you, Jada Berklee. Because of you, I was able to forgive my mother. Because of you, I've learned love is not a weakness, but a strength. A strength I'm not willing to let go."

Tristan wiped her cheek. It was only then that Jada noticed she was crying. As he cradled her face in his hands and looked into her eyes, she knew he was telling her the truth. This wasn't acting. This wasn't pretend. This was love.

"You are my magic, reina," Tristan said.

Too overcome to speak, Jada leaned forward and kissed him. She hoped it said everything she was feeling because she couldn't do a better job than he just had. When they pulled away, Tristan went on with absolute certainty.

"Let's do this for real. No more games or fake dates. No more pretending. Only us."

"I like the sound of that," Jada said, finding her voice. He pulled her close and she rested her head against his shoulder. As the Ferris wheel continued to spin, they looked out at the enchanting landscape. With the city twinkling far below them, Jada relished the comforting promise of new beginnings.

# Several Months Later

*Here we go again*, Jada thought to herself as she stared Tristan down. They'd been through this same scenario over and over, but their latest explosive argument might finally put an end to everything.

"I'm tired of your constant screwups. I'd be better off without you," Jada snapped.

"If that's how you feel, then maybe we should go our separate ways." Tristan's retort stung, but it wasn't like she hadn't seen it coming. She buried the pain, looking back at him unflinchingly.

"Maybe we should," she replied.

"And *cut*! Excellent job, you guys," Donnie, the director of *Love and War*, said to them. "I think we've got it."

At his approval, everyone hurried to prepare for the next shot. Shooting on location for such a big film had been a change for Jada. Filming the massive action flick, they'd traveled from the English countryside to their current locale in the lively Venice streets. Not to mention the plethora of fake explosions and shootouts they'd left in their wake. The intense schedule and travel were bearable, though, with Tristan at her side. She gave a relieved sigh, happy that the current scene was over. Tristan kissed her on the forehead.

"You did great. I loved the hatred in your eyes, baby," he teased her, leading her to stick her tongue out at him.

Watching them in amusement, Donnie shook his head and laughed. "Yes. The crackling tension yet obvious longing. You two are the perfect couple," he said.

"I couldn't agree more," Jada said to him, but she secretly traded an intuitive look with Tristan. He returned it, winking at her in understanding.

They'd both given up on the idea of being the perfect couple a long time ago. Jada had her flaws, and Tristan sure as hell had some too. But he was hers. She was his. For the next ten or twenty years, for forever, Jada planned to keep it that way.

# Acknowledgments

The title for Jada and Tristan's story couldn't be more accurate. While I've always wanted to be a published author, my vision on how I would reach this goal definitely went "off script." I had the set idea that most writers have of writing something great, then querying and pitching until my work finally got noticed.

But it was only after I joined Wattpad and wrote something completely out of my comfort zone that my writing began to resonate with people. This time, I wasn't nervously sweating as I tried to talk to an agent. People I had never met in person were reading *Off Script* online. Ranging from the US, Europe, India, Nigeria, and the Philippines, readers from all over the world were connecting with Jada and Tristan's romance.

To be honest, I had always hidden the hopeless romantic side of myself deep down. Yet, my experience with *Off Script* reminded me that love is one of the most powerful forces in the universe.

I want to thank all of my Wattpad readers for helping me realize such a fundamental truth. You all have been there from the beginning, making me feel seen and that my writing matters. I will always be grateful to you for all your lovely engagement and enthusiasm for the story and these characters.

Thank you to the Wattpad team who helped *Off Script* flourish from a small story on a huge writing platform to a novel I'm proud to put out into the world. You have all been so lovely to me and helped me grow as a writer. I'm sure I'm going to forget some names but special shoutouts to my great editors, Deanna and Fiona, my talent specialist, Amanda, Samantha, who was one of the first people to notice *Off Script*, and Grace, my point of contact for the Black History Month Feature.

I'd also like to thank my first group of beta readers. Amanda Ross, for being *Off Script*'s number one cheerleader, my cousin Halle, for always believing in me, and my moo, Andrea, for her insightful advice and endless friendship.

Lastly, I'd like to thank my family. Especially my library family, the Mountain Park Rangers! You've been so supportive as I've muddled my way through the process of becoming a debut author. Listed alphabetically, so there's no need to be jealous, y'all! Ashley Texas Walker, Brandon, Danielle, DJ MC LYONS, Linda, Lucca, Miriam, Reynolds, Savanna, and Trang.

To everyone I've mentioned and more:

We made it!

Here's to all of us and whatever chapter may come next.

# About the Author

Ashley Marie is both a novelist and screenwriter whose overactive imagination keeps her tapping away at her keyboard regularly. Despite the carpal tunnel, the Georgia native has placed as a quarterfinalist twice in the PAGE Awards for her screenwriting and found a home for her writing on Wattpad. With over a million reads on the platform, *Off Script* has blossomed into her debut novel. In her spare time outside of brewing stories, Ashley Marie sings off-key, dances spontaneously, and fosters her love of learning different languages.

Turn the page to read a preview of

★ "Filled with delectable delights and heart-tugging insights . . . Stunning."
— Publishers Weekly

24
HOURS
IN
PARIS

ROMI MOONDI

Available now everywhere books are sold.

# CHAPTER
## *one*

### M

### *The Night Before*

Mira had always believed that laughter was infectious. It had the power to spread from one delighted face to the next, but here, in the corner of this chic Paris bistro where the brash American laughter surrounded her in waves, she managed to stay immune.

She pressed her lips together tight, a defensive move to avoid being lumped in with the rowdiness of her tablemates. Mira was simply different from the loud tourist stereotype too often proven right in the train cars, cafés, and cobblestoned streets of Paris. She was different from them, *dammit*, and everyone in this bistro needed to know.

The staff seemed unbothered by the elevated noise, but was it any surprise? Each successive round of laughter meant another round of drinks: more champagne, more pricey vintage reds.

The husband-and-wife owners exchanged a knowing look as they brought out a few more bottles from the cellar. Given that they owned a restaurant off Avenue Montaigne—a notable street in the

8th arrondissement and home to the famous Plaza Athenée—Mira could only assume they were well acquainted with the platinum card–carrying demographic. Early summer was an especially busy period, with swarms of jet-setters descending on Paris, particularly on a night like this, when the glitzy Haute Couture Fashion Week had just gotten underway.

Not that Mira and her crew had anything to do with fashion. They were merely another rowdy group of white-collar Americans who just happened to be in Paris on business. The business of pushing the latest in sparkling beverages, to be exact.

The owners now made a beeline to Frank, Mira's fifty-something boss, who sat at the head of the long wooden table. Even in the soft glow of candlelight, his tailored suit and looming presence made it clear he was the one in charge. In their office back in New York, that meant rejecting an idea with a simple shake of the head. In this bistro, however, that meant being the one in charge of appraising the wine, which he now carefully did by examining the labels.

"Not a bad selection," he acknowledged, his accent a faded tribute to a childhood growing up in Queens. "We'll take both."

The owners shifted their focus to refilling everyone's glasses. They worked their way down the table slowly, starting with the smartly dressed middle-aged executives, and moving on to the younger, more fashion-forward employees.

Mira, at the younger end of the table, could feel her taste buds anticipating a fresh dose of wine, but before her glass could get some attention, it was the thirtysomething man with sandy brown hair and pale blue eyes who received his refill first. He grinned as each ounce cascaded into the glass, a smarmy look that expressed an affection for company-sponsored unlimited refills. The smarm paired well with the hair gel sweeping his shaggy hair into a greasy salesman dome.

Without all that product, he could've been one of those intensely handsome bed-headed men you'd see reading books on the subway, men whom Mira had been known to crush on during her A train trek to the office. Instead, the greasy gel had sealed his fate (and his hair) in her eyes.

Hair aside, he was tall and broad shouldered and had probably been the captain of the rowing team in college (and had likely done a good job of making sure everyone knew it). She noticed him unfasten the top two buttons of his shirt, a sign that he was probably a few glasses in.

"It's hot in here," he said, before holding his fresh glass of wine to the light. "But it's okay; I'm a *glass-half-full* kinda guy." He snickered at his own lame joke, ignoring Mira's immediate groan. After gulping some wine, he elbowed the male colleague to his left. "We men can handle our liquor, amirite?"

"It's not liquor, it's *wine*," Mira muttered, her brown eyes narrowing in disapproval. She tucked a few strands of long black hair behind one ear, frowning at the presence of this irritating dude. She'd always heard that frowning was the dangerous road to deep-set wrinkles, but up until now her South Asian genes had been good to her, and she was often still mistaken for a woman in her twenties, despite being weeks away from turning thirty-five. This ego-boosting clerical error hadn't yet occurred on the business trip, but for the moment she had other pressing problems on her mind. In addition to her latest groan, she'd served up two eye rolls, three smirks, and countless raised eyebrows in the hours since the evening had begun, all of it brought on by the irritating man-child sitting across from her.

She was Mira Attwal.

He was Jake Lewis.

3

And while they worked for the same company, the similarities ended there.

"I *know* liquor isn't wine," Jake finally said. "And so does he." He gestured to his colleague. "And everyone." He gestured to the air. "Which is why when you say it, it's kind of interchangeable." He nodded as if to convince himself that his word salad was legit.

"Thanks for the clarification."

Mira's eyes bore deep into Jake's forehead, as she wondered about the size of the brain knocking around in that oversize skull.

Mira worked in branding.

Jake worked in sales.

And aside from this five-day business trip, they'd never interacted as coworkers even once.

Of course, that didn't mean she'd never noticed him before at the office. It also didn't mean she'd never thought of him, sometimes even for an hour or two, after those rare occasions when they'd shared an elevator and she'd found herself ogling his jawline, or, depending on where he'd been standing, the outline of his ass. But did she have to admit either of those things when he was acting in such a drunken, slovenly fashion? Certainly not.

She studied his face. "Is that oyster juice on your chin?"

Looking slightly embarrassed, Jake grabbed a napkin and wiped it off.

Apart from some time spent studying his physical attributes, Mira only knew Jake from the grandiose persona he'd projected in their meetings during the past few days. She hadn't been impressed by all the showmanship, which made it satisfying to embarrass him during this dinner. Did that make her a bad person? Maybe. Or maybe it was just that his big, greasy dome of hair needed to be brought down a peg (or two).

To Mira's disappointment, his embarrassment was all too brief, his confidence now restored at the sight of the pretty waitress he'd been scoping out all night. By Mira's estimation, the waitress had been doing a very good job; clearing the plates in a timely manner and replacing each carafe before the water got too low—she was a winner. Still, Mira had a feeling that Jake wasn't interested in her customer service.

"You're back," he observed, eyes zeroed in on the kill.

The waitress's only response was a look of coyness.

As Mira wondered which pickup line he'd choose from the greasy-salesman starter pack, she saw him reach into his brown leather workbag and found herself instantly intrigued. She wondered if there was a long-stemmed rose inside that bag. It could've been a napkin and she'd be equally enthralled, as she'd been starved for entertainment since the start of these company dinners.

Night after night, she'd been a bored observer of coworkers gobbling up foie gras *this* and braised rabbit *that*, all while getting drunk at these long wooden tables—and always at restaurants that weren't even on her Paris bucket list. She'd tried to stretch their imaginations, but no one had seemed on board with her idea for a picnic at Luxembourg Gardens, or a stroll along the riverbank with handheld crêpes and the sparkling Eiffel Tower as the backdrop.

So here she was, on their final night, with the saga of Jake and the waitress as her only form of entertainment.

Jake's hand emerged from the bag, his fingers clutching a lavender-colored can of flavored sparkling water called Bloom. Jake was the top salesman at Bloom, but for the moment he was more like Vanna White as he proudly showcased the newest flavor in the company's line of botanical-based, calorie-free fizz. "Now, Chloe . . ." he started.

Mira took immediate note of the waitress's subtle wince, but judging by Jake's come-hither stare he didn't have a clue.

"My name is Colette."

He wasn't the least bit fazed.

"Yes of course, *Colette*. Now tell me: are you ready to be at the forefront of the next big thing in cocktails?" He gestured to the bar. "Let's ask the barman to whip up a little something with this lavender magic."

Colette seemed uncertain.

"I'll make it worth his while."

For some ungodly reason, the waitress started to crack, her neutral expression giving way to a hint of excitement.

At first Mira couldn't believe it, but a moment later she grudgingly realized why Jake was the top salesman at Bloom.

The waitress played with her hair, a clear sign that the mating ritual had begun.

"Perhaps I could speak to the barman."

Jake lowered his voice for the next part: "I'll make it worth *your* while too."

And there it was. The typical line used by basic bros the world over.

Without thinking, Mira reached over and patted Jake's arm. It must've been the wine. "You're coming off a little thirsty."

He turned to her with a look of faux innocence. "I was talking about giving her a *tip*."

Without another word he hopped out of his chair and followed Colette to the bar.

Mira shrugged and sipped her wine, her only entertainment now out of earshot. What remained were the colleagues on her right discussing summer camp options for the kids, a colleague on her left filming a video of herself that was bound to wind up in her Instagram stories, and the guy that Jake had been next to, who was now in the grips of a furious texting session.

Inspired by the way the aggressive texter was ignoring them all, Mira pulled out her phone in the hopes of a decent distraction.

Her eyes brightened at the stream of notifications, but the eager glow dimmed out within seconds, when she realized all the messages were from the Bloom group chat.

The company HQ in New York City had clearly heard about their stellar presentation to the top beverage distributor in Paris, and the overall reaction had been different variations of "Kudos!" and "Congrats!"

Today's big win was the latest high point in Bloom's skyrocketing success, which now included an expansion into international markets.

The brand's popularity had grown in part due to partnerships with Instagram influencers, a strategic move that Mira had suggested—despite being intimidated by the fashionable outfits and makeup filters that were a favorite among the influencing set. The social media superstars had done a great job of showcasing the artsy font and soft, appealing colors of each can in the flavor lineup, sometimes with selfies that garnered endless likes, and other times with curated shots of not-so-casual picnics—where silverware was the norm and not a single hair was ever out of place.

With the influencers locked into multiyear contracts, expansion into Europe had become the next big goal, with countless late nights and strategy decks culminating in this all-important trip. The initial thought had been to nab a bit of shelf space in European grocery stores, but in the presentation to the distributor earlier that day, Jake had mentioned the potential synergy between the speakeasy bar scene and Bloom—which would especially work in Paris, where there were now as many craft cocktail bars as in London.

With a range of flavors like elderflower, honeysuckle, and the recently-introduced lavender, Jake had been right in identifying this untapped market—even though he'd used the word *synergy* in his presentation, a loathed business term in Mira's mind, right up there with *pivot* and *take this offline*.

As Mira scrolled through the company chat, she tried her best to feel a sense of pride, and why not? The brand colors and lettering that the influencers were so obsessed with had all been handpicked by Mira. She was also the one who had convinced the head of marketing to lean in hard on the floral angle, when she'd explained how people seemed to gravitate toward that hippie botanical shit. Despite all of that, she couldn't generate the normal feelings that usually accompanied not only an amazing performance review, but her best year yet as head of branding.

Mira decided that her muted reaction was excusable, given the event that had recently unfolded in her life. Funnily enough, *the event* was also the term for the fated day when an asteroid had slammed into the earth millions of years ago. That one big event had killed off the dinosaurs and brought on a planet-altering ice age, and even though her personal event hadn't caused the death of an entire species, it was, in its own way, equally cataclysmic.

It was the reason why Mira couldn't manage any excitement in the company chat, and the reason why she'd jumped at the chance to accompany the team on the business trip to Paris. On the night before their departure, Mira had spent hours revising her Paris bucket list in obsessive fashion, a list she'd curated on and off for almost two decades. That list had been a life raft during the strict Indian upbringing that had defined her teenage years, and then the awkwardness of marriage pressure in the years that had followed. Recently, with Mira's growing success in the corporate world, there had been plenty of opportunities to visit Paris, but somehow all the buildup had made the thought of actually going seem too daunting.

But then the Bloom business trip to Paris had presented itself: a perfect opportunity to escape the event, daunting buildup or not.

Except, here she was, on her last night in Paris with not a single bucket list item checked off. Ever since she'd gotten here, it had been early team meetings over hurried breakfasts, presentations between work lunches and dinners, and then collapsing onto her bed at the end of it all, too tired to even think about venturing out on her own. Even the hotel, a lovely establishment nestled in a quiet side street of the 1st arrondissement, was closer to sprawling attractions she didn't have time for—like the Louvre—versus anything she could sneak in quickly.

As Mira sipped her wine, she couldn't escape the fact that a business trip was hardly the appropriate scenario for some freewheelin' bucket-list fun. It should've been obvious right from the start, but that was the thing with cataclysmic personal events—they had a way of clouding one's judgment.

Her next sip of wine was more urgent than the last, the liquid laced with the sweet nectar of trying to forget.

She noticed Jake reemerge from the bar, which luckily distracted her from chugging down the entire contents of her glass. She watched as he delivered a complimentary cocktail to the patrons at the nearest table. In his salesman way, he urged each of them to try a sip. Everyone was curious enough to oblige, and then, one by one, every single face lit up.

Jake hurried back to the company table and searched his bag for more cans of Bloom. "Cocktails!" he exclaimed, catching the boss's eye. "Was I right or was I right?"

Frank shook his head and chuckled. "You were *born* to be a salesman."

Mira had no interest in engaging in a Jake-centered love fest, so she turned her attention back to her phone. She noticed the glowing beacon of an email notification, and as she read the contents, every muscle in her forehead tensed into a series of knots.

"You've got to be kidding me."

"What's the matter?" a colleague asked.

"The airline changed my flight." She frowned. "It's later now and they assigned me a middle seat." She glanced around at the others. "Anyone else get a flight change alert?"

Mira's colleagues checked their phones, all except for Jake, who was still preoccupied with his precious cans of Bloom. One by one, they confirmed their flight details were the same.

"Why only me?" she scowled, immediately deciding it was white-collar racism.

"Shirley mentioned something about this earlier today," Frank explained. "She got an alert that the flight was overbooked and said she'd handle it." He smiled. "I guess it's handled."

Even though Mira didn't mind the idea of some bonus hours in Paris, she couldn't help but feel like she'd been cast off to the island of misfit marketers.

Jake noticed Mira still scowling at her phone. "What happened?" He darted his eyes around the table. "Did I miss something?"

Mira wanted to ignore him, but a part of her was sickly curious. "Did you get an email from Shirley?"

He pulled his phone out of his pocket and nodded. "Yup." He opened it and seemed confused. "Why is there another booking number? Didn't I already get this email?" He looked to Mira with desperate eyes. "Can you just summarize what it says? I really need to get back to the bar."

Mira thought about lying and telling him his flight had been delayed by twenty-four hours, but fortunately for him, she wasn't that evil. At least not yet. "You and I got bumped to a different flight; it's three hours later." She glanced at his phone screen. "I mean . . . I'm assuming you're on that flight. You should really check."

He scanned the email and nodded. "Yep, three hours later—awesome!"

Jake sauntered back to the bar, leaving Mira and her colleagues to return to their fun. Or in Mira's case, sipping wine, avoiding nauseating chitchat, and struggling to care about corporate wins.

*

After the last of the plates had been cleared, Mira emerged from the restroom to discover all her coworkers had left. All except for Jake, who was canoodling with the waitress by the bar.

*They ditched me*, Mira thought to herself.

The woman who co-owned the restaurant noticed Mira standing frozen in place.

"Mademoiselle?" she said softly. Mira turned and acknowledged her with a nod, her face slightly stunned. "Your colleagues mentioned they had to leave for an early flight."

"Oh."

"Everything is paid for, so you may continue to enjoy the evening with your colleague."

The woman gestured to Jake, but from the look on her face, she knew as well as Mira that there wasn't much fun to be had in the land of third-wheel awkwardness.

"Thanks," Mira said, "but I actually need to head out too." She adjusted her blazer. "Big morning ahead."

As Mira made her way to the exit, she inadvertently made eye contact with the hot bartender, he of tousled dark hair and tanned skin. He looked like he belonged on a beach in Saint-Tropez, and as a result she started to imagine him shirtless. Maybe pantless too.

The bartender responded by treating Mira to the sort of smoldering stare she'd previously only read about in books or seen in movies. "Care to join us for last call?" he offered, his voice the auditory version of silky fondue.

Mira looked from the bartender's handsome face to Jake, who was busy putting the moves on the waitress. After making a quick internal calculation, she concluded that the ego-boosting benefit of being hit on by a hot French bartender did not outweigh the cost of being annoyed by the very life force that was Jake.

She politely shook her head and left the restaurant.

Once outside, Mira took a moment to revel in the warm summer air. As the night breeze danced across her face, she realized something equally as important as her cost-versus-benefit math: Was she even in the right emotional state to be flirting with a man right now?

*Not even close.*

\*

Later that night, back in her quaint hotel room, Mira laid out some clothing options for the next morning.

She had already planned to use her extra hours in Paris to wake up early, take an inspirational stroll by the river, and then enjoy a breakfast at one of the places on her bucket list. She felt a nervous twinge at the thought of officially cracking open the list. Each bullet point was laced with high expectations, but it was either that, or wake up late and order room service, which just seemed wrong in a city as beautiful as Paris.

She did her best to calm the nervous feeling by focusing on her outfit; the strolling portion of the morning meant that functionality was key, but the neighborhood of the breakfast spot required something more high-end. She pushed her more practical pieces to the side and zeroed in on anything approaching fashionable.

She ultimately landed on one of her work blazers paired with a T-shirt, a pendant necklace, jeans, and her glossy white-and-rose-gold sneakers. It was hardly on the level of an Instagram influencer, but for Mira, it was more than enough.

Once cozy in bed, she grabbed her phone, set an alarm, and opened the airline app. "You better work this time," she muttered, sounding equal parts threatening and nervous. A few taps and a long pause later, she sighed in frustration.

The convenient online check-in was simply not to be.

Knowing she'd need extra time to check in at the airport, she edited her alarm for some all-important buffer, before placing her phone on the nightstand and switching off the lamp.

In a matter of moments, Mira's nervousness faded into eager anticipation.

*Tomorrow is going to be amazing.*

ı